KNOW YOUR PLACE

A novel of London love and loathing

Andy Knaggs

Published by M-Y Books

M-Y Books
187 Ware Road
Hertford
SG13 7EQ

Prologue

This was Eddie's favourite place to sit and watch the world go by. Sometimes the wind howled, and the rain teemed down, and it was easy to imagine that misery must prevail; at other times, the sun trapped him in its glare; warmed his heart, but made him shield his eyes, so that all he saw were the shoes of passing strangers, a metre away and then gone in an instant. Every day though, the growling of traffic across London Bridge provided him with company throughout another empty day, and whatever nature threw at him, this place remained at the centre of Eddie's universe; it was home.

The River Thames at its grandest ebbed by below him, but against the disorder of footsteps and babbling voices, the car and bus engines revving and whining, and the occasional party boat motoring by beneath, it was impossible to listen to the hushed sounds of the river itself until the early hours, when the city slept.

Eddie didn't mind that. He was usually still here even then – halfway across London Bridge, huddled against the elements, clinging to the blanket that was his shelter, and enjoying the river's whisper. He had no reason to be anywhere else in particular.

As a boy growing up in the countryside in Northern Ireland, probably 50 years before, he had heard people talking about London, and he had listened with disbelieving ears, and imagined with wide eyes. Many people went to London; it was bigger even than Belfast, and its call was uniquely strong, its promise seductive. It was a well-worn path: off to London to seek your fortune. Eddie had followed that path himself years ago, and it had been good to him for a while; he had drawn energy and purpose from it. Not now though, and not for some time.

These were hard times now, but he didn't blame it on the city. Life did what it did to a man, and he accepted that phlegmatically. London was still where he wanted to be; and here, halfway across the bridge, thirty feet above the shimmering water, was where he calculated the heart of London to be. He had the river, he had the traffic, and he had the people, flowing according to their own tidal patterns, mostly from his left, the south bank, across to the City to his right every morning, and back again in the evening.

He could watch the world go by, and on those days when he'd not managed to secure a source of alcohol he could think, and wait, and watch his small metal tin, long emptied of tobacco, gradually fill with coins from passers-by.

Eddie had become an avid people watcher over the years, and he indulged in it whenever he could rouse himself from fitful sleep or blurry-eyed indolence for long enough to take in what was in front of him.

And right now, as Eddie looked to his left, what was in front of him was a young man – probably about 30 years old, he reckoned; around 25 years younger than Eddie was. He stood on the bridge, not quite mid-river, looking out towards HMS Belfast, Tower Bridge and beyond, as the Thames curved away towards Docklands.

Something about the man had caught Eddie's attention as he had approached from the south side of the river and then stopped about five yards short of where Eddie, an easily ignored, shapeless figure hunched beneath a mucky blanket, was huddled. It was a dark October weekday evening, becoming chilly, and with a gentle drizzle that came and went. The evening was drawing on, although Eddie judged that it wasn't yet closing time in the City pubs, since the flow of human traffic hadn't developed into a boisterous, alcohol-fuelled surge yet.

People often staggered past Eddie after a night of boozing, but this young man – tall and skinny with a mop of fairish hair – looked more like he could still do with a drink Eddie had

2

thought, judging by the grim frown on his face as he had neared where Eddie sat.

He had walked quite slowly, almost reverentially. His face had been pale, pre-occupied, but hard-set as if steeled by some kind of resolution to action. To Eddie's surprise the young man had not continued walking across the bridge, but had stopped when nearly halfway across. He gave no obvious sign of being aware of the presence of the vagrant slumped nearby. Eddie watched with vague but growing interest, seeing the man cradle his head in his hands, looking in some distress.

Nothing happened for a minute, save for a car or two flashing past. Then Eddie saw a sudden flurry of movement, the man's arms searching their own body, and finding something; an arm pulled back and flung forward, hastily, like a nervy army recruit tossing a hand grenade for the first time; a small, shiny object flew out into the night, towards the black river. Eddie even heard a small 'plop' as it hit the surface seconds later. By now, his interest piqued, Eddie was getting to his feet and edging towards the young man, leaving his blanket behind but bringing his collecting tin with him.

The man continued to stare out at the river, and Eddie was close enough now to pick out more detail in his face. As Eddie crept nearer a tear rolled down the man's cheek and disappeared inside his coat collar. His lips were moving slowly, soundlessly.

"D'ya think that was a good idea then, sonny?" Eddie croaked, the broad Ulster accent immediately betraying his origins.

The man turned quickly towards him – more quickly than Eddie had expected. He looked defiant, but his eyes shone with moisture that Eddie knew didn't just come from the steady, thin rain. His reply was defiant too:

"I don't care. It's done. That shitty phone has done too much damage already. I'm better off without it."

A pause, then: "What's it to you anyway?"

Eddie smiled benignly; neither the question nor its tone caused him concern. "What's it to me? It's nothing to me, sonny. But this is my bridge, and you're causing a scene, so you are."

They watched each other in silence. Searching the young guy's face, Eddie reckoned he was reaching for indignation, for the excuse or maybe the will to be confrontational. Eddie sensed that instead confusion and frustration were all he could grasp right now.

"I suppose it's all to do with some lass... "

The young man answered, protested, too quickly, too loudly, summoning that indignation now.

"No!"

"No?"

"Nosy fucker."

"Oh, right you are then. There's no need for all that language now is there. I see you coming along, getting all flustered, and I thought to myself, now there's a lad who would appreciate a few hard-earned tips from the life of old Eddie Finn."

The younger man scoffed a doubtful, humourless "yeah, whatever".

"Listen, I had a woman once, you know," Eddie persisted. "Beautiful she was – as perfect as a peach. I wasn't in these rags then. But like a bloody fool I didn't realise what I had until it was too late, and I lost her. So don't be like me sonny. Do the right thing now. That's all I wanted to say. It's up to you."

The young man listened to all this in silence, then sighed and shook his head.

"Jesus, are you for real? A bloody tramp turned Agony Uncle?" The man shook his head slowly again, this time with a rueful smile. "Look...I'm sorry I swore, okay. I've just had a complete nightmare tonight and nothing you say is going to make it better."

"I got a smile from you though sonny, eh? I tell you, from under that blanket there I see young guys like you bawling over their ladies every day of the week. It's the story that never ends."

They looked at each other again in silence. Then the man murmured so quietly it was as if the words were intended just for him. Eddie could only barely hear, but he saw that the man spoke through gritted teeth:

"Well, you haven't heard this story before, I promise you. This one is a proper original."

"I've got plenty of time on my hands sonny, so please – do tell. It's not fair to keep a good story like that to yourself."

The man greeted the comment with a weary laugh: "No, no. If I did that you'd have to go in the river too, and that's the God's honest truth."

"She could be trying to ring you right now," Eddie continued, gesturing toward the Thames and by implication the discarded phone in its watery grave. "How will you make it right if you can't talk to her? You'd better get round there."

The man sighed, and looked out at the river again. "After the night I've had pal…" he started, but then paused before turning back to Eddie and speaking again in a voice full of tiredness, frustration and now a flash of anger. "It's over, it's done. Now, if it's all the same with you, I'm going home."

The younger man turned away from Eddie, and started off back towards the south end of the bridge. It seemed that the conversation was over, but Eddie persisted, enjoying the moment, raising his voice slightly even though the man was still just a couple of yards away from him.

"Hey, don't forget what I said now. Get yourself round there; take her some flowers. Be a man."

The young man stopped in his tracks and turned to face Eddie again. Eddie wondered if he'd over-stepped the mark. The younger man seemed to study him closely for a few seconds, before turning again towards the river. Eventually he nodded, and with a quiet comment of "maybe you're right" he turned on his heel once more and walked on. Eddie watched him stride away, feeling relieved, happier even. Suddenly the man stopped again, dug something out of his coat pocket, and faced Eddie again.

"Here, take this. Thanks for the advice," the man called, and tossed something underarm towards the old tramp. Eddie caught it smartly in his open tin, recognising it in mid-air as a gleaming pound coin. He didn't drop those kinds of things.

"Cheers! I hope you work it out!" he called to the man's rapidly retreating back. There was no sign of acknowledgement. In a matter of seconds, just as he had arrived, the man was gone for ever from Eddie's life.

Chapter One

Men in suits and women in high heels milled around the concourse of London's Liverpool Street Station, a blur of perpetual motion to a casual observer. If you looked closely enough though there were a few stationary figures amid the Monday morning frenzy.

Here, a station cleaner resting on his broom; there, an office worker, leaning against a wall waiting for a friend; and here, just by the escalators that take new arrivals at Liverpool Street onto the City's streets of gold, here was a shoeshiner, clad all in black – t-shirt, trousers and shoes – sitting back in the chair he reserved for his clients, reading a paperback book between jobs, occasionally flicking his fair, floppy fringed hair away from his eyes and looking up and around at the rivers of humanity that flowed past.

He viewed the streams of people impassively and with practised eyes; he heard the buzz and felt the pent up electricity, though he hardly, at this moment, seemed energised by its power. The sights and sounds of the station at rush hour were as familiar to him as the advancing lines he saw on his 32-year old face when he looked in the mirror every dawn, rubbing crusty sleep out of his eyes before getting ready for the subdued bus journey to work.

Nick Newman had been working as a shoeshiner for more than a year now, and although in his earlier years he'd had lofty ideas about the station in life he expected to achieve, he found himself relatively content with his lot.

Occasionally, as the railway station busied itself around him during the long day on duty, and he waited for his next customer, he would have time to consider the path his life had taken to bring him to this point, this moment in this place. It had been anything but a straight-forward path. A cycle of bereavement, disillusion, drug abuse and then homelessness had marred his life in his 20s, and there was no getting away from those cold facts. It had never been the plan – no-one would plan a life like that, after all – but it had happened, like it did to many young people that got caught up in the wrong circumstances, and followed the wrong instincts.

Nick was now on his second chance, and he was smart enough to know that this one really mattered. Some may have looked down upon it, but he found that he actually quite enjoyed his job. It was true that there was boredom between customers, but there were books and newspapers and attractive women around to divert his attention in these situations. It was not too mentally taxing but Nick took his pleasure from simple things – chatting to new people, the praise of regular customers, making commuters break into laughter when just minutes before they had seemed anxious or pre-occupied about the day ahead of them.

He was a familiar sight, if not a personality, to many of the commuters, and even more so to the employees of the nearby coffee and sandwich shops, the newsagents and chemists, and the station staff. One of these workers, a slim, petite girl called Vicky from the Coffee Cup bar which faced onto the part of the concourse where Nick had his regular pitch, now approached him, bringing with her a tall plastic cup of coffee with a lid on top.

Nick had got to know her fairly well over the last year, but that was mostly because Vicky, who was ten years younger than he, had taken a shine to him, even pestering him for a date. She seemed to have given that up in recent months, but she still came over to say hello when quiet moments in the coffee bar allowed. Nick knew that the regular four coffees a day that she brought over for him to drink were really just friendly subterfuge – an opportunity to flirt a little.

He saw her approaching with his coffee out of the corner of his eye, and looked up from his paperback, giving her a friendly smile. He had learned to tolerate her hanging around him. "Hey Vicks, how's it going?" he hailed her as she walked over wearing an earnest look on her face.

"Brought your coffee over dude. Shall I put it down here?" she replied. Even as she said it she was bending down to put the cup on the floor in front of Nick's black work bag, where he kept his kit. This was almost a ritual by now, he felt. He was flattered by the attention, but for Nick it was a no-go. It wasn't that she was unattractive; it was just that he had Justine, his Australian girlfriend. And that, as far as Nick was concerned, was that. "Thanks mate," he said, as she straightened up again. He knew what would happen next.

Vicky stood next to his seat in silence for a second or two, looking at the commuters rushing by. Then, without actually looking at Nick, she said: "Good weekend? Still with her?" The two questions and their answers seemed inextricably linked.

"Yes Vick, still with her."

He reached down to pick up the coffee cup, which was by her feet. She had to shift to get out of the way, and took the opportunity to look down at him. The expression of resigned disgust that he'd seen a hundred times on her face flickered across her features again. She didn't need to say anything, and nor did he: she was fed up with it; he was sorry. It was the usual Monday morning.

He therefore gave her the obligatory apologetic shrug, and sipped his coffee. "Where'd you get to this time then?" he asked, as much to end the accustomed awkwardness of the moment as to pursue genuine interest. She started to tell Nick about another weekend of drinking too much, boys and girls on the pull, scrapes and scenes, moments of hilarity and horseplay. It always made Nick wonder why Vicky was interested in him – from what he could hear, there was much more going on in her life than in his.

His weekend had been quiet. He had little money, and Justine, who worked as a secretary in the West End by day, and often did evening bar work in a Camden pub near to where they lived, didn't have much more to spare. Occasionally, at the start of a month when wages had just been paid, they would head west into town with her friends for a big night out. Mostly though, they had to scrimp and save to pay the rent on their flat, and spent their evenings either indoors watching movies, or nursing a couple of slowly consumed pints in the pub.

It wasn't exciting, and Nick longed to be able to offer Justine more. Years before, he had worked in a bank, here in the City, earning decent enough money, and with the potential to earn a lot more. He'd blown that one though. Banks didn't react favourably to finding their staff with a nose full of cocaine in the toilets. Nick had been in his mid-twenties when that had happened. It was just one horrendous moment in a run of misfortune and misjudgement that had plagued him through those years.

By the time he was 28 he had lost both parents, and a girlfriend who had taken her drug habit to its final, fatal end; other friends had drifted away, and there was no-one close enough left to halt his slide into depression, drink and drugs. He lost the job and the house in quick succession. Then he was on the streets, just another government statistic.

Nick was within a whisker of hurtling headlong over the precipice. Two years of sleeping in dirty alleyways followed, being avoided by passers-by, and sneered at by youths in baggy track suits and spiky hair. They were days of unending desperation where the only motivation he felt came from planning how to pinch the next tin of beer or bottle of vodka. He'd got good at that, but from time to time there was a calm reasoning voice in his head telling him that he was better than this; that he could find himself again.

One day he listened to that voice. A moment of clarity fought through a mind-pummelling alcoholic haze as he lay underneath some sheets of cardboard just off Oxford Street one morning. It wasn't going to be easy but he had to clean up. Fortunately he had avoided the worst – he had never been tempted by heroin, and cocaine was far too expensive a hobby for a man on the streets to pursue. If he could clean up and smarten up enough so that his appearance didn't repel everyone that walked past, maybe he could start his resurrection by selling copies of the Big Issue on street corners.

It turned out to be the turning point in his life. Some help from charitable organisations started his rehabilitation, and provided food, shelter, and counselling for the grief that still hit him, and for the remnants of his addiction. He knew he had come close to scraping the bottom of the barrel. Then, in the midst of it all, a miracle occurred when Justine Tanner walked into his life.

It happened one evening, while selling magazines outside Camden Town underground station. He managed to persuade a pretty red-haired girl with an Australian or New Zealand accent (Nick wasn't entirely sure which at the time) to part with a pound. She came back and bought another one a few days later, even though she already had that copy. They talked for a few minutes and laughed. It was more human interaction than Nick had grown used to having. Two days later he saw her again and this time, before she walked off home, she fished in her coat pocket and pulled out a slip of paper with her name and mobile phone number written on it.

Watching the girl saunter off down the road, he had stared from her to the piece of paper in disbelief. It was incredible. There was no other word for it. But putting aside his doubts, his feelings of inferiority, and what he recognised as his fear, he called her and they went out. They drank wine and talked all night. Then they did the same the following evening. Before he knew it, Nick had found a new girlfriend.

She was Australian as it turned out; a strong-minded girl of calm dignity, who had been in England only for eight months. Though it was obvious that Nick was in pieces, she seemed to accept the challenge of putting him back together as if it was entirely natural and obvious that she should do so.

He had no idea what drove her to feel this way, and one over-heated summer day early in their relationship his insecuri-

11

ty had got the better of him, and he had asked her. They had been lazing in a nearby park, lying on the grass, the back of Justine's head resting on Nick's stomach, as he reclined on his elbows with his legs stretched out before him. A three-quarters empty bottle of white wine stood beside Nick's right elbow, on the opposite side of his body to where Justine snoozed contentedly. Their conversation had grown more desultory as the day had heated up and sapped the energy from them, but it was enough to be together, warm and happy in the easiness of their laughter.

With his left hand he traced intricate little patterns on her shoulder, and coiled locks of her long red hair around his fingers, his frown as he weighed up his thoughts being unseen by Justine. He was scared of ruining everything with a misplaced word or question, but finally he broke the silence:

"Can I ask you something?" She moaned quietly, but otherwise didn't move, her eyes still shut. After a couple of seconds he saw her lips draw upwards in a lazy smile. "Well go on then babe – ask away," she breathed, rocking herself slightly from side to side to find the most comfortable bit of grass under her backside.

Nick chuckled at her efforts to get comfortable. "Okay. I've been trying to work this out for a while, but…" He hesitated, already feeling silly and self-conscious. "But…is all this really happening? It's like, there's all these men out there and… for some reason, here you are with me. I mean, I don't know if you've noticed but my prospects aren't exactly great."

He felt her shoulders stiffen a little, but the warmth and the wine that had made her feel dozy all afternoon was still there in her bones and in her blood. She half-turned her face towards him and slowly pulled her sunglasses off, looking up at Nick with one eye shut tight against the sun's glare while the other studied his face, piercing the concern in his own eyes.

"Prospects? Jeez babe, what a time to say something like that," she drawled. He shrugged an apology, and looked pleadingly at her for some sort of answer anyway. "Okay, let's sort this one out right now so you never have to say such a bloody stupid thing ever again, right?"

Justine seemed energised all of a sudden, and as if to emphasise that she was now awake and switched on, she rolled onto her side, swept a few bits of grass off her bare legs, and settled down on her front facing Nick, with her head supported by her bunched fists.

"Right." She was settled now. "Look, it's because I'm nuts about you. The whole deal: kids and stuff. I think you soft-as-shit Poms call it 'love'. But I've been waiting for you all this time and at last you're here. I knew it straight away when we met, and when you find someone that makes you feel that way, any other stuff like prospects go straight out the window." Justine grinned at the thought of the next few words she was going to say – it was a line from a well-known TV advert, with her own twist at the end.

"It's because you're worth it, you muppet! Now pass me the bloody wine, and stop being such a galah." They both laughed, and the moment quickly passed, but Nick continued to think about it. He had been hoping for something a little deeper, he supposed, but as they laughed and settled down again, he realised it was a better answer and a more important one than he had dared hope for. It was simple and honest, and it needed no further elaboration.

As weeks passed it became a magical memory for Nick; the moment that cleared away a multitude of shadows from his mind. From that day on they had just grown closer to each other. Before long, Nick had moved into the sanctuary of Justine's flat and he was homeless no more.

The next step had been to get Nick back into work, although his choices were limited because of his police record. However, the charity had a scheme to get people who were down on their luck trained as shoeshiners. He would start off working for a boss – a Polish guy called Mike – who managed several other shoeshiners, but the idea was that eventually Nick would run his own little business as a franchise. Others in a similar predicament had already done so, and Mr Desborough, who had organised the scheme for the charity, felt that Nick was smarter than most.

He had taken a few deep breaths before agreeing to do the training. It was a big moment in his life. But in the year since then he'd had no reason to regret the decision. Sometime in the next few months he hoped to take on the reins of his own franchise, and when that happened he might start taking some better money home to repay Justine's faith.

For the time being though, Nick and Justine were mostly reliant on her income for their small pleasures, and all this explained why Nick felt slightly embarrassed when Vicky asked him every Monday about his weekend. It was the same answer almost every week, and it didn't add up to much in comparison with Vicky's regular shenanigans.

Their chat was just sliding towards another one of those awkward silences when Nick had a customer turn up at his chair. It was a man in a suit, who interrupted the conversation with a curt: "Whenever you're ready."

Nick spun round, annoyed that he had not seen the man approach. "Sorry, sir – please sit here." Vicky wandered off back to her coffee shop with a goodbye wave, leaving Nick thinking with relief that that particular routine was done for another week. He got his head down and got to work on the man's shoes. Seconds after he had started a lady came and stood by Nick's customer.

Nick was too busy to look up and see her properly but out of the corner of his eye he could see her shoes – elegant, black, high heels – and the start of a shapely curve of calf. She started talking, putting a London-accented voice to the ankles.

"Anyway, you never let me finish. Your mum says you've asked them to come as well."

"Uh-huh. So what if I did? You didn't mind them coming last time."

"It would just be nice if you actually mentioned it to me first though Lee. It is my bloody holiday too. What if I just wanted it to be the two of us for a change?"

"Oh come on! Jesus, don't make me laugh Kay. Anyway, do we have to talk about it now for God's sake? I'm sure this bloke doesn't want to hear you moaning on."

A tone of mutual irritation had risen throughout the exchange. Hearing a reference to himself, Nick just concentrated on the job and tried to ignore the quarrel. The woman wasn't going to back down just yet though.

"Well, let's ask him shall we? What do you think Mister shoeshine man? Would you like it if your other half invited her nosy cow of a mother to come on the only bloody holiday you're going to get next year?"

Nick was forced to look up for the first time, and was taken aback. The woman was quite something. She was tall and slim, with long dark hair, and she glared down at Nick now with a pair of brown eyes that would stop any man in his tracks. Those eyes smouldered angrily behind the mascara, but Nick couldn't avoid appreciating her beauty. She was also already sufficiently suntanned to make Nick question momentarily in his own mind why she needed to go on another holiday. She wore a black business suit and held a plastic coffee cup in each hand.

Nick had to turn quickly back down to the man's shoes so as not to betray his own instant admiration. "I don't know," he said. "Don't bring me into it. I'm just…" He left the sentence unfinished and carried on polishing. He could feel his cheeks flushing with heat.

"See, you've embarrassed the geezer now," the man continued. "Just leave it until later Kay, when you can throw as many fucking pots and pans at me as you want. You'll have to wait though cos I'm probably going to have a few beers with Darren after work. Hopefully you'll have calmed down by then."

"Stay out all fucking night as far as I care." She spat out the sentence with startling venom. Bloody hell, Nick thought, who'd get married? She went on: "I could pour this coffee right over your head you ignorant bastard. That would take the smirk off your self-satisfied little face."

The man seemed about to respond in kind but Nick had heard enough. He shot up from his stool, dropping the brush he was using to the floor with a clatter.

"Okay people. That's enough of that. Either you both shut up and save this for later or you can get a shoeshine somewhere else. It's that simple."

He looked from one to the other. The woman looked like she was about to erupt still, anger flashing in her dark eyes. The man stared silently at the floor. Nick could see in the background that a couple of passing commuters had stopped to watch, no doubt hoping that something interesting was going to happen.

"Christ, you're like a couple of spoilt kids," Nick continued, more to fill the silence than anything else. "Well? What's it to be, people?"

The woman had closed her eyes, and appeared to be counting to ten in her head. Then she opened her eyes again, looked at Nick and said: "You know what mate, you're right. I'm sorry. I don't know why I let this arsehole wind me up."

"You started this in the first place, you moany old cow," the man in the chair retorted, giving his wife a thunderous glare.

It looked like the woman was about to snap back at him, but Nick held up a hand and with a single, sharp "enough!" cut across her. Two minutes of silence followed while Nick finished the man's shoes. The onlookers had moved along, disappointed at the anti-climax. Nick fancied that the argument still raged on above his head as he sat at the man's feet and buffed the leather; it wasn't spoken out loud but continued with every furious look that passed between the couple, he imagined.

It was with relief that he finished the job and took the man's money. The couple moved on, he without a word or look in acknowledgement to the shoeshiner, she with a small guilty smile, and a mouthed "thank you", before they headed off towards the Broadgate centre, next to the station.

Nick didn't watch them go. He was sorting out his money and his equipment. When he next turned around they had gone, and Liverpool Street Station was its usual bustling self. Nick looked up at the main clock above the concourse. It read 8.36. What a way to start the week, he thought. Mind you, what a woman. He sat down with his coffee and picked up the paperback again. Within a minute another customer had settled into the chair, and Nick was swept up in the day's work once more.

**

Kay Talbot sat back and watched the members of her team, most of them heads bowed to their desks, or intently viewing computer screens, and she reflected that despite everything that advances in communication technology had provided – emails, mobile phone, social networking – life was still much easier when you did things face to face. You could use your physical gifts to the maximum when you were face to face – and Kay Talbot was aware of the advantages that gave her if the person across the table happened to be a man.

Today though, those gifts were being neutralised. The action was happening on the telephone, and as smart, quick and tough as her mind could be, that meant that the playing field was levelled.

Kay had long known that in public relations there were two different kinds of attention. There was the kind of attention that you chased and plotted and schemed for; that you lunched journalists and analysts for, and that you wrote press releases for. This was the good stuff, and it was enjoyable enough, although a woman of Kay's expertise and political nous could handle it without having to stretch herself overly. The results could be impressive, and could be presented as great wins to your client.

Then there was the other kind, the unwelcome attention. It was usually initiated by a panicked phone call from a client. Such and such a journalist has been phoning and asking about so and so, please get them off our case. This was where, to Kay's mind, a PR professional earned his or her corn. There were some that specialised in 'crisis management'. They loved the thrill of the chase, even though it was they who were being harried by snapping journalists, demanding good answers to awkward questions.

This was one of those days, and unusually Kay found that she wasn't enjoying it. The crisis had begun at the start of the week, with a phone call from the catering firm that she represented as a director of Palmerston PR. The catering firm had won a contract two years earlier to supply meals for some of the UK's biggest airports. It had been announced in a blaze of glory for the company. There were stories all over the trade press, the managing and marketing directors were kept busy giving interviews about the importance of the contract, and even a couple of national newspapers had picked it up and printed small articles.

For the client, a company called Mighty Meals UK, this was the ultimate in press coverage. From top to bottom everyone in the firm was ecstatic. Kay was overjoyed, her team celebrated with an expensive night out in a restaurant, all paid for by the PR company, and more than covered by the increased fees that came with the PR contract extension that followed. The sore head that Kay had suffered the next day however was nothing when compared to what she was wrestling with now.

There had been a police raid at Gatwick airport. They had taken away the catering company's paperwork, and discovered that several of its staff members were illegal immigrants. Two were from China, but nobody seemed too bothered about that. It was the Somalian and the two Yemenis that were the real problems. This would have been bad enough before the terror attacks of September 11th 2001. Since that infamous day six years earlier, and then the London bombings of July 7th 2005, the issue of illegal immigrants working at airports held a whole new resonance for the British public.

Kay had fire-fought throughout that first day, dashing down to Gatwick on the train and standing shoulder to shoulder with her beleaguered client, Mighty Meals' managing director Roger Wallace, who was frightened and totally out of his depth. He was surrounded by deadly serious policemen, and intelligence and immigration officials who, when not asking questions in a highly accusatory way, were busy filling boxes with paperwork taken from Mighty Meals' personnel files.

In truth, there hadn't been much that Kay could do. No mere PR representative could prevent the security services from doing their jobs. It was going to be a matter of damage limitation when all this broke, and it did just that two days later after the police gave the story to a national newspaper.

A weasel-sounding reporter had called with a long list of questions that Kay knew she could never answer specifically. Having talked at length with Roger Wallace at Mighty Meals, Kay had discovered so many holes in the firm's procedures for vetting employees that it was obvious that they were doomed if they engaged in any kind of straight-talking dialogue with the media.

So she had beaten the questions away with a prepared statement, which said next to nothing. The company could confirm there was an investigation, and it was co-operating with the security services to investigate the degree to which these people had been checked out before being given jobs. That was the gist of it. What it didn't say was that these jobs just happened to involve working next to sophisticated aeroplanes that in the wrong hands could be turned into lethal flying bombs. The press would spell that out for everyone though, that much was certain. Well, Kay reflected, it was a complete mess. She almost hoped that Mighty Meals would get nailed.

Having sent the statement to the newspaper, Kay had then called Roger Wallace to confer.

"They're asking if we will put someone forward to be interviewed," she informed him. There was silence for a couple of seconds at the other end of the line. Kay was keenly aware that Wallace was like a rabbit caught in the headlights over this situation, and that made her even more certain that it could only work out badly for her client, and by extension Kay herself, if the company put itself in the firing line.

"Do you think we should?" Wallace ventured.

"No, absolutely not Roger. Believe me, after what we talked about two days ago, I don't want you going anywhere near an interview. If you'd ever done that media training we recommended then maybe, but even so, on this issue, it's really tricky. And when this story breaks and the TV and radio people get hold of it, the same applies then. Even more so actually. You'd get taken apart on national telly. It would be a disaster."

"Couldn't you handle it for us?"

"How do you mean?"

"Couldn't you handle the interview? I mean, isn't that what we pay you for?"

Kay had almost jumped out of her chair at that suggestion, but she had to keep her anger in check, realising that it would be unprofessional for her team to hear their boss arguing on the telephone with a client. Instead she lowered her voice to a tight-lipped, rasping whisper:

"No Roger, it isn't what you pay us for. We consult and advise but we don't run your company. How do you think it would look if Mighty Meals put up a spokesman who doesn't even work for the company to speak in front of the whole world? When Jeremy bloody Paxman asks me a question I can't just say, sorry Jeremy I'll have to come back to you on that one when I've checked with my client. You pay me to advise you, to brief you, and to issue statements on your behalf. We're a PR company Roger; we don't make food for airplane meals."

"Okay, I was just thinking out loud. I understand. Now, what do you advise me to do then?" He seemed anxious to appease Kay's anger, though she noticed that he placed extra emphasis on the word 'advise'. She took a few deep breaths before answering.

"All we can do is put the statement out, and refuse interviews. You'll get some stick but hopefully within a day or two some bloody war will kick off again somewhere in the world and they'll forget all about it. We'll say nothing outside of what we've agreed. Any media calls, direct them to me. You concentrate on working with the police to sort this out. And when this is all done and dusted Roger, make very, very sure that your procedures are as tight as a duck's arse, because in six months' time I'll just bet they will try and get an undercover reporter in to stir it all up again."

"You really think they would do that?" He sounded troubled, disbelieving of that possibility.

"Yes, totally. If I was in their shoes I know I would. This isn't a game you know, Roger. The police want the public to know they're doing their job and protecting them, and the press just love exposing all this stuff. So let's keep our heads down and get through this. I just hope to God they don't discover a bloody Al Qaeda nutter working for you. Things would be so much easier if you just gave jobs to good English people, but I suppose they want too much money."

And now, two days after that conversation, the story had broken. The newspaper had run it as a front page splash, with more promised on page seven. Police chiefs, airport bosses and MPs had all been quoted. Now Kay had the hottest telephone in England on her desk.

She had been called by four newspapers, two radio stations and two TV stations already, and it was not even half past nine yet. The phone shrilled again, and she snatched it up.

"Kay Talbot." Her south London dialect had instantly disappeared, and another voice – her 'telephone voice' – had kicked in automatically.

"Hi, it's Rob Field from Sky News. We'd like to speak to someone from Mighty Meals about this Gatwick story. Can you get someone down to the London studio?"

"Rob – great to hear from you," Kay lied. "I'm really sorry but I'm afraid there won't be any interviews."

"Oh. Why the hell not?"

"There's no-one available I'm afraid. I can send you a statement, but that's it at the moment. Mighty Meals are helping the police with the investigation and there's nothing more to say at this point. These things take…"

"Kay, this is important. You can't just brush over it. Our viewers expect answers to some important questions."

"I can't help what your viewers expect Rob. You guys give them plenty of great stuff as it is. There won't be any interview and I'm saying the same to everyone that calls me today. I'm sorry, but my hands really are tied on this one."

There was silence at the other end for a second, and Kay imagined the journalist was glowering at her down the telephone; then the TV man said:

"Kay – this really is such crap. What the fuck are these people thinking about? There are some big questions that need to be answered about security at airports. What the hell are they doing that's more important than this?"

Kay winced. "Rob, I understand you perfectly but it isn't going to happen at this moment. When it does, I promise you that you can have the exclusive. Until then, how about we do lunch sometime and I can give you an off the record briefing on what's happening."

There was another pause. Kay had uttered the magic word: exclusive. Rob Field was obviously thinking about it.

"Well…I suppose that would be something at least. What does this statement say anyway?"

"I'll send it to you if I can just check your email address. It doesn't say much that you probably don't already know though. Mighty Meals are co-operating with the police. There's not much else they can say at the moment. I'm sure you can appreciate how sensitive it is right now."

Field simply responded with a weary snort that suggested he'd heard it all before and all too often. Seconds later the conversation was over, and Kay replaced the handset. The entire morning was spent reiterating these same points to one journalist after another. At one point she had to read the statement over the telephone for a radio broadcaster to record. There was plenty of criticism flying around for the stance she took, but she knew in her own mind that it was the best way, in fact the only way with this story. It would be too easy for Roger Wallace to get tripped up on air. Soon, by way of cracking a few jokes and fibbing that the decision was not in her hands, she was even eliciting some sympathy from the reporters that called.

Her business partner and fellow director, Wilf Palmerston-Prior, came round mid-morning to check how things were going. He was posh and privately educated; the chalk to Camberwell-born Kay's cheese. It was a combination that worked though. She admired his smooth charm, and the ease with which he could ingratiate himself into the most highly esteemed of company. Wilf adored Kay, and always had since they had met working for a PR agency early in their careers. Her strength of character, her daring and her total disregard for the possibility of failure at times made him choke with amazed laughter.

They had decided to break away and set up their own agency when they were both in their late 20s, some seven years before. Wilf was a homosexual, and that was a welcome relief to Kay. He didn't take any of her crap, and he wasn't about to be swayed by her looks either.

"So, Mrs Talbot," Wilf greeted her now. "How goes the good fight? Are we winning?"

She gave him a dark look. "Wilf, I've just about had it up to here. If one more journo rings that phone I think either it or me will go into meltdown."

"Indeed, so I see from those tired, frustrated eyes of yours. But the question remains: are we winning?"

She tossed it around in her mind for a second and said: "Yeah, I think so – as much as we can on this one. We'll see what happens on the lunchtime news, and then this evening, but hopefully come tomorrow lunchtime it will all have gone away. Roger is clucking like a fucking chicken with the foxes after it, but unless something really heavy comes out of the investigations I think we might be okay."

"Excellent, I knew you were the man for the job Mrs T." It was their standing joke. She wore the trousers in the partnership.

"Plus," she said, suddenly conspiratorial, "I've got lunch arranged with the very attractive Rob Field from Sky, so I can give him a 'background briefing' off the record. Can you believe it?"

"I can believe anything of you, you brazen hussy. Anyway, can we sit down this pm and have a chat? Bring Belinda and we'll do some blue-skying on that Plaxaco pitch next week – we need some of Bel's creative spark to make this one breathe I think."

"Okay, what time?"

"3pm any good?" She nodded that it was. "Righto – there goes your phone again. The chase heats up! Back into the fray Mrs T. See you later."

She gave the phone a nasty stare before snatching up the receiver.

"Kay Talbot!"

"It's me."

She slumped back down in her chair. It was her husband. "Lee, I told you I was going to have a shit morning and not to disturb me. Which bit of that didn't you understand?"

"Excuse me for breathing. Listen, I was just ringing to tell you I'm playing squash with Dave tonight and then we might go for a curry, so don't wait up."

"Fine, I've got used to cooking for one. Now goodbye, I've got too much to do."

They hung up, and Kay covered her face with her hands for a couple of seconds, breathing hard. It was hard to believe how cold and harsh things had become between her and Lee. Displays of affection were a distant memory, and the nastiness that seemed to mark most of their conversations was getting worse.

After more than ten years of marriage, Kay could see that things were starting to crumble badly. Every conversation quickly degenerated into a bitter slanging match. Lee seemed to have little interest in anything to do with her. He ridiculed her attempts at cooking and criticised her housework, yet he was rarely there to help, and when he was there he sat on his backside watching sport on the TV, being obnoxious with apparent effortless ease.

That drove her madder than anything else. It was as if he was flinging a blunt statement in her face – that they were not a partnership anymore; that he would do just exactly as he pleased. He was no longer the charming, funny boy she had met and fallen for on holiday in Spain back in the early 1990s. Perhaps she had changed too.

They had kept their holiday romance going despite the distance between their homes back in England – he in Hertford, Kay in Denmark Hill. The fact that they both worked in London anyway had made that easier. After a couple of years the happy couple had set up home in Hertford, not far from his parents, and got married soon after. She was a high flying PR executive; he had a steady job at the bank where he still worked now. To their friends, they had seemed a golden couple. Life had got in the way though, and she could pinpoint exactly why the problems had started.

As the years went by, his desire for children grew, but Kay it seemed was still focused on her career. In fact, there was a deeply personal reason why Kay was reluctant to have a baby. Many years before, when she had been a little girl, she had lost her mother to an ectopic pregnancy. The psychological impact of that was just a starting point though. She didn't really believe that the same was bound to happen to her. But she also had a career that she loved, and a theory that there was not a maternal bone in her body.

Perhaps Lee had always assumed that he could persuade her eventually, or maybe he reckoned that the ticking of her biological clock would do the job for him. Time went by without any sign of her position changing however, and the arguments got meaner, the sly comments got more hurtful, and the grudges became deeper and more frequently aired.

The lack of a baby had come to define their marriage and it magnified every other difference, spreading like a cancerous growth until there were no physical expressions of their love to speak of. It felt to Kay as if this was her punishment for depriving Lee of children.

Kay reflected on some of this for the thousandth time as she sat waiting for the next phone call, and wondered idly whether the gulf between her and her husband had already grown so wide as to drive him into the arms of another woman. Probably, she thought. Certainly he spent more and more time out and about, supposedly drinking with his work mates, or playing sport. Did she care whether he was being faithful? The answer to that could change from one day to the next, depending on how tired or fragile she felt.

Today she was too harassed to care, she decided. She sat back in her chair and looked through the glass partition at her team of PR execs, tapping away at keyboards or working the telephones. There were four tables in the main office, and when everyone was in, each desk had two people facing each other.

They were a good bunch – young, creative and confident. Belinda, who dressed like a punk rocker and had red streaks in her short, dark hair, was the creative star. She could always be relied on to find a different angle for a pitch or a story idea, but she was also a spiky presence, with a fierce individuality that Kay adored.

Across from Belinda was Giles, who was the best writer of the team. He was also the team joker with a gift for impersonating characters from TV shows. Everyone in the team had a nickname, and Giles was generally the one who decided what it would be. Kay's immediate deputy, Sara, was away on holiday. She was a serious career girl, not long married, and a solid if unspectacular performer.

The only other male was Gavin, who was quiet and serious, but capable of moments of genius. Ruth was a feisty Welsh blonde, a PR account director with a sneeze that caused the whole office to duck in panic when it exploded with shocking suddenness. The other girls were Jasmine, a dark haired, tanned girl, always dressed in the latest fashions, who often seemed slightly detached from the pressures of her job; she was just a little too cool maybe; posh Tissy (or Laetitia), who had got the job because Wilf knew her father; and the office assistant, Steph, who gave everyone cheek but was worth her weight in gold for the account teams by doing jobs like collecting press cuttings and making up pitch props.

It was a business to business PR agency with a dozen clients, some of them very small, paying small retainer fees. Wilf looked after two very big clients, Kay another two. Mighty Meals was not one of Kay's big clients, but was demanding more attention than it warranted in fees, and Kay was increasingly aware of it.

Kay soon turned back to her desk and enjoyed the bonus of a twenty minute spell without interruption to read through some draft press releases that Giles and Jasmine had written. It was looking like she might get through to lunchtime without further disturbance, but then another call came in. She answered, and heard the voice of a lady on the other end, sounding somewhat anxious.

"Hello. Is that Palmerston PR?" the lady enquired.

"Yes, it is. This is Kay Talbot, how can I help?"

"Ah, good. I'm calling from Mighty Meals at Gatwick. There's a TV camera outside with a reporter and they're asking if they can come in and talk to someone about all this business in the newspaper today," she explained. She sounded like an elderly secretary, for whom all of this would have been mystifying stuff. There was certainly confusion in her voice. "There was an email from Mr Wallace telling us to call you if anything like this happened. What shall we do? They want to come in," she concluded.

Kay's heart was sinking. Bang goes the three o'clock meeting with Wilf, she thought.

"Alright, what's your name? Jenny? Okay Jenny, don't worry, you did the right thing by calling me. Tell them someone is coming along to see them. I'll be there as soon as I can. But don't say anything, and don't answer any questions. Make them wait outside the building; they've got no right to barge in. Take them out a cup of tea or something. Okay? I'll see you soon."

Kay heard the woman thanking her in a doddery way as she hung up. There was just time for another head-in-hands moment, muttering heartfelt curses, before Kay leapt into action. First she called Wilf to tell him that she was going to have to leave and would miss the meeting. Belinda would do great though. Wilf understood. After all, a client in need, he said in an absent minded way, was one that might agree to paying an increased fee the next time the account came up for review.

Kay packed a few things into her case and, pausing only to assign Giles to cover her telephone, she dashed out, heading for Baker Street station to catch the tube to Victoria Station, from where she could get the Gatwick Express train. Kay found a seat on the tube train easily, but as she thought over her next move, finding relaxation was a whole different proposition.

There was tension and tiredness in every limb it seemed, but Kay mentally shook herself, and attempted to focus on the job in hand: Mighty Meals, Gatwick, a TV crew, problem.

Time and again however, Lee's phone call kept bursting through as she tried to concentrate. It was only the latest in a long line of unsatisfying exchanges between the two of them, but as Kay sat silently on the tube train with just her thoughts for company she felt a familiar gloom descending in her mind; a sinking despair that she knew well but had yet to find a way to conquer, unless you counted the method that led to an empty bottle and a sore head the next day.

There was a consistent cycle to this emotional decline that she was now accustomed to. It went from unsettling gloom to a mute, hopeless despair, soon turning to a stomach-churning panic about the things in her life that troubled her: the demands of her job, the vacuum of her relationship with Lee, and the paucity of time in which to put either of those things right. A short, worthless conversation like the one with her husband earlier could, on a bad day, make her re-evaluate and consign as hopeless every facet of her life. It was happening again now, despite the importance of the task immediately at hand. It was shocking and relentless.

Kay felt self-worth draining away by the second, like blood emptying from her veins; gushing, bursting out of the tube train doors as they slid open at Bond Street, flooding the platform beyond, fouling up the shoes of disgusted passengers who were waiting to get on. She imagined she watched it happen, like a bad horror movie, observing it silently but with bitter, forlorn eyes. Kay breathed deeply and tried to fight it, tried to close the flood gates.

The next stop was Green Park, and by the time she reached it, she felt hollow. Just enough focus remained for her to rise from her seat and move robotically towards and through the open train doors before walking along the platform towards the Victoria Line, rubbing her elbow which had been dealt a painful blow by the sliding tube door as she exited just in time. Another annoyance.

It was only one stop from Green Park to Victoria, but by the time she came back above ground at Victoria, Kay's self-assurance was in tatters. It struck her as odd that she was completely aware of this slide into crisis all the way through; she knew it was happening, she recognised that it was ridiculous to let such things affect her capacity to do her job, yet there it was: it happened anyway; she experienced it creeping over her with every passing second, and it was apparent that there was nothing she could do to stop it.

Now she stood on the wide concourse of Victoria Station, to all intents and purposes a smart, attractive woman, looking up and scanning the boards for details of the train she wanted, but in fact seeing nothing more than a random jumble of letters that her fogged brain barely recognised.

It took a few seconds before she could snap out of this paralysis and focus. When she did manage to read the boards it gave her bad news: there were problems with the service, and the Gatwick Express, which should have been running every 15 minutes, was running with delays.

Was that bad news? Her eyes were drawn towards a two-storey rectangular retail unit, positioned in the middle of the concourse with platforms on both sides. According to the information board, she had nearly half an hour to wait. There was a bar on the top floor of the retail unit, just up those stairs there; she could see the entrance.

She weighed it up. One quick drink wouldn't harm, would it? It was the wrong thing to do obviously, but she could do with a little fortification – just a little something to build her up a bit, that was all – before the confrontation to come. That internal argument having been quickly won, Kay headed for the bar, feeling like a guilty cat with its tail between its legs as she sloped away.

Once inside and sitting at the bar she felt better. She ordered a gin and tonic and looked out through the glass walls of the pub, down to the concourse and the travellers gathered there; butterflies in her stomach made her feel queasy. It was all a load of shit, she decided. The thought came just like that, with no pre-amble and no analysis required. It even surprised her at first, but as she mulled it over again, sifted through the wreckage of her marriage, then tossed her feelings towards Mighty Meals onto the pile as well, she felt reassured that her initial assessment had been correct. The G&T was put in front of her and she paid with cash, before knocking back half of the drink in a single gulp.

It was always like this: after the panic and the paralysis that she had experienced on the train, came contempt for the people and things that should have been important, herself included. It was strangely reassuring to know that the same pattern she had come to expect was still repeating itself. Another lift of the glass to her lips and then it was empty. She ordered another, and five minutes later a third. The butterflies still hadn't dissipated though. With ten minutes to go before the train was due to depart, Kay ordered a fourth drink, hoping this one would prove to be the elixir that would help her to relax and be able to tackle this TV crew at Gatwick.

"Here, let me get you that," she heard an American voice over her right shoulder say. Kay turned to see who the new voice was talking to, and she found herself looking at a sun-tanned, blonde haired man, probably in his early 40s, she guessed. He wore a black suit over a black shirt, open at the collar, and by his side was a small suitcase with a fully extended plastic handle which allowed it to be dragged along on its wheels.

The man smiled broadly at Kay, all dazzling perfect white teeth, and Kay was at a loss for words.

"How about I buy you that drink? You look like you could do with some help," the American man said, and this time there was no doubt who he was speaking to, since he was looking straight at Kay. Such was Kay's surprise that she was still stumped for words as the American smiled at her and the bar tender stood by in some sort of limbo, awaiting instructions. The American took a step closer to the bar and spoke to the bar tender:

"I'll have the same as the lady."

He put a £20 note on the bar, and the barman took the move as the confirmation he was looking for; he turned to fix the drinks. The American hoisted himself onto the bar stool next to Kay, and turned to her again, flashing the big smile once more.

"Hi, I'm Mark Schrader. Did I shock you? Can't believe a pretty lady like you can ever be surprised at having a man buy a drink for them. By the way, I sure would be happy to hear you say something any time soon." He laughed quietly at his own words.

Kay took in the American's appearance. It struck her that he was quite handsome in a sporty kind of way. He was only of around medium height but he was wide enough and she guessed muscular enough to be an ex-football player or something. There was a latent power about his frame that she immediately noticed. His face was still boyish, despite the crow's feet around the edges of his eyes. It was an appealing package in a blue-eyed, star-spangled, apple pie kind of way. Clearly, he was a businessman just after a bit of harmless fun before heading home to the US, any female company being infinitely preferable to none whatsoever. Kay decided to laugh with Mark.

"I'm sorry. I'm just having a bad day. Thank you for the drink, that's very kind of you."

"Right! So you do speak. You're from London? I'm still struggling with these British accents, which is worst luck since I'm going home tonight. Well, as I said, I'm Mark."

He held a hand out towards Kay, and she took it and introduced herself. His grip was impressively strong.

"Where are you from Mark? You're flying from Gatwick tonight?"

"Yep, you bet. I'm from San Diego in California; been here on business for a few days. Love London but hell, am I looking forward to getting home. So, what brings you to this bar?"

"Oh…I'd rather not go into it. It's all very hush-hush, but you know, a work thing," Kay winked playfully, before adding: "I'm on my way to a meeting at Gatwick actually."

Mark raised an eyebrow, and Kay wondered if he had been sitting in a corner of the pub all this time and had therefore already watched her polish off three G&Ts in rapid succession – nobody's idea of the best preparation for a business meeting, and especially not an American's. The new drinks arrived before he passed any comment though, and Mark picked his drink up and proposed a genial toast: "To finding a friendly stranger from the other side of the world."

Kay chuckled, and accepted the invitation to clink glasses with the American. They chatted for several minutes before reaching the bottom of the drink, and before Kay knew it another full glass was in front of her. Mark must have made some signal to the barman to do this, since she hadn't heard him say anything and he certainly hadn't asked her if she wanted another drink.

The appearance of the fresh G&T caused a frisson of worry in her mind. She checked her watch and saw that she had blown her chance of catching the intended train. She had forgotten all about it since she had started talking to the American. Kay cursed under her breath and considered guiltily that she should call the woman at Mighty Meals and tell her there were problems with the trains. This wasn't working out at all as she had expected.

But Mark was there in front of her, looking ridiculously blond and wholesome, and he seemed to fill her eyes and ears with sparkling eyes and teeth, and uncomplicated laughter. By the time they had finished a third drink together Kay knew she was doomed. He was laughing uproariously at some pithy comment she had made about obese Americans, and Kay found her head starting to swim due to a combination of alcoholic bonhomie and high grade flattery from her new sun-bleached Californian friend, with his attractive, dazzling smile.

Before she knew it she was opening her heart about Lee and her marital troubles. He listened intently, and smiled and sympathised. He said that he was enduring a painful divorce back home. His wife had taken up with a US marine. They laughed at what complete arseholes their respective partners were.

At some point during the fourth round of G&Ts they shared, Kay was jolted towards sobriety by her mobile phone ringing. It was Jenny – the lady at Mighty Meals. Kay concentrated and started to explain that the trains were disrupted but that she would be there as soon as possible; she had to put a hand across Mark's guffawing mouth while she said this though, because he had decided that it would be funny to shout out awkward truths such as "she's in the pub!" and "it's all lies!".

She heard Jenny say something but couldn't detect the words since the bar had become noisy with the chatter of bored and delayed travellers killing time with alcohol. "Hang on Jenny – it's a bit noisy here, I'll just find somewhere quieter," Kay shouted, cutting across the words from Jenny that she couldn't make out anyway.

Kay stepped away from the bar, and walked quickly out to a balcony overlooking the concourse. Further along on the same level were some retail outlets, and Kay found a quieter spot outside these to resume the conversation. "Okay, Jenny, I think I can hear you now. I was just saying…"

Before she got any further Jenny interrupted to tell her that the panic was over; the TV crew had suddenly upped and left the site without any explanation. She didn't need to get to Gatwick now.

"Oh," said Kay, hoping to conceal her relief, "that's odd. Perhaps another story came up that they were called to. I was just about to get on the train as well, but there are problems with the Gatwick Express, so I've been waiting."

When the call ended, Kay closed her mobile phone and turned to look out over the concourse. What on earth am I doing, she wondered? I was supposed to be going to help a client and instead I just got pissed in a bar, and now some loud-mouthed Yank is chatting me up. It had been fun, she had to concede, but that didn't make her feel happy. There was an urge, and it was a strong one, to just disappear from here, get down the stairs and into the underground station again without Mark seeing her. There was a problem though: she had left her bag next to him in the bar, and she knew that he would be there waiting for her.

Reluctantly she headed back into the bar, and sure enough Mark was sitting there, grinning lasciviously. It was suddenly obvious, as it should have been all along, what the American was after, and it made her feel sick: seven G&Ts in a short space of time, followed by a brief respite out on the balcony, and now the look on this man's face jolted Kay back to some kind of common sense. This was not what she wanted, she decided.

"Hey, here she is!" Mark cried out as she sat down self-consciously next to him. He pulled his stool closer to hers and asked amiably: "Everything okay at the ranch?" She watched his manoeuvring suspiciously. The spell had been broken, and he didn't seem to have picked up that vibe yet. She knew she needed to get out of the bar right away, before it was too late, before she touched another drop of liquid.

She started uncertainly though: "Well…" Mark quickly leaned closer to her and took her hands in his own.

"Listen, I was thinking," he said softly. "I could, ya know, get a flight tomorrow, if you fancy hanging out. I bet you could show me a few sights. We could have some fun maybe?"

He tilted his head towards her in a conspiratorial way. "Whad'ya say? Don't we deserve to have a little fun?" His left hand reached up to touch her face and Kay looked into his eyes, just inches from her own. He was as drunk as she. Kay could taste bile in her mouth and she recoiled from him, both mentally and actually from his touch, pulling away sharply.

"Oh my God, I feel sick" she blurted out. Quickly she grabbed her bag and made for the exit. His hand grabbed her arm and she heard him saying "wait a second, are you okay?", but she freed herself adroitly and broke into a run, calling back a mess of words: "Bye. Gotta go. Sorry, bye. Thanks for everything. Bye, bye, bye."

She didn't look back and quickly descended the steps back to the concourse, leaving Mark from San Diego open mouthed and disappointed.

An uncomfortable thought hit home as she marched hurriedly away: only the jolt of Jenny's call had saved her; had it not been for that interruption, she might well have spent the night with a total stranger in an unknown hotel room. But she had been faithful to Lee. Kay tried to ignore the twinge of anticlimax that would bug her all the way back home.

**

The pub rocked to an ear-splitting old Charlatans tune, but the music was almost drowned out by the chants of a hundred or more football fans. Kay was loving every minute of it. She came to football with Lee only once a season, though she would have liked to have gone more often. His mates thought she should as well, but Lee was having none of it.

Now she was feeling energised by the driving beat in the background and the throaty tribal yells of the jubilant Arsenal fans celebrating a big home win. She sat in the corner, grinning at James, one of Lee's friends, and letting the surge of noise rush around her. Lee was standing up with a circle of other men, laughing and chanting boisterously with the boys. He looked happy. It was a shame that it wasn't like this more often, in different situations, Kay reflected.

They had actually got on well today. He was keyed up for the game against Derby County, expecting a big win and chattering away with the optimism that early season always brought him. Then, to her amazement, Arsenal had won the match easily, 5-0. It had been a major surprise to her the first time she had been to football with Lee that she had enjoyed it so much. She loved the atmosphere, the passion, the rhythm of the chanting, the fists punching air in unison, and the madness of celebrating a goal. She had even got stuck into a big greasy burger with onions and tomato sauce at half time.

Now, as she watched her husband across the pub being one of the lads, she suddenly realised that James was calling across the table to her. It was almost impossible – so noisy. She laughed and cupped an ear in his direction. He grinned back. "What did you think of that then?" he yelled, leaning closer to her.

"Yeah, it was wicked," she called back. "Loved it! Five nil!" She looked at him to see whether he would continue speaking, but he seemed to decide with a helpless shrug that this atmosphere just wasn't conducive to having any normal kind of conversation across the table. Kay turned instead to chat with Leila, one of the other girlfriends that came along, who was sitting next to her. Leila was studying a page in the match programme with more interest than Kay expected she could have summoned to the task herself.

"How's your dad these days, Lay?" Kay asked. Leila's father was ill in hospital and had been for a few months now. She looked up from the programme, and grimaced.

"Rough as you like mate. I said to Martin, honest to God, I don't think we're gonna get him out of there. I just wish it was all over really."

Kay grimaced back in sympathy. They chatted for five minutes, exhausting the topics of Leila's dad's illness and her job in Superdrug, after which Kay needed a break and a fresh drink. She squeezed up to the bar, where Lee spotted her and called over:

"Babe! Babe! Get us a Fosters, ta!"

One of the other lads, Darren, added with a cheeky grin "yeah, and for me babe!", getting a laugh from the circle of men. She poked her tongue out at him, and turned back to the bar, a £10 note to the fore to attract attention amidst the throng waiting to be served.

God, he must be merry, thought Kay, he's even calling me babe today. What have I done right? The guy to Kay's left at the bar was giving her sly looks out of the corner of his eye she noticed. Occasionally he would pretend as if the press of people caused him to fall against her. She bristled at the unwanted attention, feeling isolated yet surrounded.

He did it again, and she moved her left shoulder out of the way so that he had nothing to lean against, causing him to stumble slightly.

She glared at him in disgust: "Can't you stand up properly mate? It's driving me nuts." He mumbled a sheepish apology, and resumed his position at the bar. Kay did likewise and noted with satisfaction that he didn't knock into her again. Eventually she was served and then she worked her way back to the table with her gin and tonic.

James was still there, though he was now sitting where Leila had been. She was nowhere to be seen. Looking around, Kay realised that she couldn't see Martin, Leila's boyfriend, either. Perhaps they had gone home. The crowd in the pub was only just beginning to thin out as people started to move elsewhere for their Saturday night entertainment.

Kay sat down and chatted with James for a while. She had always found him to be a nice guy. He was good at listening and was actually able to have an intelligent conversation, which was more than could be said for most of Lee's mates. She liked talking to him about his job as an architect as well. It was something that she knew nothing about, but in her line of business you never knew when a little knowledge might come in handy.

They didn't have much in common really, apart from musical tastes, but he always made a beeline for her whenever they were out, and he paid her compliments and sent her funny text messages from time to time. He certainly made an effort to stand out from the rest of Lee's boozy mates. He was tall and athletic and usually tried to remain a level or two above the juvenile coarseness that some, like Darren, gloried in. She realised that James was quite shy; not awkward, just a bit more reserved. Whether it was true or not, he gave the impression that he wanted more from a Saturday night than a bellyful of beer at a nightclub, followed by a kebab and a quick grope with some bird whose name he didn't know or care about. That also made him unusual amongst Lee's mates.

During a pause in the conversation with James, Kay watched the group of men across the pub out of the corner of her eye. Darren was spinning a yarn, and the five other lads were all listening intently. One of them chipped in with a comment that she couldn't hear, and raucous laughter broke out. Kay suddenly realised she hadn't seen him before. She studied him for a few seconds. He was of average height; slim, angular even, with a long, thin nose that was bumped half way down where it had once been broken. The boniness of his nose fitted well with the rest of his frame: he seemed all elbows and sharp edges.

His hollow cheeks gave him a drawn look, heightened by dark smudges under his eyes. He looked very tired, thought Kay, but he had fierce blue eyes that brought an element of danger and maybe even a savage beauty to his appearance. His clothes also marked him out as noticeably different to the rest; much smarter and more individual than the standard Burberry or Aquascutum labels that Lee and his mates wore. He had a close-fitting button-down shirt, and instead of wearing jeans he wore narrow, dark-coloured trousers with sharp creases at the front; highly polished and expensive-looking shoes completed the look. It was a distinctively retro look, Kay noticed, but whoever this guy was, he carried his differences with ease and confidence.

Kay was fascinated, and started thinking about going over to join the group to find out who the stranger was. She let the idea go though, when she considered the way that Lee would probably react to what he would doubtless see as an interruption to his fun.

"Work alright Kay?"

It was James. He looked at her earnestly, like a little lap dog Kay thought, while raising his pint glass to his lips. She didn't really want to talk about work today. Politeness demanded a response however.

She sighed. "Yeah, not bad. Loads going on. You?"

"Alright mate, yeah. Sick of the bloody travelling though; fucking trains are a nightmare. Well, you know exactly what I mean don't you?" he replied, giving Kay a matey grin.

"I've been working from home quite a lot James, but yeah, you're right, it can be a pain in the arse."

James raised his eyebrows at this. "I'm trying to swing some of that working from home with the boss," he said. "I'm getting my computers set up and the software installed so I can do it. Once I've done that, hopefully I can swing it a couple of days a week. How often do you do it then?"

"Oh, a day or two a week I suppose. It depends on what's going on with clients, but it gets me out of the madhouse for a bit. They set me up with a virtual network, so I can still do all the work I would in the office without wasting hours travelling there and back."

James nodded knowingly. Suddenly his eyes lit up. "I tell you what Kay, we could meet up for lunch in Hertford sometime if we're both around. My treat."

Kay hesitated for a second, wondering what Lee would say, but then laughed and said: "Yeah, okay. That would be nice. I don't want you getting me pissed though, when I've got work to do."

"As if I'd do that," James protested with mock indignation. They laughed about that and then chatted for a while about bands that they both liked, making a pact with each other to go to some gigs at some unspecified opportunity. It was easy to say yes to that.

Sometime later, Lee came over to the table. It was getting towards 7.30 and the pub was much more sparsely populated than it had been an hour before. A little earlier, Kay had spotted Lee sitting at another table talking with the man with the eyes, and had wondered again who he was. She thought about asking James, but never got round to it. The conversation between Lee and the mystery man had been conducted in low voices and it was the other man that seemed to be doing most of the talking. Kay had noticed that he looked at Lee with scary intensity, his eyes hardly deviating from Lee's face, as if he wanted to memorise every detail, every line and hair.

Whatever it was that Lee and his friend had been discussing had not left her husband in cheerful spirits however. He walked up now behind James and butted straight into the conversation that Kay and James were having.

"Right, come on bird. Time to go home. I want to get a chinky in Hertford as well."

"We're talking Lee. Can't it wait 10 minutes until I've finished this drink?" Kay protested, unable to mask her irritation.

"No, it can't fucking wait Kay. There's a train in 10 minutes, and we're going to be on it. So get your arse moving."

She knew there was little point in arguing with him, and started slipping her jacket on while getting up from the chair, thinking dark thoughts. James was silently contemplating his three quarters-full pint of Guinness, perhaps wondering whether he should leave the drink and catch the train with them. He made no move to do that though.

As Kay moved around the table to join her husband, he grabbed her arm and pulled her along, leaving James with the comment that he would phone him during the week. Seconds later they were out in the cool early evening air and walking

41

quickly towards the train station. It was like a forced march in full army kit, thought Kay: one, two, one, two, get a bloody move on you men!

She wrenched her arm away from Lee's grip with a howl of pain, but carried on walking beside him, giving him a malevolent glare and demanding: "What's wrong with you, Lee?" He didn't answer though, so she kept on at him. "I've had enough of you talking to me like a piece of dirt, especially in front of your mates. Do you want them all to know what an arsehole you are?"

"Yeah, whatever Kay. You're mistaking me for someone that gives a shit. All I want is a break from this non-stop fucking moaning. Is that too much to ask?"

"Oh, piss off Lee. Don't talk to me. Let's just go home."

They tramped on in silence until reaching Finsbury Park train station. As they got to the steps up to the platform, Lee skipped to one side where there was a dimly lit part of the station and quickly unbuttoned his fly to take a leak up the whitewashed wall. Kay waited for a second on the first step before taking a few slow, deliberate steps upwards. Half way up, there came the first rumbles of a train pulling in, and as Kay turned to shout down to Lee, she found him already springing up the steps and past her towards the platform. She rushed after him and followed him onto the train, sitting opposite from him. Quickly, he had his head buried in his match day programme. It felt like any conversation was forbidden.

Seconds later the train hauled itself away from the station and towards Hertford North, from where they could walk home via the Chinese takeaway shop.

There was silence all the way to Hertford. Kay felt herself deflating by the minute as she stared out of the train window, not really even seeing the streets and the lights flashing by. How had it come to this point, she pondered? How could two intelligent adults decide to stick with a situation like this – one that was driving them both to despair? Or was it only Kay that felt punched in the face by this emptiness?

Stupid, futile questions, Kay told herself as she looked at Lee and saw her husband still engrossed in the football programme. Like a schoolboy finding out some amazing fact for the first time, he had one eyebrow raised, presumably about whatever he was reading. He looked idiotic, Kay decided. It was a childish side to him that once – and this seemed many moons ago now – she had found endearing.

She looked out at the darkening countryside again. Should she just give in and agree to have a baby? Was it time to call an end to this stubborn resistance? Would that allow them to play happy families again – except this time there would be three of them in the family? She had asked herself the question thousands of times already; several times every day, for a couple of years at least. The answer was always no, and all that had changed over time was the reason.

It went far beyond the tragic death of her mother now. How could she even contemplate starting a family with a man like this – a man that had reacted in the way Lee had, when he deemed that his "rights" were being denied? Where was the respect for her rights and her wishes? Only rarely did she feel an emotion that was reminiscent of the old feelings of love she'd had for Lee – and he seemed to reciprocate even less frequently. She would have to be foolish to imagine that adding a child to this marital mix would bring an end to the mutual hostility.

So why was she still with him, when there was a complete vacuum in the space where a loving relationship ought to be? As the train rattled through Enfield Chase, Kay thought back to the days when she was a young girl with her life ahead of her, dreaming the usual dreams of girls her age.

In her mind she could still vividly remember the excitement she had expected to feel about the man she must be destined to marry. He was perfect in her imagination: tall and handsome obviously, maybe even rich, but most importantly he would be

kind and considerate, gentle and loving, attentive and respect-
ful. They would be equals in everything, but there would be
that spark, that special way he would look at her and talk to
her, that would make her feel like she was his princess. He
would be her clown and her father-figure, whenever she
needed either.

Kay felt the train start slowing down. Well, that had been
the dream, she thought. It's never going to happen though is it.
In her mind, that was a statement of fact, not a question. She
had married this man for good and bad; she must see it
through to the end somehow. Anything else was an admission
of failure and that, she realised again, was why Kay and Lee
Talbot were still, in name at least, a married couple. It was for
appearances' sake; it was so that his mother wouldn't be upset.
Without thinking, she gave an audible sigh at reaching the
usual conclusion. Lee looked up, as if he'd only just realised
that she was there.

"Jesus, we're here," he cried, jumping up in surprise, and a
glance out of the window showed that he was right. While he
had had his head buried in the football programme, and Kay
had been lost deep in her thoughts, the train had arrived at
Hertford North.

As they walked home from the Chinese takeaway shop 30
minutes later, Kay decided that she had finally had enough of
the stifling, silent deadlock, and she asked the question that
had first occurred to her back in the pub.

"Who was that guy you were talking to at the end?"

Lee looked at her blankly. "The smart looking guy in the
pub, with the nice shoes," she helped. "You were sat together
near the jukebox before we left."

"Why? What's it to you?" he said. He sounded wary. Their
walking pace slowed, and Kay chose her words carefully.

"Just that…I haven't seen him before, that's all. He's not
one of the usual gang at football is he?"

Lee snorted derisively: "As if you'd know who the 'usual
gang' is."

"Yeah, alright, you only let me go once a year so I suppose I don't know the usual gang that well, but anyway, I've been three or four times now and I haven't seen him before."

"He's just one of the lads. He doesn't live up this way or anything, but he knows some of the others and...." Lee seemed to decide against finishing the sentence, except for a shrug, the meaning of which Kay couldn't be sure about. Was that because he didn't know anything else about the guy, or because he didn't want to talk about it, she pondered for a second?

"Does he have a name then?" she persisted. Lee had quickened his stride again and was moving briskly on, head bowed as if battering against a strong wind. Kay, following half a pace behind Lee, started to repeat the question, but Lee stopped abruptly and turned to face her, forcing her to halt in her tracks and take a step back, like a race horse refusing a fence.

"His name's Billy, all right? He's one of the guys at football. He does some shit job cleaning graffiti off walls. That's all I know about him Kay, so just forget about it. Enough fucking questions."

Lee hurried on again, mumbling something inaudible. Kay was stunned. She took a deep breath and watched him making off towards the house they shared, now only a few hundred metres away. Slowly, and with the apparent reluctance of an unhappy schoolchild dreading a day at school, she started walking along in Lee's wake.

He was in the living room, sitting on the sofa with his coat still on when Kay pushed the door open and walked in two minutes later. She took the bag of Chinese food through to the kitchen, draped her own coat over the back of a chair, poured herself a large glass of red wine from a bottle on the side, and wandered back into the front room. Lee was still on the sofa, picking vacantly at his food, his coat by his side. Kay picked up the coat and hung it on the post at the bottom of the staircase.

She was more than accustomed to Lee's moods, so this evening should not have been a surprise or a problem for Kay, but somehow, something seemed very wrong in his temper tonight. It was as if something had spooked him. She sat on the armchair across from the sofa, and took a sizeable gulp of wine down. For several seconds she studied the rim of the glass, tapping her finger upon it in a short tattoo.

"Well…" she hesitated. "Well, I'm sorry Lee. I didn't mean to upset you. We had a nice day earlier, and then this evening…I don't know what happened but I'm sorry. I won't ask again."

That expended all of her will to speak. It felt as if every time she opened her mouth it was only to take another step deeper into a dense minefield for which there was no map. Lee glanced up at her briefly, and she saw for the first time that his eyes were awash with tears; and behind the tears, in that momentary glimpse, she believed she saw confusion and fear.

Right there, in her husband's eyes, was confusion and fear, and she had no idea why. A stab of inadequate shame made her wince inside.

Before she could summon further words though, Lee was gone – up and out of the front door into a night growing chilly, and Kay was left to look with mute despair at his barely touched plate of Chinese food, some spilled onto the sofa cushion in the sudden disturbance when he had left. Slowly, but it seemed with deliberate dramatic purpose, a discarded fork slipped from the sofa to the floor. Kay didn't see it finally fall, though she heard it hit the floor. Her head was in her hands, and bewildered tears dotted the carpet by her feet.

Chapter Two

Nick was woken from a deep slumber by a sharp pain in his left arm. He heard himself emit a half-hearted "owww" in recognition of the burning sensation that lingered. With some reluctance, he forced his eyes open, and found himself facing the digital clock radio that sat on the small table at the side of the bed he shared with Justine. Familiar territory at least, even if his head was reeling from persistent internal hammer blows.

A fleeting thought: oh God, why do we do it? He was lying on his right side, facing out of the side of the bed, and he suddenly realised that his upper body was feeling distinctly chillier than his legs and feet. The duvet that should have covered his arms and shoulders had disappeared, or perhaps it had been pinched; it was certainly elsewhere anyway.

"Morning, you noisy bastard."

Ah, Justine; there was the answer to the duvet mystery. She sounded alert but there was some effort in her voice – effort and pain. Nick was still sleepy-headed, but he guessed the sequence of events. "Ugh, sorry babe. Snoring again?" He stretched his arms out as he settled on his back, and accompanied it with a noisy, wordless groan. The exertion exhausted him.

"You bet," said Justine from beneath the covers. Nick could only see a shapeless lump under the duvet to his left, but he knew she was there, and he could hear her shallow breathing.

"There's no need to be so violent though," he complained. "Can't you just give me a shake, and then perhaps a little kiss to welcome me into a new day?"

"Nope. It's tough love babe. I'm hoping that one day you'll learn never to snore within hitting distance of me, and that way we'll both be happy."

Nick chuckled softly and reached out with a foot beneath the duvet to poke Justine in the back of the leg. She giggled and shifted to try to move her body out of his reach.

"What time is it? I've been awake for ages but I just couldn't face opening my eyes. It hurts too much."

The way she said it made it seem so unfair, like a young child about to burst into tears when it couldn't have its way. Nick flicked his eyes over to the clock again, having not registered in the slightest what the digits were the first time he had looked.

"It's 9.54. God, were we supposed to be going somewhere today? Everything's a blur after that last game with the tequilas. Can I have some covers back by the way? It's bloody freezing out here."

Justine quickly turned over to face Nick, appearing head first from beneath the quilt cover, her red hair falling haphazardly across her face. She dragged the covers up with her and was soon nestled against Nick's side, nuzzling his chest. A happy sigh told him all was well and the snoring was forgiven.

"We were supposed to be going shopping – not that we've got any frigging cash," she said, her voice muffled against his skin.

"We could still go," he yawned "I could be technical advisor – as usual."

"Yeah, but we haven't got any frigging cash!" Her voice was louder with pretend impatience, then softer again as she said: "We blew it all on booze last night, or had you forgotten?"

"Mmm. Yeah, I'm still piecing all that together. I hate it when we play truth or dare with those two. I always find out things about you that I'd rather not know."

"Oh, you can talk – Mister bloody Perfect!"

They had spent an evening playing drinking games at the nearby flat of Brendan and Nicole, two Australian friends of Justine's, and by extension now friends of Nick. It had got very messy, Nick reflected, but very funny all the same – even the revelations about some of Justine's former love interests back home. Justine was still resting her head across Nick's chest as he looked down at her. He played with her hair, running his fingers through it over and again.

"Hey Just."

There was a groan in response. "Hey," he tried again, a bit louder. She turned to meet his eyes with an enquiring frown. He said: "You know, despite everything I found out last night, I still think you could be the girl for me."

That brought a small, indulgent smile to her face. She wriggled upwards so she could plant a kiss on his lips. "You're forgiven too, my gorgeous man."

Weak sunlight was sneaking through the not quite fully drawn curtains, and Justine looked towards the gap between them for a couple of seconds, studying the tiny drifting particles of dust that the beam of light illuminated, before snuggling back down. After a minute with no sound but their breathing as they dozed, she emerged from her slumber again to say: "You know what we need? We need paracetamol."

"You're right. That's exactly what we need. And a fry up. Actually…shit! We do need more paracetamol – there's only two tablets left... "

Almost before the words had left his mouth, she sprung away and in a single swift movement swung her legs out of the bed and was off, giggling and calling back as she headed out of the door: "Last one there's a drongo!"

Nick didn't carry much spare meat on him and was also quickly on his feet and chasing headlong after the slap, slap of Justine's bare feet heading for the bathroom cabinet where the painkillers were kept. He got to the door just as she tried to force it shut behind her and he barged a shoulder against the swinging wood in time to wedge himself in the way. On the other side of the door she pushed against him with all her strength but when he pushed back Justine stood no chance, giving way slowly but surely amidst giggles and protesting shouts of "no!" and "I need to use the loo!"

Then he burst in and she lunged for the cabinet, grabbing the box of pills just before Nick. They wrestled, breathless giggles bursting through the exertion, until finally Nick yanked the box free of her grasp and dropped to the floor, exhausted by the sudden burst of activity, but still laughing.

"You bastard! I knew I should have hit you harder when you were snoring," said Justine, slumping down on the toilet seat, chest heaving, defeated and a little angered at that fact.

He caught the hint of hurt in her voice, and looked up, concerned. Suddenly the laughter was gone and once more the only sound was their breathing, heavier now after the struggle. Nick forced himself to sit up cross-legged on the bathroom floor and studied the bath rug for a second. It was time for magnanimity. He broke the pills out and held one out for Justine.

"One bullet each, my love: if we're going to do this, let's do it together."

Her face broke into a beam. "You, my lovely man, are a gentleman. Yes, let's do it together. I can't think of anything better."

An hour or so later, after paracetamol tablets, showers, and fried eggs and bacon prepared by Justine, they were both ready to leave the flat. They decided to mooch around some of the shops in Camden and see if anything took their fancy, although funds were tight. It was not until gone midday that Justine decided to check her mobile phone and found that she hadn't switched the phone on since turning it off in the early hours of the morning when they had staggered to bed.

Soon after she had righted that situation and put the handset back in her bag, the phone chimed to announce that a message was waiting. They were walking around an outdoor market that was teeming with people; where the low hum of talking voices, the chirpy calls of stall-holders, and the reggae beats of a Rasta guy and his music system, all made for a rich mélange of sounds. It also meant that when Justine squeezed the phone to her ear she still couldn't hear the voice message that had been recorded.

They had stopped walking and were standing by a clothes stall. Justine made a face, and said: "Uh, I think it's mum, but can't hear for shit here. Let's go in there babe."

She pointed to a café further along the road, and he followed her in. It was noisy in the café as well, but they settled at a table, and Nick indicated two cups of tea to the Turkish man behind the counter. Justine was playing her mobile phone message again, and Nick knew straight away that something was wrong. His girlfriend's face had dropped quickly after the initial happiness at hearing her mum's voice all the way from Melbourne. Now she looked aghast. Her face then crumpled momentarily but Nick saw her fight to regain her poise. Eventually she took the phone away from her ear and reached out to hold Nick's hands across the table.

She kept her eyes on Nick's hands and he could see her fighting tears away. When she spoke, her voice wavered unsteadily. "Babe, I'm going to have to go back home for a bit. Dad's in hospital, he's had an accident." She looked up at Nick's face. He looked intently back at her, feeling a moment of fright at this sudden need for him to show strength.

"Let's get out of here, let's go home," he said, abruptly pushing his chair back with a scrape. "Cancel the teas mate. Sorry," he called to the man at the counter, as he led Justine back out into the street. She staggered along on Nick's arm as if in a daze, but soon they were back in their sanctuary, their own space, and he sat her down on the sofa, putting himself at her feet on the floor.

"Okay Just. What did she say?"

He could see that Justine was still desperately keeping her emotions in check, but it was obvious that they were very close to the surface. She stumbled through the next few sentences, looking glassy eyed.

"Mum just said to get in touch as soon as I heard the message. Dad has had an accident and he's hurt bad, and she

51

needed to hear my voice, and if I could fix it to show my face that would be even better." Suddenly she gave way to an angry outburst: "We've got no fucking money Nick. How are we going to get back to Australia?"

It wasn't meant as an accusation against Nick. It was a cry of frustration, and tears did at last flow. Nick was next to her on the sofa in a flash, holding her close and rocking her gently. She gasped choked apologies as she wept.

Soon the tears came to an end, and she forced a weak smile up at Nick. "Just when things were getting good for us, eh babe," she said softly. Nick repeated her sentence absent-mindedly while he cast about for the right words. Then he brushed some tears from her cheeks, and propped her chin up with his forefinger, forcing her to look at him.

"Listen Just. We're going to be fine. We don't know what's happened yet do we, so you've got to phone your mum right now, so she can hear your voice. And one way or another we're going to get you on a flight to Melbourne as soon as we can. I'll speak to Nicole and some of the others; see what we can get together."

"No babe, you've got to come with me too. I need you there with me," she protested.

"Well, we'll have to see with the money. If we can, then I will. Anyway, you've got to phone your mum. She needs you right now."

Justine looked vacantly out of the window for a second, as if turning her eyes towards the east and home, where her family was in such distress. She seemed at a loss for words suddenly.

Nick stroked her cheek and said: "Justine, phone her now. Don't worry about the time. Do it now."

Justine doubtfully eyed the handset that Nick had retrieved from her handbag, but then took it from him all the same. "Jesus, I'm shit scared Nick." She was shaking.

"Nonsense," he countered gently. "You're a brave, tough Aussie girl. You don't get scared." He smiled, and with difficulty she choked a small laugh out.

"Yeah, right, you soft Pommie bastard. Hold my hand Nick. Don't let go."

He could see that her eyes were filled with dread, but she went ahead and made the call. It was getting towards 10.30 at night in Melbourne but her mum answered quickly. Nick watched for reactions on Justine's face throughout the call; there was an occasional weak smile, but mostly she showed little outward emotion, apart from her vice-like grip on his hand. It never loosened until the call was done ten minutes later.

Justine sighed deeply and placed the handset on the sofa. Nick watched her stand up and walk on unsteady legs in the direction of the bedroom. He was about to open his mouth to say something when she turned back and looked at him with hurt in her eyes. As she spoke her voice was soft, but over-flowing with pent up emotion.

"Babe, dad's in a pretty bad way. I'm going to lie down in the bedroom for a while. Come and see me in a bit will you? Thirty minutes, something like that. Maybe an hour. I just need a bit of time. Then we can talk. Bring me something strong to drink."

She disappeared into the bedroom and the door clicked shut, leaving Nick to wonder in admiration at the strength of this woman whose life he shared.

**

Things moved quickly for Nick and Justine in the week that followed news of her father's accident. Phil Tanner worked as a construction site foreman in Melbourne, where he lived with Justine's mother, Maria. He had a long background in con-struction, and was highly experienced at his job. However, none of that helped him that day in September 2007. He was conferring with some of his workers on site when a careless bulldozer driver accidentally backed into a stack of metal girders nearby. The air was rent with the screech of iron as the girders gave way, and fell like an avalanche onto Phil and two of his men before they could scamper clear of the danger.

Phil Tanner was now in hospital in a coma, with serious head, leg and internal injuries, and his wife was spending every waking hour at his bedside. It was too early to say if the 55-year old would ever recover.

Nick and Justine, with hardly any money of their own, had scraped funds together from some friends and two hundred Australian dollars that Maria Tanner had transferred electronically to her daughter's UK bank account. They had enough to pay for a single ticket from London to Melbourne – about £750 for the earliest available flight they could find on the internet.

Reluctantly, Justine had accepted that it was not going to be possible for Nick to travel with her. There was the lack of money for one thing, but also it would require a lengthy application process for Nick to gain a visa to enter the country, and the process would take even longer in view of his prior conviction for possession of a Class A drug.

Justine also had to obtain permission from her employer to leave at short notice. Her bosses were sympathetic though; there would even be a place for her when she returned, they assured her. It was more than Justine could have hoped for, and the gesture left her, not for the first time in recent days, with tears welling up in her eyes.

And so the flight which would take Justine the ten thousand or so miles back to her homeland was booked. She was to depart from Heathrow Airport at around 8pm on the next Saturday night – just one week after hearing the desperate news of her father's accident. After a stop in Dubai, she would not reach Melbourne until Monday morning. Nick's mind boggled at the thought, he having never travelled much further than a package holiday to Greece before.

Friday evening brought a mixture of emotions for both of them as they stayed in to pack her things for the trip. She had decided to take two large cases, carrying about half of her clothes. She had no idea how long she would be gone for, but if either of them even thought it, neither voiced any fear that she might not return. Many times already she had said that her life was with Nick. He still saw that commitment in her eyes.

So they laughed that Friday night, and Justine cried a little as well. She was pleased in one sense to be going back to Australia to see her mum, and she reckoned that perhaps she would even catch up with some old friends back in Melbourne. However, the circumstances were ghastly so there was fear as well: fear of that first sight of her stricken dad lying still and silent in a hospital bed; fear of what the future would hold for him, and for the Tanners as a family; fear of leaving Nick behind just as they were building their lives together.

No friends came over that night. Justine had arranged to drop in and see Brendan and Nicole on Saturday afternoon. She wanted the last night in England to be a special night between her and Nick.

They awoke at 7.30am to feelings that lurched between disbelief that Justine was about to fly back home, and a creeping dread about their impending split. With Justine weeping quietly in his arms again, it all seemed so unreal to Nick. All too soon it was time to leave for the airport in mid-afternoon.

Justine was quiet as they lugged her cases to the tube station; deep in thought. Nick felt sick in his heart. It was actually happening and he could do nothing to stop it. Their conversation was muted as they sped towards Heathrow on the Piccadilly Line; just occasional flashes of forced cheerfulness. Faced with the prospect of his girlfriend spending an unknown period of time on the other side of the world, Nick could find nothing useful or helpful to say.

They had barely spent an evening apart in the 18 months since they had met. She was not only his best friend, but almost his only one. His social circle was made up almost entirely of her friends. How would that work out with Justine not around? He had no idea. How would he cope living alone in the flat in her absence? He was about to find out, but he wasn't looking forward to the experience.

What worried him most was the vacuum that was about to be left in his life. She was just there so much, being Justine, with her own scent, her own funny turns of phrase, and her own soft affection from which he drew his strength. How could he replace this, he wondered? Then he scolded himself silently for being ridiculous: she would only be gone for a short time, and she would be on the end of a telephone every day.

They left the tube at Heathrow, and oddly, thought Nick, their mood seemed to cheer as they walked together to the airline check-in area. The airport was busy with excited holiday makers, and weary travellers curled up on seats, waiting for delayed flights to be called. Justine held onto Nick's arm as she pulled one of her cases along on its wheels.

"You okay babe?" she asked, squeezing his arm. "You were very quiet on the tube."

"I was thinking that's all. No more salads and plenty of pizza for the next few weeks for me. Can't wait!"

She smacked his shoulder playfully, and shot him an amused look. At the check-in desk they joined the back of a long queue that shuffled forward tediously slowly. Once her heavy baggage had been handed over, Nick and Justine wandered off to locate a café. She calculated that she still had nearly an hour before she needed to go through security to the departure area.

They sat, drank tea and had a sandwich, laughing at fellow travellers whose appearance, behaviour or mannerisms tickled their sense of the absurd. Somehow Justine seemed fairly relaxed – far more calm than Nick would have been had he been faced with a 24 hour plane journey.

She reached across the table to take Nick's hands in her own, and gave him an appreciative smile. "Nick, I just want you to know that I've really been made up by the way you've helped me through these last few days. You've been ace, so great, and I'm going to miss you heaps," she said.

"It was nothing…"

"No babe, it wasn't nothing. I'm so lucky to have you. I couldn't have asked for any more, and I won't forget how great you've been."

Nick could feel himself choking up inside. When he spoke though, he somehow managed to disguise the wavering in his voice.

"Just, I've never even met your dad, but I really hope things work out okay. I'll be here waiting for you, whatever happens. You know that don't you?"

"Yeah, of course. Well, I bloody hope so anyway – you're living in my flat!"

They laughed easily, and Nick sat back, relieved that she didn't seem to expect any great farewell speech. Seconds were ticking away, and he felt helpless.

"This does feel odd though," Justine suddenly said. "I hate having to press the pause button like this when we have so much going for us babe. I just hope you don't get fed up waiting and go off with that silly little girl in the coffee bar at work. They will all be after you, you do know that, don't you?"

He could see that she was teasing him, but he sensed that there was maybe just a little anxiety behind it to match his own. It was a reasonable reaction to be worried about what this enforced separation might mean for their blossoming relationship, and he had felt that worry himself with dispiriting regularity these last few days. He grinned sheepishly now though. "No chance of that Just. I'll be here waiting, don't you worry."

All too quickly, the time came for Justine to move through the airport towards the departure gates. They left the empty tea cups on the table and Nick escorted her to security, where a longish snaking queue stretched back from access points to several electronic scanning units. This was it then. Nick felt panic in his heart. This really was it.

They hugged tightly and silently for a long minute, and then searched each other's faces for some kind of comfort; some sign that this was not really happening. The tears were being kept at bay for now, though Nick didn't know how. Justine's kiss lingered on his lips. Then she looked closely and earnestly into his eyes, as if searching for something, before saying: "I will phone you every day. Make sure you're ready for me, every morning and every lunchtime. Okay?"

Nick felt like a schoolboy being given instructions by his mother at the gates on the first day at school. Everywhere around them though, people were saying goodbye to loved ones; Nick and Justine blended perfectly in. Once again he felt himself choking up, and his voice croaked slightly as he told her: "I love you girl. I need you back."

She kissed him again, this time a more perfunctory peck. "This is horrible. I've got to go," she whispered. She fled, it seemed, and made off between the zigzagging lines of belts that led to the end of the queue. Nick watched her moving slowly towards the front; she was looking through her bag, checking things like her passport, her boarding ticket, and her paperback book, he guessed. When she was two from the front, she finally turned to look at him, smiled sadly and blew him a kiss.

Then she was gone. All he could see was her long red hair cascading down her back for a second or two, as she emptied some money and keys into a box and then walked out of sight beyond the scanner. In a daze, Nick walked slowly away to find the exit. Already, he thought, it felt like she was only a figment of his imagination; like an angel in some fantastical dream that he had just been jolted from. The shock was indescribable. What chance was there of finding one like her in the real world?

**

58

Guilt was a complicated emotion, Kay considered, as she lay back and stared at the smooth white plaster of her bedroom ceiling. She had reasoned with herself and rationalised about these moments for weeks; she had known somewhere in the dark corners of her mind, without even acknowledging it, that it would come to this. When she had thought about it previously however, when it was something that might theoretically happen, it had seemed much easier to justify: because she was a woman, and she believed an attractive one at that; because she still had physical needs that Lee made no attempt to meet.

Then, two weeks earlier, it had become real and it was now something that could be referred to in the present tense. Half of the time she felt sick with shame. Moments of panic caused her to catch her breath every now and again.

Outside, the early evening light was just beginning to wane. Downstairs, in the front room, her laptop computer had long since gone into an energy-saving hibernation. To Kay's left, James – her husband's friend – stirred as he dozed and shifted onto his side, his back to Kay, covered by the bedclothes that adorned Lee and Kay's bed.

She looked for a while at his dark hair, and thought with silent regret about what had happened these last two weeks. She had known it was going to happen, the moment he had sent her a text message a week before that, and said he was working at home in Ware, and did she want to meet for lunch. It had been arranged for Tuesday, and he had turned up at the house earlier than she had expected, seeming slightly nervy, slightly tense. They had flirted playfully as she readied herself to leave the house. In the end they never got that far.

Drawing boldness from their jokes, James made his move, grabbing hold of Kay as she was closing down her computer and kissing her neck before saying: "Of course, we don't have to go out Kay. I'm not that hungry really. Not for food anyway... "

God, how corny, she had thought. She had seen the uncertainty in James' eyes since he had arrived though. He had been frightened, but finally he had made the big move that she knew was on his mind. And it was on her mind too. All the eye contact across the bar at pubs and restaurants, all the supposedly matey conversations, had led to that point. After the initial surprise that the moment was finally here, she had responded readily, for the simple reason that it had been too long since she had felt this kind of thrill. In responding, Kay felt James melt into her arms with relief, his pent up doubts taking instant flight.

Already it had become a weekly routine, every Tuesday. James would come round to the house in the afternoon, and he and Kay would spend the next several hours together. Then James would leave by 6pm to ensure he was gone long before Lee came home from work.

Now, on the third occasion that she and James had got together, Kay lay in her bed and contemplated what was now happening to her. Had it been a magical fortnight? It had been…nice, she thought. James was a nice guy and he had tried very hard to please her. It had been a long time since anybody had made that much effort on her behalf. Suddenly her stomach grumbled, reminding her that she hadn't eaten since breakfast. She looked across at her bedside clock, and saw that it was just after 5pm. Well, of course it hadn't been magical, she laughed to herself; he's a man after all.

Kay decided to get up and fix herself a snack to stave off the hunger pangs. Wrapping herself in her dressing gown, she went down to the kitchen, and prepared a ham and cucumber sandwich, which she started to eat in front of the TV. There wasn't much on to watch, as usual. Daytime TV, she found, was dreadful, which was handy if you intended to work at home, because there was nothing to distract you from your job.

She had been watching the TV for ten minutes or so when suddenly her mobile phone, which she had left next to her laptop across the front room, rang. Perhaps it's Wilf, she thought, leaping up from the sofa. The display screen of the phone informed her otherwise though. It was Lee.

She answered the call with a curt: "Yes?"

"Kay, I'm just round the corner at the shops. Do we need anything?"

Kay froze for a second, as the implication of the words sunk in. "What do you mean, you're round the corner?" she asked, sounding as unconcerned as she could. If Lee was where he said he was, he could be at the front door in five minutes.

"What? I mean exactly what I said." He sounded impatient already. "Do we need anything?"

"How come...it's early for you to be home..."

"Yeah, I knocked off a bit early today, if that's alright with you. I know you've been skiving off all day – er, milk, have we got much milk in?"

Kay had a hot flush, but she fought to keep calm. She moved quickly into the kitchen and checked the contents of the fridge.

"Yeah, okay, get some milk, and a loaf of bread. And some more red wine. And whatever you want. Can you get me a lottery ticket as well?"

"You don't do the lottery, you daft moo."

A little white lie was required; anything to buy time. "Yes I do. I do the Wednesday one sometimes. I just never win so you never hear about it. Any numbers, just do a lucky dip thing."

"Oh right. Okey dokey. Maybe I'll get one for myself as well eh? See you in a bit."

He hung up, and Kay threw the phone onto the sofa in the front room, before running quickly upstairs, her mind racing.

"James! James! Get up! You've got to go, Lee's nearly home!" she called ahead, then burst into the bedroom to find James still dozing. She shook him frantically until he reluctantly opened his eyes. It took a second for the urgency of the situation to hit him, but then he was out of the bed, and running around the room collecting his clothing, which had been carelessly strewn on the floor.

It was like a scene from a Carry On film Kay thought, as James hopped around trying to put his socks on at the same time as buttoning his shirt, all the while muttering the word "shit" over and over. She would have laughed had the implications not been so serious. Within a minute he was dressed and, stopping only for the briefest of kisses, Kay pushed him out of the front door towards his car and slammed the door shut in his wake. She then dashed back to the bedroom to tidy up and hastily dress.

A quick glance in the mirror told her that she looked acceptable, although her hair was a bit dishevelled. She pulled it all back in a ponytail. A hair-up day for a work-at-home day – it seemed sensible enough. She was panting heavily though after the last two crazy minutes of activity. Kay silently thanked God that Lee had phoned ahead, for it could only have been divine intervention that had made it happen. She smirked at her reflection in the mirror at that thought.

The humour of the situation was all too obvious, now that she felt reasonably hopeful that James could have made his getaway before the front door was within Lee's sight. Hopefully he would therefore be suspecting nothing. Kay laughed quietly and took several deep breaths, before heading downstairs to the front room, where she settled at the laptop again, and switched it back on.

Seconds later she heard the key turn in the lock and her husband came in breezily, swinging a carrier bag in one hand and dropping his briefcase on the sofa as he went through to the kitchen.

Kay looked up at him as he came back out into the front room. Everything seemed fine in his demeanour, but then Lee could be full of surprises.

She dipped a toe in the water, while studiedly keeping her eyes on the computer screen: "Alright?"

"Your luck's out," he said in a matter of fact voice, grabbing his case from the settee. Kay had a lurch of panic.

"Why's that then?" Keep calm, she told herself. Lee was on his way to the foot of the stairs, but spun round.

"I left your ticket in there," he said, gesturing towards the kitchen. "But you've got no fucking chance, cos my numbers are the winners."

He cackled with mirth and went up the stairs, taking them two at a time. Kay sat back in the chair and found herself once again contemplating the ceiling. It felt like pure, warm spring water was gushing through her veins, but Kay knew what the substance really was. It could only be the relief of a lucky escape made good. She afforded herself a private smile and said quietly to herself:

"You don't know the half of it dearest. Not even the half of it."

**

Upstairs, Lee hastily removed his suit jacket, then loosened his tie and lifted it over his head, placing it on a bedside cabinet. The shirt, suit trousers and shoes soon followed, to be replaced by a casual top, a designer pullover, jeans, and a pair of trainers. Then he started to empty his suit pockets of various items. His wallet, keys, a few coins and his mobile phone he tossed on to the bed, before hanging the suit up in a wardrobe.

He moved quickly and with what seemed like calm purpose, humming a brisk tune as he did so. It was only when he sat on the bed and picked up his mobile phone that the shaking of his hands betrayed his highly keyed-up state; perhaps nerves, perhaps excitement. Perhaps fear. Lee pressed some buttons on the mobile phone to enter his text message inbox, and opened the most recent message received.

'Hello mate, all as planned. U drive, I will be on train. C u there 7.30' the text message read. He afforded himself a smile, and closed the message, which he had first viewed some hours earlier. Anticipation had been building in him since. This is the start, thought Lee, just the start, and here he was at the centre of it. Billy had told him that scores would soon be evened up, and Billy had everything planned, except for a few last little details, and that was what they hoped to sort out tonight.

He had left work early to make sure that he wasn't late for the rendezvous. The weekly management meeting had looked like going on longer than he hoped, but Lee had played a muted role throughout, much more so than usual, deferring often to his boss and to his own assistant. He was playacting really, trying to appear lethargic and speaking without conviction. This was just the preliminary before approaching his boss straight after the meeting and crying off home early, supposedly feeling under the weather.

Lee wasn't sure about his acting skills but it seemed to work, and his boss Lukas, a short, overweight black man with a bald head, thick glasses and a permanent sweat, had assented without Lee having to ham it up too much. Lukas waddled off to his office, several sheets of A4 paper crumpled in his pudgy fingers, leaving Lee to swiftly throw a few things into his briefcase and then dash for Liverpool Street station.

His mood had just got better and better as he journeyed back from London towards home. He felt as if at last there was going to be some purpose to his life, something which had been missing since his faith in his marriage had plummeted. The absence of children had hurt him for a long time, and had left him feeling bitter towards his wife. While he knew about her mother's fate, that was no reason for the world to end, he believed. They had agreed to discuss things, but it had gone beyond that stage now. She didn't want to know how he felt about it, so why discuss it? It was her decision, her career, and they were her ovaries.

Well, fuck you Kay, he had decided. You're pissed half of the time and you'd make a lousy mother anyway. In the absence of any hope of children though, there had been a vast chasm in his life. During these last few months an answer had crept up on him. Although he hadn't been affected by them directly, the bombings in London two years earlier had changed his focus on the world he inhabited and the people in it. It was an affront that these things were happening in *his* city. What kind of coward strapped a bomb to their body and set it off amongst a crowd of innocent strangers?

He had despaired about the situation for some time, but meeting Billy through a friend at football had convinced him that there were things that could be done to put things right; to put these people in their place. Lee had discovered an urge within himself to get involved. He had come to feel that it was the least he could do in the circumstances.

Across the other side of the king size bed was a full length mirror, and Lee turned to appraise himself in it briefly. His cheeks were flushed with the anticipation of his purpose. He wouldn't have admitted it to anyone, but the prospect of meeting up with Billy again was perhaps the biggest thrill. The guy was incredible; a visionary, Lee thought. He saw things as they were and he had the ideas to put them right.

Lee had never met anyone like him. At first, the solutions that Billy suggested had left Lee feeling unnerved. It was dramatic and dangerous, and he had needed to be convinced that this was the right way. Kay often told him that he was easily led, but it had taken Billy and some of the others a long time to eventually persuade him that this was right. Oh no, he hadn't just given in, but the doubt was now mostly gone, or at least it was consigned to a part of his brain that he could lock away and ignore more easily.

Kay was calling something up the stairs: she was making a cuppa, did he want one?

"Er, no. I'm going straight out," Lee shouted back, as he filled the pockets of his coat with the items he had taken from the suit jacket.

And Kay? Well, she had no idea. She probably thought Lee was up to no good, but she would suspect it involved a woman, Lee guessed. All of those games of squash, and nights out in town with the lads from work…well, sometimes he actually did do that. Other times, he met Billy and the others to talk and plan; to be inspired.

Right – time to get moving boy, he told himself. He smirked at his reflection in the mirror, without of course knowing that this action repeated that of his wife just minutes earlier. With one last pat on his various pockets to check everything he required was there, he hurried downstairs. Kay was back at her computer, typing something.

"Where are my car keys?" Lee asked, searching around various pieces of furniture.

"On the side in the kitchen, where you left them yesterday," Kay replied as she tapped away.

Lee found the keys and walked quickly back past Kay towards the front door. "Don't wait up," he called back to her. Her reply, which began: "As if I'd do that…" was cut off by the slam of the door behind him.

"…dearest, as if I'd do that," said Kay, finishing the sentence in the moment that followed his abrupt departure. She looked out at the gathering evening and shrugged. She heard him gunning the car engine into life outside. "Arsehole," she muttered, and went back to her computer screen. She did, after all, have work to catch up on.

**

Nick was sitting at his pitch at Liverpool Street, waiting for a customer, thinking about his circumstances. He had to laugh about it. Boy, you're a real hell-raiser these days, he told himself dryly. No sex, no drugs (thankfully), precious little alcohol, and rather more Eastenders than rock & roll.

It had been a strange couple of weeks since Justine had gone back to Australia. At first he'd found it difficult to get used to the emptiness of the flat. He wasn't there much during the day, but in the evenings he found the absence of his girlfriend made him feel unusually morose. As much as the physical company she gave him, and the sound of her voice, he missed the noise of Justine – just the fact that someone else would be moving things around in the kitchen or in the bedroom while he was there.

It was probably his imagination playing tricks on him, but it seemed that previously unheard odd noises, just small creaks and knocks, now came out of the hush of the night to interrupt his thoughts as he lay alone, stretching out to try and fill the space in the bed where Justine would usually be.

The first week had been the hardest, but he believed he was now starting to get used to her being away. Mercifully, his sleeping patterns were at least improving. Now, he would leave the Camden flat by 6am every weekday to head for Liverpool Street; he would spend a long and usually boring day shining shoes and drinking Vicky's coffee, and would be back home around twelve hours after leaving the flat to prepare and eat a simple tea, and pass the night watching television until he decided to turn in. In this way, the days soon ticked past.

At least he did manage to speak to Justine once, and sometimes twice, every day. She had sounded exhausted the first time she had called, which had been only a handful of hours after her long journey home. He thought she sounded like a little girl lost, and he was upset for a few hours afterwards, because there was nothing that he could do or say to make anything better.

The next time they spoke was after she had been to see her dad in hospital for the first time, and she was tearful and shocked at the seriousness of Phil Tanner's injuries. Nick could tell that she got some comfort from hearing his voice.

Nick had felt helpless really. He had been standing outside Liverpool Street station during his lunch break, City workers milling around in every direction, his phone pressed to his ear. His girlfriend described her feelings at seeing her dad lying prone and unresponsive in a hospital bed; how the nursing staff had explained various medical things to her and had tried to reassure her that there was a good chance that her father would recover well.

Nick had tried to hang on to every word but it was difficult to relate to. It all felt somehow distant and unreal as he stood squinting in the weak sunshine of an English October afternoon. He had tried to be understanding but everything that came out of his mouth just sounded like a dumb platitude. It had actually been a relief when Justine had filled a sudden silence between them to say:

"Well, I guess I'd better let you get back to work babe, and I've got to get back to mum too. There are some people queuing for the phone as well. Listen, take care babe, eat good things, change your socks every day, and don't watch too much crap on TV. I'll speak to you tomorrow. Love you babe."

And then she was gone again. It all made for an emotional rollercoaster for Nick. On the one hand, he looked forward to hearing her voice; on the other hand, he found that the conversation was difficult and that he would be pre-occupied for hours afterwards, thinking about what she had said, about the distress that was audible in her voice, and about his own feelings of inadequacy.

As the first week ended and the second week began, Nick thought he heard a different inflection in Justine's voice. She was more upbeat, more together, more like the practical problem solver that he was familiar with. It didn't make him feel any happier though, because he was unable to avoid the feeling that she was coping with this better now without him. Already, as he had feared might happen, things felt like they were changing – but was it just him thinking that? Imagining it? Being paranoid?

She had asked him early in that second week what he thought about the idea of eventually moving to Australia more permanently. She was testing the water, he reckoned, just in case she felt unable to leave her dad stricken on the other side of the world. There was a major potential problem with that though: Nick's criminal record. He had cracked the old joke that "you don't need a criminal record to get into Australia any more", but the fact was that Nick had been convicted of possession of a Class A drug. His first research indicated that there would be a great deal of red tape to go through if he ever wanted to emigrate to Australia.

"I could check what the score is with the embassy?" he had suggested.

"No, don't worry. It was just a thought really." She sounded suddenly distracted, as if something else had caught her attention, or perhaps because she had completely forgotten about Nick's past and its implications until that moment.

Their conversation moved on, but Nick kept reflecting back on that point of the discussion later. The whole situation had started to eat him up just two weeks after Justine had departed. He wanted her back, and he wanted their life to return to how it was before her dad's accident.

He didn't deserve this, but somehow, unfathomably, in his mind at least, it was all starting to unravel. In an attempt to alleviate some of the anxiety he had started to feel, Nick had spent an evening out drinking with Brendan and Nicole, Justine's Australian friends. The attempt was a vain one though, and instead only served to heighten his anguish.

They had met up in the pub along the road from Justine's flat, and had been joined at various times by other regulars and some other Aussies that Nick was less familiar with. Much of the conversation seemed to revolve around places in Australia and none of it meant anything to Nick.

As he had sat in the pub, a difficult truth had become obvious to Nick. It was that without Justine, the whole dynamic of his relationship with these people was completely altered. She was the reason why he knew them and socialised with them. Without her he found that he didn't really know why he was keeping their company. A moment of silent dismay had jarred Nick's mind as this thought hit home.

He had no other real friends outside of Justine's circle. There was no immediate family left and he had lost contact with all his old childhood friends over the course of several years. The truth was stark: without Justine, he felt alone. Another tremor of panic had shaken his wandering mind.

Needing time and solitude to recover, Nick had excused himself from the table and went to put some money into the jukebox. He was reeling from the uncertainty that now hung over what had seemed to be an ordained course for his life. He told himself to calm down; that she could be back in a week or two and all this silliness would have been for nothing.

He had got through the rest of the evening without any more sticky moments, though his sleep was piecemeal that night. And now here he was, just a few days later, sitting at his Liverpool Street pitch, reflecting again on the unsettling ebb and flow of his emotions.

It was mid-morning. The initial rush was over and Nick found that he generally only had a few customers every hour at this time of the day. A low murmur of voices hummed around him, although the frequent station announcements still rang loud if not entirely clear. For a few minutes Nick sat back and watched people on the concourse. He found it interesting to just watch people; to study their faces and mannerisms. Often there was humour, as someone scanned the platform board hung up high, looking for the time of their next train; then, upon realising it was due to leave at any minute, they would suddenly break into a mad rush for the ticket barrier, hurriedly grasping for their ticket from pocket or bag.

Nick had developed the kind of keen eye for such things that only an observer with plenty of time on their hands could have. The minutes passed by very slowly during the working day until he finished at 5pm. This was part of the reason why he had suffered so badly from Justine going to Australia; he had a lot of time on his hands and it was hard not to spend it dwelling on what might or might not happen. He felt in better control of his emotions now though, and the worst moments were always in the evenings, when Justine's absence bit deepest.

Suddenly a young businessman in a dark grey suit and with prematurely thinning hair approached Nick for a shoeshine. He took a seat and Nick got to work. Sometimes he found that customers were happy to chat, sometimes not. Nick didn't mind either way, although he did enjoy a laugh and a joke at times. This guy was immediately on his mobile phone though, and stayed on it for the entire duration of the shoeshine. He seemed to be relating the events of a meeting to a colleague. The deal was clearly in the bag. Nick listened in, purely because there was little else to occupy his mind as he went through his practiced movements on the man's black shoes.

When the job was done the man nodded and pressed a five pound note into Nick's hand, before marching off still talking on the phone. Nick resumed his vigil, looking out across the concourse. A party of what he took to be foreign students were standing 20 yards away, laughing and babbling loudly in what sounded like Spanish. They had formed a tight circle, crowded around their overloaded back packs. Nick guessed that they were waiting for a Stansted Express train back to the airport. After a few minutes an older woman joined the group and, swinging their backpacks onto their shoulders, they trooped off behind her to catch their train.

Nick decided that he fancied a coffee and quickly walked over to the Coffee Cup bar to place an order with Vicky. She brought the beverage over a few minutes later and stopped to chat, but after just a minute her colleague Jez called out that a queue was building up.

Nick daydreamed while another ten minutes ticked by, and then decided to read some of his paperback book. Just then a middle aged businessman he had shined for on numerous occasions came through from the Broadgate area.

"Nick my man!" the man hailed him while still five yards behind where Nick was sitting. Nick looked over his left shoulder.

"Mr Gillespie. How's it going?" The man had given Nick his business card months before, so quite unusually he even knew this customer's name.

"Very good Nicholas, very good. I'm in need of a polish up if you can fit me into your busy schedule."

"Ooh, well let's see – Monday week? No, I'll tell you what, maybe just a quickie right now Mr Gillespie, but I'm expecting a rush at any minute. The usual?"

Gillespie took his position on the seat, with Nick bent forward on the stool in front of him. Gillespie liked to regale Nick in a posh English gentlemanly voice, as if the master was addressing a favourite servant. Nick didn't spend too long analysing these things though, and it meant nothing to him either way. He did a job, he got paid, and even if the humour was a little forced, it was still infinitely better than waking up frozen, filthy and another step closer to your maker after a night under a scummy blanket in a London back alley.

"Off anywhere nice Mr Gillespie?" Nick enquired as he smeared black polish on the man's brogues. They were already pretty darn clean thought Nick, but if he's paying then I'm shining. Gillespie was some sort of big hitter in a City investment firm, although Nick never remembered the specific details from one visit to the next. His suits and shoes were always expensively tailored.

"Just a meeting over in the West End," Gillespie replied to Nick's question. "More damned lawyers. Drive me insane, bloody bloodsucking bastards."

"What's that all about then?"

"Oh, never you mind sonny Jim. It's no business for anyone with an ounce of common sense."

"I'd hardly say that includes me Mr Gillespie, but whatever you say," Nick laughed, knowing that Gillespie wouldn't be able to resist telling him about it in minute detail anyway. After a couple of silent seconds Gillespie, evidently enjoying the game, blurted out: "Oh, alright you scoundrel, you've forced it out of me!"

It turned out to be a deal involving a global pharmaceutical company that wanted to build a new research facility in the UK. There were Government kickbacks, incentives, political lobbying, local opposition, and moral dilemmas – a long list of complicated dimensions. Nick soon lost the thread of it. The good thing about working as a shoeshiner though, was that every conversation, whether interesting, humorous, boring or just awkward, had a finite duration and a convenient exit point.

That exit point soon came. The shoeshine was finished and Gillespie paid his money and walked off laughing at another of his own wisecracks. Nick watched him go and shook his head with a laugh of his own. At least old Gillespie was a bit of a character, he thought, settling back into the seat that his customer had just vacated. Reaching down for his paperback book, Nick looked around quickly to see if any more potential clients were looming nearby.

Immediately he noticed an attractive woman, tanned and slim, long dark hair, dressed in a smart business suit, walking directly towards him across the concourse; striding forward past some cash machines that were installed underneath the steps that led from street level down into the station. Unmistakably, she was looking straight at Nick as she now passed the bottom of the escalators that were immediately in front of Nick's position, just yards away. The expression on her face was serene and composed, giving nothing away.

Some reflex inside Nick made him swallow hard for reasons he had no time to think about. He knew her, recognised her immediately, although he knew next to nothing about her except for her first name, which came to him from a corner of his memory straight away. Then she stopped walking and stood before him, no more than ten feet away; fixing him with a shy smile, rooting him to the spot. Almost subconsciously, Nick had slowly risen from his seat as she approached, and now they stood facing each other.

"Well…hello again," said the lady that Nick knew only as Kay. She seemed slightly embarrassed, apologetic even. "You might remember me from a few weeks ago – my husband and I had an argument here while you were shining his shoes."

"Yeah," Nick replied, then paused. "I do remember."

Why did he suddenly feel like this? It was as if he was standing alone in the middle of a floodlit football pitch, in a stadium packed with thousands of people, squinting in the dazzling light, frozen under their scrutiny. The big event was just starting. His mind raced, but there were no thoughts of Justine; there was no time for calm reflection. Instead, the pounding behind his ribs suggested to Nick that his turmoil had only just begun.

**

It had been anything but a serene day for Kay Talbot. She had woken late, and found the opposite side of the bed untouched from the night before. A half empty wine bottle on the bedside cabinet was a stinging reminder of where this marriage – this emotional vacuum, as she had morosely contemplated that it was the night before in the emptiness of the house – was taking her. There was another bottle, an empty one, in the sitting room as well, and an unloved bottle of gin was left by her laptop, the screw top by its side.

Kay had risen and stumbled into the sitting room in her dressing gown, her head thick, and her mind confused as to why her alarm had failed to sound at 7 o'clock as she had expected. She had switched on the TV and watched the breakfast news in some misery for a few minutes. It was already 8.15 in the morning, and somehow she was supposed to be in the City for a meeting with a client at 9.30. Lee had slept on the sofa, if the presence of a pillow at one end of it was anything to go by. She had no recollection of him coming home. Ten minutes later Kay had reluctantly shuffled into the bathroom and showered.

It was Wednesday and James had been over the day before, hence the wine. She was aware that she was drinking more and more, but on Tuesday evenings it seemed to reach its weekly peak, as if nothing less than a bottle or two could start to wash away her guilt. This particular Tuesday had been even worse than normal though. A week had passed since Lee had nearly caught them, and Kay was spending an uncomfortable amount of time dwelling on how close that shave had been. Should she finish the fling with James before disaster struck, or instead find some other way of going about it? Hours spent thinking about it didn't seem to translate into rational ideas though.

After dressing, Kay had walked to Hertford East train station, claimed a seat and waited for the London-bound train to depart. By then it was 9.15, and she had decided to call ahead to her client, a small company that developed software, to let them know that she would be late. There was bad news for her though: if she couldn't get there for 9.30 she would have to wait until 1 o'clock in the afternoon, she was told. The client had to fit in a meeting with someone else before that as well – someone who might actually turn up on time, although that particular barb went unsaid. Kay bit her lip in disappointment, but had no choice other than to agree to the re-arranged time.

She had then decided that she would spend some time in the West End office before heading across London for the afternoon meeting. It would have been a good plan, and one that made some productive use of the day, but for a delay caused by a defective train on the line ahead of them. Kay eventually discovered the reason for the hold-up after sitting outside Broxbourne station for half an hour, not moving. It took until 10.30 before the train moved at anything quicker than a crawl.

By then, Kay had realised that by the time she would now get to the office in the West End it would be time to leave and head for the City. She might just as well head straight for the City and kill whatever time was remaining by doing some of the paperwork that she had with her.

A rising tide of impotent frustration had accompanied all of this delay, a tide that only her hangover had stopped from becoming loud vocal rage. Ordinarily she would be seething, but today, feeling this awful, it had almost felt like a blessing to be stuck on a slow moving train without having to engage with humans. So drinking did have its perks, she had allowed herself to chuckle.

Kay stayed on the train all the way to Liverpool Street, arriving at 11.15. There was a bar on the station, by the passage that led through to Broadgate, where Lee worked. She could have called her husband to see if he fancied an early lunch with his adoring wife, but that thought drew only a grim, private smile from Kay. Yeah, right – like he's going to say yes to that. Instead, she had gone into the bar and ordered a vodka and orange.

The pub was dimly lit, with most of its orange glow emanating from various flickering fruit machines. There was a slightly unloved feel about the décor and its upkeep, as if the proprietors viewed the place like their customers presumably did – a temporary stopover before moving on elsewhere.

Kay had taken a seat near the entrance and that was where she was now sitting, trying to ignore the smooth looking middle-aged man that seemed to be staring at her from across the pub. She busied herself by sending a text message to Wilf to let him know what her plans for the day now were. Having done that, she removed a sheaf of papers from her case and started to flick through them. The pile was made up of two draft press releases that Gavin had written, some briefing documents in preparation for a new business pitch, and some blank templated sheets for staff appraisals.

She started to read through Gavin's work, noting out of the corner of her eye with relief that the middle-aged man across the bar was finishing his drink and readying to leave. The man swished past her on the way out, and in his wake Kay laid the sheets back down on the table and breathed a little more easily. She drank some of her vodka, hoping that it could get her back on form after the excesses of the night before. Sometimes it worked.

Instead of then picking the press release up again though, Kay found her mind wandering to other things. Lee. How much longer could they continue like this? Motherhood – was there even the inkling of an urge yet?

It was always the same questions, every single day, over and over in a continuous loop; and it was even more annoying since there were never any answers that made sense, other than a negative response to the last question. So in her mind she quickly skipped around these long unsolved problems, and moved on to a fresher subject that she hoped there was a chance to make sense out of – James. Why was she doing this with Lee's friend? Actually, this question was becoming tired as well now, but something about the answer was obviously troubling her, because the question was a recurring one.

She went through it again: she was doing this because James held out a hope of something; not a real future in any positive, fulfilling sense, but the chance to grab at something that made her feel valued and wanted, amidst married desolation. Okay, so the psychological aftermath was messy and unsettling, she conceded, but for a few hours she could escape. That was important.

It was the finer detail of their little arrangement that was vexing Kay most now. She had almost no idea what Lee was up to from one day to the next. She didn't know when he might come home from work, nor what would happen if the scenario played out slightly differently to the occasion two weeks earlier, when only an uncharacteristic phone call home by Lee had saved Kay and James from being caught red-handed. It gave her the willies. There had been many other days when Lee had come home unexpectedly early or unexpectedly late as well. It couldn't be relied upon, that much was certain.

She had considered that perhaps they should meet somewhere else, but there seemed to be issues with every option. James' dad still lived with him and rarely went out. Kay couldn't even bear to imagine how she would look the old man in the face. So James's place was a no-go. They could find a hotel somewhere. However, that idea suggested that this was becoming too much of an organised event to Kay's mind; it required planning and could leave a trail that might still betray them, and Kay wasn't comfortable with that.

Pillow talk with James had not solved the issue. In fact, he had seemed surprised that it was actually an issue – as if it had not even occurred to him that this was a problem, despite the fact that Lee had nearly walked in on the two of them in the marital bed.

"Don't you two talk to each other? Can't you just ask him?" James had said, meaning that Kay should check with Lee what time he intended coming home. It sounded like a laughable idea to Kay.

"No, I bloody can't. Not every Tuesday anyway. He'd start getting suspicious if I started doing that. God, we haven't bothered with any of that for ages. But I need to know when he's coming home, because there have been a few times that he's turned up early when I didn't expect him to. Funnily enough, when he does turn up early, he usually goes straight out again. God knows where."

The clueless stare past Kay and out of the window behind her had told her that James had already lost interest. Why are men so fucking useless, she had wondered? That was the odd thing about this James situation. When they had just been friends they had always enjoyed chatting, but now that things had moved beyond friendship, there was precious little to talk about when they met. They just went to bed for a few hours, then he slept, and then he went home. Kay would then resume her work. There was no romance, it was purely physical. That was at least an improvement on life with Lee these days though, she had to admit.

What to do, what to do, Kay pondered, as she sat in the bar at Liverpool Street. She lifted her glass and drained the rest of the vodka, before gathering her things together and walking out of the bar, still lost for answers. On impulse, she decided to wander along to a nearby newsagent to buy a glossy magazine and then she would sit down for half an hour of escapism. There was a waiting area outside the bar – just a few seats – to which Kay returned with her magazine a few minutes later. She settled down to read.

A couple of minutes later her mobile phone started ringing. She saw Wilf's name on the display and answered the call.

"Kay, where are you?" He sounded flustered.

"I'm at Liverpool Street, reading some of Gav's stuff that I brought with me. Didn't you get my text?"

"Yes. We could really do with you here though. The shit has hit the fan with Mighty Meals."

Oh God, not again, thought Kay. "What's happened?"

"It's not a crisis management job; it's more of a 'sack Belinda' job. She told Roger to fuck off and certain other things about two hours ago. You've had a long email from Roger threatening to pull the account, which nobody knew about until he called here and blew my head off down the phone because you hadn't replied."

"Well…" Kay searched for words. "Why didn't he call me on my mobile?"

"I don't bloody know! He just didn't. He came through to me instead, effing and blinding and demanding that we either sack Bel or he's taking his business elsewhere."

"Hang on, why did Bel tell him to fuck off? What's been going on Wilf? Everything was okay yesterday when I talked to Roger."

"That doesn't bloody matter Kay. She's got to go. We can't have our people talking to clients like that."

"No, I agree, of course – but Belinda is a great worker Wilf. The fucking trouble I have with Roger and that account, and all for two grand a month. Is it worth losing Belinda for that?"

"Whoa there, Kay; are you suggesting we tell Roger where to stick it? That's ludicrous. We've got a business to run in case you'd forgotten. There are twenty thousand Belinda Frosts out there." Wilf sounded very angry now, and Kay could feel her willingness to fight this battle evaporate in the face of his ire. She felt tired and irritable after drinking too much and then getting up late. She didn't need this now. There was a second or two of silence as Kay tried to find the right words.

"Kay? Are you still there?" Wilf thundered.

"Yes, yes. I was just thinking."

"Don't think. Phone Roger and tell him he won't be dealing with Belinda anymore. He's bloody furious, and I can't say I blame him."

"Look, why don't we just move Bel off of the account?"

"Jesus Christ, Kay! You're just not thinking are you? What's wrong with you these days? I will not have staff in this company talking to customers in that way. If she's unprofessional enough to do it to once, then she'll do it again, and next time it could be a big client that really matters. So no fucking way. She's out. And you and I need to have a chat as well – about you. That will have to wait though. I've got to prepare now for a big meeting with Voucharo this afternoon. Then I'm out for two days in Ireland with Lordship. I know you can't do it today but Kay, I want this situation sorted out by the time I'm back."

Kay had been unsuccessfully trying to interrupt several times during this tirade, but the last comment made her face burn red with fury. She retorted sharply: "Oh I see. I've got to do all the dirty work, have I Wilf? I don't see why you can't manage it right now if you're so fucking keen to see the back of her."

She heard a sharp intake of breath at the other end. Then he came back at her angrily. "I don't believe this. Kay – fucking sort it!" The line clicked abruptly, and he was gone. Kay stared in dismay at her phone for a few seconds, trying to think quickly about what to do. It was impossible for her to clear her mind though. In all their years of friendship and partnership, Wilf had never spoken to her like that before. They were supposed to be equals. Kay felt badly shaken by the confrontation.

Okay, it was true that Mighty Meals was her account and therefore her ultimate responsibility, but Wilf was there in the office, on the spot. He could sort this out himself, right away. Kay could hardly sack Belinda by telephone, could she? Kay cursed out loud to release some of her anger. Another woman sitting nearby gave her a curious look. Kay suddenly realised that four or five people sitting or standing nearby would have heard one side of her heated argument. The embarrassment made her redden even further.

She took a few minutes to try and calm herself down. Having opened the magazine again she soon found that she wasn't really reading the words or even looking at the pictures. Her mind was racing too quickly to take any of that in; racing, but without producing any coherent thoughts. He had said to her: "What's wrong with you these days?" He had actually said that. What did that mean? What had she already done badly to cause Wilf to say something like that?

Mighty Meals had been the big challenge recently and Kay had dealt with it. No-one, so far as she was aware, knew about her extended drinking session at Victoria Station and the brush with Mark from San Diego, when she should have been going to Gatwick.

She might have been able to convince herself that the incident remained a secret, if only she could banish from her thoughts the other thing he'd said: "You and I need to chat as well – about you." Momentarily she had felt cowed by that – like a trainee being reprimanded by a new boss. She had been too tired, too weak, to challenge him. That feeling had passed now though, and had been replaced by more anger. How bloody dare he speak to me like that, Kay demanded sullenly.

A quick look at her wristwatch told Kay that the time was 11.35. She decided to go for a walk around the Broadgate Circle to clear her mind, and so she sauntered off through the retail outlet-lined passageway that led towards that place. Her walk took her past Lee's office, which she ignored and put behind her at a brisk pace.

It was a chilly early October day, and she quickly regretted leaving the comparative warmth of the shops, deciding that one swift circuit of the outdoor ice rink the centre of Broadgate was enough. From time to time a pulsating headache broke through her paracetamol-bolstered defences to remind her of the excess of the night before. As she wandered back towards her previous sanctuary near the concourse she dallied to look in a few shop windows.

It occurred to Kay as she mooched around the aisles of a pharmacy that once again her mind had been distracted away from her work. She was thinking about James and Lee again, and she scolded herself silently. There was too much shit hitting the fan with work right now for this, she reasoned. Resolving to phone Roger and find out what had happened, Kay left the shop and was soon sitting back in the same seat outside the bar.

Once again she removed her mobile phone from her bag, and fished out Roger Wallace's direct line from her contacts. The phone rang at Mighty Meals several times before Roger's voicemail message started. Kay cursed as Wallace's recorded message went on; then she took a deep breath and spoke after the beep.

"Roger, this is Kay. I've spoken to Wilf and heard there are some problems. I just wanted to talk things through with you. I'm on my mobile today, not in the office. Speak to you soon hopefully."

She hung up and stared vacantly across the concourse from the windowed section where she sat. A minute later Kay called the main office number for Mighty Meals, and her call was answered by the same middle-aged woman that had contacted Kay at the office those weeks before when the scandal at Gatwick was breaking.

"Hi – can you tell me if Roger Wallace is in the office?" Kay asked, employing her polite telephone manner.

"Yes, he is in," the reply came. "Who is it calling?"

"It's Kay Talbot from Palmerston. I just tried his direct line but I got his voicemail. Is he free do you know?"

"I can try his line again for you. He was in a meeting though. Hold on." The line went dead for a second, and then the silence was replaced by some orchestral music.

Kay sat and pensively chewed her bottom lip with the handset pressed to her ear. An odd thought came to her quite randomly. She imagined Lee walking past, coming from the left of where she now sat, heading for the train home, as he did most days, wearing that same unsmiling expression of indifference that she knew so well on her husband's face; walking quickly, expecting the world to get out of his way. Suddenly Kay's phone sounded a warning beep. The battery was low. Oh great.

Come on Roger, she urged. She saw the scenario again in her mind: Lee walking past, barging his way through, ignorant of anyone around him, glaring at the ones who didn't get out of his way quickly enough, as if, by some arrogant logic, they had less right to be there than he did. She'd seen it many times. She'd even visualised such a scene while lying next to James in the marital bed, hoping fervently that Lee was not about to walk through the door downstairs. The orchestra continued with dainty melodies, followed by swirling crescendos, crashing cymbals, the violinists' elbows working furiously back and forth. She didn't know who or what the music was, but it was quite relaxing in a funny kind of way she thought, although she would have preferred something a bit heavier. Her handset emitted another warning beep.

Looking out across the concourse, she saw a big group of young people – twenty or so – with rucksacks gathered in the middle, some looking up at the board for platform details, others laughing amongst themselves. Ideally, she thought, she would have some way of knowing exactly when Lee was getting the train home. That way she could make sure that James was long gone before Lee reached the house. Of course, it was impossible to get that piece of information though without asking Lee himself, and that would make him suspicious. She would have to think of something else, Kay accepted.

The large group of travellers started moving off in ones and twos, shouldering their packs and heading towards one of the platforms. The classical music continued to soar and swoop in Kay's ear. Where the fuck are you Roger, she sniffed. The phone beeped another low battery warning, and Kay sighed in exasperation. Come on Roger!

Just then, from left to right as Kay looked, a man dressed in a black T-shirt and black trousers walked out from behind a brick pillar that stood between Kay and the concourse, and she watched as he popped his head into the entrance to the coffee shop to Kay's right. After a couple of seconds he turned and walked back, right in front of Kay, and then disappeared from view behind the pillar once more. He didn't reappear, still walking, on the other side of the pillar though. He must have stopped behind it for some reason. Kay's mouth dropped with sudden inspiration. He had sat down behind the pillar, and she could see most of the right side of his body from where she was sitting.

She afforded herself a secret smile, and congratulated herself: Kay, you're a bloody genius! This is the answer! This is how I can do it! Okay, calm down, deep breaths. Don't get carried away. But yes, this was the answer. It was perfect, and she allowed a mighty beam to spread over her face as she pretended to study the fingernails on her free left hand, still waiting for Roger Wallace to answer the phone. It was the shoeshine guy of course – the one who had suffered Kay and Lee bickering just weeks before. A plan had burst to the forefront of her mind. Yes, the shoeshine guy; that was the answer. There were ways in which she could use him.

Abruptly, silence filled her right ear, causing her elation to freeze. For a moment she expected Roger's voice to come on the line. Two seconds later though, she could still hear nothing but the same vast and stupid silence. She removed the handset from her ear and looked at the screen, pressing a few buttons hopefully. It was blank; a dull, black screen that wouldn't change, wouldn't spring back to life, no matter what buttons she pressed.

For a few seconds Kay refused to believe it was true, and tried to switch the phone off and on again, desperately hoping that somehow this would spark it into life. It was no good though – the phone was dead, and on it were Roger's numbers. She groaned. For good measure, the headache waiting to ambush her sallied out and thumped at her temple again, causing Kay to instinctively reach a protective hand up to her brow in despair.

She thought for a minute. She had a fair idea what Roger's office number was, so she could ring again using one of the public telephones on the concourse. If the number in her head proved to be wrong, then there were two other options: she could call the office and get one of the guys to look it up; or she could call directory enquiries. Okay, no problem, back in control.

Now – the shoeshiner. Kay saw that a girl who was wearing one of the yellow shirts that the coffee shop staff wore was talking to him now. After only a short conversation the girl suddenly spun around to look towards the coffee shop, and then trotted back across the space between the pillar and the shop, again passing from Kay's left to right, waving back at the shoeshiner as she went.

There was a big temptation to walk straight over to him and pour this amazing idea that Kay had conceived all over his unsuspecting head. Kay resisted that urge though, telling herself instead to be patient, and think this thing through again, study the angles; there was no rush. It struck her that maybe this was the first sensible thought that she'd had all day.

Kay tried to sit still and rationally assess the plausibility of her plan, but found that she was too excited. She needed to be on the move, as if the very act of movement would generate the spark for her mind to work more effectively. Quickly checking that she'd put everything back in her bag, Kay leapt up from the seat and started walking quickly, passing the brick pillar on her right, but giving it a wide berth as she passed by. She continued on past a photo booth next to Platform 1, and moved towards a small pastry kiosk by the entrance to Platform 3.

Only then did she stop, turn and look back. The shoeshiner was still sitting there, his eyes blankly surveying the concourse straight ahead, his arms folded. Kay noticed that his shoes were quite smart and impressively polished. Well, you would hope so, she giggled to herself. Fleetingly, she wondered how anyone would come to be doing such a job.

Kay studied him for a while. He had quite fair hair, fashionably shaggy and probably ready for a good cut. It was long and thick enough to come down around and over his ears, and there was the hint of an overgrown parting to one side of centre. His face, Kay noticed, was impassive but had an honest countenance. Sometimes, she reckoned, you could look at a guy and be certain that he was a bastard. That wasn't so with this guy. His eyes held a steady gaze. He looked trusting and solid; disinterested in, or maybe just at peace with, everything around him. She knew he was English, because she had already spoken to him those weeks before, and that was good. She didn't want to have to explain all this to some Eastern European that could hardly speak the language.

Roger Wallace suddenly loomed in Kay's mind yet again. She decided to get that phone call out of the way, and then she would approach the shoeshiner. She would offer to buy him lunch so they could chat. As she watched, his gaze started traversing towards her, like the slow swivel of a gun turret on an armoured vehicle, seeking its target with deadly inevitability. Kay felt compelled to turn away and face the pastry kiosk so that their eyes would not meet across the 20 yards or so of concourse that was between them. Embarrassment flushed in her cheeks.

Not yet daring to turn around again, Kay strode further up the concourse away from the shoeshiner, passing underneath the huge platform information board suspended from the ceiling far above. Only when she had got as far as Platform 12, right up towards the other end of the station, did she look back again. Nothing had changed. The shoeshiner, now a smaller figure in the distance, was sitting arms folded, waiting for his next customer.

Looking around, Kay located some public telephones across the concourse, over by the exit to Bishopsgate, and she headed over in that direction. Unaccountably her hands were shaking as she dialled the number in her head that she hoped was Mighty Meals, and fumbled in her purse for some coins. She had a sick feeling in her stomach, and it seemed that everything around her – the people, the echoing station announcements, the general noise – was converging into a single accelerating roar that rushed by, pounding at her, causing her to catch her breath. Everything was urgent, everything was happening too quickly, and she couldn't control a spiralling feeling of panic. This was crazy. It had to be more than just a hangover, setting her on edge.

Although it had started ringing at the other end, she slammed the phone back onto its hook before there was an answer. She needed to calm down. What's wrong Kay, she asked herself? She looked nervously around, half expecting that the gathering pre-lunchtime throng of people had stopped going about their business and were now watching her with curious, accusing eyes. In her mind's eye she imagined a squad of station staff in orange high-vis coats, accompanied by grim-faced police officers, marching up and hauling her roughly away, as she screamed for their mercy and understanding.

Nobody was taking any notice of her though. Everything was normal, except for her mind, which seemed to be in the process of falling apart, thought Kay ruefully.

She counted her coinage out, and found that she had £1.25. A few forced deep breaths later and she felt ready to pick up the telephone receiver again. She punched the numbers in and soon heard the familiar female voice:

"Mighty Meals UK, how can I help you?"

Kay forced a coin through the slot. "Hi, it's Kay Talbot again from Palmerston PR. I called a little while ago."

Kay watched the small display on the telephone with quiet alarm. Right before her eyes and out of her control, the money left in the system counted down ludicrously quickly. She fed its voracious appetite until there was no change left in her purse. Talk quickly Kay…

"My mobile phone has died. Can you pass that message to Roger Wallace? Shit, I'm about to run out of money. I have another meeting now but I'll try again later or first thing tomorrow."

She just about heard the woman start to speak: "Wh…" and that was it; the money ran out and cut her off. Reluctantly Kay placed the receiver back again. Too late, another thought came to her: Kay you silly cow, why didn't you just change up that bloody fiver in your purse for pound coins before you rang? Anyway, she knew, or at least could reasonably hope, that a message should get through to Roger, and they would speak soon enough. A measure of relief washed over her; a small blessing on this God-awful day.

Kay looked up at the station clock overhead and saw it tick on to 11.50. Perfect, she thought. The shoeshiner would probably be going to lunch soon, so she'd better get over there now and commandeer his company for half an hour. She strode purposefully back across the concourse towards the Broadgate end. When she was still thirty or forty yards away she stopped again by some free-standing panels that displayed printed timetables behind clear plastic coverings, and she pretended to read the timetables. In her mind she rehearsed her sales pitch. This was what she was I'm good at, she told herself – selling ideas.

She was about to resolve herself to the job in hand when another unwanted moment of self-doubt crept in, forcing her to hold back for a few more seconds, and making her angry with herself. Get on with it, her inner voice urged; do it now

Kay. She obeyed, and moved off again in the direction of the shoeshiner. He was reaching down to take something out of his bag. Smile and sell the idea, Kay repeated over and over in her mind. It was a mantra she used often, and somehow it seemed appropriate again. The shoeshiner had taken a paperback book from his bag and was reading.

As she walked towards him Kay felt rising excitement; a private thrill that only she, in the entire world, knew what was about to happen. She moved unstoppably onwards, looking straight at him as he was flicking through the book. Just then he turned to look over his left shoulder as an oldish man in a suit arrived at his chair from that direction, pumping the shoeshiner's hand energetically like an old friend would. They smiled and laughed as the shoeshiner stood up and vacated his seat for the man.

"Oh, bollocks… " Kay swore, and came to an abrupt halt in confusion, right next to some cash machines. A man heading for the machines tried to swerve around her but failed to adjust sufficiently in the split second he had to react to the sudden obstacle in his way. Kay took a blow on the shoulder, as the man accidentally bumped into her. He looked daggers at her and mumbled: "Jesus Christ, love. What are you fucking playing at?"

Kay raised a hand in contrite apology, then looked back to the shoeshiner, who now had his back to her, bent forward at his work. The old man was talking animatedly. Kay retreated towards the timetable panels again but kept an eye on the shoeshiner's progress. Nerves fluttered and bile came into her throat once more. She had managed to gather up her courage to walk over once, only to have to abort. Could she do it again? Right at that moment, Kay wasn't at all sure.

She steeled herself once more. The poor guy can't earn much money shining shoes all day. Kay persuaded herself that in many ways, she was going to be doing him a favour. The customer was now getting to his feet and reaching for his inside pocket, presumably to get his wallet. Kay hesitated a second longer. Go now, her inner voice demanded. She obeyed it, and made a beeline for the shoeshiner again; he was exchanging a joke with the old guy, who then made off towards the underground station laughing, and tucking his wallet back into his inside jacket pocket.

This was surprisingly fun. Kay walked quickly, looking straight ahead at the shoeshiner, who was settling back into his chair. It seemed to Kay that everything around them had somehow faded into the background; it was just Kay and this man, a complete stranger dressed all in black; they were centre stage and everyone around was taking their seats for Act 1, Scene 1. The curtain rustled in preparation for a majestic opening swish. Kay couldn't help but smile.

She was just 20 yards away now. He was reaching down for his paperback again. Fifteen yards. He looked up, straight at her, almost causing her to falter, and actually causing her to catch her breath in yet more consternation. What am I fucking doing, she asked herself. The shoeshiner's expression seemed to challenge Kay: go on then Kay – I dare you; see it through to the end. There was a defiant glint in his eyes.

This was madness. Kay was terrified, without quite knowing why. Just walk straight past, and keep walking until you get to Moorgate, she ordered herself. Her legs weren't listening though, and they stopped moving just a few feet in front of the shoeshiner. He looked at her inquisitively. Well, he's wondering what in God's name you want of course Kay, she raged silently.

Then words came out of Kay's mouth: "Well, hello again." It felt like a strong start. She was surprised at how even her voice sounded, considering the awkwardness of the moment. "You might remember me from a few weeks ago – my husband and I had an argument here while you were shining his shoes."

There was a flicker of recognition in his eyes. "Yeah," he said. The eyes appraised her with laser precision – all the way down, and then all the way up again, where they met Kay's expectant gaze. "I do remember." There was no smile; not even a blink to give Kay any respite. The pressure was on. It was time to sell.

Chapter Three

The face of the shoeshiner was fixed with a frown, prompting Kay to say: "It's okay – I don't usually bite."

She winced. Was that the best she could come up with? She had tried to make it sound jocular, but instead it just sounded lame and unconvincing. In the awkward pause that followed, she tried to gauge his reaction. He couldn't, she reckoned, have looked less impressed.

Kay hesitated in the face of that solid rampart, but then jolted herself onward, a forlorn hope with no breach yet to exploit. "Look, I'm sorry to bother you; I can see you're busy but can you spare me ten minutes? It's a bit difficult to explain here but I just wondered if I could maybe buy you some lunch and make a sort of proposition to you."

She heard herself saying those words and couldn't help but wonder whether she had finally lost the plot.

"A proposition?" Nick repeated, and left the word hanging in the air between them, demanding some further explanation. He looked at the woman's pale face and noticed that there were small beads of perspiration on her forehead. Her eyes, dark though they were, looked both exhausted and full of adventure; oak doors to who knew what mystery.

"God, I haven't even introduced myself!" she said, affecting a laugh, and then stretching out a slender hand towards the shoeshiner. "I'm Kay."

At first he merely looked at the hand, and a heavy second passed before finally he reached forward and briefly shook it. "I'm Nick. Nice to meet you," he said, taking care to make the greeting as perfunctory as politeness allowed.

Kay beamed and tried again: "Cool, nice to meet you Nick. As I say, I wanted to ask you something, and I'd love to buy you a sandwich or…"

"Sorry but I haven't really got the time. I have to talk to my girlfriend during my lunch hour. Why would you want to talk to me anyway? I don't really do ladies' shoes."

Short shrift. Kay carried on smiling and persisted regardless, although she shifted uncomfortably from one foot to another as she did so.

"Oh. Well, can you call her a bit later? Honestly it won't take long."

Something that may have been anger flashed in his eyes: "Well no, actually. Not that it's got anything to do with you, but she's in Australia visiting her dad who's in hospital and this is our time when we catch up with each other. She'll probably call any minute now."

In fact, Justine wasn't due to phone until between 12.30 and 1pm – still more than 30 minutes away – but Nick didn't feel the need to explain this. "So I guess you need to make it quick here and now before I get another customer," he ended.

Kay was at a loss for a response, and blankly contemplated the floor as her mind raced. When she looked up, his eyes seemed to be mocking her, but she also saw something in them which persuaded her that he'd be a hopeless card player. She would call his bluff.

"All right Nick. I'll just stay here for a while, and wait until after you've finished chatting and we can talk then. I don't need to get anywhere in particular, so that's no problem for me."

She followed that up with a defiant look, holding his eyes with hers to see what emotion would flair up in them next. He hadn't expected that response, and it showed plainly in his surprised expression. However, he wasn't about to give in that easily.

"Do what you like. No skin off my nose," he said with a shrug of his shoulders.

"Look, I know this seems a bit strange. All I'm asking is that you give me five minutes to explain. You could help me out with something, and there's money or whatever you prefer in it for you. Please – let me buy you a beer and I can explain."

"I don't drink when I'm working love."

"Alright, I'll buy you a fucking orange juice then. Whatever you want, it's on me."

Nick gave her a thin smile she noticed, as if he registered her impatience as a small victory. Even so, shaking his head he leaned down and started packing his kit into his bag, muttering to himself.

Kay watched him, feeling relieved, then said: "There's a pub just round the other side of this big pillar, with some seats and tables outside it. Let's go round there."

Nick stood up, placed a small laminated sign bearing the words 'At Lunch' on his stool, then lifted his bag from the floor, and turned back to Kay, who was looking around the concourse. "Okay," he said. "God knows why, but I'm ready."

Kay led the way round to the pub, finding that there was no-one sitting at either of the two tables outside the bar. Nick settled at one of them while Kay went in to buy some drinks, which gave him a couple of minutes to reflect on this unusual situation. He had no idea what this woman thought he could do for her, but he reasoned that it wouldn't cost him anything to find out. She was also talking about money, and she obviously had more of that than sense, he reckoned.

There was one thing that he had already decided about her: she was just a normal south London girl, who mostly covered her accent with a put-on business voice; mostly, but not quite entirely. Nick wasn't going to be intimidated by the power suit therefore. If he didn't like what she said, she could keep her money – even though it would be useful for getting out to Australia and Justine.

Kay soon returned carrying a glass of vodka for her and a coke for Nick. She slipped into the chair opposite him, and for a second or two there was an awkward silence as Nick waited and Kay eyed her drink and composed herself. She cleared her throat softly but then started laughing. Nick raised an eyebrow.

"God this is awkward," she muttered. Nick shrugged. She continued: "How much do you charge for a shoeshine anyway?"

"Why – do you want one?"

"No, I was wondering earlier on, that's all. What is it – five quid or something each time? Times however many people a day."

"Listen, I'm not telling you how much I earn. It's got nothing to do with you. Okay, so it's probably not as much as you get in your fancy office job but so what? We're not all obsessed with money." Nick felt as riled as he looked.

"I didn't mean it like that," Kay protested. "I was just interested that was all. God, you're a bit sensitive aren't you?"

"Sensitive?" Nick almost growled the word, and it scorched the air between them like a blow torch. Kay didn't seem to sense the heat however.

"Yeah, sensitive. Let's face it mate, you're cleaning shoes all day. It ain't the best job in the world. You could probably do with a few bob or two." That sounded terrible even to Kay. All she had managed to do so far was cause offence.

"Hang on a sec," Nick retorted, visibly bristling. Kay felt miserable. "I see you've given up any effort at being polite now. Did you bring me round here just to patronise me and wave your money in my face? Because if you did, fuck you, I'm going back to work now. You don't know anything about me or my life, but what I've seen of yours ain't much to write home about."

"Okay, okay. Look that came out wrong…"

"You're damn right it did. I thought you must be clever in your expensive clothes, but obviously I was wrong."

The confrontation hung in the air for a few seconds. Then Kay sighed deeply and smiled. Nick could see that it was a frustrated, tired smile.

"Please, let me start this again," said Kay. "I didn't mean to offend you; I really hoped that we could be friends."

"Friends? Why on earth... look can we just get on with this? My girlfriend will be calling soon, so the meter is running."

"Okay, okay. Right, here goes," Kay took a deep breath. "So – this is going to sound as mad as a box of frogs I know, but…oh God, what am I saying…look, it's like this: I think my husband is having an affair, and I think you could help me find out what he's up to."

She immediately felt like a complete fool, and willed the ground to swallow her up. Nick's reaction was to look quickly up at her in surprise. He hadn't known what to expect, but it certainly hadn't been that. He shook his head, as if trying to unblock a troublesome ear. "Sorry, say that again; I'm not sure I heard it right."

"I said, I think that bastard husband of mine, whose shoes you shined the other day, is having an affair and you could help me find out what's happening."

Nick looked away again, finding himself temporarily lost for words. Kay's eyes were boring into him though, and with another baffled shake of the head he forced himself to look back at her. "You were right, that is mad. How the hell will I do that then?" he demanded.

She leaned towards him and smiled. "Well, here's what I thought: I reckoned that since you were here every day, you could let me know when he gets on the train to come home. Not every day though – probably only once or twice a week. And I'll pay you for it in cash up front. Yes I know! It sounds ridiculous, but honestly, that information would really help me catch him out."

Nick was gobsmacked. "Is this a joke?" he asked, after a few seconds of silent disbelief.

"No, honestly Nick; it's not a joke. I'm not pulling your leg. I'm serious."

"You're crazy. How long did it take you to work this one out?"

"Work what out? Look, it's quite simple." Now it was Kay's turn to look away, such was her discomfort. When she had heard the words coming out of her own mouth she had realised that the whole thing sounded idiotic. She wanted to run away now.

Nick stepped up the offensive: "Did you stop to think that I might not recognise your husband? Did you stop to think that I might be too busy working to see every Tom, Dick and Harry that walks past? By the way, it gets kind of busy here at about 5 o'clock you know."

Flustered and embarrassed, Kay reacted sharply: "Look, his name is Lee and I'll give you a bloody photo of him. He works round in Broadgate, and he normally catches the 5.45 train to Hertford East, which is where we live. Won't you have finished working by then anyway? Just hang around, keep an eye out, and send me a text if you see him – that's all I'm asking you to do Nick. And I can give you a hundred quid every time you do it. Now, does that sound like a worthwhile use of your precious time?"

Nick's eyes widened. "A hundred quid? Just for sending you a text message? You've clearly got more money than sense Kay."

After a second, she sighed and shifted in her seat, wearing a resigned look which seemed to suggest that acceptance of her own failings was an emotion that she was familiar with. "Yeah, you're probably right about that Nick," she finally laughed softly; then more urgently she added: "It doesn't make me a bad person though. Look, I know this is all a bit weird but honestly, it would really help me. Please, please, please... "

She managed to pull off a face that was both disconsolate and kittenish at the same time, and Nick felt a twinge of pity. There was plenty about this situation that didn't make sense to him, but despite it all she seemed sincere. It appeared to mean a lot to her, and he couldn't help but admire her chutzpah, if that was the right word, in not only dreaming up this hare-brained scheme, but also in approaching a complete stranger and suggesting it to him.

And certainly £100 would make a big difference to him – he could put it by to pay for a trip to Australia if necessary. Justine might ask a few questions about how he had got the money together so quickly, but he could maybe construct some sort of believable story to explain, and it most definitely wouldn't include becoming a part-time private detective on behalf of an attractive woman.

Shaking his head again in bewilderment, but this time at his own impending agreement to take part in the plan, Nick reiterated the arrangement she had proposed: "So, let me get this right. You're going to give me a picture of your husband – Lee was it, you said? Then, when you want me to look out for him, you're going to give me one hundred quid in advance. Er, will that be cash? I'm not about to give you my bank account number, so you can forget that."

"No, I understand that, of course. We can meet up. That's no problem. I work at home a lot but my office is in London, so I'm here quite often. It will probably be Tuesdays that I need you to do this, so we could meet on a Monday night and I can give you the money then."

Nick momentarily considered asking what was special about Tuesdays, but instead he let it pass. "And how long does this go on for? I mean, when I've done it once, will that be it?"

"I don't know. We'll just have to wait and see."

"And how does me telling you that Lee has got on a train tell you whether he's having an affair or not? I don't really understand that."

"Well…" her mind sought frantically for something convincing. "It's a complicated situation Nick, and I'm still working it out myself; but that's the whole point of me asking – it helps me put some pieces together."

It didn't sound particularly impressive, but it was all she had. There were questions that Nick had asked that she hadn't prepared an answer for. It was all a bit half-baked, all a bit desperate. Well if the cap fits, she thought. Forcing another smile, she put her embarrassment to one side and went for a quick resolution:

"Will you do it then? Is it a deal?"

Nick slowly shook his head, inspecting the table top in front of him. He still seemed mystified by the whole thing. Kay felt frustration welling up inside her again, but then Nick spoke and blew the frustration away.

"Okay. I'll do it. God knows why but I suppose I could do with the money if I'm honest."

Kay was grinning broadly now, mostly out of relief that this difficult conversation had finally ended in her favour. She reached forward and grabbed Nick's hand to shake it.

"Thanks Nick. I really appreciate this. You must think I'm a right weirdo."

"Ha, ha; well, there do seem to be a few sandwiches missing from the picnic Kay, let's just say that."

She laughed, and relaxed back in her chair. It seemed a good moment to laugh at herself, and if that was the price she had to pay, then fair enough. Five minutes later, Nick got up and departed, leaving Kay to finish her drink. They had swapped mobile phone numbers, with Kay testing Nick's there and then to make sure she had it right. She said she would return that week with a recent picture of her husband, and she jotted down Lee's office address, which Nick promised to go and check out in the next few days.

Kay was left to contemplate the new arrangement for a few minutes, before heading off for her meeting. Had she really approached this stranger and asked him to do this? It seemed crazy, a childish invention, even to her. In justification, this was simply where her life had taken her – clinging to what seemed like small pieces of happiness or peace of mind amidst the flotsam and jetsam of her marriage.

She had to keep living, she told herself; had to grasp at the passing moments of tenderness that she found with James. The moment she gave up, she was certain, there would be no hope of salvation.

She swigged the rest of her vodka down, gathered her bag together, stood up, straightened her suit, and headed off through the station, walking once again past Nick's pitch, still vacant except for the lonely little 'At Lunch' sign propped up on the seat. She couldn't help but glance over at the chair as she swayed past. She thought of the shoeshine guy's earnest, trusting eyes; eyes that belonged to her now. Her new friend, and her very own private spy. Perhaps it hadn't turned out to be such a bad day after all.

**

Nick watched Kay saunter past and saw the triumphant smile, from the sanctuary of Vicky's coffee bar, where he was ordering his lunch. He felt slightly dazed by the whole thing. It was the most bizarre conversation he had ever known. Still, whether he liked it or not, he appeared to have a new friend now, and one that promised financial benefits as well.

His mind was troubled though. Should he mention this to Justine? She was due to call at any minute, and he couldn't even begin to work out how he would explain the last 20 minutes of his life to her.

For a start, there was the guilt he felt at the undeniable flicker of anticipation inside as the lady that he now knew as Kay had walked up to him.

But he was also a little angry. Kay had managed to get under his skin, and make him feel defensive by the way she had spoken to him at first. Yes, he was just a guy that shined shoes, that was true, but he hadn't always been. He had fulfilled supposedly much more impressive jobs with ease, but all that money and pressure hadn't brought him anywhere near to the happiness that he had found since meeting Justine and starting this job, so he refused to accept the notion that anyone should look down on him or his trade.

The prospect of the money helped him to overlook her initial condescending manner of course. He had no money,

Justine had none, and he recognised that this offer could be his ticket to Australia.

There was something else which had helped him to put his reservations aside though. It was a certain way that she had about her, just something in her demeanour, in the way her eyes had dropped to the floor with what seemed to be a resigned sadness; something in the smallest of tremors that he had noticed in her fingertips as she had played with her glass, and in the small yet audible measure of strain in her voice as she had tried to explain her position, battling her own embarrassment.

She seemed vulnerable, he thought, and it intrigued him. Obviously things weren't good in her marriage, otherwise she would not have been talking to Nick in the first place, but there was a deeper anxiety that he thought he could sense, something calling out for help; and it was that which had finally driven him – as surely as her looks and her money – to decide to help her out.

He wondered at this as he sat on one of the steps outside the main entrance to Liverpool Street station, across from the chaotic MacDonald's store, eating a sandwich from Vicky's shop. What was it that he had seen or felt in Kay that had touched him so unexpectedly? At this moment, he couldn't articulate it, and nor could he explain the giddiness he now felt.

He checked the time on his mobile phone. It was a quarter to one; Justine should be calling at any minute. His mood sunk as he realised that there was just no way he would be able to answer the phone to her right now. His head really wasn't in the right place; there was too much confusion and he knew that she would immediately sense that something was different, and that would just make the situation worse. He munched unhappily on his sandwich for a few minutes, staring vacantly ahead, his thoughts having turned to mush as soon as he had contemplated talking to Justine. It was numbing.

The warmth of the sun was surprisingly strong to Nick, who had been inside the station since early morning, so upon finishing his food and finding himself feeling drowsy, he relaxed back against the wall behind him. It wasn't that comfortable but the sun felt good on his upturned face. He closed his eyes and waited for the familiar chime of the ringtone. The City buzzed past him as he dozed. It was really quite peaceful and relaxing in the sunshine.

It seemed only a few seconds later that he jerked forward again, and his eyes sprung wide open. Momentary alarm: Jesus! I nearly went to sleep, Nick chided himself. He pulled his phone out again; the time was 1.04. Jesus, he had gone to sleep. It had been 20 minutes since he had sat down, but there was no missed call from Australia. Justine hadn't rung. Nick debated reluctantly what that might mean for a couple of seconds. Then he pulled himself upright again, shook some stiffness from his shoulders and headed off back towards his pitch to start working again. A cocktail of emotions played on his mind, but with a triumph of willpower he closed them off and focused on boot polish.

**

The offices of Palmerston PR were situated in a peaceful side street off of Marylebone Road, one of London's busiest thoroughfares. The surrounding relative tranquillity of cafés and small family-run boutiques that she walked past gave no clue to the turmoil that awaited Kay as she hurried by at 4pm, after finally completing her delayed meeting in the City.

There was plenty of turmoil in her own head too because, after waking up in a booze-soaked mess, and then fighting with Wilf on the phone about the still unresolved Mighty Meals disaster, she had arrived at her meeting in the City to find that what she thought was going to be a conversation with the client about renewing their PR contract, turned out to be an unwelcome chance to meet the new marketing and communications manager they had decided to employ. There would be no contract renewal, but there would be a handover of duties.

Her main contact, the deeply apologetic James Westley, informed her that they might consider using the PR agency for occasional project work, alongside and at the direction of the new man, the treacly Dennis Benson, whose soft, limp handshake unavoidably brought to Kay's mind the image of a wet fish. It would be helpful, said Westley with a tactless smile, for Palmerston to work with Dennis for six months during the handover period.

Kay was shattered – not because she had any passion for the client or its accounting software business, but because she knew that stacking this on top of everything else that had gone wrong that day, Wilf would definitely now be on the warpath. Why had she not seen this coming? Was she working hard enough to get close to her clients? Wilf would ask both questions and more.

Such had been the all-consuming feeling of demoralisation that Kay had felt as Westley announced the decision, that she had been incapable of kicking very hard back at him. She simply had no stomach for the fight today. The decision was made anyway, but indeed, why hadn't she seen it coming? It was a bloody good question. The answer was clear to her, and judging by the earlier conversation with Wilf, it was pretty clear to him too. Kay's attention had not been total these last weeks and months.

She had accepted the truth of that grim judgement in her own mind as she travelled towards Marylebone on the tube, wedged in by loud American tourists on the Metropolitan Line, probably on their way to Madame Tussaud's. Her job and her life felt like they were careering out of control, and there was nothing she could do as the minutes, the hours and the days slipped away from her. There was no opportunity to stop everything; sit down, take a few deep breaths, work out what to do next, and then proceed. Things were just happening and all that she could do was try to react, usually too late, and then react again to the next thing; and on and on. She felt dizzied and worn down by the whole thing.

So Kay was feeling less than pugnacious as she walked towards the office, but she was resolved in her mind that the first thing she had to do, so that she didn't blunder into anything without knowing the full picture, was to borrow Giles's mobile phone charger and get some life into her own mobile. She needed to check whether Roger Wallace had called and left any messages. Then she would check emails, quickly talk to Belinda to get her side of the story, and then she would ring Roger and sort this out. And only then would she call Wilf and tell him about Stonebook Software, with whom she had just met, with disastrous results. It had been a truly dreadful day, and perhaps the worst was yet to come, she pondered glumly.

Still, there was the encounter with the shoeshiner – her new friend Nick – which had been difficult but ultimately success-ful. She would send him a text message later to cement their new-found business partnership.

The receptionist, a slightly dim-witted girl called Colette, greeted her with her customary bored indifference as Kay swung open the doors at Palmerston PR. "Afternoon Colette!" Kay called with deliberately over-egged enthusiasm as she breezed past, drawing a non-committal grunt from the girl. Yeah, I know how you feel, Kay sighed to herself, climbing the few steps to the office doors.

Before she even got there though, she could hear loud voices from inside. A man and a woman were shouting at each other. She had thought that her spirit was already at rock bottom, but it now sank further. She burst through the doors, and stopped as they swung shut behind her.

There before her, in the middle of the room, was Wilf – red faced, eyes blazing – and Belinda – Kay's star; resolutely intransigent, mocking and cynical but always loyal, though now positively mutinous it seemed. They were standing toe to toe, hurling insults at each other. All around them stood the other staff members, mostly at a safe distance, apart from Gavin who was standing closest to the two protagonists, and who Kay guessed had been attempting to pacify things. Kay's entrance brought the show to an abrupt halt. All eyes turned towards the doors that Kay had just walked through.

Kay took it all in quickly and with instant anger. There was an urge to scream at Wilf, which she struggled to suppress. He stood, eyes focused on the floor, looking shame-faced; as well he might, Kay thought. Whatever she did or said now could not surpass this situation for its sheer stupidity and lack of professionalism.

"Wilf!" she yelled, shattering the silence. He reluctantly forced himself to look up and face her fury. "What the hell is going on?" He hesitated, and Kay set off at a rapid march past him, towards her office at the other end of the room.

"I'll have a word with you later Bel," she warned, as she stormed between the two of them, and then barked back at her business partner: "Wilf – in here now please!"

Frustration and embarrassment made Wilf pinch the bridge of his nose and squeeze his eyes tightly shut for a moment, but then he followed sheepishly along behind her.

**

A day from hell was over, and Kay slumped back in her seat on the homeward bound train, closed her eyes for a few minutes and mulled over what had happened. A crestfallen Wilf had hardly been able to look Kay in the eye when they had talked in her office. His planned meeting at Voucharo had been postponed until the following week, and he had therefore decided to take the Belinda matter into his own hands, with the shameful consequences that Kay had walked in upon.

Wilf's mood was not helped by Kay's news about the reduced fees from Stonebook. At that moment, as they discussed the situation in Kay's office immediately after her return, they were both unaware that Mighty Meals was also withdrawing its business. Roger Wallace had reached the end of his tether after Belinda's frank exchange of opinions, followed by his inability to reach Kay. Despite the garbled messages she had left that day he had decided that Palmerston PR's management vacuum, as he put it, was the final straw.

Neither Kay nor Wilf knew this as they talked however. Kay discovered it later when she called Wallace, finally getting through to him at 5.20 in the evening. He was aloof, but his anger had cooled off. He said however that the matter was already beyond redemption in his eyes; there was formal notification of his decision in the post.

Kay had begged him not to make a hasty decision and asked that they speak again the following day. He had said he might call her when he got the chance, and hung up, leaving Kay with the distinct impression that one way or another that opportunity would not present itself to Roger any time soon. She popped up to Wilf's office upstairs but he had left for the evening. Belinda was also getting packed up to depart when Kay came back downstairs.

"I can't hang about," she said to Kay. "I've got plans to meet someone." She seemed subdued.

"Okay Bel, we'll talk about it tomorrow then. I need to find out from you what happened with Roger. I've heard his version. He's being an arsehole anyway, but there you go... "

"Have I still got a job?"

Kay had sighed. "I hope so. We'll talk tomorrow."

And now Kay was on a train, rattling through North London and on into the southernmost parts of Hertfordshire. It had been, without a shadow of doubt, the worst day ever in the history of Wilf and Kay's business; the worst day in their friendship in fact – a friendship that was hanging by a thread right now. He was pissed at her and she was now pissed at him. So, Kay mused, at least we both have some ammo now. She knew that she ought to phone Wilf at home and talk to him about Mighty Meals, but she just couldn't face it; she had to admit that that was the sad truth.

For a few minutes she stared out of the window, feeling low of spirit and weary of limb. There had been one decent thing today though, and that was the encounter with the shoeshine guy at lunchtime. She should definitely text him and say hello again, since he was her passport to at least a little fun and intrigue in the midst of this maelstrom of work disasters and unhappy wedlock.

Kay felt some disbelief that she had plucked up the courage in the first place to approach the guy she now knew as Nick. She afforded herself a private smile at her own daring, and at the confused surprise that she had seen in his eyes when she had explained what she wanted him to do. It's not such a big deal really, Kay thought. He just has to keep an eye out for Lee and tell her when he boarded his train home. That was all. If it worked out, maybe she would even start seeing James a bit more often.

She spent a couple of minutes composing a text message on her phone, trying to be as self-deprecating as possible, trying to get the tone of the message right. Although this guy Nick had a serious air to his nature, behind that steady gaze there was a dry sense of humour and gently mocking wit that she had already been on the end of.

So she tapped out on her mobile: "Hey Nick, my man! It's Kay the nutcase frm earlier. Hope all is cool. Will stop by tomoro with money and pic. Hav a nice nite x"

The text message sent on its way, she pocketed the handset again, and checked her whereabouts out of the window of the train: she was just coming into Cheshunt; another twenty minutes yet. She closed her eyes again. What a day.

**

Nick didn't hear the beep of the incoming message because his mobile phone was in the front room and he was in the kitchen flicking through a pizza flyer, trying to make a decision about what to get in for tea. It was Wednesday evening, there was a football match on TV at half past seven, he had a couple of beers in the fridge, and he intended to enjoy a night in.

There had still been no call from Justine. He didn't know what that meant and it was a worry, so earlier in the evening he had called her mobile and left a message. There was nothing else he could do now though, and he hoped that there was a totally harmless explanation for her not calling. When they had spoken on Tuesday there had not been any problems. She had still been worried about her dad, but she was talkative and affectionate to a degree. Well, there was nothing he could do about it right now anyway, and he settled for hoping that she would call when she got the chance.

Nick decided on a pepperoni pizza, and walked through to the front room looking for his mobile phone. Kay's text message was waiting for him, and he read it without showing any emotion. Then he called through his pizza order, turned the volume up on the TV and settled down on the sofa. Should he respond to the woman, he wondered? The text message didn't demand a reply, but he guessed she had sent it to keep the arrangement they had come to fresh in his mind. Maybe she was anxious about it.

It soon occurred to him that if he didn't reply, even if only to acknowledge the message, it would keep preying on his mind all evening. On the other hand, he didn't really want to encourage a conversation too much. In the hours since lunch time, as certain thoughts had sunk in, he had come to view earlier events with a certain cool detachment. She – this Kay woman – was obviously off her rocker, and had a bit too much money to spare. Actually, Nick reconsidered, maybe that was slightly harsh; perhaps she was just a little eccentric. He was simply taking advantage of that.

Anyway, he should just text her back something neutral; get it out of the way, and then he could look forward to football and pizza, he told himself. Seconds later, his two letter reply, "OK", was on its way back to Kay. Nick jumped to his feet and headed for the kitchen again to start on the beer.

**

Less than 24 hours later, Nick was standing at the foot of the steps leading down from street level into Liverpool Street station. He felt decidedly awkward. His pitch, where he had been working all day shining shoes without any notion of embarrassment, was a matter of yards away; yet now, without having the accoutrements of his trade to justify his presence here, he felt like an imposter.

No-one among the hundreds of people that thronged the concourse could possibly have guessed his purpose. They were all far too busy reading evening newspapers or looking up at the platform information, to notice Nick, or to notice that he was perhaps the only person there who showed no interest whatsoever in the platform announcements. Nick was looking to his left, beyond his shoeshining pitch, along the tunnel of shops that stretched from the station concourse towards Broadgate Circle. He had been told by Kay Talbot just that morning that it would be from this direction that a certain Lee Talbot would come walking.

In Nick's pocket was a folded white envelope, with five £20 notes inside. Incredible – someone that he barely knew had just given him £100, and she had hardly batted an eyelid in doing so. He had counted the notes several times since Kay had left them with him at 9.15 that morning; it was the physical proof that the conversation he recalled from the previous day with this mysterious woman had indeed been a real one. He hadn't been totally sure of that when he had woken at 5.30 in the morning, stretching his arms out towards the space where Justine should have been.

But real it certainly was, and he had experienced odd feelings of familiarity, an easy pleasure, when he saw her approaching him on Thursday morning, armed with a modest, self-conscious smile. She looked tired, but damn fine, he thought. She was a survivor.

Alongside the money, Nick also had in his pocket a picture of Kay's errant husband, Lee Talbot. Nick had been able to summon up a vague mental image of Lee from the encounter a few weeks before anyway, but the picture, which Kay assured him was quite recent, was helpful nevertheless. How easy it would be to pick out one guy from the constant movement of people around him Nick didn't yet know, but that was why he was still here at Liverpool Street a few minutes after 5.30 on a Thursday evening, when he would normally be on his way home. Tonight was a dry run for the real thing. It seemed a good idea, if only to make sure that he had the right guy.

His fingers again felt the smooth surface of the photograph in his pocket. He had studied it more than a dozen times already, and he could see many of the small details of the picture in his mind's eye. He was confident that he could do this, and for a hundred quid, who would turn it down?

Much to his relief, he had also spoken to Justine at lunchtime. She had apologized about the day before, and said that she and her mother had been running around sorting things out and she hadn't had the chance to call. Was that really it, he had wondered? Was she telling him everything? Nick decided that he wouldn't push her further, since he had things to keep close to his chest as well. Phil Tanner was still in a coma anyway, and so there seemed to be no end in sight to the current situation with Justine in Melbourne and Nick in London. No end, that was, until he had saved up enough money to get out there and join her. Thank you Kay Talbot then, Nick laughed to himself.

Nick kept his eyes trained along the walkway towards Broadgate. Apparently Lee had been wearing a dark blue suit, a light blue shirt and a red and blue striped tie when he had left for work. Of course, it was possible that Lee might not be getting on his usual train today. He might be doing any number of things instead, so Nick had accepted that he might well be completely wasting his time. For that reason, he had decided that if he still hadn't seen Lee by 6pm, he would head for home. There was no particular reason to rush home, since there was no-one else there anyway, but nevertheless standing around in a busy train station for no particular good reason was not Nick's idea of an evening well spent.

So hurry up and get on the bloody train Lee, he thought impatiently, studying the face of every man that came hurrying along from Broadgate, most of whom had their eyes raised to the platform information boards, which made it a little easier for Nick to get a good look at their faces. However, the ones that had their faces buried in newspapers, walking and reading at the same time, were more of a problem. He prayed that Lee was not a keen newspaper reader.

Nick checked the time: 5.35. There were still ten minutes before Lee's usual train departed. He hoped that the guy would come along early to get a seat so that Nick could check him out and then go home. A couple more minutes ticked by, with Nick leaning back on the wall behind him, attempting to look nonchalant. He could feel more and more impatience creeping up on him, and to ward that off he took out the envelope again and quickly checked his money.

Suddenly he saw a man that he thought might be Lee, and he felt a sting of excitement. Is that him? The man in question passed behind a tall Indian guy and a woman and Nick lost him for a second. When he reappeared a second later, the next sighting brought disappointment. Nick saw that the man's upturned face looked a fair bit older than Lee's should. Almost at the same moment, he noticed that the man's open necked shirt was white, not blue. Oh well, close but no cigar.

Nick's vigil went on. A sudden idea: he looked up at the platform information board and sought out the 17.45 to Hertford East. There it was: platform three. The platform was almost directly opposite where Nick was standing.

He surveyed the area around it for a better vantage point. There was a French pastry kiosk to its right as he looked, then scanning to his left, there was the ticket barrier itself, which extended to cover the entrances to platforms one and two also. Then there was a photo booth, and then a plain white, metal-lic-looking panel several metres long which ended at an entrance to the London Underground station. To the left of the tube entrance as Nick looked began the row of shops, starting with a pharmacy, which lined the passageway towards Broadgate.

Nick turned his attention back to the pastry kiosk. He reckoned that from there he could probably get a better view along the passageway to Broadgate. Nick set off, threading a path through the crowd on the concourse.

He reached the kiosk, and turned around so that he now faced out to the concourse. When he looked to his right towards Broadgate however, he found that this position didn't in fact afford him a better view at all. There were too many people crossing his line of vision, and a brick pillar – the partner to the one that he worked in front of all day – stood guard, resolutely blocking the view that he had hoped to get along the passageway.

Worse, Nick now felt exposed standing here in front of all these people, and was therefore even more self-conscious than he had been before. At least back there by the stairs, nobody was likely to notice him; he had been just a guy standing around. Now, he was a guy standing around in full view of everyone, hanging about by a croissant parlour and looking nervously from side to side.

Bad move Nicky boy, he told himself. His embarrassment caused him to turn away and pretend that he was interested in the pastries on sale in the kiosk, although he didn't take in a single word of the options advertised. This was stupid, he realized; he wasn't even looking out for Lee now, and that was the entire reason that he was here in the first place. He would be better off back by the stairs.

He whirled back round, away from the kiosk, and turned slap bang into a commuter heading for the platform. Face to face, they bounced off of each other with some force. "Shit, sorry mate," Nick spluttered. The man glared at him, and Nick realised with shock that this was his quarry. This was Lee. The clothes were as described, although he didn't now have the tie on. While Nick had been looking the wrong way, Lee had walked right up to him.

"What the fuck are you playing at, you dick-head?" the man snarled, and Nick took a step to the side, apologising again. The man didn't give him a second look as he sped on through the ticket barrier, and then along the platform towards the front of the train.

Nick exhaled deeply and watched him go. It was definitely Lee: around six feet tall, the same height, pretty much, as Nick was himself, but more thickset than the shoeshiner, and with short, dark hair, ruddy cheeks, and eyes that seemed to gleam with indignation. Yep, that was Lee all right.

Nick watched him saunter to the front of the train and felt an instinctive dislike. He couldn't put his finger on it: perhaps it was the way he had spoken weeks before, during that argument at Nick's shoeshine pitch; perhaps it was the quiet desperation he saw in Kay's eyes, a desperation that Nick assumed this man had caused; or maybe it was just an air about the man, which Nick had picked up again, even in that second or two that he was close to Lee just then – an air of indifference to anyone around him.

Probably it was all three, Nick told himself, casting a final malevolent glance in Lee's direction, and seeing him step onto the train near the front. His job done, the shoeshiner smiled to himself and walked off to catch a bus home.

**

A wisp of smoke curled lazily towards the discoloured ceiling. An obese man with scarce tufts of hair dotting the back of his otherwise shiny head, stubbed a cigarette out forcefully in an ashtray that was already half full of dog-ends. Across the table from him was another man – skinnier and younger, sunken eyes, short spiky hair.

"Billy, we've got to be careful with this. We can't just get anyone involved. How well do you know this geezer?"

The younger man, whom the bigger man had just addressed, took a swig out of his pint glass, and betrayed just a little irritation with a sigh. "I told you already. I haven't known him that long, but he's sound. I met him up the Arsenal. He's well up for it. I've had him watched; I know all about his job, and I know all about his missus. She's a sort by the way, but they're not ringing each other's bells at the moment from what I hear. I've got half a mind to go round there myself. Anyway…"

There was silence for a second, before Billy continued. "You know, I remember when you used to trust me Custer. What the fuck have I done to lose that?" Billy sounded offended.

"Billy! Course I trust you mate. We've just gotta be sure, that's all. If it turns out he's filth or, even worse, a fucking journo, we'll be in deep shit." He thought for a second or two before adding: "We do need good blokes on the ground though. Every one we can get."

"Custer, he'll be here soon. You can meet him yourself, and if you don't like him, then I'll do it alone."

Custer raised a surprised eyebrow. "He's coming here?"

"Yes mate. I told you he was going to come along. He really wants to meet you; fuck knows why he wants to meet a muppet like you, eh?" Billy laughed quietly at his own remark.

Custer showed no sign of taking umbrage though, continuing: "Okay. We shouldn't have too many of us in one place though, you know, but I suppose for a little while there's no harm. So he's going to do the job with you Bill?" Custer was looking at Billy earnestly, and speaking to him in a low voice. The pub around them was not busy, and anyone walking past could easily have heard snatches of their conversation.

"You're going fucking senile mate!" laughed Billy. "Don't you remember anything I tell you? Yes, he's going to do the job with me. I want to make sure he's solid, so I want to see him at work. Just trust me on this Custer. Do me a favour eh?"

Custer nodded silently and took a mouthful of his beer as he reflected on these words. Billy waited and regarded him through narrow eyes, sipping some of his own drink. Custer was a top man, but after years of boozing the guy was not a pretty sight: loose skin sagged on his jowls, and tiny jagged blue and red veins crept across his cheeks. His eyes were bloodshot, and beneath his double chin, a well-worn polo shirt was tight around his bloated frame, one collar pointing upwards, the other folded under itself – the result of too many hot washes. He was still the boss though, even if he didn't look it.

"You've got pride of place Bill," Custer continued. "That's how much I trust you. We decided on Monday that you are going to kick the whole thing off. I've got other boys out there on the ground just waiting for the signal. And you are the signal Billy, so do not fucking let me down."

Billy nodded with undisguised appreciation. "Nice one Custer, nice one. I won't let you down."

Just then, a man and a woman walked past their table and went up to the bar, and both men stopped talking to watch them go by. Then Custer turned again to Billy.

"So – when will you be ready to go?"

"I reckon two or three weeks. We're still doing a bit of groundwork, but we're nearly there mate. I've got the exact perfect place in mind to get him."

"Say no more Billy," Custer quickly interjected. Billy smiled and sipped some more lager from his pint glass.

"It's going to be good Custer. Top fucking draw. Couple of weeks and then everything will be just right. Can't wait to get stuck in."

"Yeah, I know Bill, but you mustn't until we're all ready. It's got to be coordinated or there's no point; no impact. You know what I mean? I'll give you the green light. Anyway, good. Good to see you're on top of things. Do you need anything from me?"

"Nah mate. Got the tools, got the manpower. Two, three weeks – just give me the word Custer and off we go, eh?"

They both laughed quietly, and chinked glasses in celebration. Custer started to light another cigarette – a liberty that he had "negotiated" with the owner of the pub. Billy was a good boy, he thought; smart as they come, both in his head and with the clobber he wore. He made Custer feel like a bundle of old rags.

Just then the pub door swung open, and a suited man walked in, peering into the gloom. Billy, whose eyes were well adjusted to the dark in the room, turned to look towards the door, then back round to Custer, and said: "Talking of manpower."

He got to his feet, and called out to the newcomer: "Lee! Over here! Alright son."

The man had spun round towards their table, and his eyes lit up as he saw a familiar face. Another suit, thought Custer, as the new man walked quickly over. He looked keen, looked capable though. Billy had his arm around the man's shoulders, welcoming him as a brother might. He turned to Custer with a wide smile.

"Custer, this is Lee. Lee, this is Custer. Let's do business."

**

Kay had been dreading the weekend that started two days later for a single specific reason: Lee's parents were over from Basildon, staying for the weekend. Not only would she and Lee have to play at happy families the whole time that his parents were there, but Kay would also have to contend with Lee's mum and the stony, disapproving look that would follow everything that Kay said or did.

She knew exactly what the real thoughts were behind that expressionless façade: why haven't you given me the grand-child that I long for? Lee was an only child, so Kay could at least partly understand why Jean Talbot held her in such barely concealed contempt. It was regrettable and just very unfortunate for Jean that the woman who was married to her son was not interested in having children. But Kay was not about to compromise her own life for Jean Talbot, nor anybody for that matter.

They walked into Hertford town centre that Saturday evening – a chilly October night – and ate an adequate Italian meal in one of the town's restaurants. The meal was okay, but the conversation was awkward and punctuated by several uncomfortably long silences. Kay felt like she was suffocating in these people's company, but at least it gave her a chance to reflect on the past week as she picked unconvincingly at her pasta and salad, and put away her white wine slightly faster than polite company would have deemed acceptable.

After dinner they wandered over cobbled streets round to a couple of pubs, and eventually they settled down in a pub at the side of the river. John Talbot, Lee's dad and very much a wider, shorter, white haired version of Kay's husband, was telling them about the estate in Basildon where he and Jean lived. A Muslim couple had moved in next door, and John, Jean and Lee were laughing at some of the stories John was telling about them: their clothes, their customs, the aloof way they regarded John and Jean.

Kay smiled because she thought she should and gritted her teeth harder. People all over the country were probably taking the piss out of women that wear burkas right at this very moment, she thought, and they probably all think they're as funny as you do John. It was boring and Kay's mind wandered elsewhere.

She had managed to save Belinda's job, though it had caused another row between Kay and Wilf. The two were now hardly talking, which was bad for the business and awkward for their employees, who endured every day knowing that their bosses were at odds with each other. It was a mess and needed to be sorted out. Kay and Wilf had been friends for so long that Kay thought that somehow they must be able to reconcile their differences.

It had got personal though. Wilf had slammed Kay about her drinking, pointing out that not only had he noticed her performance crumbling, but so had the staff, and so had Roger Wallace at Mighty Meals – now an ex-client, but one who had spelled out a few home truths to Wilf on the telephone. That was serious, and it had been a massive jolt for Kay.

Looking at Palmerston PR's reduced account list now, it was clear that things were very tight. So tight that if they were to lose any more revenue they would have to start thinking about letting people go. They needed to win new business, and Wilf had criticized Kay on that score as well. It was about time that she bucked her ideas up and brought some new accounts in.

Wilf's instructions had been stern: "We need new business from you in the next six months Kay. I want a list of prospects by the middle of next week and some thoughts on how we can win them." Kay had been about to respond but Wilf spoke first again.

"Before you say it Kay, I'm going to do the same as well. Perhaps we've all been a bit too casual around here recently. It's time to get professional."

They had left it at that. For a couple of days Kay had been shocked into abstaining from evening bouts of drinking, but then this Saturday evening with Lee's parents had come around, and there was no way that she was going to get through the night sober, she decided.

While the conversation at the table continued, Kay excused herself and walked off to the ladies' toilet, where she locked herself in a cubicle and sent a text message to James. She was looking forward to receiving some affection, and wanted to let him know. The response was almost immediate. Absolutely girl, it said, can't wait. That brought a rare smile to her face.

She washed her hands, checked herself in the mirror and then went back to the table to face the rest of her ordeal. Even Lee, who was not usually attentive, seemed aware that Kay was finding the night difficult, squeezing her hand in unexpected sympathy after she sat down. Soon she faced an inquisition from Jean about her job.

Kay answered diplomatically for a few minutes, but Jean still seemed distinctly unimpressed at the end of it, concluding with the tart observation that she was "sure it was important really". Kay stared back for a long second afterwards, fighting off an urge to bite back at her.

She wondered how long it would be before the inevitable big question was asked by Jean. The men were talking about football now, and Kay could feel Jean closing in, sensing that despite all previous evidence she could make a difference. Almost as a nervous reaction Kay drained her wine glass with a flourish and stared unhappily out of the window. Maybe she should quickly make friends with the men and join the conversation about football, to avoid the other conversation that she knew was approaching fast.

"I think they should stop mucking about with it and kick it in the bloody goal," Kay blurted out. It was one of the things that she had picked up from talking to James and some of Lee's other friends at football matches. Apparently Arsenal passed the ball around too much, instead of shooting at goal when they had the chance.

"Yeah, all right Kay. Thanks for that," said Lee, winking at his dad. "We weren't even talking about the Arsenal you silly cow." Lee was smiling, but there was mockery in his eyes. John chuckled and gave Kay a patronizing, pitying smile, while Jean bit her lip and looked out of the window. Kay felt her face redden, and decided that it was a better idea to just listen instead. That would be much easier.

The conversation she was dreading began as they walked back to the house through a thin rain shower. Drops of water soon settled and glistened on Kay's cheeks and her coat. Heads down, the four of them marched quickly, but Jean was there at Kay's side as soon as an opportunity presented itself – or so it seemed.

"Have you decided anything about what we spoke about yet, lovey?" The last word was Jean's customary term of address, but it always seemed totally incongruous to Kay, considering their mutual antagonism. It was once again time to decide whether to hurt Jean's feelings, or to protect them. Well, Kay quickly concluded, she had asked for it.

"Er, yes."

They walked a few more paces, hunched against the drifting rain. Jean seemed to be expecting a longer answer, but when it didn't come she pressed further.

"So do you…"

"It's not for me, mum. We've talked about this before."

"I know, but I thought you might have changed your mind by now. You know Lee would love to be a dad."

"Yes, I know. But I'm not keen on being a mum, and it's my life too."

Kay couldn't bear to look at her mother-in-law. There was silence for a few seconds. The men were a couple of paces ahead, braced against the weather, walking quickly, also in silence. I know exactly what you're thinking Jean, Kay told herself. You're thinking that I'm a selfish bitch, but then what does that make you, since you only want me to have a baby to make you and your son happy? We're all bloody selfish, but this is my body and my life, so I'm entitled to decide.

"Well…" Jean at last said, managing to convey her affront in just that one word, but Kay heard the emotion in her voice and knew that the conversation was already over. They walked back to the house without another word. Kay was pre-occupied, debating whether to say sorry but not knowing how she could say it without making things worse. Instead she kept her thoughts to herself.

Back at the house, Jean was very quiet. She seemed pre-occupied too, and Kay could imagine the boiling anger that lay beneath that subdued exterior. Blaming a headache, Jean soon announced that she was off to bed and departed meekly, almost as if she was in a trance. As his mother left the room, Lee gave Kay a long and meaningful look that wasn't particularly friendly. The men were cracking open some beers and Kay suddenly felt lost and lonely in their company.

Ten minutes later she was in bed herself, listening to some music through her earphones with the lights switched off, trying to block out all feelings, and all sensations. A few tears rolled onto the pillow that she hugged. Kay felt as devastated as Jean had looked when she had shuffled, glassy-eyed, out of the front room to retire for the night. Tuesday night couldn't come quickly enough to take this pain away. After too long, blessed sleep at last came to relieve her.

**

Kay Talbot and her secret lover hadn't been the only people looking ahead to Tuesday with some anticipation that night. Despite his previous ambivalence, Nick spent that Saturday evening drinking with Justine's friends Brendan and Nicole in Camden. As the night wore on though he found he was increasingly distracted by thoughts of what was to come during the next week.

Brendan and Nicole were making a special effort to keep in touch with him, and he had assumed that it had been a request from Justine. They were loud and boisterous but good fun. He realised now that they wanted to be friends with him, even in her absence. It made a big difference to him. They talked about Justine mostly that evening, and the Australian couple listened intently to the latest update from Nick. There wasn't much to say really: Justine's dad was still in a coma, and she and her mum were still visiting Phil Tanner every day to sit by his bed, hoping against hope. Justine seemed no closer to returning to England, and Nick wondered how long it would be before this temporary situation became permanent.

However, she was still phoning virtually every day to chat, even if those chats were becoming shorter, with less to say that hadn't already been said many times. She did talk enthusiastically about meeting up with her old friends in Melbourne, and Nick could not help but feel slightly peeved every time she mentioned seeing Craig, an old school friend who she talked about frequently.

There had been no real suggestion that there was anything more to this than friendship, but she talked affectionately about this Craig guy, while Nick was on the other side of the world feeling unavoidable twinges of jealousy. Nor could he easily stop those twinges without asking Justine a direct question that would make him sound jealous and paranoid; so he feigned interest in Craig's fine qualities and privately seethed.

There was little in his own life that he could tell Justine about. Work was work, and then he stayed in most nights. They spoke of shared dreams, but he couldn't be sure how long these would last, given the distance between them. And he found that he was completely incapable of mentioning the strange situation with the enigmatic married woman he had become friends with, and his soon-to-begin life as a private detective. How the hell could he ever explain that one? It sounded ridiculous in his own head, let alone across a distance of 10,000 miles, on a shaky phone connection.

The only reason he had agreed to do it in the first place was to get some extra money that he could put towards traveling to Australia if necessary.

So why, he had wondered that Saturday night, and several more times between then and this moment now on Tuesday morning as he travelled on the bus to work, why was he so keyed up about this? It was a very simple errand: stand around, look out for the bloke, send a text message, go home and wait for another envelope of cash the following week. What could be easier or, in fact, less exciting?

But it was certainly something different in his life – a diversion from the mundane routine that saw him rise early each weekday to spend the day buffing scuffed shoes, biting his tongue at pretentious City types, laughing at their jokes at the right moments, and at the end of the day heading back to the Camden flat for a night in, alone with the TV.

Being asked to carry out this small task made him feel just a little more useful to the world, and after the bad years before he met Justine – those days of vacant hopelessness on the streets – it was a feeling that Nick could savour. He was healing; that much he was sure of.

Now there were only a few hours of work to do before he earned that first £100 advance that she had given him. An amazing act of good faith and trust, Nick considered. It was true that she knew where he worked, but if his bosses had suddenly decided to move him to another part of town, then that would no longer be the case. Maybe she hadn't thought about that. Maybe she had so much money that it didn't matter.

Nick's bus turned the last corner before it reached his stop at Liverpool Street Station, and he made his way down the stairs from the top deck, still deep in thought. Half an hour later, he was at his usual pitch. It was 7.30 in the morning, and the station was getting busy all around him. Customers needing a shoeshine frequently interrupted his attempts to read a newspaper.

Soon after 8.15, Nick was standing by his seat, sipping a coffee brought over by Vicky and watching with dull, over-familiar disinterest as the pulse of the station quickened, and waves of people swept through the ticket barriers.

Suddenly, right there, was Lee, walking away from platform four and then heading past Nick towards the Broadgate Circle and his office. A stroke of luck – now Nick even knew what clothes Lee was wearing today: a light grey suit and a pale blue tie. Nick watched him slalom through the rush, looking purposeful, moving fast as he always seemed to do, a soft black case clutched to his thigh.

Nick smiled to himself. "Thank you, Lee Talbot," he muttered. "I will see you later."

**

That Tuesday afternoon was a difficult one for Lee. He had a three o'clock meeting arranged with his boss Lukas Baptiste. It went badly. Baptiste had asked Lee to identify some potential investment strategies and the risks involved, for a number of the bank's highest value clients. It was a task for which Lee should have spent some time thinking, doing preparation and research. Baptiste had even given him a week's notice to put it together.

Instead though, Lee had found other things to do – online shopping, chatting to friends and generally just looking after immediate work requirements; it was only that afternoon, in the short period between returning from the lunchtime pub with his friend Dave, and sitting down with Baptiste at 3pm, that he jotted a few ideas down on paper. It was obvious to Lee as he walked through the corridor to Baptiste's office that his boss was not going to be impressed.

Fueled by lager and general disdain of the hierarchy above him though, Lee found himself to be curiously unconcerned about the whole thing. He had discovered within himself a rebellious streak that he didn't remember being there even a year before. Lee had always been a diligent worker, though he knew that he was easily distracted. He had taken his career seriously enough to rise to management level at a fairly young age, and a few years earlier had been told that some of the senior directors considered him to be a rising star in the firm.

Part of the problem was Lukas Baptiste, who had joined the bank only within the last six months. He was of Nigerian descent, the son of a lawyer that came to Britain for education, and stayed. There had been an instant and mutual dislike, which wasn't helped by the fact that Baptiste had got the job that Lee had also applied for. For the first two months, Lee had watched Baptiste's actions like a hawk, glorying in the errors that the new man sometimes made as he found his feet in the job; making snide comments about Baptiste behind his back to undermine his authority.

The fact that Lukas Baptiste didn't confront Lee about it only made the disrespect that Lee felt become greater. Once, early in the feud, Baptiste had approached Lee and asked for his advice on some professional matter. It was a big mistake, never to be repeated. The look of triumphant one-upmanship that was written all over Lee's face said it all, but Lee went further, humiliating Baptiste in front of the whole office in a loud voice:

"Oh Lukas, you don't even know that? How embarrassing. Oh, you want my help, do you?"

As his staff turned to listen, Baptiste had tried to bluster through. Peering down at the seated Lee through his spectacles, and suddenly sweating, he said "don't make a thing out of it; just tell me Lee". Lee continued to make it awkward though, and eventually Baptiste had stormed off and found someone a little less smug and a little more discreet to help him out.

After that, Lee's air of amused superiority over Baptiste became almost unbearable for everyone in the office, apart from Lee of course, who was oblivious to the tension it caused.

And Lee might still have been entitled to feel that he held the upper hand in this atmosphere of antagonism, had he kept his own eye on the ball. During the last couple of months though, other things had turned his head. In his rare introspective moments he would acknowledge that his situation at home was a part of that.

Really though, it was his burgeoning friendship with Billy Filler, the young guy he had met at football, that had made his career fade out of focus. Befriending Billy had awoken something inside Lee that he had scarcely imagined existed. The unexpected desire to seize the initiative, to cut through the crap and really make a difference – it now burned strongly in Lee's breast.

Lee had no respect for Baptiste, and in any case he had more important things on his mind than the intricacies of investment banking. Lukas Baptiste represented much of what was wrong with modern day Britain, to Lee's mind. His appointment to the job instead of Lee deprived a true-blooded Englishman of opportunity. Billy had impressed upon Lee how unjust it was, and Lee found the arguments to be persuasive.

So it was that Lee entered Baptiste's office without bothering to knock that afternoon, armed with a single A4 sheet of paper marked with seven or eight lines of Lee's untidy handwriting – the sum of his week of preparation.

He emerged twenty minutes later, shaken, humiliated and angry. Baptiste took one look at Lee's notes, turned to face Lee and stared at him with contempt. Then the tirade began, although it was delivered in such a calm, measured fashion, and such icy detachment, that Lee found himself feeling even more unnerved than if the same words had been shouted at him.

Baptiste said he knew how Lee felt about him. He knew what was in Lee's mind, and what was in his soul. It was ugly and it had no place in society. It didn't belong in a professional workplace such as this one either. Baptiste had come up against Lee's sort before; he had beaten them then, and he would not lose this time either.

Lee had a choice: he either got over his problem with the colour of Baptiste's skin, or he found another job. He could expect no support from Baptiste in finding one though. If he wanted to carry on undermining Baptiste in the office, then he would find him up to the challenge. Baptiste's own superiors had also been informed about the nature of this clash of personalities.

And this so called report that Lee had presented – well, it was pathetic, almost the final straw; and it showed the depth of Lee's contempt for Baptiste. Every hastily scribbled word in Lee's spidery hand spoke more eloquently than Lee ever could of his own ignorance and misplaced arrogance, said Baptiste.

Right now, Lee's professional competence was under question. Baptiste had been told when he had joined the organisation that Lee was a great deputy: committed, knowledgeable, and trusted by the staff and the management.

Baptiste had seen no such evidence. He had watched as Lee's standing amongst his colleagues had crumbled away in recent months. He had observed as Lee had coasted through the last few months, sitting through meetings barely concealing his lack of interest. He had made costly mistakes through not caring or not concentrating, and only the diligent checking of his colleagues had prevented some serious problems with clients.

In short, he was no longer up to the job it seemed. Lee had got away with it until now because over the years he had built up a large amount of goodwill amongst his bosses. Baptiste didn't claim to have perfect eyesight, but he was damned if he could see how, judging by Lee's current performance. Anyway, that goodwill, from the company CEO Bernard Molyneux down, had been expended. Lee was drinking in the last chance saloon.

Speaking of which – Lee had clearly spent some time this afternoon in the pub. Baptiste could smell it on Lee's breath. So, it was like this: the patience of the senior management was wearing thin; Bernard had instructed Baptiste that one more indiscretion from Lee Talbot and he would find himself on the receiving end of the company's disciplinary process.

And that was before he had sauntered into Baptiste's office today, after a few lunchtime beers, to offer up the most inept piece of analysis it had been Baptiste's misfortune to look at. It was embarrassing. Lee could be assured that Baptiste had it within his power to set the disciplinary wheels in motion right there and right then, and (look at me Lee), after all the mocking and downright insulting comments behind Baptiste's back, and the poisonous looks that Lee probably kidded himself that Baptiste hadn't noticed, why the hell should Baptiste not do so?

It was only out of the kindness of Baptiste's heart that Lee was getting one more chance. This was his wake up call. Get this work done properly by Thursday lunchtime, or Bernard Molyneux would get to hear about the latest in Talbot's fast-growing line of cock-ups. Personally, stated Baptiste coolly, he didn't care whether Lee stayed with the company or not. There was clearly no respect between them, but that feeling had originated with Lee, and Baptiste was professional enough to get on with the job. Either Lee did that as well, or his prospects at Benning Rowe were not looking bright.

"Now get out of my office. It makes me angry just looking at you."

Baptiste sat back, arms crossed, eyes fixed on Lee, daring a riposte, but Lee didn't, perhaps couldn't, even look at him; he rose unsteadily to his feet, turned and went out of the door, closing it gently behind himself. As he walked along the corridor outside, the shame of his departure stung him fiercely. Back there in Baptiste's room, his mind had gone utterly blank. He had needed to escape from Baptiste's withering stare. But now his mind was awash with anger and humiliation as he tried to come to terms with all that his boss had said.

He saw Diane, one of the secretaries, approaching along the corridor. Lee was too devastated for any kind of contact with his colleagues yet. He stopped abruptly in the corridor, intensely studying the sheet of paper in his hand, or so he made it appear, but his panic was total and his eyes didn't register any of the inadequate words that he had written on it. Then he turned and hastily walked back in the direction from which he had come, affecting as if he had forgotten something important, but actually fleeing from Diane; from all of them.

He reached a gents toilet door along the corridor and Lee was inside in a flash, bolting himself inside the cubicle. There, at last, shocked tears fought with furious insults, both outbursts coming spluttering and gushing out in waves. Head in hands he cursed Baptiste, cursed Molyneux, cursed his lunch buddy Dave Ramsbottom who should have warned him about all this, cursed his wife. They were all to blame, yet he was the one being punished; he was the one being victimised.

Right at that moment, as he choked back tears of impotent fury, he was effectively a child again; too feeble, too helpless to hit back in a man's world.

**

It was a few minutes short of 4pm before Lee felt composed enough to venture out of the cubicle and head back to his desk. He was a changed man. Already, anger and humiliation was being channeled into indignant determination to rise to Baptiste's challenge. Yeah, he would do this stupid work for the tosser. He would show everybody who was the best around here. Baptiste was damned right that Lee hadn't been trying, but now he would try and Baptiste would be left a million miles behind.

Lee worked at a feverish pace for the rest of the day, feeling more focused, more motivated, than he had felt for as long as he could remember. It surprised him. Lee hadn't thought he could get so fired up about anything these days, outside of the Arsenal or his conversations with Billy. But here it was: he was bent to the task, moving from one screen to another, one account summary to another, making calls, jotting down notes, and printing off pages with swift efficiency. Cold fury drove him on until, soon after 5.30, his desk mate Robin Ashmore downed tools, and switched off his own computer, bidding Lee a good evening. Lee sank back into his chair, feeling a sort of grim delight at the progress he had made.

At this rate, hitting the Thursday lunch time deadline would be a piece of piss, he reckoned. The office was emptying quickly, and Lee watched people moving about for a couple of minutes, noticing the banality of their conversations for the first time in a long time.

After a while, he saved the document that he was working on, checked some emails and shut down the PC. He felt quite tired now; tired, but satisfied. No, not satisfied actually, he reflected. This was actually exhilarating; a rediscovery of his own prowess. Even the look that Robin had given him as he had got up to leave had been something to savour for Lee – a look of bewilderment mixed with grudging admiration at the super-slick activity that had been going on across the desk from him for the last hour or so.

Lee quickly checked the time on his mobile phone: 5.40. If he legged it now he had just enough time to make the 5.45 train. Maybe he would even talk in a civil fashion to the missus when he got home. Hauling his jacket on as he walked, Lee went out to the lifts, passed them by and bounded down the stairs instead. He checked out by waving a plastic card he took from his pocket at an electronic sensor by the reception desk. It was home time in the City and Lee joined the stream of people walking urgently towards Liverpool Street station.

It had been an odd day, he allowed himself to reflect as he strode quickly away from Broadgate Circle. A few lunchtime bevvies and a laugh with Dave, then the humiliation of Baptiste's dressing down, and the private tears of despair; then the hardened resolve, and the prolific, thrilling feats that had propelled him to the end of the working day.

Lee walked out onto the crowded expanse of the concourse and looked up to check his train was on time. Who would have thought that getting a bollocking by your boss could work out so positively? The train was running on time; it was there on platform three ready for Lee to board, with a minute and a half to spare before it was due to leave. Almost without breaking stride he was through the ticket barrier, and on his way home.

Across the concourse a few seconds later, unspotted and of no regard in any case, a young man in a black T-shirt and black trousers, slipped his mobile phone into his pocket, and with a barely perceptible private smile, walked off to the escalator to head for the bus stop. Lee Talbot wasn't the only man to have satisfactorily finished his work for the day.

**

Five minutes earlier and twenty or so miles to the north, watchful, impatient eyes were fixed on the clock radio next to the Talbot marital bed. All was still, all was quiet, apart from Kay's own shallow breathing and the heavier breathing of James next to her, slumbering as, post-coitus, he usually did.

There was just an occasional distant sound of passing traffic outside and the constant hushed electric hum of the house.

Kay found herself imagining the scene at Liverpool Street: Lee sweeping out of his office building and storming through the crowds; Nick, bless him, waiting patiently for the sighting. Perhaps the text message was already written, and her spy's thumb was hovering expectantly over the send button. All this – this subterfuge; this game – has been manufactured by you Kay, she told herself. It was funny, but she kept the laugh to herself, not wanting to stir James.

Ah, yes: James. It was another illicit meeting between the two of them, the same as the week before, but somehow slightly different in two ways. It was more passionate for a start, which surprised her. James's passion for Kay seemed to be growing with every visit.

He had her to himself for four hours; time which he used urgently and decisively. Then he slept, leaving her to cuddle up to her pillow and wonder at the normality of it all, the routine that this acquiescence had already become. No chocolates, no flowers, no wining and dining: just sex. It was certainly uncomplicated, thought Kay, and like most men, that just about summed up James. Perhaps it had once summed up Lee as well, but if she was honest, she wasn't really sure what thoughts went through his mind any more.

The other way that today was different to the week before was in this period right now, as James slept and Kay's mind worked through the day's emotions. Since that almost fateful occasion before there had been anxiety that Lee might walk through the door at any second. Not today, though. Today she was more relaxed, even though she knew that her plan was far from foolproof – Lee could, after all, walk past Nick in the rush hour at the station without being seen. That was certainly a possibility, but nevertheless, this new arrangement did give her some peace of mind.

Or at least it would, when Nick sent the text message. Kay's mobile phone lay next to the clock radio, and she turned her gaze towards it. Any minute now, she thought. A sudden moment of alarm caused her to reach over and pick the handset up. What if she had missed a text during the afternoon? She quickly saw that she hadn't. Even so, she switched the phone to silent, since she didn't want James to know about this arrangement. If he heard the phone beep right before she told him it was time to leave, he might start asking awkward questions. It was better to play it safe, Kay decided, reaching over and putting the handset back down next to the clock radio.

Any minute now. From outside she heard the waspish buzz of a motorbike going through the gears, and a minute later there came the muffled shouts of kids horsing around as they passed by the house. Come on Nick, it's time, Kay demanded silently, impatiently; and to her amazement, just then the display of her mobile phone lit up in response. She grabbed it again and smiled as she read the words in the incoming text message:

"The eagle has flown!"

Top man, Nick; you are a top man. With her back to James, a wide smile spread itself across Kay's face at all this exciting secrecy. First, sneaking about behind Lee's back, and now sneaking about behind James' back as well – she really shouldn't be enjoying this quite so much, she thought, but what the hell; she deserved it. Thank you, Nick.

She put the phone back down and relaxed for a couple of seconds. There was work to do, and as ever she would be sitting at her laptop and her paperwork for most of the evening to make up for the afternoon's lost hours. She did love it when a plan came together, though. Anyway, the fun was over and it was time for James to go. She snuggled up to him and kissed the back of his neck a few times. He groaned in response.

"Is it that time already babe?" he asked. He sounded sleepy and disorientated.

"Afraid so. We can't have a repeat of last time, can we my love?"

God, did she really just use the word 'love'? Did she really mean that? Well, that was a question for another time. James showed no sign of stirring from his slumber, so on a playful whim she gave him a sudden firm push in the small of his back, causing him to fall, feet first, halfway out of the bed, with a surprised yelp. Another hefty shove and James departed from the bed – quickly confirmed by a thud as his upper body hit the floor. Kay might even have heard the bitter curses that followed, had they not been drowned out by her own gales of laughter.

Chapter Four

Curled up and tucked inside a small enamel pot on Justine's dressing table were ten crisp twenty pound notes, stashed away and left untouched until Nick needed them to pay for a flight to Australia. Most evenings, as he wearily undressed for bed alone, he would quickly check that the money was still there – his wages of sin, he liked to think, although it wasn't much of a sin, on reflection. And it would eventually enable him to be by the side of his Justine.

Twice now he had waited after work on a Tuesday evening, spotted Lee Talbot heading for his train, and sent a text message to the man's wife telling her that simple fact, though he had used a different "code word" each time. This was his own contribution to the game – and it was a game, he was sure of that. Being given £100 for the most ridiculously easy piece of espionage ever conceived…well, he couldn't take it seriously. It was obviously some game between Kay and Lee Talbot, and Nick had just happened to be in the right place, and with the right circumstances, to benefit financially from the warring couple's situation.

Continuing the playfulness, and to gently mock Kay as well, in his first text message Nick had therefore sent the words: "The eagle has flown"; the second time he continued the joke with: "Elvis has left the building". He and Kay had laughed about it when she stopped by at Liverpool Street to give Nick his pay packet, in advance of his second spying mission. Despite that little bit of fun it hadn't been a particularly cheery conversation. She seemed distant and distracted, and he could tell that she didn't want to talk much. When he asked her how her weekend had been, she had answered as briefly as she could, and at the first opportunity it seemed, had said: "Anyway, I've got to go. I'll let you know about next week."

She had then made off towards the tube entrance, watched by a puzzled Nick. He had a constant stream of customers that Monday, so he hadn't really been able to think about it for the rest of the day. But it kept returning to his mind that evening and for the next few days. Was it work? Was it Lee? Was it some other problem? Finally, and angrily, he made himself acknowledge that since he knew nothing about her life, it was pointless to speculate.

In any case, he should have been thinking about Justine. Their daily phone calls were now happening only every other day, and Nick hated this distance that was between them. He could feel things crumbling slowly, and he fought against the perception of inevitability that was creeping up on him. Phil Tanner was stable but still in a critical state. The doctors couldn't say how long this would go on for, and Justine was proving to be somewhat more of a home girl than Nick had imagined her to be. The mere thought of leaving Australia while her dad was still in hospital was impossible for her to comprehend.

So Justine and Nick continued to live separate lives, and whenever they spoke Nick felt what seemed like an increasingly unbridgeable gap between them. They did however still talk about Nick going out to Australia and that was a comfort of sorts. Perhaps when they were together again all the dark shadows would disappear, Nick figured. He could only hope.

That had been the last, nervous thought he could recall having while lying in the depths of his bed on Sunday night before sleep mercifully caught up with him. He remembered it the instant he woke up on Monday at 5 a.m. though. Another day with doubt gnawing at his mind lay ahead, with little but boot polish and brushes for company.

Before 6 a.m. Nick was at the bus stop, queuing with the usual pale, puffy-faced handful of fellow commuters who daily shuffled mutely onto the bus, barely acknowledging each other or the driver in their sleepy stupours. Nick himself shuffled on in line, waved his bus pass at the driver, who was barely looking in any case, and then took a seat near the back, next to a window, upon which his head was soon resting, his eyes scrunched shut, dozing in and out of a near-sleep.

By 6.30 he was at Liverpool Street and getting set up. The station had an atmosphere of hushed anticipation at this time of day, with cleaners and shop workers busying themselves, and passengers from the earliest train arrivals walking with blinking eyes into the glare of the concourse. By 6.45 Nick was ready and waiting for clients.

Slowly the station came to life around him, with a thin dribble of commuters turning into a near non-stop surge between 7.30 and 9.30. From then on, the pace of the day fluctuated with periods of inactivity spent reading or just sitting thinking dull thoughts, punctuated by flurries of custom. Nick had stopped wondering about the vagaries of his working day a long time ago. It was just as it was.

Lunchtime came and went and Nick found that his mind was troubled: where was Kay? Would she not be visiting to pay him for the following Tuesday evening? The arrangement was clear – if she didn't give him the money in advance, he wouldn't fulfil his part of the deal. As it ticked onwards towards 3pm, Nick found the absence of any word unsettling. In a quiet moment, he sat and looked out across the concourse, not particularly noticing any of the usual human activity, and reflected that the thought was bothering him more than it should be. But where was she? And more to the point, he convinced himself, where was his money, which he needed to fly to his girlfriend's side?

Nick was polishing a customer's shoes a few minutes later when he heard his mobile phone beep inside his pocket, announcing the arrival of a text message. He wanted to reach for it straight away but he fought off that desire, and instead carried on shining while half listening to his customer moaning about some political story in the newspaper. Maybe it's Justine, he thought, but then Justine isn't due to ring until tomorrow; so hopefully it's Kay.

As he got towards the end of the job, Nick was annoyed to notice that another man was lurking behind his seated customer, waiting his turn it seemed. The man came forward and sat down as soon as the first guy stood up to pay for his shoeshine, and Nick had no chance to check his mobile phone as the new customer was chatting away at him already. Nick gritted his teeth and got to work. The man was exceedingly well-spoken it turned out, and Nick quickly found his voice irritating. He was talking about his holiday plans, some sort of trekking adventure in Nepal it transpired.

Eventually the man asked whether Nick planned to go away for Christmas. Nick wasn't in the mood for friendly banter, or even just polite conversation. He simply replied: "I can't afford holidays doing this job, sir."

The man was silent for a minute, and Nick imagined that he was trying to get his head around the concept of not having the wherewithal to go on holiday three times a year. No mate – difficult to believe I know, but no skiing at St Moritz, or scuba diving in the Seychelles for me this year, Nick thought.

The silence gave Nick the chance to brush up and finish, and he thankfully slipped the man's money into his bag, and wished him a good holiday walking in the mountains. The mobile phone was in his hand a second later.

It was Kay! Nick hurriedly read the message through twice, before pocketing the phone again and resuming his seat to think about a reply. Kay's text message was a long one: "Hi Nick sorry can't get there yet, mad day. Got your money! Can you meet for quick drink at 7ish tonite? Let me know, beers on me Kay x"

Nick weighed it up. It would mean hanging around after work, but that wasn't such a high price to pay to get another bundle of £20 notes. It wasn't as if he had any particular reason to get home on time anyway. A big smile spread across his face. Would he meet Kay for a drink? Well, okay then; just as long as she behaved herself.

**

Kay watched the screen of her mobile phone as the message to Nick was sent, and then placed the handset back in her handbag. Through the glass partition between her and the rest of the office she could see a few of the staff gathering in a bunch around Belinda's desk, all of them with notebooks, pens and sheets of paper to hand. They were getting ready for a meeting that Kay had emailed everyone about that morning.

At the far end of the room was what the staff called the "chill out room", a small square-shaped room decked out with sofas and beanbags to assist the process of relaxation. It was also the usual venue for these types of meeting, since Kay had refused to sanction Giles and Gavin's request to put a pool table in there. Gathering some sheets of paper of her own from her desk, Kay now breezed out of the office, and headed towards her team of bright young things.

"Right, come on you lot. Stop gassing. Let's get to it!" she called, passing by the crowd at Belinda's desk and heading for the chill out room. Young Steph, the office assistant, was at her desk near the door to the room, and she looked up as Kay went in.

"Do you need me for this KT?" she asked. She had a pair of scissors in one hand, and various bits of newspaper and magazine pages littered her desk. Kay stopped in the doorway and turned towards her.

"Are you feeling brilliant Stephy? I only need you in here if you're feeling brilliant."

Steph gave Kay a sideways look that suggested she was too over-worked to be in brilliant form today, though there was also a mischievous glint in her eyes.

"Yeah, of course I am boss. More brilliant than any of that bunch of losers you've got with you, obviously," said Steph, as the rest of the team lined up behind Kay at the doorway. There were laughs and jokey expressions of disdain from the team. Ruth poked her tongue out at Steph, who continued: "It's just that Wilf wanted this done so he could look at it, change it all, get me to do it again and still send it out tonight."

Groans and more laughs came from the team, and Giles started playing an imaginary violin. Kay raised her voice above the tittering.

"Giles! Stop being an arse. Give Steph one of your hugs and tell her that we love her but she's excused from this meeting so that Wilf can have his cuttings ready."

Full of mirth, the team trooped into the chill out room and sat down, as Giles drooled a lustful "come 'ere darlin'" and made a grab for the reluctant Steph, who tried to twist away from him. She was sitting down though and found that it was impossible to escape. Cries of disgust from the office assistant suggested that Giles was over-doing the affection; Steph recoiled from the sloppy wet kiss he planted on her cheek, yelling: "Eeeuuurrghh! Giles, piss off, leave me alone!"

But she joined in the laughter as Giles finally let go and walked through to the chill out room, calling back to her with one of his special nicknames: "Don't pretend you didn't love it Wiggle." An exasperated Kay finally dragged Giles into the room and shut the glass door behind them, rebuking him between her own giggles that he should stop it because they needed to get started.

It still took a few seconds for the group to settle down. They seemed excitable today, and had been since lunchtime when Gavin had uncovered the revelation that Jasmine had a new boyfriend whose name was Toby. The mickey-taking, especially from the boys, had been merciless since then, but all this joviality was in stark contrast to the way that Kay felt inside. She and Wilf had gone through the business figures over the weekend, and they didn't make for happy reading. It was quite simple, Wilf had warned: either they pulled in new business quickly, or they would have to let people go. If it reached that point then the jokes and the japes would soon fall flat.

This meeting had therefore been called. There were some new prospects around – Kay had a couple, Wilf had one, Giles had mentioned a company he had worked with at his previous PR agency, and Sara claimed that she had a couple of possible new clients. They needed to decide who was most likely to come in, and how they could make that happen. Despite the importance of the meeting though, Wilf had one of his own clients visiting, so he had left this one in Kay's hands.

Now Kay invited each in turn to explain who their prospect was, what sort of company it was, what sort of PR activities they could require, and what sort of fees Palmerston PR could hope to accrue. The prospects ranged from smallish companies that would probably only need occasional project work at £1,000 a time, up to Giles's suggestion which was a large pharmaceutical company that had been paying £14,000 per month at his previous employer. He said the client had not renewed its contract at that agency and had taken PR in-house, but he had heard from an old contact that that experience had gone badly; so he thought it was an even chance, and he had already arranged lunch with the company's marketing director for the following week.

Kay quickly totted up the combined value of these prospects. It came to about £25,000 in fees per month, which would make a useful difference to the company's outlook. But at the moment that £25,000 was a value that only existed in theory. It was a best case scenario and they would probably be lucky to get half of it, so if Giles could bring in his pharmaceutical firm, that would be a massive bonus.

Having explained all this to the team, Kay changed tack. "Okay guys. As I said in the email I sent, what we're thinking of doing is arranging some sort of bash where we can invite these people, spend a bit of money on them, give them the treatment, and hopefully cement a relationship or two. We can get some of our best customers there as well so they can tell the new people how great we are. So it's PR for us as much as anything. There is a budget, but that's between me and Wilf at the moment. Come up with the right idea and maybe we'll spend more. Anyway, let's have some ideas thrown into the hat."

She looked around expectantly. Giles quickly chipped in: "Wilf's got contacts at the Houses of Parliament hasn't he? Couldn't we arrange some sort of reception and dinner at Westminster? I've been there a few times for that sort of thing. The place just reeks of supremacy."

The rest of the team looked at Kay for a response. She shook her head slowly but decisively. "I mentioned that to Wilf on Sunday, and it would just take too long to get it approved by the people there; and then again just to get everything arranged takes ages. We really need something that we can do sooner."

Giles shrugged and seemed to accept that explanation. Kay looked around again. "Anybody got anything else?"

Ruth opened her mouth to speak, but Gavin beat her to it. "I had a look at this website earlier – it's a company called Top Draw Events."

Gavin had taken photocopies of a printout from the internet, and was passing them around the team as he spoke. "I reckon this would be perfect. Basically, they do corporate hospitality for all sorts of sports events and cultural stuff like opera and theatre. I went to one of their events during the World Cup last year when England played."

He turned to address Kay specifically. "If I've understood this right Kay, what you want is something not too high-brow, not too formal, and something probably involving a lot of alcohol so that people relax and have a good time. So I looked at the schedule that these people had online and thought: perfect."

"Which one?" asked Ruth who, like the rest, was scanning down the A4 page.

"The London Bierfest."

It wasn't Gavin that said this though; it was Kay. Gavin grinned with laddish pride and nodded: "Correct."

There was a mixed reception: excited hoots and whoops from Giles and Belinda; groans of disbelief and disgust from Ruth and Sara; a reserved smile of non-commitment from Jasmine. Loudly, so that she could be heard over the din, Sara started to say: "Trust you Gav, typical bloke... "

Kay raised her voice to interrupt. "Guys, settle down!" She paused as the banter came to an end. "Gav, I think I like it. Tell me more."

Sara seemed to object quite strongly however, her curses sounding incongruous coming in such a well-tailored Kensington accent. "Oh, fucking hell Kay. It's such a boring idea; it's just a glorified piss up. Surely we can come up with something a bit more creative and a bit more fun."

"What, like an evening of charades?" Giles goaded her. She shot him a deadly look across the room, and told him to piss off.

Kay listened to them argue amongst themselves for a few seconds, quietly smiling at the passionate response that Gavin's idea had sparked. Then she stepped in again: "Right! Shut up everyone. I want to hear more about this, and I'm in charge. What's the cost Gav, for a start?"

Gavin was ready with the information, producing another set of photocopied sheets from inside his notepad. He gave all but one of them to Jasmine to pass around the room, and started to read out the most important points from the sheet still in his hand: "Okay, it's at Old Billingsgate Market on the Thames, near Tower Bridge and London Bridge. There are two evening functions; you can see the dates – they're Wednesday and Thursday nights. The cost, as you can also see, is just over a grand plus VAT for a table of 10 people. You get unlimited beer, you get served by sexy ladies dressed up as Heidi, you get German food, but we'll gloss over that, and best of all, you get an Oompah band!"

There was laughter all around the room, even from Sara, although she managed to look annoyed at the same time. Kay waited for a few seconds for the excitement to die down, but the commotion went on and she found that she still had to raise her voice again: "Gav! You need to phone these people right now. This is less than two weeks away, and they might have sold out already."

"No need KT," answered Gavin, in the manner of a man in total control. "I've already done that and reserved us a table for the Thursday. I just need to call back and confirm before 4.30 today. I knew you'd like it – not that I'm saying you like a drink or anything boss, obviously."

Sara raised an eyebrow in Kay's direction, but Kay let the comment pass. She believed that Gavin had come up trumps, as he so often did. Sara was still looking reproachfully towards Kay however. Kay met the challenge head on: "What's wrong Sara? You don't look happy."

"I just think it's a rubbish idea. If we used our imagination a bit more we could come up with something a bit better than just saying to these people 'come and get pissed with us'. I can see that it appeals to the boys because all they think about is beer and breasts anyway, but these are clients we're trying to impress, business people, and I think it's the wrong message to send."

Giles was booing childishly, as was his wont in the frequent moments when he had not engaged his razor sharp wit and intellect. There was little in between with Giles. Kay thought for a second before answering. "I hear what you're saying Sairs, but I disagree. It does appeal to the boys yes, but I also noted down when you were all presenting leads earlier that every one of the contacts is a man too. It might seem a bit lowest common denominator to us refined ladies, but we have to appeal to their basic instincts. I think they will love it. I know I will, and I have a feeling Jasmine might enjoy it too. And as for Bel, well…"

"And what will Wilf think?" Sara still sounded solidly opposed.

"I reckon Wilf will go for this," Kay replied. "He'll understand what we're doing."

"Well, you can count me out, that's all I will say. It's not my cup of tea," said Sara with apparent finality.

Ruth had kept quiet while the discussion was going on, but she now piped up. "I think I'd rather not go as well Kay, to be honest. Rob would divorce me if he knew I was going to something like this and not taking him!"

Kay nodded: "Okay, okay. Well, we can't all go anyway, but Sara you have to go – two of these prospects are your contacts, so you have to be there. I don't care whether you hate every second, you have to be there. Ruthie, I guess you and Steph are our volunteers to answer the phones the next day while the rest of us feel shit," chuckled Kay. "There are six prospects, so that leaves four spaces, but we were going to invite some customers like Tony Goodman from Urban Stripe and Rob Schneider from Spears and Yorke. So that leaves only two of us. Shit, maybe we need two tables if everybody accepts."

She turned to Gavin again. "Right Gav, get back to these people. Tell them we want the table, and sort out the invoice. Ask about a possible second table. Giles and Sara, get on to your contacts this evening by phone and invite them. We need to get definite numbers quickly. I'll speak to the rest of them. Okay…" Kay looked around at the mostly expectant faces of her team. "Let's roll!"

**

"How much longer Billy?"

The words were spoken sulkily, and Billy sent an irritated glance towards the speaker.

"Any minute now Lee. Patience… he'll be along, don't you worry. I've been here at this time of the day every day for the last week and a half. This character is a creature of habit, I tell you."

Lee shifted uncomfortably in the car passenger seat and looked blankly out of the windscreen at the road outside. It was a wholly unremarkable English street, like thousands more the length and breadth of the country; there was nothing to recommend it or distinguish it whatsoever. Darkness was beginning to fall, but visibility was still good. That fact made a thought occur to Lee, and he turned to Billy, who was sitting behind the steering wheel of the stationary vehicle.

"Isn't it still a bit light? Surely we want darkness don't we?"

Billy huffed with his own impatience. "That, Lee, is one of the reasons why we're not doing the job yet. Give it a couple of weeks and it will be plenty dark. Especially down there."

Billy nodded his head towards the entrance to an alleyway across the road and ahead of them to their left. The alley, which was mostly screened by bushes, branched off at right angles from the road on which the car was parked. Silence descended upon the interior of Billy's car once more. After a few tense seconds though, a third voice spoke; a measured, precise English voice that came from a man hunched low on the rear passenger seat.

"Are you sure about this imbecile Billy?"

"It will be fine Mister P. We're still getting familiarised but it will be fine in a few…"

"He seems bloody immature for an important job like this," said Mister P dismissively. "In fact, if you don't mind me saying, every question he asks is more fucking stupid than the last."

It was only after this statement that Lee realised the invective was aimed at him. He was the "imbecile". He glanced uncertainly back at Mister P, and then questioningly at Billy: what should I say, his eyes asked; should I say anything?

Billy kept his eyes trained on the windscreen, but his lips curled in a tight smile. He said: "Mister P, Lee will be okay. He's just a bit nervous because he's never met you before and you're a very important man. Isn't that right Lee?"

Lee nodded a weak assent. A second later Billy stiffened in his seat, and his eyes fixed on the car's internal rear view mirror with renewed interest.

"Okay gents, here comes our man."

In the wing mirror on his side, Lee could see a man approaching along the opposite pavement, coming from behind the car and towards the alleyway. He looked stocky and athletic, and moved quickly along the street – almost feline in the lightness of his feet upon the concrete. He wore a light grey hooded track suit top with the hood up, and Lee struggled to make out any facial features at all, save for a dark smudge around the jaw line, which he assumed to be the beard or heavy stubble that he had seen in photographs.

The man drew level with the car and continued walking past on their left, and from the back of the car came a sinister hissing sound, which made Lee's skin crawl. It was Mister P, he realised, who was sitting upright and alert, leaning forward and looking venomously at the passing figure. Even Billy looked slightly disconcerted by that, Lee noticed – especially when Mister P began to spit calculated, ice cold words at the fast receding figure:

"There you go Abu, walking on my streets as if they belong to you. Oh yes indeed, but not long now until the filthy blood of you and all your followers will wash down these streets. And you'll be back where you belong, Abu. In Hell, Abu, yes that's where. I wonder what the virgins are like there, Abu."

The figure at whom these words were directed had now disappeared around a corner further up the road on the left, and Mister P sunk back into his previous position of repose as if nothing of note had happened. Billy made no reaction to the words at all, save to study the steering wheel for a few seconds. Then with a shrug he turned the ignition key and the engine burst into life. Lee swallowed hard, his mouth bone dry.

Billy glanced across, managing a smile that looked only slightly forced. "So, there you go," he grinned. "Simple. Job done. Fancy a beer?"

**

Nick sat at the bar nursing a pint of lager, and reflected that the Duke of Abercrombie pub was a dark and gloomy place to meet on a Monday night. It was ten past seven and Kay was late. He had originally suggested the Railway Tavern across the road, but she had insisted on this place instead.

It struck him as an odd choice. He thought she would have been more of a trendy wine bar type of girl; somewhere that the City's bright young things would hang out and let off steam. Perhaps that was exactly it. Perhaps Kay calculated that there was less chance of being seen by anyone she knew, completing this illicit transaction in such a place.

If so, she was probably right about that. There were only two other drinkers in the pub – two middle aged men, joking together at a corner table about pieces of skirt in the office, from what Nick could hear.

The door of the pub suddenly opened, and a thin beam of weak evening light heralded the arrival of a pin-stripe suited Kay Talbot, an evening newspaper raised above her head to cover it from the rain. Wiping her feet in the doorway, she saw Nick at the bar and smiled apologetically before pushing the door shut behind her.

Nick could see a few spots of moisture on her cheeks from the rain, and though weariness was written across her face, her eyes still sparkled. How can you be that exhausted but still look so good, Nick wondered? She was wrestling with her newspaper now, trying to cram it into her bag as she walked towards him, and making a mess of the job.

Watching her struggle with the paper, Nick started laughing. Finally she was at the bar and ready. "Bad day?" asked Nick, trying to sound more concerned than sardonic, but failing.

"Don't even go there mate," Kay laughed back. "I've had a serious fuck-off day today."

She saw a £10 note in Nick's hand and gestured dismissively towards the money. "Put your money away Nick, it's my round. What can I get you?" she asked, sounding as if no further discussion on the subject would be entertained.

She ordered Nick a beer and a red wine for her, and they stood in silence side by side as the bar tender prepared the drinks. The oddness of the whole situation suddenly smacked Nick right between the eyes. He felt utterly tongue-tied. He and this woman knew next to nothing about each other. What on earth were they doing? This was how he imagined a blind date would be: so nervous and eager to please the other person that movements became clumsy and words awkward until the ice was broken. How to do that now though? He needed to think of something amusing to say, but his mind had gone completely blank.

She was staring at the rows of bottles and glasses on the rack behind the bar, and seemed to be getting her breath back. He wasn't sure what was going through her mind, but she didn't seem as painfully aware of this deafening silence as Nick did.

Mercifully the drinks came, and they moved over to a table in one corner of the pub. Kay led the way, biting her bottom lip in despair. The gulf between them just then at the bar had seemed huge and impenetrable. She had wanted to run away, to flee in the face of this new and impossibly difficult situation she had put herself in. After a whole day spent battling with journalists, battling Wilf, battling with clients at times, she felt like she had nothing left in the tank. And she'd convinced herself, that this part of the day would bring respite, hopefully even fun. Words had deserted her as she stood at the bar though, and it had left her in shock.

Then Nick spoke, and noise, any noise whatsoever, was welcome. It didn't add up to much, but it meant everything to Kay at that moment. She couldn't have known how his own desperation had forced him to say the first words – the first coherent sentence – that came into his head.

"Is it raining hard?"

He could have looked out of the window and answered that for himself, he realised, but it was a start at least. Kay gave a weary smile in any case. "It just started really. But I do have an expensive hairdo to look after. Do you have that problem too?"

Nick greeted the question with a small, priceless smile. His hair was of fairly average length, but it wasn't styled in such a way that a downpour would be catastrophic. "Oh yeah," he replied, "all the time. That's bloody English weather for you though isn't it?"

They both laughed, and nodded rueful English agreement, and somewhere inside them both the tension went down a notch. Kay was looking at her wine glass, which she held around the stem with her left hand. Their laughter died away.

"Anyway," she said, suddenly looking up, "how was your day Nick? Clean lots of shoes?" It was meant to be light-hearted, but instead the words sounded clumsy to Kay, maybe even patronising. Nick didn't seem to take offence though.

"Well, yeah. I had my usual working day of City wankers rabbiting into mobile phones and the occasional normal person that wants to chat."

"Do you enjoy it? I mean, it must get a bit dull, mustn't it?"

"Yeah, it can be, I suppose. Nothing exciting tends to happen – apart from when you and your husband decide to have a slanging match, obviously – but it's not the worst job in the world. I like meeting people, and I meet lots of them, even if some of them are total prats."

Kay seemed to be listening intently, and the invitation was apparently there to keep talking, so Nick did. He gave a brief laugh and said: "There was a bloke earlier – when you texted me actually. Really posh bloke, going on about all these holidays he has. I said I couldn't really afford holidays with this job and he looked at me like I'd just beamed down from Mars. I don't think it had ever occurred to him that we don't all go scuba diving three times a year."

Nick laughed again, before reverting back to serious mode: "It's a funny conversation I have with my customers really – I mean, I'm just shining their shoes; I'm nothing to them really, and it can be annoying if people act all superior. I guess I'm used to it these days."

Nick was taking a sip of his drink, and Kay had a question.

"Was I a superior bitch when I came and spoke to you then?"

"God, yeah," he laughed, wiping his mouth with the back of his hand.

"Really?" Kay wasn't sure whether Nick was joking. He hesitated for a second, and then adopted a conciliatory tone:

"Honestly? Yes, it was a bit like that. You said a few things that almost made me get up and walk away. It was touch and go at one point."

Kay found that hard to hear. A simple apology would have sufficed, but she was nervous and her mind was a little scrambled. Instead, when she spoke it caused more confusion: "Well, there's the small matter of the money I suppose."

Nick inferred from that that she wanted to hand over the £100, night over. Disappointment stung him, which he didn't expect, but he reached hastily for his drink to finish it.

"Right, yeah. I suppose I ought to be getting on too."

"No, no silly. I meant, you didn't walk away that time because you needed the money," Kay explained. It seemed a long and laboured explanation to her. "I've got nothing to rush off for," she added as an after-thought.

Nick said: "Right, I see." He put his drink back down and thought for a second or two, before eventually agreeing that indeed it probably was the money that had made him agree to his task. Kay was upset to hear how her manner had come across to Nick in that previous meeting. It was a million miles away from the way she had wanted to come across to him, and in its own way, Nick's honesty was another small dent to her confidence. She wanted to make up for it somehow though, and at last an apology arrived.

"Well Nick, I'm really sorry if I was rude before, or if I acted superior, or anything like that. I didn't mean to be, but I suppose I was just embarrassed more than anything. I still can't believe that I went up to a complete stranger and asked him to do this. You looked at me like I was a complete nutter."

Nick laughed and felt embarrassed as well. "What can I say? It's hardly a conversation you expect to have is it?" He paused, then said: "Has it been useful anyway?"

Kay made a face, momentarily confused. "Sorry, has what been useful?"

All too easily, it had slipped from Kay's mind that Nick only saw one side of this arrangement. He didn't actually know what the real purpose of his text messages was – to enable Kay to dispose of her lover before Lee got home. She could have kicked herself for forgetting that at this moment, of all moments, as she sat opposite Nick.

"You know, these texts I send you – has it been useful at all?"

She covered her tracks quickly: "Oh yeah, definitely. It's kind of helping me to build a picture about what he's actually doing, as opposed to what he says he's doing."

There was more hesitation between them, as Nick looked earnestly at her; innocently in fact, Kay thought, as she felt herself blushing with guilt. Even so, and without really meaning to, she added just a bit more decoration for effect.

"It's difficult for me to even talk about it Nick, it hurts so much. I can only ask that you trust me when I say that this does help me. I know that's a lot to ask because you don't even know me, and there must be all sorts of questions... "

"It's all right Kay," he interrupted, his concern at her obvious distress evident on his face. "Don't worry about it. You don't have to explain everything to me. I don't really need to know I suppose."

Kay felt herself retreating unavoidably to her coquettish best. "Ah, thank you Nick. You are a sweetheart." An appreciative smile fluttered towards him.

"I won't pretend that I haven't wondered about this quite often though," Nick said after a moment. He took another sip of lager. "Sometimes there's not much else to do but sit and think when I'm bored at work."

It sounded like an invitation for Kay to talk more about it if she felt able to, but she decided she had probably already spread it on thickly enough. It was best to leave this conversation for a time when she had actually concocted some kind of plausible background story, rather than playing the emotional card like she had just been forced to do. Anyway, she was warming up now – starting to relax in this guy's company, seeing different shades to his character, and enjoying her glass of wine while she did so. It was time to change tack, she decided; time to find out a bit more about this shoeshine man.

"So tell me about your girlfriend – what does she do?"

He raised his eyebrows in mild surprise at the question – it was clearly an unexpected change of topic; now the beam of attention was back on Nick. He looked slightly bashful, Kay noticed.

"Yeah, her name is Justine. At the moment she doesn't do anything. She's in Australia."

"Oh…how come?"

"Well, she is Australian for a start, but her dad had an accident and he's in hospital, so she went back to see him and help her mum through it."

"Is it bad?"

"Yeah, it is pretty bad by the sounds of it. He works on a building site and a load of metal girders or something fell on top of him. It happened a few weeks ago now, and he's still in a coma, so she's really worried about it."

It struck Nick as he spoke these words that he hadn't really had to explain this to anybody before. He had explained some of it to Vicky in the coffee shop, who hadn't really known what to say, but that was about it. His friends were Justine's friends and she had told most of them what had happened before she left for Melbourne.

"So you don't know when she's coming back then?" asked Kay.

"No," Nick replied. The one word answer felt inadequate, but it summed up his numbness about the situation.

"What does she do when she's in London?"

"Bloody hell, lots of questions Kay." The words came out more pointedly than Nick had meant. Kay wasn't expecting it and reacted hastily and with more heat than she would have intended also.

"God, I'm sorry. I'm just keeping the conversation going while we have a drink Nick. It's not much fun if we sit here in silence, is it?"

They were back to square one again. Nick looked slightly crestfallen, suspecting it was his fault that they were suddenly at loggerheads. It was Kay who apologised first though, taking a step back from her own frustration.

"Look, I'm sorry Nick. I'm just interested in people, I suppose; what they do and why. It's part of my job, but really I'm just a nosy old bag. You can tell me I am if you like. Tell me to stop poking my nose into other people's business."

She was relieved to see him smile at the invitation. "No, it's alright Kay. I'll pass up that opportunity," he said. They both seemed to relax again, and instinctively reached for their drinks to toast the outbreak of peace.

"So, what is it you do? I'm guessing it's some kind of office job," Nick said.

The fleeting thought occurred to Kay that Nick hadn't answered her own question yet – the one about his girlfriend's job. She wondered if that was deliberate, or whether he had just forgotten. Oh well.

"I'm in PR, Nick. I'm a director at an agency that represents various clients. We do things like arranging events, putting stories in the media, and trying to protect our clients when there's bad stuff going around."

"Right. Anybody I would have heard of?"

"What the clients? Er, probably not really. They're mostly big kind of industrial companies and a few smaller software companies. We don't do any big retail or consumer brands that you'd know."

Nick looked only mildly impressed. Kay wasn't sure how much she would have to explain about her work: some people were very savvy about the media world, while others really had no idea how these things worked. How much would a shoe-shiner understand the world she inhabited?

"So you're a spin doctor. Also known as a liar," Nick said, laughing. Kay laughed along, though her amusement was somewhat less genuine than Nick's. She had heard it a million times before, mostly from her own husband. It was best to laugh along with it she found, so she cracked her usual joke:

"Yeah, didn't I tell you that Alistair Campbell is my hero?"

"Oh no! You are joking, I hope," Nick cried in disbelief. He was still laughing though: "I can't stand that bloke; he comes over as such an arrogant, smug bastard."

Kay found herself torn between wanting to say things to please Nick, and also wanting to refute his accusation about her profession. Would it spoil the moment if she did that, she wondered? She took a gulp.

"Now Nick, I feel I must defend myself. It's not about lying really."

"Well if it's not, then it's certainly trying to stop the truth coming out; same difference to me. I read newspapers and I watch the news on the telly, and sometimes you just think that thing is only on there because of PR. So maybe that's good PR I suppose, I don't know... "

Nick was smiling as he said all this, so Kay took it in good part, but she countered: "Well, it's a battle that's been going on in some shape or form since humans first walked on the earth, so I'd say it's almost human nature – one person wants to find the truth, and another person wants to stop that from happening if they can."

"Maybe," Nick mused. "Still sounds like I'm right though."

Kay couldn't quite believe that she was having this conversation with the guy who shined shoes at the train station. The last thing she had expected to happen tonight was that she would have to philosophically defend the job she did. She was impressed. She decided to laugh it off.

"Okay, you win I suppose!"

"You must be pretty good at it, if you can afford to go around giving money to penniless shoeshiners."

"Thank you. Yes, I am good at it. Are you penniless Nick? You seem quite intellectual for a shoeshiner."

He looked a little cross by that observation, which made Kay feel clumsy and tactless once again. There was a harder edge to his voice as he countered: "I haven't always done this, you know. Years back I was a City boy, and I worked for a bank. I was suited and booted every day, three hour lunches on the piss and all that. Then I had a few problems and I ended up losing my job. I was in a right mess. I'm lucky to still be here."

"What happened then?" asked Kay, before adding slightly gingerly: "If you don't mind me asking that is."

Nick shrugged, and then stroked his chin briefly with the fingers of his left hand before answering. It was something that Kay had noticed he did quite frequently when asked to explain anything. She enjoyed watching the gesture. He was obviously taking their conversation seriously, and Kay was enjoying that too.

"Most of it went up my nose. That's the truth of it," Nick said. "I just lost it for a while. But I saw where I was going early enough to stop before things got out of hand and I hit the really heavy stuff. It was bad enough though. I'm still recovering, and I think I probably always will be. I was even on the streets for a while. You wouldn't have wanted to throw any of your money at me then Kay, I'll tell you."

They both laughed, and Kay gave Nick an appreciative smile. This night was proving to be far more intriguing and enjoyable than she had anticipated a night spent talking to a man that shined shoes for a living could be. God, what a stupid, blinkered way to have thought, she chided herself.

Anyway, it turned that out he was very sweet, with his honest and earnest way of looking at the world. He had an interesting story to tell, and now that he had relaxed a little, he seemed to be enjoying telling it to Kay. It was time for more alcohol, she decided, and refusing to listen to Nick's protestations about her paying again, Kay headed for the bar to reorder.

When she returned, Kay got comfortable back at the table and asked: "So Mister, what's the next little phrase you're going to text me with? I really liked the Elvis one."

Nick chuckled, and winked conspiratorially: "Well, that's top secret my dear. I could tell you but, alas, then I'd have to kill you. I've got a great big long list of them though that I wrote down when I was sitting at work the other day. It helped kill a slow twenty minutes."

"Yeah, right…you do make me laugh, funny guy. I just thought of a couple for you when I was up at the bar anyway."

"Really? Excellent. Come on then, show me what you've got Mrs Hotshot PR maestro."

Kay took a deep breath, as if readying herself for a big performance. "What about: the horse has bolted?"

Nick raised an unimpressed eyebrow. "Mmm," was his non-committal reaction. "Well, I assume that wasn't the best one out of the two."

"Oh balls," Kay sighed, "what's wrong with it then? That was actually my best shot so I think I'll keep the other one to myself."

Nick shook his head with heavily over-hammed dissatisfaction. "Not nearly dramatic enough I'm afraid. A bit more imagination and a lot more drama darling – that's what we need. I've got loads of them lined up girl, so don't you worry about it."

"I see. Okay, well you're clearly a lot better at this than me. I'll have to go back to the drawing board obviously Nick."

"Come on, tell me what the second one was," Nick persisted, relishing the exchange.

Kay giggled: "No, I'm not telling you now. I'm too embarrassed. Anyway, you still haven't told me any of yours, oh master of silly bloody code words."

"I'm not bloody going to either," he laughed. "You've got to pay me cold, hard cash before I tell you, and they cost a hundred pounds each. Speaking of which…"

"Yeah, yeah, I've got it all here. I've taken the cost of your beers out though; this ain't flipping charity you know."

"What!" Nick cried out in mock alarm.

The men across the pub turned their heads in unison to see what was happening, but only saw Nick smiling towards them sheepishly. They quickly turned back and resumed their conversation. Meanwhile, Nick studiedly brushed imaginary specks of dust from his shirt and affected to regain his composure as Kay tittered, eyes flashing with happiness, all signs of the previous weariness gone.

Eventually Kay's laughter subsided, and as Nick took a mouthful of his drink, Kay looked suddenly wistful as she gazed out of the window at the street lights that were beginning to bathe the road outside in an amber glow. It was as if she had just remembered some big hole that existed in her life.

She was still gazing outside when, in a softer voice, she said: "You know Nick, I was a bit nervous coming here tonight. I didn't know what to expect; how we would get on or anything. It's all just so weird isn't it?" She was laughing again, softly, self-deprecatingly.

"I mean, I know it was my idea – all of this that has happened in the last couple of weeks. I'm a total scatterbrain and I know that sometimes I have just the silliest ideas, but…"

Kay sought the right words: "…but this has been fun, hasn't it? I think it has been anyway. I've enjoyed talking to you, when I haven't been putting my foot in it. We could be friends couldn't we?"

Nick watched her, and wondered about this unexpected change of mood: suddenly it seemed that she needed his confirmation that her company was acceptable. She could swing instantly between confident, smart peaks of hope, fun and excitement, and then despairing lows, when she was needy of appreciation and assurance. It was a roller-coaster of emotion, and it was startling to Nick how quickly the transformation could come.

He left a host of questions unasked as he lowered his voice: "Hey…yeah, of course it's been fun. And of course we can be friends. We are already, aren't we?

She looked at Nick mischievously as she raised her wine glass to her lips, taking a big gulp down.

"Right, finish your drink – let's go somewhere else. Somewhere a bit brighter than this horrible pub," she said.

She threw the rest of her wine down her throat, and then turned her attention to her bag, and Nick was left a little bewildered again. He contemplated his drink, three quarters full of liquid and sharing a table with Kay's freshly drained glass. How can you reason with this, he asked himself. Well, whatever was next, he decided, he was prepared to run with it.

"What are you like?" he mumbled, taking up the glass. "Okay, just give me a few seconds to get rid of this." He got about half way down the remainder of the lager before next taking the glass away from his mouth. Kay was watching with a critical eye.

"Come on," she ordered. "Down in one. Hurry up."

"All right, all right; nearly done."

Nick's head tilted back to accommodate the final flow of lager. Then he was finished and with a flourish he smacked the empty glass back down on the table.

Kay was off heading for the door straight away, and Nick hurried along behind, dragging his coat on and catching up as she stepped into the night and turned left, away from Liverpool Street station.

"Has anyone ever told you that you're completely nuts?" Nick grumbled, shoving his hands in his pockets against the sudden chill. Kay laughed the question away, her mood swing obviously complete.

"Yeah, all the time. It's the only way to be, believe me. Anyway, come on, I'm paying, so stop bloody moaning." She flashed him another mischievous smile – she seemed to be buzzing; feeling good, he guessed, to be in charge once again, after letting her guard slip for a couple of vulnerable seconds. They made off into the London evening, laughing and mocking each other as if they were the oldest of friends.

**

It was gone 11pm and drinkers were beginning to tumble out of Camden's pubs, by the time that Nick jumped off the bus at the end of his road and headed for the flat. It had been an interesting evening, one that he had thought constantly about as he travelled home.

It had lasted much longer than he had expected. He had thought that he would meet Kay, have a quick drink, she would give him the money, they would have a polite chat, and then off they would go on their separate ways. Nick had been prepared for that in his own mind, despite the nervousness that had nagged at him as he sat at the bar of the Duke of Abercrombie waiting for Kay to arrive.

Then there had been those initial moments of panic when she had first arrived, and they had both searched their own minds for words, and searched the other's face for clues as to why this situation was now a part of their lives. Once again now, with his footsteps echoing in the North London night, Nick recoiled inwardly at the memory of those awful, hesitant moments.

It was a bad vibe that soon passed from his mind though, happily thrust back behind the memories of the laughter, the drinking, the conversation – and the frequent uncertainty about what would happen next when in the company of Kay Talbot, as he now knew her name to be.

There had been more mood swings from his female companion, and Nick had handled them, managed them, tended to them like a prudent gardener. Unexpectedly, but gloriously, his own words seemed somehow to bring her back to a contented frame of mind. It all felt somehow slightly magical to him.

The clear skies of early evening had given way to light drizzle as he walked home from the bus stop, giving his jacket a sheen that gleamed in the light of the yellow street lamps. The rain couldn't douse the fire that was blazing in his heart though, and nor could it stem the frenzy of thoughts that fizzed around inside Nick's head.

These really were crazy thoughts, he had told himself all the way home, and he did so again as he reached the front door of the flat and took the key from his pocket. Once inside Nick poured himself a glass of cold water, and sat down in the front room, leaving his damp coat across the back of a chair to dry. It was pure madness to imagine that anything could happen between him and Kay Talbot. There was a gulf between them and the lives they led. Whatever problems she might be having with her husband, there was no way that Nick could ever provide her with the kind of lifestyle to which he assumed she was accustomed. He was a bloody shoeshiner for Christ's sake.

There were many other reasons why it was ridiculous and he went through the list in his mind: money, lifestyle, career, looks, and ambition. There were probably lots more too, but anyway, it was stupid to imagine that he could be anything other than an occasional friend.

There was another voice in his head that countered this though, telling him that the list he had made ignored the real evidence. It ignored the great time they'd had, the way he had been able to make her laugh with such ease that Nick had begun to feel like a lucky gambler who knows the result before the dice are thrown. It baffled and delighted him time after time. And anyway, she wasn't really from a social level beyond him at all. She was just a girl from south London who had done well in her career because she was good at it.

Most of all, he remembered the way she had looked at him, and the way that made his stomach catapult. He remembered being at the bar buying drinks halfway through the night, having insisted upon buying a round. He had wheeled around to say something to Kay, and found to his surprise that she was already looking intently at him. Despite his astonishment, he had managed to make a joke out of it:

"Are you checking me out?"

She had simply laughed and smiled back. No answer, no denial, and no embarrassing admission. Her dark eyes just flashed back at him with that happy mischief that had captured her during the evening. It had sent his mind into a spin, so he had just laughed, shaken his head in capitulation, and turned back to the bar. After that, he had felt like a king for the rest of the night. He was sure that there was a special intimacy in the way she looked at him, and it made him tingle with anticipation. It was better than just a good memory. It was magnificent and triumphant.

Feeling more than a little drunk, Nick took his water through to the bedroom, where he took a small wad of £20 notes from his pocket, and tucked them inside Justine's enamel pot on the dressing table. Then he struggled out of his clothes, turned out the light and fell into bed. Ten minutes later, the bedroom was bathed again in light as Nick switched on the bedside lamp, sat up and stared vacantly at the wall opposite.

After a while he asked himself out loud: "How the fuck am I going to sleep tonight?"

His hand rested on the pillow at his side where Justine's head would normally be, and he studied that hand for a few moments, noticing the small hairs above the knuckles, the bitten down fingernails, the tiny pores, and the maze of lines that made it something unique. Again he spoke aloud, more of a sigh.

"Justine…" A long pause followed; then he repeated the word. He felt idiotic. He didn't know who he was talking to. When he next spoke, raw emotion made his voice waver. "You need to come back soon babe, cos I'm losing this. It's just getting so hard."

The silence that followed the words thumped Nick in the chest. Where was Justine when he needed her? They were supposed to be together. They were best friends and life partners, or so Nick had believed, from virtually the day they had first met. Now, all of those certainties had fallen into shadow. He suddenly felt very tired and aggrieved. He was shocked with guilt, for having thought about another woman in the way he had thought about Kay. It was just wrong. He was being tricked – surely. A moment later his mobile phone, which he'd left on his side table, chimed a single time.

He looked at it in surprise, wondering what information was presented on the lit up screen. After a few seconds the screen faded to dull black again as Nick watched it, and only then did he reach across and pick it up. It was a text message from Kay; a short, sweet message to send Nick hurtling into a blissful sleep.

"Nite nite xx"

He put the phone down, turned the light off and settled beneath the covers again. Within 15 minutes the sound of carefree snoring announced that sleep had claimed him.

**

The 10.42 train from Liverpool Street to Hertford was almost deserted that Monday night. A smattering of City workers were heading home after a day in the office followed by a night in the pub, their eyes shot through with tiredness and booze, munching on Macs and fries, hunkering down in the corners of the carriages and hiding with second-hand Metro newspapers.

No-one wanted to talk. No-one, that is, apart from Kay, who sauntered along the platform all the way to the front of the train, to save walking extra yards at the Hertford end. She carried a brown paper bag with a burger in it and felt guilty about that, but the impending calorie injection was well deserved, she reckoned. In truth, she felt dizzy with excitement and she was bursting to tell anyone who would listen why that was so.

Sadly, no-one entered the carriage she was in until the train reached Tottenham Hale, almost 15 minutes after departing Liverpool Street. By then the combination of too much red wine and the gentle swaying of the train as it headed north, had nudged her into drowsiness. She was distantly aware that a person had sat nearby, but she never even saw what they looked like. Her head was heavy and hanging down, her disorientation over-powering. Kay dozed, instead of talking.

It would have been worrying, except that Kay knew that at Hertford East the train would reach the buffers. She wouldn't be jolted out of drunken sleep in some far flung destination miles from home. The worst that could happen was that she would find herself back at Liverpool Street. Some kind of survival instinct kicked in anyway though, and she dragged herself up to stand by the door as the train left Ware. Hertford East was next.

Once there, she stepped off the train to meet rejuvenating cold, fresh air. Just a ten minute walk home; she'd be in bed before midnight. A spring had returned to Kay's step, just as there had been back at Liverpool Street. She thought about the night out in town, and her companion in drinking: Nick; Shoeshine Nick; lovely Nick. There was no way to keep the smile from her face. She felt humbled yet electrified; moved, amused and animated. Awoken. She ran out of descriptive words for how she felt. This was no press release. But he was, she thought for the twentieth time (maybe it was the hundredth), just an amazing guy, a really special guy.

The whole world was full of arseholes. People like Lee and James, and half of her customers, and some of those self-important hacks she had to deal with. There wasn't a good, pure or honest bone in their bodies. They were mean-spirited and arrogant. They were full of themselves.

And now she knew this for certain, because she had found someone who was different; someone who treated the world as he expected it to treat him, and yet didn't seem to hold a grudge when it let him down. What a lesson it was. Kay felt herself bursting with elation.

The hard moments at the start of the night were forgotten. They had soon discovered an easy rapport and after that it was plain sailing. Kay was approaching the centre of Hertford now and the lights of a kebab shop up ahead were beckoning. She was peckish enough for chips, even after her burger earlier, and she also wanted to send Nick a text message. It would be easier to type what she wanted to say if she could stop walking, and the shop would be the perfect place for that, rather than this cold street.

Her fingers got busy tapping the buttons of her mobile phone as soon as she had ordered her chips. It was a clumsy job though, with drink jumbling her many thoughts, and causing her to press the wrong buttons frequently. Soon her chips were wrapped, and she retreated to a corner of the shop to keep warm while she finished her text message. Even before she had finished typing the message though, she knew that she wouldn't be able to send it to Nick. It was too much; too girly, too overblown, gushing with lovey dovey emotion.

It was the drink talking.

Kay started deleting bits and rewriting others, tinkering over and over, getting frustrated at her inability to grasp the right words or sentiment. She read it through again: still no good. It went: "U r the man Nick! Best night ever. Cant wait to c u again xxx". It would frighten him to death. Fucking hell – her chips were getting cold as well. The Turkish blokes behind the counter were babbling away in their language and eyeing her up. God, the pressure! It was ridiculous! Now she was flustered. No way could she do this now. There was no way she could concentrate. Why was all that excitement, all those warm feelings, just draining away?

She deleted the whole thing, put the phone back in her bag and made a rushed, noisy exit from the kebab shop, high heels clattering on scrubbed floor tiles. The men were laughing behind her. Five minutes later she was home, to be greeted by Mister Sarcastic himself, Lee, who was still up. He decided he wanted to ask her where she'd been and to have a conversation about it. Kay fought a tricky rearguard action. In the end she gave him what was left of her chips, and went upstairs to bed. It felt like her eyelids were propped open by matchsticks, she was so tired.

She got into bed, and knew that the moment had gone. There would be no long, sentimental text message to Nick. She was too exhausted, and he was probably already asleep anyway. Even so, she grabbed the phone again and quickly wished him goodnight; she even put a couple of little kisses in the message as well. She always called them e-embraces; sweet and harmless, just like him, just like her. Hehehe... she smiled herself to sleep.

Chapter Five

Lee Talbot was late for something and it showed. Firstly, there was the speed at which he tore along the street – somewhere between a brisk walk and a jog, his face beetroot red, his forehead glistening with sweat, his chest heaving as might be expected of a man, even a fairly young man like Lee, who had just run 200 metres or so from the train station.

Further clues that this fast-moving man was pushed for time were the petulant demonstrations of impatience, the muttering and the agitated flinging of hands in the air, his neck craning first one way, then the next as he waited for a gap in the rush hour traffic that would allow him to cross the Seven Sisters Road. He stared at every passing car with loathing in his eyes, as if each was driven by the world's biggest and most dangerous idiot.

Having finally succeeded in crossing the road, the last clue was the cold fury vented upon a little old black lady that dared to stop abruptly in the street in front of him to check her bag. He only narrowly avoided walking straight into her, such was his distraction, and he yelled a venomous volley in her direction, to "get out the fucking way", ignoring the insults she hurled back at him as he continued down the street.

He hurried on, paying no heed to the stares of passers-by. He felt like an alien in this place, but then this was Tottenham in North London, and his distaste for the area was instinctive owing to his football allegiance, as well as the ethnic mix of the local community. Why the fuck did Billy and Custer want to meet in this shit hole, he wondered? Up ahead he could now see the outside sign of the pub they were to meet in. The sign had seen better days, and had flaky paint peeling away in parts.

Thirty seconds later, Lee went in through the doorway, and saw Billy at the bar ordering some drinks. It was a relief to see a friendly and familiar face. He walked across to join him.

"Alright Billy. Sorry I'm late mate. Fucking trains been up the spout," he said as he reached the bar, where Billy hadn't yet seen him and was still concentrating on the barmaid. He turned upon hearing Lee's voice, and gave a relaxed grin.

"No worries feller. Just in time to buy the beers."

"Is Custer…" Lee started, still feeling pensive.

"He's over there in the corner," said Billy, pointing to a dingy and secluded part of the pub where the carpet was ripped around a battered darts oche. "Now, give me a tenner, and take these over there," Billy ordered with a grin.

Custer seemed as suspicious and unimpressed with Lee as he remembered from their first meeting a few weeks before. He was a man of few spoken words when it came to conversing with Lee, and usually addressed Billy directly instead. Lee could almost reach out and touch the distrust. Custer greeted him now with a curt: "About time. Sit down."

Lee did as he was told and gave Custer his fresh pint. Several uncomfortable moments ensued as Custer contemplated his drink in silence. Lee wished that Billy would hurry up and join them. Billy, as sharply dressed as ever, eventually came over with the last of the three drinks. Everything he wore seemed made to measure. There were no baggy jeans, or t-shirts worn loose. It was always tailored shirts and trousers, and immaculate shoes. Along with those fearsome blue eyes, Billy's dress sense was one way that he distinguished himself from the crowd. Lee could only guess at how he afforded such a wardrobe – Billy worked for London Underground, cleaning graffiti away as far as Lee knew. It didn't strike him as a high paying job.

The table where Billy now joined Lee and Custer was well chosen. The dartboard was secluded from the rest of the pub, stuck at one end, with a wood and glass partition shielding most of the area from the other tables. Custer had been looking down at his hands, seemingly deep in thought, but he sat up quickly with Billy's arrival.

"Right," Custer said in a low voice. "As usual, no names, no places, but talk me through it from the top again Billy."

Billy raised an eyebrow towards Lee in a gesture of mock impatience with the older man. Then he started talking – quickly but, like Custer, quietly. "It's simple. The two of us meet at the suggested point. Travel to X. It will be dark by this time. We'll be well covered up. We walk down to the alley, wait there and when A comes along, we do the job. Split up, and meet at Mister P's car at position P. Then we get the fuck out of dodge."

Custer nodded slowly. "How well do you know X?"

"Do you need Tesco's or Sainsbury's? I know it like I've lived there all my life, as you well fucking know. Fucking shit-hole."

"Yeah, yeah – I know; but what about Lee?"

The question was still directed at Billy. He answered obligingly: "He knows it well. We've been down there a few times now. Would you say you know the ground well Lee?" Billy turned to him. Lee coughed to clear his throat – surprised to suddenly find that he was the centre of attention and was even required to speak.

"Yeah, I feel pretty good about it…"

"Pretty good?" Custer was looking sternly at him.

"Well – no, I feel very good about it. We've been through it loads of times. We've been over the ground several times and I'm familiar with it. It's fine."

Custer gulped a mouthful of beer down. He still looked unconvinced, and he turned back to Billy with questioning eyes. Billy saw Custer's expression and spoke up quickly. "Custer, it's fine. We're ready to go. Just give us the fucking date and we'll get this thing started. Then it's up to the rest of the boys, yeah?"

Custer grunted in affirmation. Then he said: "Tools?"

"Yes – all sorted. We're ready to go," Billy repeated. They talked like this for another 10 minutes, the conversation

168

swinging to and fro between Custer's questions and Billy's patient replies.

Lee listened with rising excitement, despite Custer's unconcealed disdain for him. These are the final checks, he thought to himself. It's really going to happen. Then he noticed a girl standing at the bar, and looking over at them. Custer was talking, and Lee thought that Billy had been simply concentrating on what Custer was saying, but suddenly Lee realised that Billy had also seen the girl. She was in her mid-twenties he guessed, not particularly pretty but with an athletic-looking body, which her scant clothing did little to conceal.

"Hang on a second boss," interrupted Billy, and abruptly he was up and away, walking towards the girl at the bar. Custer slumped back in his chair and watched as Billy reached the bar and started talking to the girl, who smiled a little nervously, and at one point looked over his shoulder at the two other men sat in the corner. She was nodding her head earnestly as he talked. Then Billy dug a small piece of white card – perhaps a business card – and a biro out of his jacket pocket, which the girl used to write something down. He put the card back in his pocket, spoke a few more words, and the girl laughed. Then he kissed her on the cheek, and came back towards Custer and Lee. The girl walked off towards the door of the pub.

"I've pulled," Billy reported, sitting back down. Custer stiffened in his seat with sudden irritation, but he kept his voice low.

"For fuck's sake Billy. This is serious. Keep your shagging for some other time."

"Custer, I saw she was dossing me and I didn't know if it was innocent or if she might be old bill or press. I still don't know, but she was showing a bit too much interest in us and I didn't want her listening in. So I went over and sorted it out, okay? I think she's alright though. Anyway, I've got somewhere to park the bike tonight by the looks of it."

He started laughing, and Lee was unable to suppress a smile; Custer raised his eyes to the ceiling, muttering "Jesus H

Christ". He then turned to Lee and told him that he needed to speak with Billy alone for a while, so he should make himself scarce. Lee nodded and started pulling on his coat to leave.

"Lee, there's another boozer a bit further along the road called the Dragon," said Billy. "Wait in there for me and I'll be along in half an hour or so."

In fact it took almost an hour for Billy to turn up at the Dragon, and he found Lee feeding coins into a fruit machine when he arrived, whacking the buttons in a detached, disinterested manner. They bought more drinks and sat down again. Billy had a more serious head on now.

"Okay mate. We've got the green light to go," he said. "This is it."

"Fucking hell. When?"

"Custer has a couple of things to sort out, so not next week but the week after. And the plan is exactly as we talked about before. We meet at the rendezvous at 6.30. After we leave this pub tonight, don't call me or text me or anything. We don't meet to talk next week. Take the missus out or something. Just assume that we are good for Tuesday week, and if anything changes before then I'll get in touch with you. Got that?"

"Yeah, no worries," nodded Lee.

There was a sparkle in Billy's eyes now, he could see. This was it, and Billy and Lee had the honour of starting it off. Lee silently wished he could let his dad in on the secret; the old feller would be so proud. Rules were rules though, and there was to be no talking about this job outside of the immediate circle of planners. Custer had made that very clear.

Lee and Billy talked about football for a while, with Billy relating some stories from his travels with the Arsenal boys – the triumphs on the pitch and in the streets nearby; the drinking and the camaraderie. The day that Billy and two others had fought their way out of a pub in Fulham against a dozen or so Chelsea boys. The way Billy described it, it seemed like a miracle: the Chelsea thugs much bigger, nastier and uglier than real life; the Arsenal lads, smarter and quicker on their feet and in their heads.

Lee lapped it all up, loving the tales of derring-do and the way that Billy shrugged it all off with a laugh as "a way of keeping it interesting". Billy eventually finished his pint with a long swig, and glanced at his watch. It was after 9.30 now.

"Right Lee, my old son. You've got a wife to go and look after, and I'm going to chase up that bit of stuff from earlier, and we'll see what bed that leads me to by the end of the night – know what I mean?"

Lee finished his own drink and stood up. "Okay Bill. Tuesday week it is then, yeah?"

Billy grinned broadly, and from his pocket took out the card with the girl's phone number on: "Tuesday week. It's going to be fucking epic mate. Oh, and if you see any Tottenham boys on the way out, give them a whack for me."

Lee left Billy sitting at the table, tapping numbers into his phone, and headed for the door. The last thing he heard before stepping outside was Billy's voice greeting the girl on the phone with a supposedly suave, "hello darlin'". Lee chuckled to himself. He was a character was Billy, of that there was no doubt.

Lee pulled his coat tight around himself against the rain and set off for the train station. The traffic was still heavy along the high street, but Lee was in no particular rush now. The next destination that mattered in his mind was a fortnight away yet.

**

It was 10.30 that same evening and Kay was curled up on the sofa, glass of wine in hand, eyes on the TV screen, from which trumpeted the familiar theme music of the BBC's Newsnight programme.

It was part of Kay's routine to catch the evening news programmes, to understand what had happened in the world that day and, with a professional head on, to think about the treatment of certain news stories – how views were represented, who was interviewed, what pictures were shown, what bias there might be. It was as much a part of her job, she considered, as pitching to prospective new clients, organising publicity-driving events or writing press releases. She expected her team to do it, and therefore she had to do it herself.

Tonight though, Kay was finding it difficult to concentrate on the stories that were being covered. It was the usual news of British troop casualties in Iraq, political intrigue at Westminster, and Champions League football results. These sounds came out of the TV set, but the words scarcely registered with Kay.

For the last three or four hours she had grown increasingly annoyed. Where the hell was Lee? She kept asking herself the question, over and over. Nick had sent her a succession of text messages from Liverpool Street, explaining firstly that there were delays on lots of the services because of signal problems, then that Lee was on the train, another five minutes later to say that the train was still in the station, and finally that it had left about 15 minutes later than scheduled. As was now customary, she had woken James from his sleep after receiving Nick's second message, and he had dressed, and kissed her briefly on the way out. Then Kay had got on with the work she should have been doing that afternoon.

Preparations for the big night at the London Bierfest had moved forward quickly. It was now just two nights away, and they had almost filled two tables for the event. A couple of spaces remained, and it was Kay's job to fill one of those with another guest. She knew that her afternoon should have been taken up making calls to achieve that, instead of entertaining James, and she felt bad about that, but not bad enough to have rearranged things. By the time he had left and she got down to telephoning, many people had left their offices. She had only got through to leave voicemail messages. What the hell, she would follow up again in the morning. It would be fine.

She had got on with reading some case studies and doing some other paperwork for the PR business, but she found herself increasingly distracted as the evening went on. Ordinarily, Kay would have expected Lee to have got home at about 6.30. That was four hours ago now, and he was still not home. It was bloody annoying.

It wasn't that she missed him, nor was it frustration at missing out on spending more time with James. What really bothered Kay was the fact that her husband was obviously up to something, and she had no idea what. Was it a woman? Would she have even cared if it was another woman? A difficult question to answer, and all she knew was that it made her mind race and her heart pound with an emotion that she didn't want to think of as jealousy, but she guessed probably had to be. Kay felt decidedly miffed. She had been the one playing games behind her partner's back, as far as she had been aware.

Maybe Nick had made a mistake, and it hadn't been Lee that he had seen getting on the train. She couldn't believe that though. Nick just seemed too solid and reliable to have got it wrong. She indulged herself by thinking about her new friend for a while, enjoying the memory of their recent evening out.

Before 8pm she had given up all attempts at work, and curled up in front of the TV, accompanied by a bottle of wine. Where was Lee? There was that thought again. God Kay, she had thought, whoever would have guessed that you could feel envious of anything that rat bag got up to. She was getting fed up with thinking about it.

At about a quarter to nine she had tried to alleviate the irritation by calling Lee's mobile phone, although pretending to be the concerned housewife would never wash. It had diverted straight onto his voicemail messaging system, as if the phone was switched off. She had hung up, cursed her husband and poured more wine.

Now, for the umpteenth time in the evening, as the clock ticked towards 10.45, Kay tried to put thoughts of Lee and another woman to the back of her mind so that she could concentrate on the TV news. Suddenly, and to her relief, she heard a key turning in the lock of the front door, and seconds later Lee breezed into the sitting room, carrying just a thin blue polythene bag.

He passed Kay on his way through to the kitchen, without saying a word but glancing briefly at her upturned, quizzical face and flashing an amused smirk. Smugness suited him so very well, Kay always reckoned. Perhaps it was another woman then. She knew that Lee wouldn't be volunteering any information, so Kay piped up above the rustling sounds of paper and thin polythene and the harsh chink of a plate being placed clumsily on the kitchen worktop.

"Had a nice night, darling?"

She put a sarcastic emphasis on the last word of the enquiry, which she knew would rile her husband. There was no immediate answer, but a few moments later Lee came back into the sitting room, and sat down in the armchair across from Kay. He had a plate on his lap that was almost overflowing with doner kebab, salad and chips. He crammed some chips into his mouth and started chewing, before answering with his mouth half full.

"Wonderful, darling." He emphasised the same word as Kay had, in the same way, and then did it again. "Played squash with Dave after work darling. Then we had some beer. Is that okay darling?"

It was a rhetorical question as far as Lee was concerned, and Kay didn't bother to answer it anyway. She felt her eyes smarting and her cheeks burning, and she looked back at the TV screen to try to hide from him any visible signs of those physical reactions. She damn well knew that Lee had not played squash with Dave, because when they played together they did so at a sports facility in the City, and Nick had told her exactly what time Lee had got on the train. So he couldn't have played squash with Dave after work. It was impossible.

He had just lied to her, of that there was absolutely no shadow of doubt. Kay seethed: Jesus, the bastard! He just barefaced sat there and fucking lied to me. Anger boiled within her, but she was careful to avoid giving any indication that she might doubt his story. Lee wasn't watching her anyway; he was finding his takeaway far more appetising to look at.

Kay tried to listen to the news instead, but the voice of the TV presenter was now being accompanied by the irritating noise of Lee chewing on his kebab. The air in the room seemed still and heavy with the tension of sharing the same space as the married couple. Kay felt the tension strongly. There was a distance of about three red-carpeted metres between the sofa and armchair where the two of them sat, but they might as well have been on opposite sides of the world.

On screen, a TV reporter was delivering his piece to camera outside the Houses of Parliament, in time-honoured fashion. Kay's ears were deaf to it though; already she knew what she needed to do and how. She needed to find out what Lee was up to – whether it was an infidelity to cancel out her own, or whether it was something else. He was definitely lying to her though and she needed to know why; she also knew exactly the right man to find out for her.

She saw Nick in her mind, and felt comforted. Actually, it was more than that, she realised. She was looking forward to seeing him again; really looking forward to it. That twinkle in his eye whenever he looked at her was a thing to cherish, maybe even encourage. Why couldn't Lee be funny and sweet and sincere like Nick? She was a lucky girl, that Australian lady of his.

Kay knocked back the contents of her wine glass, rose from the sofa, and unsteadily picked her way between shoes and coats that littered the floor between her and the sitting room door. Still bristling with silent fury, she stopped at the door and spoke to Lee.

"I'm tired and I'm going to bed. There's football on in a bit. Don't think it's Arsenal though – are they playing tomorrow?"

Some sort of affirmative grunt came from Lee. Kay added quietly: "Okay, night." She heard another meat-and-bread-munching, uninterested noise from her husband's overcrowded mouth, and she carried on walking to the staircase and up to the bedroom, taking out her mobile phone from her pocket on the way. It was time to initiate another meeting with her shoeshine friend.

**

Nick awoke on Wednesday morning feeling refreshed after an early night. He had gone straight home from Liverpool Street after texting Kay about the train delays. It was the second week in October and the nights were starting to draw in. There was a chill in the air, and he'd had to pull his coat tight about him to keep the cold out as the bus snaked its way back to Camden in the thickening darkness.

At home he had cooked a quick pizza and watched TV for a little while, but finding nothing of interest in the schedule he had switched it off at about 8pm, and gone to his bedroom. The flat was silent and felt devoid of warmth – both the physical kind and spiritual or emotional warmth – without Justine's smile or her laughter to energise the rooms.

Nick had read for a while, but soon grew tired of that since he'd been reading for most of the day at work. He could never say that he didn't get the opportunity to get his head into a good book these days, he had laughed to himself.

He had heard Justine's laugh as well earlier that Tuesday, when they had spoken for ten minutes at lunchtime. There was no progress in her dad's condition still, but she sounded a bit brighter and more optimistic than she had seemed of late. Nick didn't like to hypothesise about why that might be, especially as it sounded like she was spending more time having fun with her old mates than sitting anxiously by her dad's bedside. Nick didn't want to feel suspicious or paranoid, but the frequent mention by Justine of her friend Craig was a sharp point that continually jabbed at his own pride. The accumulation of these small cuts was starting to become a painful sore.

It would probably have been much worse for Nick, had he not been able to very quickly turn his mind to other things –

either the next pair of shoes to polish, or the thought of Kay Talbot. It was as if a switch had been flicked and suddenly she was everywhere in his mind. He knew that was not a good situation, but it also felt completely out of his control. He kept seeing her face in his thoughts and in the faces of strangers – at times smiling and mocking him gently in that way she did, at others looking tired, anxious and vulnerable, in that other way of hers, which made him feel sick and angry all at once.

He had tried to resist these thoughts at first; had tried desperately to focus on the worry of Justine's situation. There was no fight in him to turn off these daydreams though. A woman that he still barely knew had come to dominate his thoughts every spare moment of the day. It was a part of his life that he could tell no-one about, because who would ever believe such a story? This weekly task on Kay's behalf had become the most important thing he did in his world, and that wasn't merely an idle thought that had shaped in his head; it felt like a basic truth, part of the fabric of his existence. Already, he couldn't imagine being without it.

Over the years he had learned about the importance of feelings that were deeper than mere physical attraction: acceptance of a person's differences and faults; friendship, companionship and trust; freedom of expression. This all added up, Nick reasoned, to what people called love. He had never really thought about it when he was younger, but he sensed it quickly when he met Justine, and it had been blossoming day upon day, until she had left for Australia.

The thoughts and feelings that he was experiencing now about a different woman seemed to magnify these emotions, distorting them out of all proportion. Every morning since the night he and Kay had gone drinking in the City, Nick had woken to find that he had a new constant companion – a colossal edifice of sheer care about the well-being of another person, over whom he had no control and very little contact. It was thrilling and frightening.

Nick felt puny alongside these feelings, and helpless against their persistence. They were just there, in everything he did, whether it was taking a morning shower, queuing at the bus stop, polishing shoes, or just eating, drinking and sleeping. He could think of no words to adequately describe how this made him feel.

So when Nick awoke on Wednesday morning he lay in bed looking at the ceiling for a few seconds, appraising these feelings with wonder again. Kay's face stared back at him, and he tingled with the pleasure of that vision. Eventually Nick rose, and showered and shaved. Back in the bedroom getting dressed, he switched on his mobile phone.

Seconds after connecting to the network, the arrival of a text message was announced with a beep. It was from Kay – exactly the person he hoped it would be from, although there was no reason to expect to hear from her on a Wednesday morning. He guessed that the message had been sent late the night before.

"Hey Nick my man. Need to talk tomoro…keep ya fone on xxx"

Nick read it four times over. It was ridiculous to analyse such things, but it had three kisses in it, and she had said "Nick, my man". Her man? That was a stunning thought. There was nothing that he could imagine wanting more. Did she know that? Was she playing with him? His head spun just at the idea of it. Nick pocketed the mobile phone, checked he had everything he needed, grabbed his coat, took a deep breath, and headed off into the chilly, dark morning.

The day took on its usual rhythm: customers came and went; there were periods of inactivity when Nick read his book or newspaper, or simply sat and watched people; seemingly a solitary, immobile rock in a swirling tide of movement, as the City went about its business around him. Outwardly he appeared to be a source of calm in the teeming rush around him.

It wasn't so, however. There was turmoil raging inside. He knew he should have been thinking about Justine, and about how he could get to Australia to see her. Right there at the front of his mind however – pulverising all other thoughts – was Kay. He felt some guilt, but he accepted it, and knew that it was futile to fight that guilt and the butterflies in his stomach that came with it. When would Kay call him though? Why did she need to call him? Were her emotions in the same turmoil as his? The excitement and the anticipation kept circling him.

It wasn't until after lunch that his mobile started to ring, triggering a burst of joy mixed with panic. It wasn't Kay calling though; it was Nicole, Justine's friend. Nick fumed with impatience as he answered the call.

"Hi Nicole."

"Hey Nick, how are you babe? Can you talk?"

"Yeah, no problem. Just sitting here at the moment."

"Cool. Listen, we were wondering – me and Bren – whether you would be up for a pub quiz tomorrow night? We haven't seen you for a bit so if you fancy it, it would be great to meet up."

Nick thought. He had nothing else planned he realised and it sounded pleasant enough. After only a brief hesitation he found himself replying: "Yeah, okay mate. Where is it and what time?"

"It's in that Walkabout near us, do you remember? We'll be there about 7.30 and it starts at 8.30. And don't you worry about money, we've got you covered."

Nick wasn't going to accept that. He responded quickly: "No, no. I'll pay my way Nicole. I've got a little bit put away."

"Okay, well, if you're sure Nick. How are you anyway?" Nicole continued. "Have you spoken much to Justine? I got a text about a week ago."

Nick felt another one of those flashes of guilt. "I'm fine Nic. I spoke to Justine yesterday as it happens, and she seems okay."

"Jeez, you guys must be missing each other like crazy."

179

Nick felt his cheeks burn. "Yes mate, it's a bit tough at the moment." That was vague enough to be worthy of some small measure of self-congratulation, he reckoned. Nicole went on chatting for a little longer and it sounded like she wanted to talk, which was nice, but it was a conversation that Nick found he would rather not be having until the following evening, when he might be ready for it in his head.

He had no choice but to interject, saying, "listen mate, sorry to rush you but I've got a customer come up, so I've got to go,"; he had to smile, surveying the empty space in front of his pitch, where there was no customer to be seen. With a quick reply of "okay, no worries Nick – see you tomorrow", Nicole hung up, and Nick relaxed back in his chair. Well, he reflected, tomorrow night would be a nice little diversion from routine, if nothing else.

On the day went, and Nick grew more restless as the minutes crawled by with no phone call from Kay. He wanted to just phone her number and get the waiting over and done with, and during the quiet periods when there was no pair of shoes to shine or client to talk to, when he had just his book for company, the waiting gnawed at his nerves.

Relief finally came not long after 4pm, when his mobile chirped again, and he saw Kay's name on the screen. What looked like a possible customer was heading his way across the concourse. How bloody typical. Nick pretended he hadn't seen him, hurriedly grabbed his 'Back Soon' sign, placed it on the chair, and turned away from the man walking towards him, although Nick just glimpsed that the man stopped suddenly in his tracks, wearing a look on his face that was somewhere between personal affront and weary resignation. The man changed direction to head for the tube entrance, with a disgusted shake of the head.

Nick, ringing mobile in hand, wandered a few steps along the sheltered shopping area leading towards the Broadgate Circle, and after a deep breath to try and settle a heart that felt like it was about to somersault, he answered the call. A flash of inspiration came to him as he pressed the button; a silly comment to make Kay laugh, he hoped.

"Hello, Nicholas Newman Executive Footwear Associates. A shine a day helps you work, rest and play."

There was a delighted giggle at the other end of the line.

"Nicholas Newman eh? Executive footwear – is that what you do? Very posh I must say. How are you babe?"

"Well, Kay, what can I say? I've got a queue of twenty men here waiting for me to give their shoes a bit of a sparkle, and they're all giving me the evil eye now, but I told them tough, they'll have to wait."

"Ha ha – now Nick, I don't want to get blamed for a major disturbance of the peace at Liverpool Street. Maybe I should call later?"

"No, no. Sod them, they can wait. All right, if I'm honest the queue is actually about twenty people shorter than I said! How are you anyway? Seems like ages since I saw you two days ago."

That was certainly true for Nick. The two days since Kay had dropped by with his latest pay packet had seemed interminable. Kay laughed wearily.

"It's been mad, but I'd rather not go into it Nick. My life is a succession of ridiculous situations and arguments with people I hardly know or don't want to know. Anyway, enough of that boring rubbish; I wanted to invite you to a do tomorrow night."

"A do?" Nick was genuinely surprised.

"Yeah, there's an event that we're doing where we're taking some customers and some prospects out for basically a night of drunken lunacy. But there's a spare seat going, and I thought it would be a good way to say thank you for helping me out recently."

"Er…" Nick had to think for a few seconds. This was unexpected. "I don't know. I mean, there'll be other people there, won't there – your work friends and your customers; what will I say to them? Surely I can't tell them the truth, can I? Can I?"

Nick had stopped walking now and was leaning against a wall outside one of the shops, his head bowed down with the concentration required to hear Kay's voice above the general hubbub of the station. Kay replied after a moment's hesitation.

"I thought you could act up a bit. Pretend to be a businessman that might need a bit of PR."

"Act up a bit? Fucking hell, Kay. I'm a shoeshiner, not bloody Laurence Olivier."

"I know that, but honestly, you'll probably only have to chat about your 'business' for a little while, make polite conversation, and then change the subject. Talk about football or fast cars. Man things. I'll be there to help you out. Anyway, if it all goes to plan everyone will get plastered and no-one will care after a while."

There was silence while Kay waited for Nick's response and Nick wondered what on earth to say. He wanted to turn the offer down because it sounded like an uncomfortable night. How could he turn it down though? It was a chance to see Kay Talbot – the woman that he had been obsessing about for days.

"Please, please, please. I'd love to see you again," Kay said softly, to fill the silence. "We get on so well when we're pissed." Nick heard Kay giggle again at the other end of the line. He sighed with resignation.

"I must be mad. This is right up there with someone asking a total stranger to spy on their husband for them. Okay, I'll come. But you've got to promise to look after me Kay."

She laughed. "Well, we'll have to see about that. I am a married woman you know."

A note of humorous mischief was audible in her teasing voice, and Nick felt himself redden; disarmed in an instant. He started to splutter: "No, I mean, tell me what to say and stuff. I don't know who these people…", but Kay interrupted:

"I know what you mean Nick. Don't worry. I'll call you again tomorrow lunchtime and give you a full briefing. You'll be brilliant. Honestly Nick, you're cleverer than most of these people. Don't you dare start getting all inferior on me."

Nick weighed up that piece of advice for a second before saying: "Alright, whatever you say. Anyway, what time do I have to meet you, and where?"

Kay explained about the London Bierfest: that the venue was Old Billingsgate Market, down by the Thames; that there was music, unlimited German food and beer, waiters and waitresses in traditional German costume, and an oompah band to get people in the mood for quaffing steins of beer. Nick laughed at the silliness of the whole idea.

"Jesus, and you call this work? It's just a jolly up isn't it?"

"Yeah, of course it is. It is work though. Wilf will be there and a couple of the other guys. It's all about building relationships Nick, building relationships."

"Sure."

"Yes it is – now less of your lip young man. Seriously, if we don't turn any of these prospects into real money, I'm not sure how much longer I'll have a job."

The laugh that followed her words made Nick doubt that the situation was quite that precarious for her, and he laughed along.

"Have you got a suit by the way?" she suddenly asked. Nick found that he had to think about that one.

"Er…shit, good question. Yeah, I have but I haven't worn it for ages. God knows if it still fits. I'd better try it on tonight when I get home."

Kay was laughing again: "Oh my God…when did you last wear it?"

"I can't remember. Listen, I go out with an Aussie – they think you're over-dressed if you're wearing a pair of trousers that go all the way down to your ankles."

Kay laughed and said: "Okay, look, don't worry about it too much if it doesn't fit. After all, we're supposed to be trying to impress you as a potential client, not the other way round, so just a shirt and trousers will do. Anyway, we need to decide what kind of business you're in." She paused to think. "What was it that you said when you answered the phone earlier? Nicholas's Executive Footwear or something, wasn't it? That will do – you know all about shoe care don't you, so you can baffle them with your waxes and polishes."

Kay's enthusiasm for the plan entertained no argument. By the time the phone call ended a few minutes later, Nick was committed to an evening pretending to run a nationwide shoe shining business that was looking to expand rapidly and was considering using PR to enhance the esteem and the image of the humble shoeshiner. There were just two good points for Nick to cling to: it would only have to be for one night; and he would get to spend another evening in the company of Kay, even if there were going to be dozens of drunken business people at the event, who would no doubt be competing with him for her attention.

It was only after Nick had put his phone back in his pocket and walked back to his seat that he remembered the arrangement he had already made to meet up with Nicole and Brendan the following night. He swore softly, and decided he would have to phone Nicole to cancel it as soon as he left work. That would give him a few hours to concoct an excuse. It never occurred to him to call Kay back and say he had forgotten about previously made plans. Without having to think about it, his choice had already been made.

**

There were so many excitedly chattering voices all around, that the feeling that this was one of the most eagerly anticipated nights in the City of London's calendar was inescapable. Kay Talbot, with Giles standing to her left and one of her prospects, Andrew Moloney from Western Wonder, to her right, took in the scene around them.

The night was fresh and becoming quite chilly, but despite that more than a hundred business people, probably 80% of them men, were gathered around, talking and drinking pink champagne on the Yellowstone reception area in front of Old Billingsgate Market. Shouted greetings to a regular flow of new arrivals added to the jovial atmosphere, as the crowd waited for the organisers to open the doors to the London Bierfest.

Just a hop, skip and jump away, the River Thames flowed silently by. In the gathering darkness, the lights of passing boats twinkled out on the river, while the area where the drinkers were congregated was bathed in a neon glare. The lamplights from here cast their glow out onto the black surface of the water, each tapering to a shimmering apex halfway across the river, pointing towards the South Bank. HMS Belfast sat impassively there at its anchorage, the old warship's guns aiming at the sky as if still standing to attention after all these years. To the right and left of Old Billingsgate, vehicles and pedestrians hurried across London Bridge and more distantly Tower Bridge, as another day drew to a close.

Those people heading for home weren't among the chosen few – this select band that had a ticket for a night of alcoholic revelry by the river. It felt good to be here. Kay could see Wilf ten yards away, talking animatedly with a potential customer. He seemed to be loving this, despite the cold. Well, thought Kay, he's surrounded by men; Wilf would enjoy this, wouldn't he.

She was trying to keep her nerves in check. This was a big night for her and Wilf, and the business they had grown together. Much depended on having good conversations and getting good business out of the evening and its aftermath. Giles knew that, and he seemed unusually tense as well. Anxiety about the state of the business was only a part of it for Kay though; she was looking out for Nick. She had told him to get there at 6.30 and it was a little past that now. He'd had to go home after his normal day working at Liverpool Street, get changed and then head back into the City. Maybe there were problems with tubes and buses.

When they had spoken at lunchtime he sounded a bit agitated, as if he was having second thoughts about this event, but she had tried to reassure him that it would be fine. She had asked him a few questions about his 'business', just to test out how he might reply. She had coached him, in the same way that she sometimes coached her clients in media training: say this, don't say that; wear these colours; don't look at the floor or at the camera; make eye contact with the reporter; relax; smile. They were mostly simple, obvious things, but things that could be easily forgotten under the pressure of performance or examination.

Nick had responded to the coaching, but he still sounded a little unhappy about it all when Kay had needed to end the phone call and dash off for a meeting. There was never enough time to talk to him, she thought as she stood and scanned the paved area towards London Bridge, hoping to see Nick's willowy frame come into view. The pavement was still crowded with strangers though. Giles and Andrew Moloney were talking again, and had now been joined by Rob Schneider from Spears and Yorke, one of the PR agency's existing clients.

Kay pretended to listen, but she was thinking about Nick still, and feeling anxious on his behalf. Maybe he would duck out of the whole thing, she mused. No, actually he wouldn't. He had a steadiness about him that she had noticed with some wonder when they had met up. He seemed to take things in his stride, weigh them up, decide on the next move, and then act. He was deliberate and solid – qualities that Kay admired since her own life seemed to be a constant panic of meetings, arguments and deception. She was always trying to keep up with developments that just seemed to happen. That was the right way to put it as well: things just *happened* to her, and she seemed to have no control over them.

It was a daunting spiral, but Kay found that some degree of calmness descended upon her if she thought about Nick and saw his face in her mind's eye. She trusted him and she liked the way that he seemed to trust her too. He made her laugh, which was priceless. All of this made Nick a special friend, but there was more to it than that. There remained strong feelings that she had been trying to avoid confronting. It was simmering below the surface, yet she kept putting herself in positions where those feelings could be reinforced. Right now was the perfect example: she couldn't wait to see him again, that was the truth of it.

Where the hell was he though? She glanced slyly at her watch, hoping her guests wouldn't notice. It was nearly 6.45 and surely any minute now the Bierfest organisers would start admitting people into the building and out of the cold. A slight shiver confirmed that desire.

The pink champagne was going down well though – a little too well perhaps, thought Kay, but she was feeling more nervous than she had expected to be and the champagne was currently all that was on hand to fortify her. Kay had Nick's ticket in her pocket, and he was the last remaining guest they were waiting for, so she would have to wait outside in the cold for him if the doors opened and they all went inside before he arrived.

It had been odd telling Wilf earlier about who her newest prospect was. She had been in the office and was about to pick up the telephone to call up to his office, when unexpected self-doubt had stayed her hand before it reached the receiver. Instead she had scribbled some words quickly on a piece of paper, getting the most important parts clear in her mind. Then she typed it all into an email, tapping at the keyboard hastily and with frequent, furtive looks through the glass partition and across the office to make sure that no-one would approach and catch her in the act.

This all felt sneaky and ridiculous, which brought to mind the situation with James and Lee, and she had contemplated how these feelings were becoming increasingly commonplace in her life. The email was written without interruption eventually, and she had sent it to Wilf, who had replied soon after with questions: what kind of fees were likely for PR activity? What kind of PR activity? When might it commence?

Kay had cobbled together a reply, pulling numbers and words out of the air, but ensuring that they were none too impressive. She didn't want to over-state the attractiveness of Nick as a potential client, because she knew that if she did, Wilf would consequently be all over him at the Bierfest. That had given her an odd feeling as well: the thought of Nick being the centre of attention, and of his own focus not being on Kay, as it always had been when they had met up so far. She'd never thought about that before, and it wasn't much to her liking.

In any case, the email back to Wilf had seemed to satisfy his immediate needs, and Kay had heard nothing back from him until 4.30, when he came down in his suit and tie to round up the lucky ones that were going to the event. There had been plenty of laughter as the party-goers had left the office, leaving Ruth and Steph to attend to the phones.

A voice nearby suddenly broke into Kay's reverie, and she whirled around to see that Andrew Moloney was looking at her and smirking; behind him people were starting to move towards the now open doors of the venue. "I said, I think we're going in now Kay," Moloney laughed, noticing her distraction.

"Sorry Andrew – miles away. I'll see you in there. We're still waiting for another guest to turn up, so I'll have to wait out here with his ticket. Anyway, we're tables eight and nine; they've probably got a table plan in there."

Moloney nodded and moved off towards the door with the rest of the crowd. Giles stopped next to Kay, and said: "Want me to wait boss? It's a bit cold out here for a lovely lady to be on her own."

Kay studied his face, expecting a wisecrack to follow what had sounded like sincere concern but, coming from Giles, probably wasn't. He smiled. "Well? Don't just look at me, boss. Can you understand English?"

"Yes, piss off Giles. Is that good enough English for you? Now go and look after the guests, I'll be fine thank you. I'm sure he won't be long."

"Righty-o boss. Just point me at those Fräulein…"

Kay laughed and manhandled Giles so that he faced the entrance to the venue, and then she pushed him in that direction. Soon she was virtually alone outside, with just a security man on the door for company. Kay walked across to the wall at the river's edge, and leaned against the bar along the top of it, watching the boats chugging by and the people walking along the bridge. The temperature had dropped and her breath turned to white vapour mist, floating momentarily in front of Kay before vanishing into the night.

She found herself studying each vapour cloud, absent-mindedly wondering about the natural laws behind why they formed. Another odd thought came: these little clouds; each one was like a second of your life; there just for a moment, and then gone. You couldn't stop it and you couldn't get it back. Kay proved that to herself by grabbing at the next couple of misty breaths with her hand. She seemed to catch them, but when she opened her hand there was nothing there, nothing remained… gone forever.

It hit her in a way that she didn't expect, as she watched each little cloud disperse in the early evening air: it was telling her something. It was telling her that she had to make the most of every second as it slipped through her fingers, because every single one was unique, and every single one was important. This was her life, and she had to do something with it. It was up to her to change it somehow; to make it better.

A small voice inside Kay's head demanded to know what the hell was wrong with her – why was she having these stupid, pointless reflections?

But a more insistent voice wondered how many millions of precious, unfulfilled seconds she had already let slip by, and how many more were still to pass. Here she was, about to get stupidly drunk for no reason other than to try and make money. At home she had a husband who didn't care whether she was happy or sad, and who rarely bothered to speak a kind word to her any more. It was all shit; none of it meant a thing, she thought to herself. It was all pointless. A tear threatened to roll down her cheek and Kay hurriedly wiped it away before it could fall, telling herself to get a grip.

Tipping back the champagne glass, she finished the drink, and placed the glass on the floor near her left foot. Her eyes still observed the mystery of her breath turning to vapour and then disappearing. Vaguely she became aware of the distant sound of laughter and music from inside the venue. London was all around; she was right at the heart of it standing here, but she had never felt more alone.

For God's sake, where was Nick? More strongly, she felt her stomach tighten with nerves. Nick, Nick, Nick. It kept coming back to him. Was that why she was so pensive tonight? Nick was on his way, which perhaps explained why she was standing here shivering, looking at the Thames, and childishly trying to catch her own clouds of cold breath as they eked away.

She needed to steel herself for the evening to come. She decided that the tear she had wiped away was merely caused by the cold breeze. Suddenly, there was someone next to her, nudging her right elbow, and sharing the view towards the river.

"Don't do it lady."

Kay's head spun to her right, and Nick was there, looking down at the water, then looking up briefly and smiling self-consciously before turning his eyes back to the river. Kay cried out: "Nick!" and flung her arms around his neck, surprising them both with the force and the joy of the embrace. Nick had to take a step back, with Kay's arms linked round his neck. He was shocked by the welcome. For a long two seconds Kay stayed there, with her head nuzzled beneath his chin.

"Was I just in time then?" he asked, trying to sound light-hearted. "It looked a bit serious from back there. I was worried you were going to throw yourself into the drink."

Kay looked up at him and smiled, her face seeming to Nick to shimmer under the lights, and he was struck dumb momentarily by the vision. Kay was laughing now.

"You saved me! You're my hero!" she cried, getting inquisitive looks from the security guard on the door, and from a young couple that were passing along the pavement nearby. Nick could feel himself blushing madly. Kay still had her hands linked behind his head, and she stepped forward to hug him again. Nick was taken aback once more and looked quickly from side to side as if checking who was watching. Was this allowed, he wondered? He patted her shoulder a little awkwardly. Kay was saying something, but her words were muffled by his coat.

"I can't hear a word you're saying down there. What was that Kay?" he chuckled. She looked up at him again, her eyes sparkling with good humour, and replied:

"I said, you bastard, I'm fucking freezing from waiting here all this time. The least you can do is give me a cuddle and warm me up."

They both laughed and he took the bold step of pulling her closer to him as seemed to be instructed. Kay, her head buried in the folds of Nick's coat, was fighting to regain her composure. The release of happiness at Nick's arrival had been a sensation. She had been staggered at the intensity of that moment, and the line about being cold had given her much needed time to think. Anyway, this was nice, snuggling up with this man. She was supposed to be working though. Reluctantly, though trying to cover up that reluctance, Kay pulled away from Nick's grasp. He looked totally flummoxed by the previous minute of his life, she thought; and a little bit proud too.

"How do I look?" he said, spreading his arms wide, and doing a twirl for Kay. The suit looked good, and Nick looked a different man in it to the one that she saw shining shoes.

"Oh yes, look at you – very smart, very handsome," she nodded appreciatively. "How about me?" Kay did a twirl too.

Nick couldn't keep the grin from his face. This was going like a dream. All that worrying; the couple of brandies he had sunk for Dutch courage at home while getting ready, and the pint in the pub round the corner that he'd needed to fortify himself a little more; trying to keep his head from spinning away with crazy hopes and gut-wrenching fears about what the night might hold. Never in his wildest dreams had he imagined she would be this pleased to see him.

"Kay, you've looked amazing every time I've seen you, but tonight…my God, I think we need to invent a new word to describe this vision before my eyes."

She laughed: "Okay, let's discuss what that new word might be later over beer. But now… " She offered a hand for him to take while adopting the posh tones that a genteel lady might have used at an English garden party a century before: "Nicholas Newman, businessman extraordinaire, purveyor of fine footwear, the entertainment awaits. Come; let's tarry no longer."

Nick took her hand with a slight bow of the head and, proceeding with the poise and measured pace of a King and Queen approaching the throne, they walked together to the door, giggling as they went, which somewhat spoiled the regal effect. Kay gave the security man the two tickets, and they stepped inside, feeling the instant blast of warm air. The noise of the music inside the venue suddenly pounded their ears, as if someone had turned an invisible volume dial from one to ten with a quick flick of the wrist. They walked on together towards the source of the din.

**

Four hours later, Nick was sitting alone, drinking steadily and watching a sweating crowd of men and women cavorting on the dance floor, as a live band hammered out some classic 1960s numbers. The guy who had sat next to him for most of the evening, who worked for a company that manufactured toys Nick had discovered in the course of their conversation, was up there on the dance floor, wearing a silly plastic, horned Viking hat and dancing badly in amongst a big group of men gathered in a circle around some women who were strutting their stuff rather more capably. Kay was one of those women.

The men were whooping, cheering and clapping their hands as the women shook and shimmied in the middle. Kay's colleague, a young guy who had been introduced to Nick as Giles, seemed to be one of the most vocal cheerleaders – even though his boss was a main object of attention. Nick didn't even need to see the women's movements to know that the dancing was getting raunchy. The reactions of the men, who probably outnumbered Kay and her fellow female dance partners by about ten to one, said it all. They sounded like a pack of baying wolves.

Across the table from Nick sat another of Kay's work-mates, a girl called Sara, whose eyes betrayed the fact that she had hit an alcoholic brick wall, though her head was still inclined towards the man sitting next to her, suggesting that she was actually listening. Nick could remember that the man's name was Rob. He was talking enthusiastically and gesturing with his hands about something. Sara was concentrating hard, fighting the effects of the drink, and beginning to lose the battle as her eyelids drooped.

Nick took it all in. It had been a funny night: not funny in a laugh-a-minute sense particularly, though it had had its moments; rather, Nick had found the night to be equal parts discomfort and sheer delight. The latter was generally when Kay had leaned across to catch his willing eye and include him in the conversation, or otherwise to intervene and save him from the toy man – what was his name again, Nick wondered as he watched the man sway on the dance floor in a rhythm that was only vaguely related to the one that the drummer was thumping; Norman, that was it.

The passages of awkwardness and boredom had been pret-ty excruciating though. Thinking about it, those parts had generally involved Norman, or Kay's business partner Wilf, who was highly intellectual and more than a little camp to Nick's mind. More than once Nick had looked across at Kay in panic when Wilf had asked him something complicated about his "footwear business".

The food had been passable, though Nick wasn't much bothered about when he might next be eating German cuisine again, he decided. The beer was excellent, the waitresses were real head-turners, and the musical entertainment had been both hilarious in the case of the oompah band, and now adrenalin-soaked with the soul band hitting its high octane straps.

But what now? Nick had been sitting alone for about ten minutes. Kay was throwing herself wholeheartedly into her dancing, and Nick felt slightly lost without her. He didn't much fancy dancing himself, and there was a growing temptation to make himself scarce while nobody was looking. Just disappear and bring this strange and awkward night to a blessed quick ending. Send Kay a text, talk to her another time to thank her and apologise for leaving. It would be so easy to sneak out. He reckoned that glassy-eyed Sara wouldn't even notice, and Rob had hardly spoken to Nick all night. Nick still had some beer left in a stein in front of him, and he took a big swig from it while he considered what to do next.

Finding Kay waiting outside Old Billingsgate seemed a long time ago now, and Nick could feel himself teetering on the brink of drunkenness. That seemed to be a consistent theme on nights involving Kay, he noticed.

The high of that moment when Kay had flung her arms around him outside and shown him such affection had gradually dissipated during the evening. It had been replaced firstly by a reluctant acceptance that she was, after all, working tonight, so she couldn't devote her attention to him. But as jealousy and feelings of his own social inadequacy had slowly invaded Nick's thoughts, making him fall increasingly quiet at the table, even that feeling had slowly deteriorated.

Nick had another swig of the beer, and scowled with dissatisfaction at the taste – it was the flat liquid at the bottom of the glass. That summed up his mood and made his mind up for him: it was time to make a low-key exit. He'd done his bit for Kay, and she was having fun; now it was time to go home, drink some water, get to bed and hope that the next day's hangover was manageable.

He looked around one last time: the coast seemed clear. The revellers were still going hard at it, and Kay was in the middle of it; Sara and Rob were still in earnest conversation. Nick rose silently to his feet, and walked self- consciously towards the door, feeling like a cat burglar making his escape, and hurrying with greater urgency the closer he got to the cloakroom, from where he needed to retrieve his coat. A blonde waitress dressed in German folk costume was standing near the cloakroom and flashed him a wide, perfect smile. "Good night sir – thanks for coming," she beamed at Nick as he went by. Nick waved back at her, and proffered his coat ticket at the cloakroom door.

Seconds later he was out in the cold night air. A hefty breeze was blowing along the Thames, and Nick pulled his coat around tightly as he battered his way into the wind, head down and heading towards London Bridge. He wondered what the time was, but to check his watch would have meant taking his hand out of his pocket, and the cold blast of the wind dissuaded him. Never mind, it was going to be a late night, whatever time he now finally reached his bed. Gradually the muscular strut of the soul band's beat faded away behind him.

Recollections of moments from the evening re-played inside his head as he walked: the disinterest from Wilf when they were introduced, who obviously considered Nick to be small-fry in the grand scheme of running his business, and had no idea how right he was; the laughter, cheers and wisecracks around the table as the oompah band swung into its first number; Norman and his hopes for a bumper Christmas with the company's new range of toys; Nick and Kay both poking uncertainly amid much humour at the mysterious, curiously tasteless and cloying dumpling-type food that was part of the traditional German food served up – knudel, the waitress called Birgit had said it was called. Whatever it was, Nick would not be seeking out the recipe with any urgency.

He remembered Kay's bright and frequent laughter as she made small talk with Nick and Norman at the table; the eye contact; the knowing and encouraging wink; the increasing loudness of her voice as she got drunk; the dancing on stage. The welcoming hug when Nick had arrived. Yes, that had been the best bit.

Nick realised suddenly that he had mistakenly walked past the passageway that would take him back to Lower Thames Street, from where he could walk along to Monument tube station. He was virtually under the bridge itself now and that passage was back behind him. To his right he saw a couple of steps leading up inside an enclosed staircase that he guessed went up to street level at the end of the bridge. He veered in that direction and skipped quickly up the first few steps into the concrete shelter. What was that he had heard as he mounted the steps? It had sounded like a muffled shout of some kind. Maybe it was just a trick of the wind.

Ahead of him now was a flight of several steps that provided access to the main road, from where pedestrians could walk into the City in one direction, or instead across London Bridge to the South Bank. Even though his nose was tucked into his upturned collar against the cold, it still registered the stench of stale urine in this sheltered place – reminiscent of the generally squalid ambience of the stairwells at a typical inner city block of flats.

Then he heard the noise again – definitely a shout – and it brought him to an abrupt halt. He recognised the voice: it was Kay and the word she was shouting was his name. He turned back towards the river and Kay arrived on the run a second later. Beads of perspiration glistened on her forehead and cheeks – Nick guessed from her dance floor exertion, but perhaps from running after him as well.

She gave him a puzzled look as she came to a stop in front of him. "Nick, where are you going?" she gasped. The run from the Bierfest, which was probably only one hundred metres or so, had left Kay breathless. He thought about making a comment on her fitness, or lack of it, but he could see that this wasn't the right moment. She looked a little hurt, a little concerned and a little confused. He decided he should explain.

"I was just going home Kay. I had a nice night but I have to get up early."

"You didn't even say goodbye," Kay responded accusingly.

"Well, you were busy from what…"

"God, I wasn't dancing for long. I came back to the table at the end of the song and Sara, the useless fucking cow, didn't have a clue where you were, but Rob said he thought you'd gone, so I came after you."

"Well, you didn't really need to. I was going to text you," explained Nick.

"I did need to Nick, because I never got to talk to you about what I wanted to. It's been a bit difficult, what with that boring bastard Norman sat there, and Wilf ear-wigging me all night."

Nick looked beyond Kay to where he could hear the river lapping at the stone banks, just twenty feet away over Kay's shoulder. They were standing inside the concrete shelter, which provided some refuge from the cold wind, but it was still a rank and gloomy place to stop for a conversation. Kay was looking at Nick as if expecting some sort of response. He couldn't stop himself from silently cursing because he had been so close to escaping, even though Kay, this amazing woman, was here in front of him. A warm bed had beckoned, but now she wanted to chat some more.

"Besides," she continued with a coy smile, "we were having fun. I didn't want you to go yet."

Nick sighed. "Well," he started, then paused, "…well, can we at least get out of here? It stinks of piss."

Kay nodded in agreement, stepped forward and took Nick's arm, and together they walked up the steps, fifteen or so, that brought them out on to the street at the north end of London Bridge. The contrast was immediate – lights, traffic, gusting wind, and fresh air, instead of the hushed, dark, dank stairwell they had just come from. Kay tugged Nick's arm towards the centre of the bridge and Nick, unthinkingly, complied. They took slow, seemingly deliberate steps away from the City, and away from the tube station that Nick had been intending to travel home from. He looked as if he was deep in thought, lips pursed, eyes fixed on the pavement ahead of him as they strolled side by side.

Then he spoke: "What's this all about then Kay?"

They walked on a few more paces towards the centre of the bridge. Nick saw that Kay was looking around at the lights of London and the occasional passing vehicle with a serene expression of contentment on her face, and he wondered why. She shivered slightly and huddled closer to Nick as they walked.

"I want you to help me again," said Kay, her voice quivering slightly with the cold. "Something is going on with Lee and I want you to help me find out what."

"I thought I already was helping you. Where are we going by the way?"

Kay stopped walking, causing Nick to halt also. They were about mid-river now and over Kay's left shoulder Nick had a fine view of HMS Belfast, and beyond that, Tower Bridge, its lights twinkling in the night. It was a stunning view but Nick scarcely noticed it.

"I'm not sure where we're going actually. I just started walking in any old direction really," said Kay, looking left and right to both ends of London Bridge. "Shall we find a pub?"

Nick laughed. It seemed to be Kay's default solution for most situations. He quickly checked his watch and found that it had just gone 10.45. They did have enough time for a drink if they found a pub quickly. Nick didn't particularly want more alcohol though, having already made a mental switch to prepare for work and an early start the next day.

"I think we've probably had enough to drink for one night, don't you?" Nick smiled. She sighed and visibly wilted. Suddenly, she looked incredibly weary, Nick noticed. All evening long she had been flying high; being the vivacious host, laughing, joking and dancing. Now it was as if a huge weight had descended upon her shoulders once more. To Nick's alarm, Kay suddenly staggered a couple of paces away from him, until her momentum was checked by the light grey stone wall behind her. It was all that stopped her from falling into the inky black water of the River Thames, whispering by fifty feet below.

Nick had instinctively reached out to grab her arm as she had stumbled backwards, but Kay managed to steady herself against the cold stone and started giggling. "Oh my God, I think you're probably right babe. Looks like I've had a few too many."

Nick laughed softly along with her, then said: "Kay, to be honest, I've got half an eye on getting up early for work tomorrow, so I'd rather not carry on drinking. You still haven't told me what this is all about though, and it's bloody freezing standing here."

He laughed again, and Kay smiled back; then she seemed to summon up her powers of concentration once more. "Yeah, you're right, this wind is going straight through me," she began. "Well, as I said, something's going on – with Lee that is. The other night, after you texted me about the delays, he didn't get home until gone half ten, and he said he'd been playing squash with his mate up here in town, had a few beers after squash and then got the train home late from Liverpool Street. But I know that's a lie yeah, cos you told me he got on the train and it left Liverpool Street at about 6 o'clock. So he went somewhere in those four hours, but I don't know where."

"Have you asked him where he went?" Nick asked.

"No, silly billy. I can't say 'I know you got on the train at six Lee' can I, because how would I know that? I only know that because you told me; because we're watching him. So…so I just went to bed and left him downstairs with his kebab, but I was laying there thinking about it, and it was driving me mad knowing that he had lied but not knowing why, so I texted you. Then the next day I had the idea of inviting you tonight so I could ask you to do me another big favour…"

"Which is…Oh God…you want me to actually follow him now don't you?"

"Well…yes, I guess that's it really."

"Fucking hell, Kay." Nick had to turn away from her and bite his tongue to prevent more expletives bursting out. When he turned back a second or two later, he saw that Kay looked confused by his reaction.

She mumbled: "What's wrong? What…"

"What's wrong? Are you having me on? This is fucking crazy Kay. In case you hadn't noticed I'm a bloke that shines shoes, not a fucking private detective. Am I supposed to walk along a safe distance behind and jump into the shadows every time he turns round? What if he notices me? In fact, he's seen me before, probably loads of times, so what do I do if he recognises me and challenges me? I could get done over, and your money won't do me a lot of good then will it?"

Nick glowered at Kay, taken by surprise by his own fury. Kay looked distraught. There were just two paces between them, filled with the swirling vapour of their hot breath. Kay raised a coat sleeve to the corner of one eye and ham-fistedly rubbed away a tear. When she spoke, she sounded like a complaining teenager. Nick could hear how shaken she was.

"Why are you being like this? I thought we were friends Nick. I thought you liked me. It's just a favour…"

"You think I just like you, Kay? Jesus, that doesn't even start to describe how I feel about you. I'm not bloody interested in Lee, and I couldn't give a toss about what he…"

Nick stopped talking mid-sentence. Something about the look on Kay's face brought him to a juddering halt. It was extraordinary how she changed so quickly; that thought briefly fluttered in and out of his mind, but he was barely capable of the act of thought right then. They eyed each other across a divide of about three feet. It was only a second, maybe two, before either of them moved, but Nick remembered every imaginable fragment of those seconds afterwards, so rich were they in utterly concentrated sight, sound and emotion. The insistent breath of wind, the far-off honk of a car horn, the previously only dimly acknowledged lights of Tower Bridge in the distance, suddenly in sharp focus behind Kay, as if someone had just slipped the perfect lens into a broken pair of spectacles.

Kay – watching him it seemed – stood just there, still shivering. He saw the hint of a smile, but it was the eyes that completed the transformation: they shone with what he hoped was happiness. Nick was aware, somewhere in the outer reaches of his consciousness, that he was transfixed; that a magic spell was at work somehow; that the platform for his anger had collapsed in that unbelievable instant. He wanted to move, to reduce the distance between he and Kay, but in those slow-motion particles of time he was just never able to galvanise any part of his body to respond.

Then Kay did it. She stepped deliberately towards him, reached a hand to either side of Nick's head, and he was liberated by her kiss. It was two minutes before either could pull away, and it was Kay who did so, uttering a disbelieving "oh, God", and burying her face against his neck. They stood there for more long seconds, with Nick holding Kay to him, oblivious to the cold and to passers-by, and feeling his heart strangely sinking with fear and apprehension, while stabs of excitement and joy punctuated every slow second; Kay wept quietly into the fabric of his overcoat.

At last she was ready to look into his face again, and her own face was shining now, happiness and tears glowing in

London's illumination. She laughed self-consciously as Nick wiped away some tears with a thumb.

"I must look a right state."

Nick didn't laugh with her but he smiled a tired smile: "You look beautiful. I can hardly speak Kay."

She kissed him softly again, and said: "Thank you. I meant all of that, Nick. That wasn't a mistake. I know I'm a bit drunk, but….it's what I want, I think – as much as a woman can say half-pissed and freezing cold, in the middle of London Bridge."

They both laughed, and he pulled her close to him again. There didn't seem to be any words within his grasp that could explain how he felt, and he was too scared to talk anyway, in case he spoiled this moment. Instead he clung on to her and enjoyed the closeness, the touch of her hair, the odour of her perfume. Kay started weeping again but that soon seemed to pass. He heard and felt her pulling herself together once more, still enfolded in his arms. What now, he wondered? His own senses were still stunned.

Kay looked at him, this time with a new inner resolve he thought, and when she spoke her voice was stronger, though still a little shaky. The tone of Kay's voice told him who was in charge as she linked a hand in his hand and pulled him back towards the City, in the direction from which they had come just a few eternal minutes before:

"Come on, we need to find a taxi," she ordered him. "I've been waiting long enough."

**

It wasn't a dream. Nick felt sure it must have been, but his eyes had just flicked open and confirmed what the weight pressed against the right side of his body, and the smooth skin his fingers felt, had suggested. It was Kay.

Implausible yet wonderful, here she was, curled up in the bed he was supposed to share with Justine; and the world, as represented by Kay's tranquil, sleeping smile, was at peace as far as Nick was concerned. He looked down at her and felt a staggering moment of completion. How on earth would he ever get used to this – this happiness? It felt ridiculous in its sheer scale; so ridiculous that Nick almost laughed out loud as he contemplated it.

Work was blown for the day, and for all he knew it was blown for good. He'd known that was going to be the case when, just after five o'clock in the morning, he had felt himself slipping helplessly at last towards a blissful sleep. He didn't need to look at the bedside clock to know that he was now irretrievably late for work – the brightness outside the bedroom curtains told him that much.

The inevitable confrontation with his boss could wait though. Things had changed fundamentally in Nick's life during these last few hours, and he needed to re-adjust. He spent some minutes silently watching Kay's face, admiring and adoring the serenity it radiated as she slept; finding it hard to come to terms with the prospect of this sight becoming the first thing he would see every day, as he fervently hoped it would.

What would happen when she woke? Would she look at him with alarm, and then grab her clothes, mumbling apologies and excuses for having made a terrible mistake, as she headed for the door? He couldn't believe that would happen – not after the things that Kay had said the night before, as they held each other on London Bridge, then in the taxi that sped them back to Camden, and then in the early hours of the morning here in this room; surely all that had been real, and true, and destined to be. Despite himself though, he still saw Kay's imaginary flight enacted in his mind's eye.

Nick noticed from the bedside clock that it was almost 9 o'clock in the morning. He had turned his mobile phone off hours earlier, and he expected that it would now be jam-packed with abusive messages from Mike demanding to know his whereabouts this morning. He really should call Mike right now if he wanted to keep the job. Just tell him that he had been sick all night and then collapsed into sleep and had only just risen, or something like that; anything to try and deflect some of the trouble. Nick stared up at the ceiling and thought about that for a minute.

Then a soft voice broke into his reverie: "Penny for them." He turned and saw that Kay was looking up at him, studying his face for something; frowning at his pensive expression he guessed.

"Oh, I was just, ah…nothing much really. I was just thinking about work." He felt taken by surprise. It wasn't the way he'd wanted to welcome her to the day. She groaned and buried her face against his chest.

"Work…don't say that word Nick. It hurts too much."

Nick felt Kay relax against him, exhausted by the effort of speaking even those few words it seemed. Well, she hasn't run away yet, that's one good thing, he thought. There was silence apart from their breathing for a few seconds. Nick felt tense though. These were new pastures in their relationship.

As so often with Kay, he felt a spell needed to be broken, or perhaps it actually needed to be cast. They knew so little about each other, and there was usually some initial awkwardness that maybe a comment or a meaningful look between them would overcome.

Here was that awkwardness again – Nick perceived it was there anyway, and he wondered if Kay did too. He strongly felt the anticipation of that next sweet moment which would sweep them across the invisible line again. She would know what to do, and in fact here she was, shifting her weight to allow them to face each other directly, in spite of the dark hair falling across her eyes; clambering astride his thighs, and then leaning down to kiss him on the lips – a long, searching kiss.

When she stopped, she smiled down at him, locks of her hair intruding in the few inches of space between their faces. She whispered a "wow" and continued to watch him, smiling, her head swaying slightly above his as if she was feeling woozy. There was no sound, apart from the low hum of electricity in the flat, and further away the occasional murmur of distant cars. Anyway, Nick was barely aware of anything outside the confines of the long, dark hair that framed Kay's face.

He went to speak: "Are you…" Kay whispered a soft "sshh" sound and put a finger to Nick's lips.

"These moments are ours," she whispered. "Ours for ever…nothing else matters."

Once more she leaned towards him and they kissed again. Nick surrendered to the inevitable, forgot about Mike, and banished guilty thoughts of Justine from his head.

Half an hour later, Kay skipped from the bed and went out to the bathroom, leaving Nick to relax beneath the covers. As he rested, he heard a faint beep coming from the direction of Kay's clothes piled on the floor. Nick guessed it was her mobile phone, indicating that a message was waiting. It reminded Nick of his own predicament with work, and he reached over to grab his mobile phone. He switched it on, and waited for the network to connect. Soon the display showed him that there was a voicemail message. The number that had called was Mike's, and it was timed at 7.42 in the morning. Nick listened and found that in fact Mike hadn't left a message, but had hung up with speaking after the recording had started, leaving no clues as to how he felt about Nick's unexplained no-show.

Nick thought for a few moments, preparing himself for a difficult phone call. He could hear Kay running taps in the bathroom, and decided that coffee was in order before calling Mike. Pulling on his dressing gown he wandered through to the kitchen. It was getting on towards 10 o'clock now. Nick changed his mind: call Mike immediately, the coffee could wait.

He took a deep breath and rang the number. Mike answered quickly, sounding gruff and impatient, his Polish accent coming across as even more abrasive than usual: "Where in hell are you? You fancy long weekend? Why do you not call me?" he demanded. Nick tried to explain: he had been vomiting most of the night, and had not slept until about 5 o'clock. He must have set his alarm wrongly because it had not gone off, and he had just woken up. He was really sorry. Mike seemed unimpressed. "You work Monday, and then you come and see me. I will decide what we do then; today is too busy."

Nick ended the uncomfortable call there and with a heavy sigh leaned against the kitchen worktop, contemplating the floor tiles for a second. Well, it could have gone worse, he reflected; much worse. He had another day's work to come at the very least.

Nick was watching TV in the front room when Kay finally joined him again, dressed in her clothes from the night before. She looked pale and tired but, to Nick's eyes, heart-achingly beautiful. She walked in while speaking on her mobile phone, and Nick guessed from the irritation in her voice that she was talking to her husband. It reminded Nick of the first time he had set eyes on her, as she and Lee had argued at Liverpool Street that morning, several weeks earlier. It seemed like years ago now. Kay wasn't taking any prisoners by the sound of it:

"Yeah, well thanks for asking if I had a nice night... I told you, I'm round Sara's. We had a late night, there were no trains, so I slept here, rather than spending a hundred quid on a taxi back to Hertford just so that my dear hubby could insult me... are you accusing me of lying?... what? No, Sara's asleep... fuck off Lee, I'm not waking her up to talk to you. Anyway, she's got a day off today – she had the sense to book it in advance... what? Oh God, whatever. Look, I'm going to hang up now okay? Bye. Get back to your work. Bye."

Kay snapped her phone shut and parked herself on Nick's lap, linking her hands behind his neck and giving him the strained smile that he'd seen before when she had mentioned her husband.

"Sorry about that," she said. "Lee's being a prat for a change. Well, I suppose he's right this time, but he doesn't know that does he. Anyway, we need to talk babe."

Nick laughed. "Yeah, not half. There's a lot to say."

"Well, yes, there's that, and we will have that conversation. But it should be obvious that this wasn't an accident or a mistake. I've been waiting for someone to make me feel like this since I was a little girl, dreaming of Prince Charming sweeping me off my feet. And it turns out my Prince Charming shines shoes…"

"Damn right he does…"

"…and that's fine. I don't care about any of that crap. I just want to be with you, and prove to myself that these crazy thoughts going round my head really are true."

Kay was looking at Nick earnestly throughout this, and he had a feeling that there was a 'but' coming. Kay didn't disappoint. "But," she continued, then paused momentarily for emphasis, "we never finished talking about this thing with Lee, mainly because other things suddenly became more important last night. But I still want you to do this for me."

Nick had actually felt himself involuntarily twitch with distaste at the mention of Kay's husband's name. He studied the area of carpet by his feet for a few seconds, avoiding her gaze. A curse hovered just behind his calm exterior. She waited and then suddenly squeezed his neck slightly more firmly, forcing him to look up and be confronted by her imploring eyes.

"Say something Nick," she demanded, before adding with feeling, "…please."

Nick's words tumbled out in a rush, and he wasn't able to hide his disappointment:

"So you're staying with the guy then? Despite all this? Despite him being a complete arsehole, you're staying with him?"

"Oh Nick… Look, I'm not lying or pretending. I'm not tricking you or playing you around. I want to be with you. But I'm married to Lee and that means lawyers and things will get involved, so it's going to be messy and I need to do the right things. I need to know what he's doing."

She waited for him to respond, biting her bottom lip anxiously, but her grip on his neck had relaxed, and she was playfully twisting his hair in her fingers. The combination knocked all the fight out of Nick. He could never say no to this woman, and she seemed to know that – she sensed it and used it, he was sure. It wasn't even a close contest.

"Oh, for God's sake. All right, I'll do it. I must be an idiot. Anyway, when?"

Her smile was more one of relief than triumph: "Thank you babe. Probably next Tuesday, but I'll let you know."

They hugged for a minute, before Kay asked about Nick's boss. Nick replied:

"He was…annoyed, I think. But he said I've got to go and see him after work on Monday, so at least I've still got a job for another day."

"God, I'm really sorry. I'd hate it if you lost your job because of me."

"Kay, I wouldn't change this for the world. I don't care how I get punished now; it will have been worth it."

He could see that her eyes were watery with emotion, and his own emotions were running wild too. Every second that he held it together felt like a mighty victory.

"When can I see you again? I know you're a busy woman and stuff but…"

"Soon Nick, soon. I need a couple of days to think about what's happening and work out what we do next. Please don't take that the wrong way. But my head is spinning so fast at the moment, I can hardly think. You've got Justine to think about as well. I totally promise I will call you on…" she thought for a second or two, "…Sunday. We can talk sometime on Sunday. I might even be able to get away and meet you maybe, I don't know."

"Okay, okay." Nick accepted the meagre offering like a starving man being thrown a few seeds. It was hope for the future. There was a perfect stillness in the room for a second. Nick felt it pressing down upon him. His mind was reeling from the events of the last 12 hours, but it felt so meek to just watch Kay gather her things up and start to switch her mind on for work.

Too quickly she was ready to go, and the front door was open, cold air rushing in, chilling the dressing-gown clad Nick's feet and lower legs as the pair clung to each other again in the doorway. Kay started laughing playfully, tearing herself away from Nick, and then rushing back dramatically to his arms. Finally he raised his voice and despite his own laughter ordered her out of the door: "Go! Get out! Call me, I'll be waiting, but go! My feet are bloody freezing!"

She backed away from him and out of the door, though their hands were still clasped. "Right, I'm going. It's been lovely darling; the best. Which way is the tube station – that way? Okay, laters."

She leaned forward and kissed him one last time, leaving him with instructions to go back to bed and dream sweet dreams. He watched her walk away, and saw her turn back once to smile and blow a farewell kiss. He returned it, then closed the door against the outside, and leaned back against it for a few seconds of stunned, silent contemplation.

Her sudden absence felt savage and strange. It was like having an arm cut off, yet feeling quite relieved about losing it, such had been the concentrated intensity of their moments together. Now there was respite. She was gone and that hurt, but he desperately needed some time and space to think, and to make sense of this new situation. What the hell happens next was the first question that came to mind.

Chapter Six

It was Saturday morning in the Talbot's Hertford residence. Lee stretched his limbs under the duvet, and tried to focus on the ceiling, feeling mildly confused. From time to time a dull thudding in his head intensified, making him wince. This was his punishment for a night out in London with his work mates. A double figure tally of pints, plus the curry and the Flaming Sambucas at the end of the night, before the last minute dash to Liverpool Street to get the last train home – all this added up to create the irregular but persistent hammering inside Lee's skull.

He had the bed to himself but he could hear Kay occasionally moving about downstairs. She had been asleep before he got home, and had not stirred as he fumbled about drunkenly in the dark, struggling to get undressed. It all started coming back to him now. Lee had eventually decided that he really couldn't get undressed without some light to see by, so he had waddled out of the bedroom with his shoes still on and his trousers already around his ankles, to remove his clothes in the spare room, and not disturb Kay.

It had seemed like a good idea, until he had leaned for support on the vacuum cleaner that Kay kept in there, while wrestling with a hard-to-remove sock. Inadvertently, and making a ridiculous din, the appliance and Lee came crashing to the floor. After that, he had bounced off the walls on his way back to the bedroom, where he discarded the clothes on the floor, and edged between the sheets. Sleep came soon after.

Now, eyes wide open again, he saw that the time was almost 11 o'clock. The world was bustling around outside and he was still in bed feeling like death. There had to be salvation in paracetamol, but that would mean getting up. He decided to think about it for a bit longer.

Soon though, Lee's mind wandered elsewhere, and he felt a pleasant tingle of anticipation. Today was a quality day of quality sport, and he had arranged to meet with James in one of the local pubs to watch it on TV. There was an England football match at 3pm, and then at 8pm there was a Rugby Union World Cup Semi Final to watch as well – England versus France, no less. He would probably still be in the pub with James to watch that.

A top drawer day, he reckoned. Bring it on. Maybe he would even see if Kay wanted to come along as well. Uniquely among Lee's mates, there seemed to be some sort of friendship between James and Lee's wife. He often asked Lee how Kay was.

Anyway, Sunday would therefore be a bad hangover day. Then it was just another boring week at work, before he and Billy would get busy, and a new chapter in Lee's life would begin. It would be dangerous – he couldn't ignore that. He was excited and scared out of his wits in equal measure, and it was good to feel alive at last.

With that last thought, Lee reluctantly swung his legs out of the bed, and then slowly and unsteadily stood and straightened up, feeling like an old aged pensioner in his stiffness. He shuffled to the door and took his dressing gown off of the peg there, wrapping the gown around himself as he moved along to the bathroom.

In there, he found the box of tablets that represented his first step on the road to recovery. He gulped two down with water, then studied his face in the mirror for a few seconds, deciding that he didn't much like the look of the bleary-eyed, saggy-cheeked apparition that glared back, little tufts and clumps of hair jutting out of its head at unintentional angles. Upon his tongue he could still taste the chicken madras of the previous night. He decided it was time to progress to step two of the recovery plan: coffee.

This would probably involve some sort of confrontation with Kay, he realised, but even with a sore head he was up for that. It was she, after all, that had failed to come home on Thursday night and had claimed to have stayed at Sara's place. His conscience was clear, but what about hers, Lee wondered? It occurred to him that they hadn't actually spoken face to face since Wednesday evening. What kind of marriage had this turned into? Did he really need it any longer? He growled at the mirror in response: there would be a better time for those kinds of questions, he supposed. One day it would become his priority.

He walked quickly to the top of the stairs and started to descend, thinking that if he was to whistle a jaunty little tune and affect some sort of breezy indifference to his condition he might deflect whatever harsh words she had ready for him. The moral high ground would be h…

"Shit!"

Suddenly, solid ground was no longer there. His left foot had slipped straight off the carpet at the edge of the stair, at the same moment that he was raising his right foot to reach for the next step down; suddenly he was in mid-air, unable to control his progress. His head jerked backwards as he uttered a startled yelp and groped for the banister with his left hand. Complete panic, curses, and a blur of thoughts: oh God, broken legs or worse happening to him in this next second or two.

He braced himself mentally for the pain, knowing he was done for. Then his backside hit a stair and he bounced downwards, still out of control, still worried about his legs being wrenched beneath him and snapping like twigs, or pitching him headfirst towards the radiator across from the rapidly approaching foot of the stairs.

His feet touched the carpet of the living room floor and that, together with his hand at last locating the wooden banister, stalled his downward momentum. Lee came slithering to a halt, feet stretched out before him, his backside on the bottom step. He felt shocked and ridiculous and started to mutter a heartfelt expletive, but then his embarrassment reached a whole new level: Kay's laugh rang out; a high-pitched, mocking laugh that to Lee's discerning ears contained no trace of concern.

"That was good! Can you do that trick again I wonder?"

Lee looked angrily up at Kay, who was sitting on the sofa chuckling with a hand half covering her mouth, as if that would mask her amusement. He started to pull himself upright, rearranging his dressing gown as he did so. His fury was obvious though.

"Yeah, very fucking funny Kay. I nearly break my fucking neck and all you can do is piss yourself laughing."

Lee stormed past Kay on his way to the kitchen, casting a single malevolent look back at the offending staircase as he went. She heard him muttering more poisonous swear words as he noisily cast about for cups and ingredients in the kitchen, and filled the kettle with water. Her laughter had just about subsided by the time he came back out from the kitchen bearing a steaming coffee mug. He slumped down in the armchair to Kay's right and gave her an accusing stare.

"Thanks for your concern Kay. I could have been badly injured and you'd be too busy pissing yourself to even call me a bloody ambulance."

Lee's indignation bristled, but Kay responded dismissively. "Shush your noise Lee – I'm trying to watch the telly."

Lee's eyes looked across at the TV screen for the first time since he had come into the room. Kay was watching a cookery programme of some kind. Lee had to have that thought twice for it to register properly: Kay is watching a TV programme about cooking. She never did that – never in all the years he had known her. She never wanted to cook great food for Lee. So was this the turning-over of a new leaf? If not, then who was the intended recipient of her soon-to-be-discovered culinary skills?

"Anyway, why didn't you put your slippers on, you idiot? Then you wouldn't have fallen down the stairs."

Kay said this without taking her eyes from the TV screen. Lee watched her for a few seconds, trying to decipher from her eyes and her mannerisms whether she was hiding something. He was still watching her when she repeated herself, this time with rather more hostility in her voice:

"Well? Are you listening to me Lee? Why didn't you put your slippers on? It's not the first time you've come down the stairs like that, is it?"

She was looking straight at him now but though she was pursuing the conversation, something in the tone of her voice also suggested more than the usual indifference to something she considered trivial. And perhaps it was trivial. Lee shrugged unhappily, feeling despondent about this swift and bloodless defeat.

"I dunno," he ventured. "I didn't really think. My head fucking hurts."

"Oh well."

Kay seemed to consider the matter closed and was concentrating on the television once more. There was silence for several seconds, during which Lee built up reserves of animosity towards her. She serenely ignored him. It was so obvious, Lee silently seethed. There was a new man in her life; it was as obvious as the nose on her face. Then his anger broke out into the open.

"Cooking something nice for your new boyfriend then?"

That took her by surprise, he fancied. She had visibly flinched, but she recovered her poise quickly, and snapped back:

"What are you talking about Lee? Are you accusing me of cheating on you?"

"Well, something happened on Thursday night…"

"Oh, piss off. You knew that we had the work do and you knew that I was staying round Sara's. So if you don't believe me then you're calling me a liar."

"Well, it was very bloody convenient that Sara was asleep when I phoned wasn't it. And it was very bloody convenient that she had the day off on Friday according to you, so there was no point in me calling the office. We'll see, shall we – maybe I'll call on Monday and check it out."

Kay was unable to keep a lid on her anger now. "Lee, you really are an arsehole. You're making up lies to suit yourself now. Does it make you feel better because you're feeling guilty about being a complete shit for the last couple of years? Look! I'm still here, despite everything. I put up with you coming in at all times of the night with no explanation. I put up with you insulting me and ignoring me because of all the baby stuff. I put up with your mum looking down her snooty fucking nose at me for the same reason."

She ran out of breath. A second's worth of hefty silence passed. Lee took a nonchalant sip from his coffee.

"Looks like I hit a raw spot there dear."

"Oh fuck off. Just make it up to please yourself you pathetic child," Kay thundered again. Then she rushed past Lee, saying stroppily that she was getting dressed because she had shopping to do. Lee heard her run quickly up the stairs. He studied his coffee for a while, deep in thought. He was now convinced that there was something going on. He was sure that he had seen panic in her eyes, and her cheeks had burned red with guilt. How convenient it was that the human body should betray its master in such ways.

But the question remained that if she was seeing another man, who was it? She had the kind of job that brought her into contact with lots of people, so there were always possibilities there, and Lee wouldn't know any of these people. They rarely talked about her work, so his attempt to dredge up any names she might have mentioned frequently was fruitless.

She spent a lot of time working from home though, and that, now that Lee thought about it, was a perfect opportunity for her to be unfaithful. He was away in London, and she knew that he wouldn't be back until the evening. So it could be someone local. He wasn't aware of her being particularly friendly with anyone however. Maybe it was the postman or the window cleaner he thought, clichéd as those scenarios might be. He had to admit that he wasn't at home frequently enough to have any real idea.

Maybe it was someone they both knew, from amongst their circle of friends, he wondered. Most of those were already married. But Kay was a good looking woman, and men were, after all, men. There was Michael and Penny, who lived two doors along, but Lee couldn't see Kay with Michael. He was too much of a mouse, surely.

There were the football lads, who Kay knew to varying degrees, but she didn't really like those guys, apart from James maybe. Yes – apart from James. Lee let that idea percolate for a while. Well, it was possible he supposed, in that Kay and James got on well with each other, and James did some work from home occasionally as well. So in theory there might be opportunities for them to get together while Lee was working in London. This was his mate James though; they had been friends for years, and James wouldn't do that to him. He simply wouldn't.

Lee finished what remained of his coffee and rose from the armchair to grab hold of the TV remote control, which was on the sofa where Kay had left it. He switched the television channel onto a football highlights programme and stood watching for a few minutes, fists shoved into dressing gown pockets, before deciding it was time to get showered and dressed. He would get some breakfast – a serious fry up – at the greasy café down the road, and then he'd go to the pub and meet James.

Kay was sitting at her dresser doing her makeup when Lee wandered back into the bedroom having already set the shower running in the bathroom. He retrieved his slippers from beneath the bed and stood behind Kay as she pulled faces at the mirror, testing her lipstick, checking her eye shadow.

"I'm, er, meeting James for a few beers today," Lee began, sounding matter of fact. "We're going to watch the football and then there's egg-chasing tonight. It's the semi-final, England/France, if you fancy it. I know you like James."

Kay glared at him via the mirror in silence for a few seconds, her eyes studying his it seemed for clues; then she snapped her makeup case shut and hastily started gathering her things together to leave. Her face was flushed once more, and her brow was furrowed. He noticed that she avoided eye contact with him before leaving the room carrying her handbag and mobile phone.

"It's not funny Lee," she said quietly, sternly, from the doorway. "Don't make jokes out of these things."

Then she was gone. Lee stood for a while and looked from the mirror to the door and back, his mind trying to decipher what that episode had meant. Sometimes, he reflected, you just dangle a little bait, and you catch a bigger fish than you had bargained for.

The sound of running water intruded into his thoughts and reminded him that the shower was on. Interesting, he thought as he went through to the bathroom. His headache had disappeared now as well.

**

Kay was outside in a hurry, but once there she had no real idea where she was going. It was simply a huge relief just to get out of the house and away from her husband. She felt wearied by the emotional and professional tension that seemed to accompany her every day; and Lee's accusations, had he ever known it, were shocking both in their timing and in their uncomfortable accuracy. It seemed just a matter of time before he worked it out, or before some mistake gave the game away.

Facing that probability and its implications, for her and for James, filled Kay's heart with dread. She needed space to think, but her mind was in a complete fog as she walked into Hertford town centre and then roamed aimlessly around the shops.

First Lee, then James, and now Nick: it was becoming a horrendous mess. What did she want from any of these men? Eventually she grew tired of walking and sat down on the low white stone wall that surrounded the town's war memorial, set in the middle of a roughly triangular public area with shops and bars on all sides.

Cars and Saturday shoppers went by on their business but Kay was mostly oblivious to them. Her cheeks were wet with a few tears that had escaped, and she sucked in the fresh air, in the hope that it might help clear some kind of pathway for sensible thoughts. An elderly man who was walking past even stopped and asked her if she was okay, evidently because he saw the remnants of tears on her cheeks. Kay smiled weakly, thanked him, and blamed it on the wind making her eyes water. The old man hesitated but then moved on.

Every thought now came back to Nick. She hadn't spoken to him since leaving his flat on Friday morning. That was only a little over 24 hours earlier, but although she had said that she would call him on Sunday, that seemed an age away right now. Kay wanted to hear his voice; to take comfort from it. She needed to hear him again express the feelings he had shared with her in the small hours of Friday morning, and voice once more the future he hoped there would be for them. She needed it again because she had a hard decision to make.

She was part of the way there already: James, to her mind, was history. The feelings that she had imagined she had for him before Thursday night and Nick, were now completely dead. Their affair had mostly been about several moments of weakness when she had taken what attention was on offer because her husband offered none. If her expectations of what Nick represented to her were correct, then there was no requirement for James in her life any longer.

Telling James would be difficult though. She wanted to call him now and break the news, but he was about to meet her husband for a day of drinking, so this was actually about the worst possible moment to ditch him.

There was a chance that Lee might pummel the truth out of James if he followed up his earlier line of questioning, but Kay thought that unlikely. The two men's conversation wouldn't get much further today than the merits of the England team's back four, Kay reasoned, and James was too careful to let their secret slip by accident. There was plenty for him to lose as well. Kay accepted therefore that the moment to finish her affair with James would have to come on another day.

So the choice was Lee or Nick, and she put her mind diligently to that. It was true that with Lee she had a nice home, a good income, and every mod con that she could wish for, but that was about it. It was possible, she supposed, that one day they could reconcile their differences, but it seemed a very remote chance. If Kay's point of view never changed and they never had a child, she was sure that Lee would always hold that against her. He would keep it in his heart and let it eat away at him, and from time to time it would spring out at her, ugly and vicious. So really, the possibility of reconciliation was dependent upon Kay hearing her biological clock ticking, and feeling an urge to do something about it.

Just thinking about the concept of a biological clock made Kay bite her bottom lip with added unease. She had been keeping a secret to herself for a few days now. In the middle of all the recent goings-on in her life she had misplaced her contraceptive pills and missed out two consecutive days. It was very bad timing. Privately panicking, she had caught up again on Friday evening when the pills had turned up in the washing basket, but it was yet another thing to worry about.

There was nothing she could do about it now though. She just had to hope for luck. Kay buried that anxiety away again, smiling instead at thoughts of Nick. She resumed her assessment of the men in her life, and accepted that Nick would not be able to offer her all the trappings that she was accustomed to – at least not in the short term, in his present job. Kay believed he had more to offer though, and she intended to help him do that. Anyway, none of that mattered really, because her feelings towards him were deeper than any she had ever known.

It was all very simple. The world was full of romantic clichés such as pounding hearts, wobbly knees and gut wrenching butterflies, and Kay was feeling every single one of them as she thought about this man, right now, sitting on her own, with just a coldly indifferent monument to the town's war dead for company. Nick made her feel wanted in ways that Lee hadn't come close to for years, if ever. So the choice was either a life of happiness dressed in rags, or one of soulless, opulent misery. She had to smile at those melodramatic words; she should keep them for a press release some time.

But there was no way she could reasonably make a decision without seeing Nick again. At once it became a matter of urgency to call him; she was waiting for his voice to answer the ringing phone seconds later. As she waited, Kay also decided that she needed to get out of the centre of Hertford as well, since Lee and James might walk by at any minute, and Kay really didn't think she could face that.

She set off at a brisk pace, deliberately in the direction of Hertford North train station, which seemed the route least likely to cross the paths of Lee or James. After three or four rings of Nick's mobile phone he answered, and Kay had to smile at the instant warmth she felt course through her at the sound of his voice.

"Hello," Nick answered. "I was just thinking about you."

"Ahh, thank you. I couldn't wait until tomorrow. Can you talk?"

"Yeah, absolutely, I'm not up to much; just sitting around the flat, daydreaming."

"I see – what were you daydreaming about? Was it clean or filthy? There is a right and a wrong answer by the way."

"It was pretty raunchy stuff Kay. I'd better not repeat it in case someone is listening. In fact, it was so hot that the phone could easily melt in your hand."

She giggled. "That was the correct answer darling. Sounds like you need me to come and help you out a bit."

"What, now?" He was laughing as well, she could hear.

"Uh-huh."

"Oh, you really are too good to be true. Go on then. Hurry up, I'm waiting."

It was all so easy. Twenty minutes later Kay was on a train into London, still on the phone to Nick, still laughing, and feeling more alive than she ever had in her life. Thoughts of opulent misery were forgotten more quickly than the unremarkable Hertfordshire towns that the train passed through on its route to the capital.

**

One of Kay's situations came to a head the very next day. Before that however, she'd had to endure a torrid night of fear and alarm, having returned home from Nick's during the evening. She had still been awake, lying in bed, happily contemplating the last few hours with Nick in Camden, and regretting the necessity of having had to return to Hertford, when Lee staggered home in the early hours. Kay heard a crash as he tripped over the doorstep and fell through the front door. She murmured a quiet prayer that he wouldn't come up to bed in that state.

Kay had squeezed her eyes shut and tried to find sleep, but occasional sounds had carried up the stairs, keeping her nerves on edge. Lee had knocked some things over, had been sick in the toilet, and then she had heard him move back into the front room, after which all went quiet. By then it was 2am, she saw from the bedside clock. God had answered her prayers it seemed, and sent Lee into slumber; she thanked the Lord for listening to her, even though she called upon him so infrequently.

After a while, though, she had started to hear more small sounds. It was an odd whimpering noise, as a dog that was locked inside a room might make while pawing at the door.

The sound came again, unmistakeably. It had taken Kay a few seconds to realise what the noise was, and it made her shudder: Lee was crying downstairs. He had been out drinking with James all day, and now he was downstairs snivelling this strangely haunting sound, punctuated now by occasional random shouted obscenities. She couldn't be sure what it meant, but it wasn't likely to be good.

Instant dread sent killer butterflies fluttering in mad disorder inside her tummy. It couldn't have been the sport that was causing the tears: England had won the football match and had then won the rugby match as well to reach the World Cup Final. Lee should have been cock-a-hoop. Kay had even seen some of the football match herself at Nick's, who she had discovered had only an armchair interest in the game. But even if the sport had gone badly, surely not even Lee was immature enough to cry about it, Kay reasoned.

No alternative scenarios sprang to mind however, so perhaps Lee had challenged James about having an affair with his wife, and it had all come out in the open. Kay shrivelled at the thought of that. God only knew what might happen next if that was what had happened, she thought. Sleep was out of the question now anyway, just in case she needed to defend herself. A longing for the protection that Nick would have given was inevitable.

The night had dragged on for Kay, with the stillness of her room frequently shattered by the sounds from downstairs. She felt pinned to the bed, her muscles frozen in suspense, fearing that the slightest move would betray her presence. Eventually, the noises had died away, and the most welcome snores she had ever heard had replaced them. Kay started to breathe easier once more, and soon she also had slept at last.

The memory of the night's fear came back to her as soon as she opened her eyes on Sunday morning. She found however that when she eventually steeled herself for the confrontation and crept down the stairs, Lee was not there. He was nowhere to be seen. Kay still hadn't seen him by the time her mobile phone rang as she worked through her ironing during the afternoon. It was James, and she answered the call.

"Hi James," she said, struggling to inject some enthusiasm into her voice. She wasn't prepared for the riposte however.

"Kay – what the fuck have you told Lee?"

"Sorry? I haven't…"

"You must have said something cos he got pissed and started asking me questions yesterday."

"What? You didn't tell him did you?"

"No, of course not, you stupid cow. But he's become a very suspicious man for some reason."

Kay's mind raced. She couldn't think of the right thing to say so after a pause, James carried on speaking: "Why would he suspect anything Kay? Why would he? If you haven't said anything, and I certainly fucking haven't, then why would Lee give me all that shit yesterday? Tell me that."

James's voice had an unusually aggressive edge to it, which was impossible to miss; he hadn't told her everything yet, it transpired:

"Then, when we left the pub and we went to the kebab shop, he was still giving me a load of abuse about you, and I was saying 'come off it Lee, I wouldn't do that to a mate'. I was shitting myself. But he just lost it. We were in the queue and he started swinging at me. I took one in the mouth and we had a wrestle, and then some blokes started pulling him off me, and he went fucking mad; started on them, whacked a couple of them, and then he legged it out of the shop, and I haven't seen or heard from him since."

"Oh my God…" Kay sat down unsteadily.

"Is he there? Did he come home last night?" James continued.

Kay tried to get her thoughts together quickly. "Er, yeah. I mean, no, he's not here. I haven't seen him today; he'd already gone out before I got up this morning, but I heard him come in at about two this morning. He was sick downstairs and then he fell asleep on the settee, so I didn't know about any of this."

"Well, you'd best get hold of him pretty fucking quick girl. He's losing the plot about something. And by the way, you can count me out of this thing now. I've had it."

"What do you mean 'count you out'?"

"This thing: me and you, Kay. It's over. Fuck it, I don't need the grief any more. It was fun while it lasted but bollocks to all that. Thanks but no thanks."

"So that's it?" Kay could scarcely believe her luck.

"Don't try and change my mind Kay."

"I'm not…"

"We're finished. Don't keep phoning or texting me, cos I won't answer…"

Kay suddenly shouted: "James!"

He finally fell silent, and then she spoke more calmly, but with a sense of satisfaction that was deeper than he could ever have imagined: "Right, thank you. James, I won't keep chasing you – I promise. It was never all that anyway. Now piss off out of my life. Bye."

She snapped the phone shut, hearing just the first syllable of what was perhaps a word of protest from James before he was cut off. Kay put the phone back on the table and resumed her ironing with added vigour. After a minute she stopped again and looked over at the mobile phone. What if James phoned back? She would ignore it. In fact, she decided, she would delete his number right now to prove that to herself. He was forgotten already. That task done, she turned up the volume on the radio, went back to the ironing board, stretched a blouse across it, and with the iron smoothing out the creases, and the radio blaring out pop music, Kay set her vocal talents to work.

**

Another week shining shoes had gone by, and it had been a frustrating week. It was Tuesday evening again, and Nick had time to reflect as he stood and waited. It had seemed as if his life was on hold since the moment that Kay had left his flat on the previous Saturday evening.

She had paid him for the coming Tuesday that day, adding another £50 to the usual £100 because she wanted Nick to do more, to go further; she wanted him to wait outside Lee's office and then follow him wherever the journey took them.

Nick had done exactly that, and so it was that, after a brisk walk back into Liverpool Street Station, following Lee closely, and then about 45 minutes sitting on a train, watching Lee like a hawk from the far end of the train carriage, both men had arrived at Hertford East station. It was the end of the line and everyone alighted. Nick continued to follow Lee as he walked for another five minutes through streets that Nick had never seen before. Eventually, Lee had walked up to and entered a smart looking terraced house with a white door. He hadn't needed to knock to get in because he used a key taken from his pocket to open the door.

Nick's sinking feeling had started some time before that, in truth – even before the train had reached Hertford in fact. As Nick then dallied on the corner of the street, looking with a mixture of curiosity and dark humour at that same closed white door, the situation had seemed pretty clear: whatever it was that Kay had suspected Lee might be getting up to on this particular night was clearly not happening. He had just gone home instead. Nick imagined that the pair of them were probably arguing behind that door right at that moment.

So he had swiftly moved back around the corner, out of sight of the house, and sniggered to himself – a reaction triggered as much by helplessness as anything else. It was possible, he supposed, that this house with the white door wasn't the same house that Lee and Kay shared, but the odds certainly suggested that it was. Nick had taken his mobile phone from his pocket and started composing a rueful text message to Kay.

He had only managed to tap in a few words though, asking what colour her front door was, when he was surprised to find

Kay standing there in front of him, smiling sheepishly. They had laughed at each other, savouring the silliness of the situation, before she kissed his cheek and led him away from the house and back towards the train station, still chuckling.

"Oh well," she began. "Sorry about that Nick. How silly do I feel now?"

"Not half as silly as me I reckon. Nice place you've got there by the way."

She had explained that she couldn't stay out for long, since she had made up an excuse to Lee about needing to visit the local shop for some bits and pieces, just so that she could escape from the house for a few minutes. She had guessed that Nick would be outside somewhere.

"You're welcome to take in the sights of Hertford while you're here if you like – it won't take long," Kay had laughed. "Or you can get the next train back home and enjoy the rest of your evening. I am so sorry that I wasted your time babe."

They were already nearly back at the train station, and Nick had stopped on the opposite side of the road to the station entrance, and turned to face Kay.

"Come back with me," he had said. "It's driving me insane knowing you're in the same house as him." Kay had hugged him briefly, and then pulled away.

"Nick I'd love to, but you know full well that I can't. Anyway, I have to get up early tomorrow to get the Eurostar to Paris, so I need an early night."

Nick raised an eyebrow: "Romantic break?"

"Ha, ha. No, just work. I'll save the romantic one for us, I promise."

They had talked and laughed for a couple of minutes, and then with a kiss and another apology, she was gone. Nick was lucky with the trains, and had only needed to wait for five minutes before one left for London. He had looked at his watch, and chuckled again: he'd been in Hertford for less than 30 minutes. Well, at least there had been the consolation of having seen Kay.

Nick had received a few text messages from Kay during her Paris trip, and he had heard even more from Justine, who sounded bright and happy. It was maddening. One woman was in Australia, another was in France; Nick had felt in a bizarre kind of limbo, with guilt pulling at one arm, and desire at the other.

Those feelings had remained with him throughout the weekend that followed, until Sunday night, when Kay called Nick on her mobile phone, breathlessly marching around the streets of Hertford in a state of panic. She felt unwell, and she'd had to get out of the house, she explained. Lee was indoors and seemed to be going completely off the rails; Nick learned then that Lee had even beaten up one of his best friends the weekend before. Kay said she needed some respite and needed to hear Nick's voice again. He had heard shakiness in her voice.

"Something is about to happen; something terrible," she had said. "He's in a right state. He can't keep still; he's pacing around the house, being nasty to me, shouting at me, at himself, at the walls at times; just weird, horrible insults at no-one in particular. Then he'll go quiet for a while, but his hands are all over the place. He can't keep them still, for fidgeting. The thing is, it's not like an unhappy state he's in. It's almost…well it's like he's excited about something; like he's building himself up for something."

"Have you asked him about it?" Nick had asked.

"Yeah, of course. But he's not telling me anything. No surprises there I suppose. The way he's been tonight though, I think whatever it is, is happening very soon."

"So you want me to follow him again."

"I promise you Nick, this will be the last time I ask you to do this for me."

"And what if nothing happens again? What then?"

Kay gave a nervy, uncertain laugh: "Well…I'd better not promise I suppose. I don't want to do this Nick but it's scary at the moment."

"I just want to know what's happening Kay. We said the other night about there being no secrets, but I get the feeling there are lots of things you haven't told me yet and I've hardly seen you all week. It's killing me."

"I know, I know. It's killing me too. I will tell you everything when the time is right, but I don't even know what's really happening yet. Look, I'd better go back now babe, even though I'm scared out of my mind."

Nick had heard real fear in her words, and he had pleaded with her to come down to London instead. She had insisted on staying in Hertford though. Nick had slept badly that night, continually fretting about the situation.

And now here he was, two days later, at just before 5.30 on Tuesday evening, leaning once more against the same wall outside Lee's offices where he had waited a week before; tall, plush office buildings reared up on every side of him, and the wall surrounding the Broadgate Circle's central ice skating rink was several metres away in front of him.

He had money in his pocket, delivered to him the previous morning by a pensive looking Kay; he had a job to do for her and he was prepared to travel for it. He didn't know where to, and he didn't know why. He couldn't even quite decide whether he might prefer another wild goose chase to Hertford like the week before, rather than whatever it was that Kay feared was about to happen.

To Nick's mind, Lee's behaviour didn't suggest another woman was involved. This situation seemed more sinister now. Nick could only swallow hard and wonder what was about to happen.

About thirty metres away to his left was the entrance to the building where Lee Talbot worked, and Nick had his eyes focused on that entrance, watching for his man to emerge. Quite frequently, small groups of office workers or single individuals walked out and headed off for the train home, or the gym, or a local pub. Not for the first time, Nick questioned the sanity of the situation he found himself in: Super Sleuth Nick. It was a ridiculous concept.

However, he told himself that this watching duty was for Kay, and his loyalty would be rewarded eventually, with the full story of Lee and Kay, and more importantly with Kay at his side for good. Now that idea made it all worthwhile. It was now nearly two weeks since they had first got together after the Bierfest, and Nick felt as if he was still in a dream world.

Nick watched as a gaggle of office workers came out through the glass doors of Lee's building, noisily laughing as they walked across a short stretch of paving, and then down some steps to the left that led towards Liverpool Street Station. Nick's eyes settled on each of them in turn, ruling them out one after another; Lee wasn't one of them. He relaxed once more against one of the reddish stone pillars that shielded Nick from view of the office entrance. His eyes remained trained on the glass doors.

Next, a couple of young guys came out, larking about. One ruffled the other's hair, and the second one instantly set off in pursuit of his friend, chasing him around a big black metallic sculpture – a hare leaping over a bell that was lying on its side – which was set into the paving stones outside the building. The sound of their laughter and pounding steps rang clear, echoing around the tall office blocks that enclosed the Broadgate Circle.

Neither of the two guys were Lee, and Nick had time to wonder, just as he had been doing a week before, what the point of the sculpture was. The two work friends soon headed off, still hooting with mirth as they went. Nick glanced at his watch: it was gone 5.30 now; Lee was going to miss his normal train unless he got a serious move on. Nick felt his tummy tighten uncomfortably with nerves at that thought. Perhaps Lee did have different plans; perhaps something really would happen tonight.

Nick tried to focus on looking out for Lee again, but it seemed all too easy for his mind to wander, just standing there, hiding behind a wall, and feeling foolish. The events of the previous few weeks ensured that there were many things to occupy Nick's mind and distract him from diligently maintaining his vigil outside the office.

There was Kay and all that she had become in his life: the first meeting, the unusual approach to him, and the task she had set him; the nights out, the text messages; the infatuation that had taken root and flowered, despite the insistence in his own mind that it was doomed to wither and die; all of that leading up to those still incredible moments on London Bridge and after – the moments that had proved him rapturously wrong in his pessimism.

Then there was Justine. The thought of her engendered a kind of hollow regret; a sorrowful resignation that time and distance, and then unforeseen events, had overtaken something good and worthy; had made irrelevant what he had believed to be the defining, life-saving love of his life. So he'd been wrong about that too. Well, being wrong is part of what it means to be a man. Nick took some small solace from that idea.

What haunted him most was that he had stood at home on the afternoon of that Friday when Kay had first woken at the flat, and he had held his ringing mobile phone in his hand, looking at Justine's name flashing on the display as the phone rang, and he had just watched it ring until the voicemail took over and the ringtone ceased.

He hadn't been ready at that point to get through a conversation with Justine; he could still smell Kay's perfume on his dressing gown, and his mind was still doing somersaults about what had just happened. He had laid down on the bed that had barely cooled from Kay leaving, and he had noticed a long, dark hair on Justine's pillow; it could only have belonged to Kay. He just could not bring himself to speak to Justine yet. It caused him to shake his head in dismay.

When he did speak to Justine the following day and on the occasions since then, she sounded happier but had little that was new to report. In contrast, Nick had all too much to talk about, but since he was living in Justine's flat, he reckoned that this would be a bad time to break that particular piece of news.

With a start, Nick realised that he had been distracted from the job in hand yet again. He tried to recall the faces of the people that had left the building in the last few minutes and found that he really had no clear idea. Nick swore harshly under his breath and hoped desperately that he hadn't missed Lee's departure. What a joke that would be. Well actually, on reflection, it wouldn't be very funny if Nick had to report that back to Kay. She was the boss. He watched the glass doors again with renewed alertness.

A few minutes went by, and Nick could feel impatience beginning to sap his concentration once more. Then a large bunch of people – perhaps ten altogether – came into view, walking through the reception area of the building. There seemed to be a good deal of gaiety in their general demeanour as they progressed slowly towards the door.

Nick tried to pick out each in turn so that he could rule them out. As the first of the group reached the glass doors and stepped outside, their chatter suddenly becoming audible to Nick, he noticed that one of the group, a man, had slowed down at the rear, and was now standing still, seemingly talking to a security guard by the reception desk, while the group went on ahead without him.

Although this man had his back to Nick, he had seen him frequently enough now to know exactly who he was. It was Lee. As Nick realised this, he saw the man raise a hand towards the group of people spilling out onto the pavement ahead of him. A couple of them had stopped in the doorway and turned back to face Lee; others, presumably oblivious to the delay, just carried on walking away from the building, talking amongst themselves.

Nick didn't hear what was said, but those who had stopped in the entrance soon continued on their way, leaving Lee still in the reception area with the security guard. Nick's feeling of relief that Lee had not escaped unnoticed while he had been daydreaming, was soon tempered by a new thought: this was it; now the job began properly.

It took only a few seconds, but Lee seemed to just wait until the others started descending the steps that led towards the train station, before making his own way towards the door. It was as if he had been stalling for time, and deliberately putting space between himself and his friends. By the time he had reached the doors, all of them had disappeared from sight.

Then Lee was through the doors and walking. From thirty metres away Nick gulped nervously and stepped out of his cover to follow. Lee walked only a few paces though, then stopped and checked his wrist watch. The action forced Nick also to stop, and he turned instinctively away as if that would prevent him from being seen by Lee. His heart suddenly pounding, he glanced over his left shoulder and saw that Lee was again moving, walking towards the steps, but at a deliberately slow speed.

Feeling exposed, but not wanting to lose contact amidst the hundreds of people that would be milling around Liverpool Street Station, Nick measured his own speed across the open space of the Broadgate Circle against Lee's dawdling pace. Lee reached the top of the grey stone steps and stopped for a moment, before slipping quickly down the first few and disappearing from Nick's sight. That was the cue for Nick to rush forward himself, past the sculpture of the bell and hare, to quickly reach the top of the steps and ensure that he saw which direction Lee took.

Having reached the top of the steps, Nick saw that Lee had crossed over a small open space that had another sculpture in the middle – a tall construction that looked like five huge, rusty metal planks standing on their ends and leaning haphazardly against each other. Lee was beyond the sculpture, walking more quickly now, and mounting more grey steps beyond. Nick was on the move again as well, thinking that Lee could be heading for Moorgate. At the top of the next set of steps, Lee went to his right along Eldon Street and away from Liverpool

Street Station, and Nick fancied that he might be proved right about Moorgate. No train home to the wife in Hertford tonight for Lee then.

Feeling a smile that he put down to unexpected excitement spreading across his face, Nick dropped into line behind the swaying figure of Lee, who now seemed to be straining at the leash as he ploughed through the streams of oncoming commuters that were heading towards Liverpool Street Station. At this end of Eldon Street, there were some road works underway; the road surface was dug up in places, and these areas were sealed off by metal wire fences. Several vans belonging to the workmen were parked here, blocking the road to traffic, but not to people on foot.

Further along, after a pedestrian crossing which Nick could see they were quickly approaching, the road widened. Nick was surprised though when suddenly he saw Lee step quickly to his right just before the pedestrian crossing and apparently go through a doorway. Hurrying forward, the reason soon became clear: it was a pub called the Red Lion, and Nick could see Lee standing at the bar, only yards away from him.

Not wanting to stop suddenly and get in the way of commuters walking behind him, Nick walked on past the pub, and turned immediately right afterwards, into another road that joined Eldon Street. There was less pedestrian traffic here, and he was able to stop and think, to quickly assess what he should do next. Should he go into the pub himself? Should he hang back out here, keeping Lee in sight until he left the pub? That could be in several hours' time though, for all that Nick knew. His lack of forethought about what to do in certain scenarios was becoming uncomfortably apparent.

Without having really decided anything, Nick re-joined the flow of people towards Liverpool Street, walking back past the pub, and then crossing to the other side of Eldon Street before stopping near a shop doorway. From here, he could still see Lee, leaning against the bar, with a near full pint glass in one hand. Lee's face betrayed nothing in particular, but he drank the lager quickly, taking a couple of long pulls almost immediately, after which half of it was gone.

There was no sign of enjoyment as he did so. Watching him, Nick got the feeling that this was just a short stop on the way to somewhere else. He knelt down to fiddle with his shoes and waste a few seconds, and then after standing upright again, looked into the shop window next to him for a few more vacant seconds.

When he turned round again, Lee was looking into his glass, and contemplating the last mouthful. Almost the entire pint had gone down in not much more than a minute, Nick reckoned. Then the glass was empty. Lee put it back on the bar, wiped his mouth with the back of his hand, and immediately headed for the door of the pub. Nick made himself appear busy, reaching into an inside pocket of his coat as if looking for something, but out of the corner of his eye he saw Lee cross over Eldon Street to the side where Nick was standing, and then continue walking in the direction of Moorgate. The chase was back on. Nick followed, matching Lee's brisk pace as closely as he could.

At the end of Eldon Street was a set of traffic lights controlling vehicle access to Moorgate itself, which crossed the top of Eldon Street to left and right. Lee and his pursuer closed rapidly on the intersection. Nick saw Lee reach the junction and turn left, towards the entrance to Moorgate tube station. He couldn't be sure that the station was actually Lee's destination though, so Nick hurried to the junction and, looking left, saw the back of Lee's black raincoat again – probably only 15 paces away now.

Nick made after him, ensuring that the gap between them remained constant. A few seconds later, and Nick watched as Lee veered left, and disappeared from view. It was the entrance to the tube station. Nick hurried forward again, urgently aware that it would be very easy to lose Lee now, somewhere in the labyrinth of platforms, passageways and escalators of Moorgate tube station.

Reaching the entrance himself, Nick skipped swiftly down a flight of eight or ten steps, then another flight at 90 degrees to the right, this one of just a few steps, and then a third flight, this one at another 90 degrees to his right. He was now under ground, and the gathering dusk out in the street was replaced by fluorescent light, the sound of traffic by the clumsy metallic clanking sound of ticket barriers opening and closing; voices suddenly seemed amplified away from the traffic above, and distant squeaks and whines told of trains arriving and leaving the station.

All of this was only dimly registered by Nick; they were sights and sounds that might come back to him in the days ahead, if ever he cared to think about it. He certainly appreciated the extra light that the station afforded, since that helped in his task of more immediate urgency: finding Lee Talbot once again. Right then, a jolting realisation came to Nick. He might well see Lee heading off in some direction or other, but he had no idea actually where Lee was going, and nor did Nick have a ticket to get through the barriers. Was he prepared to jump them? That would attract attention and delay, maybe bigger problems; that was the last thing Nick wanted.

This thought stopped him in his tracks, confused, standing in the middle of a white tiled area where the station entrance opened out into the interior. Ticket barriers were to his immediate right. A tiled wall with two cash machines built into it and various advertising posters mounted upon it was straight ahead. Between the ticket barriers and the cash machines was a ticket hall with some narrow serving windows that Nick hoped were manned. To the left of the cash machines a short corridor led to another row of ticket barriers.

For a second Nick felt completely lost. He looked around, taking in these details, but all the while searching for a sight of Lee in his long coat. He was nowhere to be seen. Nick felt panic begin to take over from what had been reasonably composed haste until that point. This situation was slipping from his grasp, and he cursed in frustration.

Just then he heard a voice, behind him and to his left, saying a few curt, economical words: "Just that mate, yeah."

Nick spun round in the direction of the voice and saw that there was a small kiosk just inside the entrance to the tube station, which he had walked straight past as he entered, without even noticing. Lee Talbot hadn't walked past it though. He was inside buying something – a newspaper maybe, or perhaps some confectionery. Anyway, that didn't matter. What mattered was that Nick had not lost his quarry just yet.

Nick grasped at this second chance with sudden clarity of thought. Buy a ticket, any ticket – just anything to get through the barriers, and then he could deal with the next development as and when that revealed itself. There wasn't much time however; Lee was just about to pay for his purchase, and then he'd be out of the kiosk and probably moving quickly again. So Nick needed to move quickly himself, and buy that ticket while keeping an eye on the kiosk door so that he would see Lee come out.

He dashed forward into the ticket office area. To the side of the manned counters were several ticket-dispensing machines. He headed towards them and, with frequent distracted looks over his right shoulder to watch for Lee, he started pressing buttons. There wasn't time now for deliberation; he found himself buying a return ticket to Kings Cross, and had no idea what had driven him to that decision, other than that it had quickly caught his eye as an option on the screen.

The electronic display of the machine showed him the amount of money required. He saw the number just a second after catching sight of Lee leaving the kiosk and walking briskly out of Nick's line of sight, and behind the wall that housed the cash machines. So Lee was now directly behind Nick, and out of his line of sight. There were ticket barriers around that side as well, Nick knew, so perhaps Lee was heading towards those. That probably ruled out one or two possibilities as to his destination, if only Nick had the time to work them out.

With clumsy fingers, Nick pulled a note out of his wallet and fed it into the machine, seething with impatience as the machine went about its business of printing a ticket and delivering Nick's change in its own sweet time. Now Nick was looking anxiously over his other shoulder, to his left, hoping to see Lee re-appear from behind the wall, having gone through the ticket barriers and then heading for one tube line or another. A couple of times Nick's eyes flicked from the ticket machine to that area behind his left shoulder where he hoped that Lee would appear; back and forth like a spectator at a tennis match, transfixed by a rally.

And suddenly there was Lee – in exactly the place where Nick was looking. He was striding on towards a sign for the Circle, District and Hammersmith & City Line platforms. At the ticket machine a light was flashing in the receptacle where the tickets and change had finally been delivered. Nick grabbed the contents without checking them and rushed to his left, to the nearest ticket barrier.

Then he was through and there was Lee, now heading down some steps that were situated before the eastbound platform. Nick gave a silent word of thanks, which was in no way proportionate to the thrill of excitement that flooded his veins. He had kept his target in view through that tricky passage of time. He realised suddenly, with surprise, that he was actually enjoying himself.

Despite his haste, Nick had the presence of mind to read the sign that was positioned above the stairway that Lee had gone down, and which Nick himself was about to descend. The sign told him that this was the way for trains to Bedford, and for travellers wanting the westbound Hammersmith & City, Metropolitan and Circle lines. Nick scanned the words hastily, on the move, and then the sign was behind him as he moved quickly on.

Lee was now out of his sight again, so Nick moved quickly through a short labyrinth of stairs and left and right turns that first went below platform level, and then climbed again. Not once did he see Lee during these moments because the sequence of turns and the distance between Nick and his target, kept Lee frustratingly out of view. At least Nick could be certain that he was still on Lee's trail though, since there was no option for either of them but to follow this passageway through to the end, or to turn back – and Lee certainly hadn't done that.

When he reached the ascending steps at the far end, Nick took these two at a time, hoping to glimpse Lee once more. He reached the top of the steps, and there was a platform almost straight ahead, dotted with waiting commuters, another of whom rushed past him from behind as a tube train came thundering into the station.

There was no sign of Lee on the platform though. Nick had stopped walking at the top of the steps and he now noticed that to his left there was another platform, this one with a stationary train at it already. It was the start and end of the line, he realised, since the train was at the buffers, 20 metres away to Nick's left.

More importantly, there was Lee – swaggering along past the rear of the train, and then swinging right to walk along the platform itself. The stationary train was now between Nick and Lee and hid him from Nick's view. Nick set off in pursuit and immediately collided with another commuter that had reached the top of the stairs, but who was sprinting for the tube train that had just pulled in on the platform to Nick's right.

Neither man stopped to apologise, or even to curse the other. The guy just wanted to get home no doubt. Nick certainly couldn't imagine that the man would be on the same kind of mission as himself – chasing a near stranger through the streets of London to who knew where, all for the love of a woman. There wasn't really even time to dwell upon it. He ran, and in seconds Nick had reached the buffers at the rear of Lee's train. This train, he guessed, was a train to Bedford, or at least it was part of that service. It was certainly different rolling stock to the usual tube trains.

Nick slowed once more to walking pace, and strode along the side of the train, with Lee again in his sights, walking just ten or fifteen metres ahead, hands shoved in coat pockets, collar upturned. Now that he had Lee in front of him again, Nick felt at liberty to relax a little.

It occurred to Nick that if anyone had been following him for the last few minutes, his behaviour would have appeared erratic to say the least: brisk walks, followed by sudden bursts of more speed; mystifying abrupt stops, and even a full-on sprint just then, for the 20 metres from the top of the stairs to the start of the train platform. It would all have seemed very odd, of that there was no doubt. No-one was immediately behind him though. It was just him and Lee for the moment.

By now Lee had walked most of the way to the front of the train, and he suddenly hopped on through an open door. Nick, watching, marked the doorway in question in his mind. It was the first one after the join between two carriages, and Nick was currently two doors further back.

He walked on for a few seconds. Lee's door was now the next ahead. There was a sudden beeping sound from the train to indicate that the doors were about to close; it hadn't even occurred to him to check what time the train was due to leave. Now he was midway between two doors, as far from either as he could possibly be; realising that he was struggling to reach the door in time, another surge of panic propelled him into a desperate sprint for the doorway ahead of him, swearing viciously under his breath at the bad luck, the sheer injustice of it all; that having done so well to stick with Lee until this point, he would now be undone by something as stupid as a sliding door closing shut when he was too far away to reach it.

He saw the doors begin to slide towards each other, seemingly in slow motion, as he ran towards them; a moment later he was somehow squeezing between and then beyond the rapidly converging doors before they met with a clunk behind him, and he was in the train carriage, suddenly acutely aware of the need to appear neither flustered nor at all inconvenienced.

Just sit down nice and quietly as if nothing untoward had happened, Nick told himself. He couldn't just sit anywhere though, and most of all he fervently desired not to sit too close to Lee.

He looked to his right, then left, and saw Lee out of the corner of his eye in that direction; he was sitting on a seat in the middle of the carriage, next to a window, and facing towards the rear of the train, which also meant that he was facing towards where Nick was standing. Lee had picked up a discarded newspaper though, and he wasn't paying attention to anything in the carriage around him, least of all the man that had just bundled noisily through the closing doors.

Relaxing again, Nick moved to his right, and sat in a part of the carriage where the doors were between he and Lee, but facing in Lee's direction, so that Nick could keep watch through the glass partitions and above the seat tops that separated them. From here he could see the top of Lee's head, and that was enough as far as he was concerned.

Nick slumped back in the seat and started to breathe more easily. He started to take stock of his surroundings. To his surprise, the train was only sparsely occupied by fellow passengers – there were probably only about ten or twelve people in the entire carriage, he reckoned. The train was moving now, pulling slowly forward into a dark tunnel. After the panic and near-disaster of almost missing the train, all was now peaceful. Nick couldn't hear a word being spoken; all the people within his field of view seemed to have their heads bowed down, concentrating on newspapers or books, or just dozing.

Nick had nothing of his own to read, having left his paper-back book with his shoe shining kit, but there were a few crumpled newspapers left on the seats around him, and he thought about picking one up – it seemed like it was the right thing to do, to fit in somehow with everyone else on the train. He left the newspapers where they were though; a sense of nervous anticipation, of being seriously keyed up for something, made him doubt that he could concentrate on reading a newspaper right then.

Instead he tried to relax, while keeping an eye on the top of Lee's head from a distance. There was a sudden splash of light outside as the train burst out of the tunnel. Its speed wasn't great though and it was moving slowly enough for Nick to read the name of the station that it now passed through: Barbican. The train didn't stop though. It kept moving and then plunged into another black tunnel.

A minute or two later the train did come to a halt. The doors opened at Farringdon, and Nick concentrated harder on the part of Lee's head that he could see. There was no movement; barely even a turn of the head to look out of the window. Half a dozen or so people entered the carriage, and one sat down close to Nick – an old guy with a beard and spectacles, who smiled thinly at Nick as he moved a discarded newspaper so that he could sit on the seat he wanted: a rare moment of human contact between strangers on London's transport system.

The doors closed and the train pulled away again, picking up speed through another tunnel, then a deserted, disused station. Yet another tunnel then closed over the train, followed shortly after by the sudden glare of more lights, brighter than either Barbican or Farringdon had been, and looking to his left Nick saw a wide, bright, modern-looking platform. He read the station name: St Pancras International. He'd never been here before. It was quite a new development, as the station had been upgraded so that Eurostar services could run from there into mainland Europe. Nick had heard from one of his customers that it was pretty smart.

Nick dragged his eyes away from the window to watch Lee as the train rolled to a stop. Suddenly, Lee got to his feet and started moving towards the door positioned between where he and Nick had been sitting. Nick registered this development calmly, surprising himself with his composure, as Lee walked straight towards him for a few paces, before reaching the door.

He stepped out, and Nick, who had remained seated until that moment so as not to attract Lee's attention, now sprung up out of his seat and followed him out of the door, pushing past a gaggle of people that were trying to board the train.

Half way along its length, the platform wall gave way to a wide exit, where there were two escalators. Lee was four or five yards ahead of Nick, walking quickly towards the upward escalator, and he continued walking despite having the moving stairway under his feet, taking the steps two at a time. Everything was a rush it seemed, but Nick matched Lee's speed, feeling uncomfortably aware that the two men were both moving much more quickly than anyone around them. He kept Lee in view through a network of brightly lit corridors, until they came to a line of ticket barriers. Seconds later they were both through the barriers and striding out into the evening air.

A drizzle had started, giving every surface a shiny coat. Lee hurried forward along the pavement at the side of the station, light grey paving stones glistening in the rain and the neon glare. He was heading towards a main road about two hundred metres ahead, and as he walked he pulled his coat tighter around himself to keep out the rain and wind. Nick, just five yards behind Lee, and looking grimly determined as he followed, did the same.

Chapter Seven

Kay felt sick, and had done for a couple of days now. For a while she had kidded herself that it was fear and worry, engendered by Lee's odd behaviour. That self-delusion had now worn off. She had done some work at home during the day, but an overpowering tiredness was upon her and she found that the need to lie down came frequently, bringing all working activity to a halt. Most of the afternoon in fact, she had lay upon her bed, arms wrapped around her stomach, feeling woozy and nauseous, her mind whirling like the spinning reels of a fruit machine jammed on constant play. She couldn't believe it; refused to.

Now evening was falling, and Kay was curled up, exhausted, teary-eyed, in front of the TV. There was nothing in particular on the television to watch, and she scarcely even listened to the sound. She was lost in thought; confused about her feelings, and about the sheer momentousness of everything that was happening to her.

Nick was only a phone call away, but she left her mobile phone untouched by her side. She was sure that he would be in touch at some point during the evening, with news about her husband. It was early yet though – only 6pm. Just the act of thinking about those two men, Nick and Lee, made tears well up in her eyes. Kay wanted all of this to be over. She wanted to be away from this place for good, but things just seemed to be getting increasingly complicated; the unknowns more immense and more frightening. She wished fervently that she had not put Nick in this position, because she had no idea what might happen. He might get hurt because of her. It was another thing to worry about.

What she needed now was courage, and not the kind that came from the lower reaches of a bottle of Merlot. Earlier in the day, Kay had roused herself to walk down to the town centre and had bought a few bits and pieces from the super-market and the pharmacy. Not everything that she had bought was now packed away in the fridge freezer or in her toiletry cabinet though. She had left one item untouched in a white plastic bag in the kitchen. Somehow she had to summon up the nerve to do something about it now.

Kay wept for several minutes, shaking gently as tears flood-ed her eyes and streaked her cheeks.

A little later she felt ready – as ready as she ever would, at any rate. She was resolved to do it now, and then maybe she could begin clearing away some of the dark clouds around her head. That prospect did at least make her eyes shine with a little pinch of tired hope. She switched off the TV set. It was surplus to requirements anyway. Swinging her legs down from the sofa, Kay hesitated – couldn't move again for more seconds; the enormity of the moment had stopped her in her tracks once more, testing her will.

She was just about ready to stand up and go into the kitch-en, to do this thing, when the mobile phone started to ring. Looking down she saw that it was Nick calling. God, what timing, she thought. Momentarily, Kay was torn between answering the call from Nick and taking advantage of her newly-found resolve to act; it could ebb quickly away again if she didn't do it now. But it was Nick calling, after all.

She picked up the phone and pressed the button to accept the call.

"Hello baby," she said. Everything else could wait.

**

In common with most cities of the world, London is able to offer any thirsty visitor a warm, Gaelic welcome, through the Irish-themed public houses that never seem to be far away, wherever you are.

Nick found himself sitting in one such pub, just five minutes after following Lee out of St Pancras station. They had walked along the side of the station, reached a main road and then turned right, walking away, Nick saw, from Kings Cross station, which was next to St Pancras. They crossed the main road at some traffic lights, and Nick had watched as Lee then went into this pub, which was on the corner of a side road that Nick saw was called Judd Street.

Nick had decided to wait for a couple of minutes before following Lee into the pub. It was a gamble of sorts, since he couldn't know if Lee intended walking in one door and then walking straight out of another door, perhaps out of Nick's sight. Having watched him demolish a pint in quick time not long before however at the pub near Moorgate, Nick reckoned it was more likely that Lee was here for at least one drink. He did not want to run the risk of being noticed by Lee, by walking into the pub directly behind him and then vying with him for attention at the bar.

So Nick had kicked his heels for a couple of minutes, watching the ebb and flow of traffic. Then he had gone into the pub. It wasn't brightly lit, apart from at the bar itself at the far end. Around the three other walls were several tall-legged tables and stools. There was also a raised dining area with tables and chairs, which Nick saw to his left as he came in. In the corner, right by the door, were some games machines, and it was from here that Nick had heard a voice that he recognised as soon as he walked into the pub. The voice came from behind his left shoulder, but he didn't need to turn around to know that it was Lee, uttering an expletive and then laughing. Nick had kept walking until he reached the bar, before taking the opportunity to look around at his new surroundings.

And then he had seen Lee, standing in that corner by the door with a drink in his hand, looking at the screen of one of the machines, with another man by his side. They were laughing about something. Nick had ordered a bottle of lager from a young guy with a wispy beard and eager eyes who was serving at the bar. Carrying his beer, Nick had then looked around for a suitable table from which to unobtrusively watch Lee and his new companion. He had soon found such a position, at one of the high-legged tables by the windows that faced out to the main road outside. From here he had a clear view of the two men.

They were playing some sort of quiz machine he could see, and were laughing loudly and frequently. What next, Nick wondered to himself? How long would they be here? Nick looked around, saw the lights flashing from the machines, heard the hum of chatter from other tables around the room, and the persistent beat of rock music from the juke box. The extent of the Irish theme seemed to be a few welcoming words in Gaelic above the bar. Otherwise, the drinks, the food, the music and the clientele were no different to what you might expect in any London pub on a Tuesday evening.

There was plenty going on in the pub, but even so, Nick felt an unwelcome finger of despondency touch him. He wondered if it was the mystery that surrounded this particular evening; not knowing where he was going or why. Or perhaps it was just being in close proximity to this man – the man who shared a home with the woman that Nick had fallen for; the man whose malevolent alchemy could effortlessly turn the sweetness that Nick found in Kay into a bitter poison.

Nick indulged himself with thoughts of Kay. She was, after all, the reason he was here, watching two complete strangers playing a silly computer game in a London pub that he'd never been to before. He had to believe that this entire experience would prove to have been worthwhile one day, when she was his for good. Now that he was thinking about her though, he wanted to hear her voice, and it struck him that this was an opportunity to call her, to update her on what was happening.

Nick pulled his mobile phone out and first of all noted what time it was. It was now 6.20. The subterfuge made Nick smile: calling Kay to tell her what her own husband was doing. Perhaps that said everything about the respective positions of Lee and Nick in her life these days: it was Nick that she trusted.

Kay answered the call after a couple of rings – not quite anxiously-sitting-by-the-phone quick, but fairly rapidly all the same. She sounded coy when she answered:

"Hello baby."

Nick kept his voice low, although there were several yards between his table and where Lee was busy playing games.

"Hello you, what are you up to?"

"Oh, just…just…oh never mind, you don't want to know, trust me. Are you okay?"

"Well, I was going to ask actually: is this an all-expenses paid trip?"

He could hear her chuckle softly down the line. "Why? Are you flying off somewhere exotic with my husband?" Nick laughed too.

"No. Well, not as far as I know. I just wanted to hear your voice really."

"Ah, you're such a sweetheart Nick."

Nick hesitated. Something was wrong. She sounded very low, very fragile.

"Are you okay girl?" he asked, tempering his voice to show concern. "You sound a bit upset."

He heard her sniff at the other end, and the fragility was still there when she replied, even though her words denied any worry: "I'm fine darling. I'll be fine."

It didn't sound like she was fine though and Nick persisted: "Kay, what's wrong? Where are you?"

There was a pause, before she spoke with a chipperness that seemed out of place compared to the rest of the conversation: "I'm at home Nick. Please, don't worry about it. I've just had a hard day; lots of arguments. Feeling a bit emotional, that's all. Ho hum."

She had done it again; that thing where she switched emotions off and on in the blink of an eye. Nick was struck by it every time. It was a beguiling ability to have, and it worried him in a way. How could he ever know what her real feelings were if she was able to control them and conceal them with such ease? One day he would ask her about it, but not now, in this pub, on the phone. He could only shake his head and laugh uneasily.

"Well, if you're sure. You just sounded a bit upset, and I was worried."

"I know. Thank you babe, but don't worry. I was upset but it's just work stuff. It's nothing really. You know how us girls like to cry our eyes out every now and then. It's good for the complexion apparently. Anyway, tell me what's happening. Have you lost him?"

The conversation had clearly moved on. Nick decided that given the situation, it was best to go with the flow. "No, no. He's here," he replied. "We're all getting along famously."

"Where are you then?"

"We're in a pub outside St Pancras, some Irish pub. He met another guy here…"

Nick looked more closely at Lee's companion for the first time, realising that he would have to give Kay a description.

"…he's a little bit younger than your man I'd guess. Bit taller, looks like he's had his nose busted a few times. Nice coat though."

There was silence for a couple of seconds as Kay considered this description; then she said: "Mmm. Not sure, but maybe it's Billy. He hangs around with him quite a lot these days I think. They both go to Arsenal."

"Ah, he's one of them is he? Now I know why I don't like him," Nick laughed quietly.

"Haha. Okay, now this might sound silly but, can you tell me what colour his eyes are?"

"I can't see that from here girl – I'm behind them. It's too dark anyway. What colour should they be?" Nick was still laughing.

"They're very blue and very piercing, if it is this Billy. You'd notice them, put it that way."

"God, are you in love with this bloke or something?"

Kay gave a tired laugh. "No, of course not Nick; you're the man for me. I've just noticed them before, that's all. Women notice these things."

They both chuckled, and Nick had a swig of his lager. This whole situation was still bugging him.

"When will you tell me what the hell this is all about, anyway?" It was a sudden change of subject and Kay seemed caught by surprise. Her laughter stopped abruptly. She said nothing for a second, and Nick had time to curse himself for blundering in clumsily when he knew that she was already upset.

"Oh Nick, please. Let's just get through tonight and I will tell you everything – like I promised."

"Okay. I'm sorry, that just came out. But it's obviously not another woman though is it – hang on…" Nick's voice suddenly trailed off. Soon Kay heard him speak again though.

"Sorry about that. The other guy was just walking past me and going to the bar. Nice eyes. Anyway, what was I saying? Yeah, this isn't about another woman is it? I thought that's what this would be but you don't seem too surprised that he's met up with this guy. I'm just wondering what I'm getting myself into here."

After a pause Kay spoke, slowly, picking her words carefully as if concerned not to say something rash. "Honestly Nick, I don't know what to expect. I really don't. He's been very weird recently. He's been nervy, fidgety, distant…well, even more so than usual. I've just had a feeling that he's building himself up for something, and I don't suppose it involves buying me flowers or anything like that. But something is going on. He said the other day that he wouldn't be back tonight, so I had a hunch that whatever it is could be happening tonight. And now he's met up with Billy, whatever that means…"

She paused again before continuing: "And now that I think of it, something weird happened a few weeks ago when I first saw the two of them talking; when we were in the pub after going to football. I'd never seen Billy before and on the way home I asked Lee who the guy was that he'd been talking to, and he got really defensive; snapped at me, went off in a huff. He was almost in tears. It just happened so quickly. Then he stormed out of the house and I've never mentioned it since, but I've wondered a few times what that was all about."

Kay's voice trailed away as she said these final words, as if even the act of talking and thinking about Lee had drained her enthusiasm. During the time that Kay had been talking, the other man, Billy, had walked back past Nick with another couple of full pint glasses, and he and Lee were now concentrating on the quiz machine again.

Nick weighed up Kay's words. A question came to mind.

"Do you think it's to do with football then? Do they get involved in that sort of trouble?"

Kay thought about that for a second. "Not that I know of; not Lee anyway. I've never seen him come home with bruises or cuts or anything after football, as if he's been fighting. Maybe Billy does, but I don't know anything about him really."

Nick murmured a thoughtful, tight lipped "hmmm". He watched the men again. They were completely focused on the flashing colours on the screen, but they seemed to be making quick work of this fresh pint. The talking and laughing between the two seemed to have been overtaken by a more serious mood. Nick could see the change in them, and it suggested to him that another move was about to be made.

"I think they might be heading off after this drink," he said, almost in a whisper.

Kay's reply was wracked with emotion. "Oh God, I'm scared Nick. I'm scared about everything right now, but I really don't know what I'm sending you into, and I'd never forgive myself if you got hurt."

Nick surprised himself with his reply. It made him sound braver than he felt. "It'll be okay darling. I'll keep out of the way. I'm not going to get too close to whatever happens. But there's no point stopping now that I've come this far, is there?"

He forced a smile and tried to make a small joke to lighten the tension that had enveloped them, murmuring: "I can't wait to get my reward for this." She laughed hollowly. There didn't seem much else to say. Kay sounded exhausted, beaten, though she denied it. Feeling helpless, Nick told Kay that he would let her know as soon as anything new happened. Then the phone was back in Nick's pocket, and he was once again alone in a semi-crowded pub, with two men in front of him that he had just talked himself into following for the rest of the evening, come what may. Nick took an unhappy swig of his drink. He badly wanted to go home.

Lee and Billy were conversing closely and quietly now. Nick checked the time – it was 6.45. Another five minutes passed, and it was obvious that a quite extraordinary change of mood had taken place since Nick had first seen his two targets laughing in the pub. Neither of them was smiling now. What was happening? A grim seriousness had descended upon the men, and Nick was disturbed by the solemnity of it.

He saw them exchange a few more words, and then Lee and Billy drained the last of their lager, putting the empty glasses on top of the machine they had been playing. Then they left the pub using the door that both Lee and Nick had entered by.

Though every bone and every sinew in his body wanted Nick to stay where he was, he made off after Lee and Billy anyway, and found them outside, crossing the main road, and walking back towards St Pancras. The streets were busy and the thin rainfall was now miserably incessant. He had two men to watch now, which he suspected would make his job easier. One of them, Lee in the dark coat, he knew well by sight; the second, taller and skinnier, was much less familiar, but he wore a distinctive long, brown coat that Nick reckoned should be easy to spot in a crowd. They walked quickly – Nick hardly expected anything else – and he pursued them with stern determination.

Back at St Pancras International, they queued up and bought tickets. Nick loitered directly behind them in the queue, barely daring to breathe, straining against the noise around him to hear which destination they asked for at the window. He couldn't hear them though, so as Lee and Billy walked off towards the ticket barriers, Nick stepped forward to the serving window and simply said: "Same please."

"Bedford single, yeah?" confirmed the man behind the counter, and Nick nodded, trying to appear nonchalant. It took a few seconds to carry out the transaction – seconds that felt interminable to Nick, as the distance between him and the two men stretched greater and greater. Finally it was done, but the men were now out of sight having gone down an escalator. Nick rushed to the ticket barrier, passed through and ran to the top of the escalator; there, only half way down, were Lee and Billy, standing as still as statues amongst a line of commuters, letting the moving stairs do the work for them. Nick kept walking, taking advantage of Lee and Billy's unexpected slow down to close the gap to three or four yards, before stepping to his right and filling a handy gap in the file of people standing stationary on the right hand side of the escalator.

Less than a minute later they were on the same platform where Nick and Lee had arrived at St Pancras a while earlier. Shortly after, a train rumbled into view, and halted at the platform. This one proved to be considerably busier than the earlier train had been. There were only a few spare seats to be had, and Nick made do with standing by a door. Lee and Billy had been able to get two seats almost facing each other, in the middle of the carriage. Nick took the precaution of facing in the other direction, not wanting to give either man a chance to see him too clearly and perhaps recall that the same face had been just a few yards away from them in the pub minutes before.

The train pulled away, picked up speed through the tunnel that it immediately entered, and then emerged back out into the open to rattle through Kentish Town Station without stopping. Nick's feelings of foreboding back in the pub seemed slightly less heavy now that he was here and moving again on this busy train. He guessed that while they were on the train nothing was likely to happen. What might happen at Bedford though was another matter. And why Bedford? Nick had never been there before, and knew virtually nothing about the place. If something nasty was going to happen, Bedford seemed a pretty unlikely setting.

He decided to send a text message to Kay, informing her about this latest development. The train seemed eerily quiet to Nick. Everyone was reading, dozing or looking blankly out of the window, probably dreaming of summer holidays or dully ruminating on their problems in life. Nick glanced over his left shoulder, and saw Lee's face, only a few yards away. It was unreal: mask-like; grim, stony; betraying nothing at all. He couldn't see Billy's face, just the back of his head, because Billy was sitting opposite Lee.

The train went quickly through another station without stopping, and then another soon after; both were past too quickly for Nick to even read the names of the stations, but he knew that he was being sped north on a journey that was very much against his will. A sequence of stations and tunnels went by as the train clattered through the suburbs of London, and out towards the counties that lay north of the capital. Nick thought about that for a minute: probably Hertfordshire and since they were apparently going to Bedford, well, Bedford-shire was a reasonable assumption too.

He closed his eyes and wished that the evening could be over. About 20 minutes into the journey the train driver announced that they were approaching St Albans, which was to be the next stop. Nick opened his eyes again. The train was shedding speed now, and throughout the carriage there were small scenes of commotion as passengers got ready to leave the train.

It soon pulled into St Albans, and several people got off, but not Lee or his friend. Just before the doors closed Nick heard a sudden tinny blast of rap music, and following close behind the music came a young black guy dressed in jeans and a T-shirt, who bounded between the closing doors just in time. He had his mobile phone in one hand, and this was the source of the music. Nick noticed a number of people in the carriage look up in surprise at the sudden noise, just as he himself had done.

The young guy swayed past Nick, who was still standing up by a door, and went looking for a seat in the area where Lee and Billy happened to be sitting. He was in luck as well, because there was now a free seat, directly opposite Billy, and to Lee's left. The guy pushed between legs and made that seat his, slumping carelessly down and turning his head to look out of the window with what appeared to be complete disinterest in everything around him.

The train pulled away once more and Nick tried to ignore the music, but it was loud, especially in comparison to the previous stilted hush in the carriage. Suddenly Nick heard a raised voice, and looking over his left shoulder again, he saw the black guy's lips moving. The guy was looking straight ahead at Billy.

"I said, turn that fucking shit off. No-one wants to hear it."

These words were spoken loudly enough for Nick to hear them clearly, and he was certain that the words had come from Billy.

The guy countered bitterly: "What the fuck's it got to do with you man? Get out of my face."

"It's got everything to do with me, disrupting my peace and quiet and everybody else's with your shitty wog music. Stick some fucking earphones on."

Nick saw that many people in the carriage had stopped reading or snoozing now, and were listening to this exchange of mutual irritation. Several people at the far end of the carriage were craning their necks, or rising hesitantly from their seats to see what the disturbance was about. Nick saw the black guy wave dismissively at Billy and look back out of the window. He clearly had no intention of turning the music off as Billy had demanded, or even of turning the volume down. Then Lee piped up:

"Oi, arsehole, don't give us that teeth-sucking shit. Turn the fucking music off."

The black guy turned in surprise towards Lee now, and looked quickly from Lee to Billy and back again. Only now did he realise that he was outnumbered, it appeared.

He sneered: "So you ganging up on me now yeah? Want to cause some trouble you fucking big boys, yeah?"

"Listen monkey boy," spat Billy poisonously. "I've told you twice and my mate has told you once. Turn that fucking shit off or I'll turn it off for you and shove it where the sun don't fucking shine."

Nick watched transfixed, as did all those people on the carriage that hadn't decided to bury themselves deeper into the pages of their books instead.

Billy now leaned towards the black guy and made a sudden lunge for the offending phone. There was a struggle as Billy grappled for the phone and the black guy fought him off, but then Lee came in to help from the side, pinning one of the guy's arms back, and quickly it was over. Billy had the phone in his hand, and with Lee still restraining their adversary, Billy rose to his feet, turned to face along the length of the carriage and hurled the phone perhaps 20 metres or so, past where Nick stood by the doors, and clattering past flinching commuters in the next section, until it slid to a stop on the floor near the next set of doors. The radio was now deafeningly silent, as was the whole carriage.

All heads were turned in the direction of the once-musical missile, and then almost in unison turned back to Billy, who straightened his coat, and sat back down again, as if nothing had happened. As Billy had stood and turned to throw the mobile phone Nick had for the first time been able to see his face properly. Kay was right: the eyes flashed with a fierce intensity; you couldn't help but notice it.

The black guy's arms were still being held by Lee, and Billy met his furious, impotent glare with scathing words. "Don't try anything stupid sunshine. Just take your punishment like a man and go fuck off somewhere else with your coon tunes."

The guy strained at Lee's restricting grip, trying to get at Billy, but Lee intensified his hold, and with a look of disgust the man soon slumped back in his seat.

"Don't feel like quite such a big man now do you?" Billy taunted him. "Sitting there with your fucking attitude: 'fuck everyone else, I'm gonna listen to my music and everyone else can go fuck themselves'. Taking the piss Delbert; taking the piss."

A middle-aged man who was sitting opposite Billy, and next to the black guy, suddenly spoke:

"Okay mate, you've made your point. There's no need to keep on at him."

He was talking to Billy, Nick could see, and Nick noticed the glimmer of a smile pass over the black guy's face at this.

"Yeah, no problem feller; just doing my bit for civilised society," Nick heard Billy reply, with heavy emphasis. The middle aged guy shook his head, briefly raised a hand and mumbled "whatever", and then tried to concentrate on his newspaper.

Nick could see that the black guy was sweating, and that Lee's hands still pinned him back in his seat. He tried to shrug Lee off, complaining: "Get your fucking hands off me man. Are you a fucking cop or something? I need to go get my phone."

He and Lee glared at each other for a long second, before Lee stated his conditions: "Don't even think about coming back here with it. Fuck off up that end, and stay up there."

"Understand?" Lee insisted, reaching forward and roughly grabbing the black guy around his jaw. His victim seemed to crumple slightly, but he quickly jerked his head free defiantly.

"Yeah. Jesus man, just leave me alone," he croaked, miserable in defeat. Nick saw Billy nod towards Lee, who released his grip, though he remained poised, ready to move quickly if necessary. Watching through the glass partition, Nick could feel his heart hammering at his ribcage. There was a moment, still and heavy with dread, when there seemed a chance that the black guy would go for Billy again, now that his arms were free.

Instead though, he rose slowly, sheepishly, to his feet, as if he was alert to the need not to make any sudden movements. Then he pushed through the legs to reach the aisle, and walked in Nick's direction and then beyond Nick towards his discarded mobile phone. Some of the passengers watched him go; others, Nick saw, had already buried themselves back into their newspapers and books, as if nothing untoward had happened; as if by ignoring everything, they could make themselves invisible. Just keep quiet and stay out of trouble; that was the maxim. You didn't know what some idiot might be capable of these days.

Nick understood that urge to hide perfectly. Unfortunately for him it wasn't possible to even imagine such invisibility, since he was standing by the door in full view of everyone, feeling just as exposed as the black guy must have felt at that moment.

A woman at the far end of the carriage had retrieved the now silent mobile phone from the floor and handed it to the black guy as he reached her. It was a nice touch, perhaps even a brave one in the circumstances. In recognition of that, she hurriedly sat back down and started to rummage through her bag, as if looking for something important. It was a tacit way of dipping back out of the limelight, and not wanting to be seen overdoing the fraternisation.

Once again there was hardly a sound in the carriage, except for the train's own roaring progress along the tracks. The black guy stayed at the far end, and inspected the damage to his phone; Lee and Billy had their heads close together and seemed to be conferring about something which Nick couldn't hear. Lee then threw his head back with laughter, and sat back in his seat again, looking pleased with himself.

Some measure of calm descended, although by now Nick's own reserves of composure were shredded. There was an uncomfortable knot of butterflies in his stomach, and he tried to breathe more deeply and slowly, hoping this might calm them. It made no difference, and he closed his eyes again in sheer desperation. The thought of Kay crossed his mind once more, and with a hand that was clammy with nerves, he reached into his coat pocket to check whether there was a message from her on his phone.

There was indeed a message from Kay, but it didn't help him. It said: "Bedford? No idea. Take care, thank u x". That was it – not much succour there. Nick felt completely isolated once more. He put the phone away and gave a loud sigh as he stretched his frame and leaned back against the glass partition, closing his eyes and praying for swift deliverance from this evening. The train started slowing, and a couple of minutes later arrived at the next stop, Harpenden. Nick saw the black guy walking quickly from the other end of the carriage towards him again, his face set hard. What now? Nick's stomach dropped with helpless dread.

The black guy reached the area where Nick was standing, just as the doors were about to open at Harpenden. Lee had seen him coming as well and spoke quickly to Billy whose seat was facing in the opposite direction. Billy stood and turned to face the approaching threat. Perhaps seeing this, the would-be assailant stopped, right next to where Nick was standing, and started to taunt Billy:

"Hey arsehole, if I see you on this train again I will fucking have you, you know what I'm saying? I will be ready next time."

Billy smirked at these shouted threats. When he spoke, he sounded unperturbed, calmly superior. "Yeah, whatever; go fuck yourself." The doors were open now and some startled people waiting on the platform at Harpenden could hear the raised voices, and were eyeing the carriage dubiously. The black guy was edging towards the open door though, still shouting abuse at Billy and his "bitch", which Nick took to mean Lee. This was clearly a parting shot; some easily mustered bravado, intended to regain some face from a safe distance. Everyone could see that, especially Billy, who was laughing, and who continued laughing even after the guy had finally left the train and disappeared into the night.

Only a couple of people got on to the carriage; most of those on the platform had apparently decided that it was a safer bet to rush along the platform and board a different part of the train. Several seats had been vacated as well, as other passengers had left the train at Harpenden, and Nick quickly took one of these seats, further away from where Lee and Billy were sitting. From here Nick couldn't actually see the pair, but that, he decided, was just fine by him. The train moved off again, and the air itself seemed shocked by the incident between these two young white men and their victim.

Nick reckoned that he must be feeling more oppressed than anyone. After all, everyone else on the carriage was just going home. In contrast, his task was to follow these two men wherever the night took them. Home seemed a long way away, and Nick felt smothered with fear and foreboding of what might happen next. Once again he closed his eyes and tried to think happy thoughts: being with Kay, the comfort of her scent, her eyes, her touch. Even so, time dragged.

A few minutes later the train slowed once more. Nick opened his eyes and looked out of the window. There were lights outside and a car park. Nick saw the station name on a sign: Luton Airport Parkway. A couple more people left the train but neither Lee nor Billy was among them. Nick fell back into his troubled, distracted thoughts.

A couple of minutes after leaving Luton Airport, the train started slowing again, and the driver announced that Luton was the next stop. Through the window Nick could see that they were in a more built-up area now. The train shed speed and was about to a halt; amidst the commotion as people got ready to leave the train, Nick saw Lee stand up. His face, which Nick only saw briefly at first because another commuter walked between them, was set in the same grim, expressionless mask that he had seen earlier.

And there was Billy also, rising out of his seat, and nodding at Lee as he adjusted his coat. The doors opened and the two men moved along towards them with other passengers. There was no doubt; they were leaving the train here at Luton. Maybe they were not going to Bedford after all.

Nick moved quickly and dutifully to follow Lee and Billy onto the platform – obstinately, like a disowned dog following sorrowfully in the wake of its one-time master, refusing to be shaken off. Swiftly he followed his targets up a flight of steps, keeping them a couple of yards ahead of him amongst the bunch of people that had left the train with them.

There was a turn to the right, another flight of steps, and then the ticket barriers were ahead. Nick saw Lee and Billy pass through these and walk away to the right, and after negotiating the ticket barrier himself, he followed them. On the station wall Nick saw a sign pointing in the direction they had taken, which said "High Town".

He hesitated. Lee and Billy were too close to him for comfort. Everyone else had gone to use an exit in the opposite direction, and it was just the three of them now. The men were only a couple of yards ahead, and Nick wanted more distance. Lee and Billy continued walking while Nick loitered. He watched them start walking across some sort of blue metal-walled bridge, underneath which, Nick assumed, was the railway track. When Lee and Billy were about 20 metres away, Nick started after them again, endeavouring to match them pace for pace, blinking against spitting rain. At the end of the bridge was a chicken take-away shop, where a couple of people were standing waiting at the counter. Lee and Billy ignored the chicken shop and instead turned left, going behind a high wall that then prevented Nick from seeing them.

When he reached the end of the bridge himself, Nick saw the two men still striding onwards along a deserted pavement that went parallel to the train lines. The kerb was marked by evenly spaced trees and lamp posts. There was a pub called the Railway on the other side of the road, but Lee and Billy had already walked on past that. Spooked as he was by the dark shadows that hung over this evening, it still occurred to Nick that this was the first pub he had ever seen Lee walk past without entering. It was enough to draw a thin, wry smile from him.

Nick continued along the road, still 20 or so metres behind Lee and Billy. His footsteps seemed to him to ring out, as if he was wearing metal-heeled shoes. Neither of the two men walking in front of him turned round to look though. Nick kept close to the line of trees that dotted the pavement edge, preferring the reassurance of some semblance of cover, just in case he suddenly found that he urgently needed to avoid being seen.

The road dipped gently at first as they walked, and then went more steeply into a downward gradient. There were some shops on the other side of the road, which Lee and Billy walked past. It was quiet – unnaturally so, it seemed to Nick. Had he lived here and just been on his way home from work, he guessed he probably wouldn't even have thought about it. But he didn't live here, and he wasn't just returning home from work. He had never been to this place in his life, and to him it seemed drab and spiritless.

He had no idea what he was walking into; no conception of what would be the end game to this unhappy night. He was following two grimly purposeful men who he found that he instinctively disliked. The quietness of the streets and the patches of darkness between the splashes of yellow street light, gave the night an eerie edge that Nick's nerves really didn't need. He pressed on, into persistent spots of rain and a sturdy wind, reluctantly focusing his attention completely on the backs of the men ahead of him.

They were about half way down the hill when a car sped past, coming from behind Nick and then shooting past Lee and Billy; immediately in its wake, as if the car itself were a signal, the two men veered to the right off the pavement, and crossed over the road, hands stuffed in their pockets, coats wrapped tightly around them. Nick instinctively stopped and watched from behind a tree. The two were heading down an alleyway that looked sufficiently narrow to force them to now walk in single file, with Billy leading. The alleyway led them away from the road, and in a few seconds Nick could no longer see them.

He stayed behind the tree for a few seconds, deliberating whether to follow. When he next peered at the entrance to the alleyway he saw that Lee had reappeared there, and was looking up and down the road. Startled, Nick pulled back behind the tree. Did they suspect they were being followed? Had they noticed him? It was an alarming possibility. However, Lee stood there scanning the road for only a few seconds before once again going back up the alleyway. Nick silently thanked the tree that shielded him, feeling its rough bark with his fingers.

After several more seconds, Nick took a deep breath and then broke his cover, crossing the road quickly and stopping by the entrance to the alleyway. He now saw that it ran in front of a modern apartment development, and he read the address on a sign outside: Milliners Place, 1 and 2 bed apartments. Between the alleyway and the doors to the apartment complex, a ramp led down to what he guessed was private car parking.

Nick turned his attention to the alleyway itself and peered nervously along its length, recoiling inwardly at the prospect of seeing Lee's face staring back at him. No-one was there though. The alley seemed to stretch for about 30 metres or so. There was a lamp post at the end, behind which were some bushes. The alleyway was closed in along both sides by head-high brick walls. Nick guessed that the alleyway was L-shaped and that there was a turn just before the lamp post at the end, which would explain why he could no longer see the two men.

He wavered for another second before venturing forward into the alleyway. It seemed intimidating in its narrowness and in the secrets it held at its far end. Every step felt like a big one now. Halfway along on the left there was a derelict property, while to the right he saw a covered car parking area, presumably for the apartments he had walked past at the entrance to the alleyway. His shoes seemed to crunch on the concrete below as he walked, like hobnailed boots on loose gravel.

It made him wince, and his own perception of the amount of noise he was making was enough to make Nick halt in despair, about level with the derelict building on the left. There was a ragged hole in the brickwork and he took a moment to study the contents of the one trashed room that he could see.

Randomly placed breeze blocks were scattered loosely around its floor, along with tattered bits of carpet and curtain, a pile of sacks of concrete mix, and a broken table with one leg staved in, as if it had received a hefty kick; part of its Formica surface was blackened and blistered by fire. General detritus and discarded litter was everywhere, though whether that had blown in on the wind or been left there by kids or junkies or tramps, who could know.

It was certainly a desperate place; home to no-one that had a choice. Nick felt compelled to stop and listen. It was eerily silent here: barely a whisper of wind, and just the occasional sound of far off car engines. It was difficult to believe that he was in the middle of a large town, so isolated and forsaken did this alleyway feel. Nick felt the chill and shivered just a fraction, yet he was also aware of beads of sweat on his brow.

Slowly, and as softly as his shoes would allow, Nick walked on, leaving the derelict house behind him, and feeling happy about that. Five paces further on it became apparent by the light from the lamp post that the alleyway did indeed take a left turn at the end. The left hand wall stopped short of the bushes at the end. Some impulse made Nick stop in his tracks and listen again. Still nothing, save the wind, a few spots of rain, and the almost imperceptible rustle of a town that now seemed far, far distant.

But what was that noise... was it the whisper of a human voice, or just the wind playing tricks? It had been just a brief murmur of some kind, but as he listened with furious concentration, every sense tuned to receive, the murmur had gone. Perhaps it was just the wind after all.

The narrow alleyway seemed to close in on him, bear down on him, and some instinct made Nick reach out with his hands to touch the walls on either side. Their cold, crusty strength against his fingers was little comfort, but at least they were something solid and definite. He wanted to be able to melt into those walls; just disappear, and then reappear anywhere in the world but here.

He knew he had to go on but the noise his footsteps had been making was still bothering him, and despite the floor being damp from the rain, he decided there and then to remove his shoes for the last few metres he had to walk to reach the end of the wall and the left turn. Another impulse that he just had to trust told him that he wouldn't be walking any further than the end of that wall in the near future. He was in no rush to turn the corner.

With a shoe in each hand, and feeling a mixture of self-ridicule and terror, he padded the last few metres noiselessly, until he reached a position just a few inches from the end of the wall on the left. Here, he wanted to stop and take stock again. He judged that he could perhaps crane his neck and see beyond the vertical edge of the wall and further along the passageway, without showing himself to anyone around the other side.

The sight that he knew would greet him was right there. Standing close to each other, half way along this next, shorter stretch of alleyway, were the figures of Lee and Billy. They were mostly hidden in a dense patch of shadow that fell between the glow of the lamplight at Nick's end and the lights of a bigger road that crossed at the far end of the alley beyond the two men. Nick now realised that it was just about possible to hear a low murmur of voices. The actual words were indistinct, so he was unable to make anything clear out of the sounds, but one of the two men was doing the talking, that was for sure: it sounded like a near constant, droning invocation; a low-pitched appeal to some unseen force or being.

Nick pulled his head back, retreated a couple of steps, and leaned back against the wall, floored momentarily by a hundred different thoughts and fears. He needed some time to come to grips with the meaning of this latest situation, and to work out what to do next. Perhaps, he thought, the best thing to do now was nothing – just stay hidden, and watch, and wait. Lee and Billy were just ten of fifteen feet away, and Nick felt utterly trapped. Fear and uncertainty sent a crawling sensation down his spine. What the hell was about to happen here?

His mind wandered for several moments, thinking only useless questions about the purpose of him being there; but then his reverie was broken by a louder voice from the other side of the wall. He could now hear distinct words. Nick moved closer to the edge of the wall again, and listened. He was sure that it was Billy's voice, and he was talking to Lee, his tone scolding and exasperated. Nick couldn't resist the urge to peep around the corner, and he saw the two men still standing in the shadows. Lee was looking down at the floor, while Billy was gesticulating and talking urgently at him. The words made Nick's blood freeze:

"…this is no time for bottling it brother. Get a fucking grip on yourself. We're about to do the job. This is what we've waited and planned for all these months. You can't just back out of it now. Custer and Mister P gave us the chance to be the first; to start the crusade that Mister P dreamed about; to win our country back, and make it English and Christian again. That's something to be proud of. I feel proud about it and you should be too. Everyone is waiting for this signal. Are you just scared or are you telling me that your heart isn't in this cause?

If so, well there is a price to pay for that brother, one that you really don't want to pay, believe me."

Nick thought he heard a snivelling reply to this from Lee, who seemed to be avoiding looking at Billy. The words weren't clear though.

"Yes brother, I am fucking threatening you," Billy hissed in response. "You'd better believe it. You're jeopardising the whole operation. Walk away from this now and you will have to watch your back for the rest of your life. You know the power we have behind us. I couldn't vouch for what Mister P would do. You're betraying me too. I argued for you to be included in this, like you fucking begged me to do. Brother, you are already too involved in this to back down now."

There were several moments of silence as Billy glared at his companion in the darkness and Lee, as if overcome with sudden weariness, slowly leaned back against the fence behind him. When Billy next spoke, it was as if he had decided to change tack; that threats were perhaps not the way to motivate Lee and make him stand firm to carry out whatever task it was that they were here to do. It was time for a softer approach, it seemed:

"Lee…Lee my friend. We're here to do something massive; something that will be remembered forever. Remember what Mister P told us: how he described the situation here, with these scum waging their holy war against innocent British people, pumping their drugs across our country and trying to destroy our way of life.

"Remember what Mister P said about July the 7th. Those murdering bastards started that from here. This is a fight for the survival of England, Lee. We have to strike the first blow and let them know who and what they're fighting against. You should be proud of the Anglo-Saxon blood in your veins; proud that you are a son of Churchill and Cromwell. We have to be worthy of their memories, and show that when the time came, and our politicians as usual just did nothing, that the

British people stood up and fought for what was right, like we always do.

"And we will win, as we always do. And you Lee will always be able to say that you were the first lion to strike a blow. Think about that – the first of the lions. The First of the Lions. Billy paused, letting the phrase sink in. Then he continued.

"We have to be brave, and accept that this is now the only way, because it really is the only way. We are at war, and I would rather die for England than become a slave in an Islamic country. Mister P calls this a sacred task Lee and he's right. And you well know that there are thousands who would give their all to be in your shoes right now, to do their duty in the middle of the enemy camp. As Mister P says, the soldiers of our Christian British nation are waiting for us to strike the first blow."

Billy took a half step towards Lee, as if to ensure that his message would be delivered securely.

"We didn't want this, but it's what we've got. Lee, when the final account is made, we'll be remembered as true English brothers, who stood strong when war was the only choice we were left with. And I'm here, shoulder to shoulder with you as your friend and brother as our moment arrives. What we have to do will only take a second to do, but its significance will ring out for centuries. Mister P saw this in his dream and I persuaded Custer to give us the job Lee, so don't fucking let me down now.

"You've got to believe in what we're doing Lee. You've heard Mister P say it: God is on our side."

At this, Lee seemed to sniff in some sort of show of doubt, or maybe even insubordination. He mumbled something that Nick didn't hear, but Billy's dismissive reply again rang clearer:

"No, of course I don't believe in all that God stuff. Personally I just fucking hate the low-life scum, and the sooner we can rid the place of them the better. You know that. But I'm a good actor, and fortunately Custer and all that lot fall for it, so here we are."

Nick heard all of this with mounting shock, realising that he had stumbled into something beyond even his own worst imagination. There was another pause in Billy's rhetoric, and Nick felt a strong urge to shatter the oppressive silence by sprinting back along the alleyway, screaming at the night sky like a madman to relieve the taut nerves in his face and chest.

After another second though, as Nick still wrestled with that urge, Billy spoke again, this time in a quieter voice which Nick could only just hear. Lee was looking sorrowfully at the ground, and Billy said: "Lee, look at me. This is it. Are you with me? Are we going to do this together? Or am I going to have to do the job alone?" Billy was reaching forward to his friend, and he grabbed hold of one of Lee's elbows as he continued speaking. "Because I'm not backing down, even if you go. And if you leave me here, we will meet again I promise you, but it won't be as friends. So are you with me or not?"

Nick watched as Lee reluctantly dragged his eyes away from the patch of concrete between himself and Billy, and focused them directly on his companion, whose own eyes seemed to glisten in the darkness with an unnatural zeal. Nick was struck by that; frightened out of his wits by it. Lee said some words that Nick didn't catch, but he did see Kay's husband nod his head briefly in Billy's direction, and Billy clearly welcomed the content of the message, as he replied: "Yes Lee; on my mother's life. Man, you had me worried there, but these things happen I suppose. People get scared before battle. Never mind; no harm done. Right, let's get ready now. He'll be here any minute."

Then Billy took Lee's arm and they retreated further into the darkness, away from Nick's hiding place, and towards the lit street that passed across the far end of the alleyway. He could hear that they were still speaking in low voices, but it was now impossible to make out what they were saying. Nick pulled his head back from the edge and fell back against the wall, his upturned face being spattered with stinging raindrops.

His mind was racing so furiously that no coherent thought was possible.

Piece by piece, things formed in his brain; vague ideas, hunches, suppositions. If he had not misheard, and if he understood correctly, then Billy and Lee – and it was now clear that Billy was in charge – were here to carry out some racially or religiously motivated attack. That was sinister enough, but it also seemed that whatever these two men were about to do was only the beginning; a starting pistol for something more organised, and larger in scale. It was a declaration of war against a community, or a faith or a particular outlook on the world. Whoever or whatever the target was, it was an act of violence, and a declaration of some kind of war; and any minute now, Nick was to be its lone witness.

What should he do about it though? Kay could surely never have suspected anything quite like this. But if what he had just heard was Lee almost losing his nerve at the last moment, then that might explain the desperate tension in his behaviour recently, which Kay had told him about. Nick's mind sifted options, and there were none that he liked, except the one that recommended he should sneak quietly in the opposite direction, get on the next train to London, go straight home and forget that he'd ever been to this miserable corner of the world.

His legs seemed leaden and unable to move though. He felt pinned to this spot, and whether it was through fear or fascination, or both, he couldn't be sure. Should he try and stop them? Be some kind of hero? That thought would have been funny had the predicament not been so serious. Instead, it was an appalling thought. How could he stop them? He was no fighter, and these men would almost certainly be armed with some sort of weaponry. For all Nick knew they were about to shoot someone.

He sneaked another look around the corner. The two men were side by side, peering through the branches of a bush towards the main road. He saw Billy point at something through the branches, and the two conferred with whispers. There seemed a stirring of anticipation between Billy and Lee, and Nick was transfixed. Gradually, millimetres at a time it seemed, they edged towards the light at the far end of the alleyway, where it met that main road. Nick tried to see who or what was coming along the road from the direction that Billy and Lee were watching, but tangled branches blocked his line of sight. He could guess anyway: their quarry was approaching, right on cue.

Both men were now facing towards the main road, with their backs to Nick. Billy was standing directly behind Lee, who was close to the end of the alleyway and the pavement beyond. One of Billy's hands was placed between Lee's shoulder blades. Metres away, Nick's mind reeled. Do something now, he urged himself; but the act of propelling himself out of his hiding place to draw their attention was quite simply beyond him.

Instead, Nick just looked on as Billy, this slim, smartly dressed and ferocious young man, took some sort of implement from the inside pocket of his coat. Nick saw it dangle from his hand for a second: it looked like a blunt hammer of some kind, with a dull metal head and a handle that was perhaps a foot long.

A thought passed through Nick's mind that this really was his last chance to interfere, but in fact it was already too late: he saw Billy push Lee forcefully in the back, and Lee was suddenly out of sight, moving to both Billy's and Nick's right along the road, hidden to Nick now by the bushes. Billy took up a position of readiness in the shadows, crouching slightly, muscles tensed, the implement gripped in both hands high above his right shoulder.

The next five seconds changed the lives of everyone present. A hooded figure was suddenly propelled by an unseen force into the entrance to the alleyway, from light into comparative dark, where Billy crouched with his murderous weapon at the ready. Nick saw that it was a bearded Middle Eastern-looking man. His eyes were at first wide with surprise but then, curiously, they seemed to find swift understanding as they registered the tall, slender figure in the shadows with arms raised.

And right at that instant, seemingly from deep within Nick's own breast, there came an unexpected and unnatural noise – a childish, melodic, cheery sound – and everybody stopped and turned to look in Nick's direction, though no-one knew until that moment that he or anyone was even there – it was just the place from where they heard a mobile phone suddenly ringing. Frozen in horror himself, Nick saw Billy's face, his confusion total, looking towards him. The bearded man was also rooted to the spot, gaping, surprise heaped on surprise; that momentary understanding put to flight by new bewilderment; and behind him was Lee's face, pale and troubled in the yellow street light.

The bearded reacted first though, and in the blink of an eye, brilliant white steel flashed and he had closed the short distance towards Billy, who was still distracted, still confused, and now completely off guard. The phone was still ringing in Nick's pocket.

Too late, Billy saw the coming danger; the man was upon him, and Billy's desperate hammer swing passed uselessly over his assailant's shoulder at the same instant that the blade punctured Billy's clothes, Billy's skin. He gave a single, anguished yelp – it sounded more like surprise than pain – and cursed in frustration and impotence as the man slammed him back against the branches of the bush with another thrust of his dagger-wielding arm. The hammer slipped from Billy's fingers and clattered on the ground at his feet.

All of this happened in a couple of seconds, to the accompaniment of Nick's feeble, jolly ring tone. Then the bearded man rounded on Lee, who was two yards away behind him, and like Nick had been paralysed by the turn of events. Lee now backed away into the glare of the street lights on the main road and cowered down, kneeling and raising an arm above his head for protection; pleading, Nick heard, for mercy. In response, he heard unintelligible words from the bearded man – unintelligible because the words weren't English. The man unleashed a furious volley of words at Lee, but he then ran off without striking again, and Lee was left in his defensive crouch, like a mere mortal shielding his eyes from the glory of the Almighty. Billy slid slowly down to the ground, still tangled up in branches.

Nick thought he heard a single gasp from Billy's lips, a futile exclamation of "oh, Jesus"; then it really was time for Nick to get away from this place, to run – run like the wind, no matter where it took him. He doubled back along the alleyway, his shoes swinging from his fingers as he ran, with no regard for the harshness of the stone floor under his feet; Billy lay flat on his back, drifting away, choking his last few breaths amidst helpless tears and bloody fingers. And as Nick emerged from the alleyway and scampered at full pelt back up the hill towards the train station, the mobile phone in his pocket at last stopped ringing.

Chapter Eight

There was desolation among many emotions on the train back to London. Nick had run half way back up the hill towards the station, choking back shocked tears, before stopping to finally put his shoes back on. Then, chest heaving, he had finished the return at a listless walking pace, staggering like a drunkard, not believing what had just happened, and his own unwitting part in it.

A voice inside nagged at him to do the right thing and go to the police; tell them everything: who the men were, what he had heard them saying, why he was there in the first place. But he didn't do that and, right now, he couldn't. The whole thing was too desperate for words.

It was only when Nick was on the train platform waiting for the next London-bound train to pull in that he even had the wherewithal to look at his phone. Then he saw that the missed call – absent-mindedly, he wondered whether there had ever been a more fateful missed call – was from Justine. Despite his mental disarray he did the maths: it must have been 6 or 7 in the morning where she was. What could she want with him at that hour? She had left a short voice message, which he listened to with dull disengagement. She seemed quite chipper, despite the hour of her day. She said that she wanted to speak to him; she even said that she was missing him at the end, and called him affectionate names.

It was too much for Nick to handle, and he tottered to the darkest, remotest part of the platform to hide more uncomprehending tears from the two strangers also waiting for the train.

Once on the train, thoughts turned to Kay, and then by extension to Lee. The last time Nick had seen Kay's husband he'd been cowering in front of the man with the knife, defeated without putting up even the slightest resistance. The sight of Billy floundering, slithering down to the cold concrete, where his blood had already splashed, had obviously been too much for Lee. It was evident that he was not as committed as Billy had been to this attack, this campaign, whatever it was.

Faced with the unexpected disaster of Billy's demise, Lee had had nothing to offer, no stomach for it. Lee knew that, Nick had witnessed it, and their supposed target had seen it and unbelievably had even taken some kind of pity on him. How else could you describe his decision to leave Kay's husband unscathed? Perhaps it was contempt.

Where was Lee now, Nick speculated? Was he still there, cradling Billy's body, weeping for a lost friend, or "brother", as Nick had heard them referring to each other? Or had Lee made a run for it too? Nick hadn't seen him at the train station; maybe they had some other escape plan – a safe house or a getaway car.

In truth, Nick didn't really care about the answers to these questions. At some point however he needed to call Kay and find a way to relate these events. Making that call was beyond him right now though, as the train rattled through the night towards London. The carriage was almost completely empty, which was a blessing because Nick fancied that he must look a right state: tear-stained and shaking like a junkie in withdrawal.

He needed time and he needed isolation so that his mind could slow down sufficiently to try and make sense of this night, if that were even possible. In search of that isolation, Nick closed his eyes, and let the swaying of the train send him into a peaceful reverie of sorts, as it took him, minute by minute, further from the crime scene that he had fled.

Anger flared soon though, and it surprised him in both its cold fury and in its target. Why had he ever even been in this situation? It had been because of Kay and her silly games. She could very easily have got him killed at the hands of Billy or Lee if he'd been discovered, given the grim intent of their mission. What might have happened if his mobile phone had rung at some other inopportune moment? The way things had transpired in those few seconds of horror and madness in the alleyway, he was lucky that the knifeman hadn't come running in his direction wielding that dagger, having dealt with Billy. Really it was pure luck that he was still alive and heading for home, and that was no thanks to Kay, who he had managed to kid himself supposedly cared about him.

It was a joke wasn't it, a big charade. Here he was, running around, putting himself in danger, doing her dirty work, and all to satisfy her girly whims. And if she was prepared to play this particular sneaky little game behind her husband's back, what might she be capable of behind Nick's back?

The train pulled in to Kings Cross, and Nick got off, head down, consumed with his thoughts and his indignation. He headed for the Northern Line on the tube network. She was using him. That was the long and short of it. He was just a pawn in her adolescent game. How could he be so fucking stupid as to believe that there was anything real between them? Nick's blood boiled and he made a decision that came more easily than he could ever have imagined.

**

At that moment of decision, tears were peppering the white tiles of a bathroom floor in Hertford. Kay Talbot rocked quietly upon the toilet seat, and knew the truth – that all the physical signposts of the last few days were telling her exactly what she had feared they did.

Kay looked through eyes blurred by teardrops at the band on the white plastic stick she held between the thumb and forefinger of her right hand. She turned back to the creased piece of paper that had come with the stick, and once again consulted the instructions on how to read this device; but it still told her the same thing she had now seen half a dozen times: she was pregnant, and the plan for her life, such as it was, was in tatters.

It was totally possible, she had to accept, but devastating all the same, and made even more so by a conundrum she couldn't unravel. She couldn't be sure if this situation was caused by Nick or by James. She had always relied on her contraceptive pills, but stupidly she had missed them for two days running. The liberation of realising her feelings for Nick had turned her life upside down and then, carried along on a wave of previously pent up emotion, she had let her guard down; she recognised that now. How strange, mystifying actually, that after years of battling with Lee about his desire for a baby, here she was, certifiably carrying one, and the one man in her life who she knew couldn't be the father was Lee himself.

It had taken hours for her to get even to this stage; savage hours of fear and self-doubt; of putting off the inevitable, and finding solace only in shocked tears. She was numbed by the immensity of the change this would mean to her life, and to her body. She thought of her mother, and the pain of that loss all of those years before. She veered at times between desperate rejection of the whole idea, and a secret, surprising thrill, which she just couldn't account for. Her, carrying a baby – it was too much to even begin to understand.

The occasional text message or call from Nick, out on Lee's trail, had punctuated the evening. It had diverted her mind from this unwanted task, and delayed the moment of truth. The last she knew, Nick was heading for Bedford. He really was an amazing man and a wonderful friend; a knight in shining armour in this selfish world. She wanted him to be here with her, giving her comfort, because it was unbelievably tough to be alone and discover this revelation about her body.

On the other hand, guilt gnawed away at her as well. Even if Nick had been there, would she have been able to share any joy with him, not being certain whether the baby was his or James's? Would she have been able to look him in the eye? It was a hard dilemma to consider when feeling so emotional.

Instead she sobbed quietly in the bathroom, feeling anger, feeling emptiness, feeling confusion, feeling elation. She sat like this for a long time, almost paralysed it seemed, as she tried to work out what should happen next.

Then, with such care that it seemed the most delicate, important thing in the world, she finally put the test kit down on the side of the bath. She cradled her head and focused on the droplets of water which had fallen from her eyes onto the floor tiles below, willing herself to stop producing them, but failing. Soon she accepted the inevitability of tears and gave up fighting against them; they were all the company she had anyway.

And the flood of tears eventually brought with it a new determination, and a bold decision. This baby was Nick's. It had to be, since only that could account for the enveloping and otherwise inexplicable love she felt towards this new life growing inside her. She wondered where Nick was now; busy following Lee as she'd asked, and oblivious to his impending fatherhood.

Kay's mind turned back to those moments when she had waited for Nick outside the Bierfest; the moments when she had watched the vapour clouds of her hot breath in the cold air; she had watched them, and tried to catch them in her hand. It had seemed at the time to be a moment that was heavy in symbolism about the direction of her life. Now she knew for certain that it always would be.

She hadn't been able to articulate it right then, and hadn't been brave enough until she'd had the benefit of a few drinks inside her. Consequently, she had needed to chase after Nick that night when he had left unexpectedly early. It had been so difficult to take that step, but it had felt like a case of then or never. She seemed to have arrived at another one of those moments now, and it was obvious what she had to do. There could be no room for fear. She had to seize the moment, and the idea came quickly: she would go and see him. She would surprise Nick by being there, outside his flat, when he came home. Maybe she would never come back here to Hertford.

Her mobile phone was in the pocket of the bathrobe she was wearing, and she quickly checked it to make sure that she hadn't missed any messages while she had been taking the pregnancy test and dealing with its aftermath. There were no messages. She decided against contacting Nick right then though, since she didn't want to interrupt anything important and cause him problems. Besides, she smiled to herself, she wanted the surprise to be complete.

Within 30 minutes, Kay was out of the house, and loading bags into her car. Two big cases full of clothes went into the boot, and numerous smaller pieces of luggage were stowed on the back seat. With scarcely a look behind her, Kay locked the front door of the house, got into the driver's seat of the car and started the engine. She checked a map for a couple of minutes, then released the handbrake and drove away, leaving one life in her rear-view mirror, and hoping to find a better one on the road ahead.

**

Billy Filler's final moments were surprisingly peaceful, and Lee might have noticed that had he not been stricken with panic, casting wild-eyed looks from side to side, from one dark, empty shadow to another. He wanted to scream for help, but was unable to make a sound. He wanted to run away but found that his legs wouldn't yet allow him to completely desert his friend. After interminable seconds of indecision he pulled himself together enough to kneel next to Billy. The sadness was crushing; the peacefulness ever more desperate and brutal as Billy's breathing grew shallower.

Lee could find no comforting words, and no words came from Billy either as he looked up at his friend for the last time. In any case, his eyes communicated better than any words could do the confusion and bitterness, the recriminations of this moment – as if it were Lee's fault. As if Lee was to blame for a stranger's mobile phone unexpectedly ringing just when the blow was to be struck; as if it was his fault that this unknown and unseen stranger had come walking along the alleyway at exactly the wrong moment. Those accusatory eyes were like a rapier piercing his heart.

It was bloody unfair, and he was about to protest as much, when suddenly he saw a renewed tension in the muscles of Billy's face. His whole body seemed to brace itself. Then he kicked out convulsively once, and after that a second time, less violently, his shoes scraping uselessly on the concrete. Then Billy's eyes softened, and his body finally yielded with one final shudder of resistance. Billy was gone. His vacant, glassy eyes looked unseeingly up at the stars. It had been no more than two minutes since the target of their intended attack had plunged his blade into Billy's chest, and then run away.

Whoever it had been coming round the corner with the mobile phone had obviously taken one look at the scene and fled as well, because Lee had never seen them. Already it seemed like a long time ago. A life had passed since then. What had been the chances of that incident happening? They had been to this alleyway a dozen times, maybe more; they had spent hours here, and in the area nearby, checking the ground, checking the movements of the man that Lee knew only as Abu. In all that time, no-one had ever interfered by walking through the alleyway.

The sheer awful misfortune of what had befallen their mission started to sink in as Lee crouched there beside Billy's lifeless body. Fucking hell, what were the chances of that happening? They must have been astronomical. How would he explain this to Custer, or to Mister P, who was supposed to be nearby in a car, waiting to take them quickly away from here to a safe house?

There was blood on the floor, trickling towards Lee's shoes, and the sight of it made several things clear to him: this was a crime scene; the person whose incoming mobile phone call had caused everything to go wrong might well have gone on to call the police; it was possible that Lee's finger prints would already be all over this place, but if he touched anything now, especially anything on Billy's torso, they certainly would be; the target, Abu, might well be rounding up more of his jihadist friends right now to come back and finish Lee off; and Mister P might drive past at any minute if he got impatient waiting for Billy and Lee, and came to see what was happening.

Lee had to get away – run anywhere. Put some distance between himself and this dingy back alley. Get back home to Kay, make amends to her in some way; build bridges. Put all this nonsense behind him.

It impressed Lee how calmly he managed to put these thoughts together, bearing in mind that he'd never been as frightened as he was right then. What he needed to do first was obvious though: get the hell out of here. He set off, jogging away from the town centre, away from Mister P's expected location, and away from the train station, which he was certain would soon be swarming with police. He headed towards the outskirts of Luton instead, not knowing exactly where he was going, and not caring. Behind him, Billy remained in the dust.

A page had been turned. One chapter was over, and the next would be different: less dramatic for sure; just a quiet life at home with Kay, out of harm's way. Okay, Custer might come for him, but he doubted it. Lee would cover himself, and Kay would help him do that. Lee would tell her everything and he would make it clear to Custer that if he caused trouble and anything nasty happened to Lee then Kay would bust the organisation apart by going to the police. It was probably doomed already, with Billy being dead. Lee had done his best, and Custer and all the others could go swing, as far as he was concerned.

He saw a bus waiting at a bus stop ahead, and decided to sprint for it. What the fuck had he been thinking of, getting involved in this? The sheer stupidity of this mission, and of the wider plan; as if they could mobilise an apathetic public – it was ridiculous. Pure fantasy. The bus driver even waited and kept the doors open for Lee so that he could hop on board, and as he claimed a seat he found that he was certain in his own mind: everything would be fine, he told himself; everything would be fine.

**

Justine Tanner looked at her mobile phone with disappointment, before slipping the handset back into her bag. What a pity, she thought, glancing up at a large clock on the wall to her left. Oh well, she needed to get a move on. She had really wanted to hear Nick's voice when she broke the news that despite the early hour, she was here at the airport and was on her way back to London. It would have been a special moment for her.

Mind you, perhaps the moment would be even more special if she didn't tell him until after her flight, when she was in England and only an hour away from being with him. It would be a wonderful reunion. Justine sipped her coffee and looked around at the bleary-eyed people around her in the café – her fellow early morning travellers.

For the last two days, Justine's dad had at last been conscious and able to talk haltingly. It had been a moment of joy for the whole family, as Phil Tanner forced a weak smile and said his first words for several weeks.

"What's up?" he had croaked, looking bemused to find everyone staring at him. They had all laughed, and for several hours Justine had simply sat and held her dad's hand, just looking at him, mesmerised by the miracle that lay in the hospital bed in front of her. When he had felt up to it, they had chatted a little, and he had caught up with her life.

Dad had told her it was time for her to get back to England and be with her man. Justine had confided that she was thinking about coming home to Melbourne for good, if she could settle all her loose ends in London, but she wanted to talk to Nick first and find out how he felt about moving permanently to Australia to start a new life. Get yourself back to England then, dad said. Talk everything through; live your lives. Make the right decision, and whatever they did had his blessing.

And so she was here at the airport, and the minutes were now ticking away. It was time to go through to her boarding gate. Would Nick call back before she had to switch the phone off? She hoped so, because she was bursting to tell him what was happening, but she didn't just want to leave a message on his phone. She wanted to hear his voice when he heard her news. Poor Nick; these last few weeks must have been awful for him, left alone in London with everything in their lives on hold. She would make it up to him; she'd see to that.

Justine drained her coffee cup, gathered her things, and stood up. With just a cursory look around the café, she wandered off, checked a screen in the middle of the wide corridor outside, and headed off towards her departure gate. The flight to London was scheduled to leave on time, and they would be making the final call for passengers soon. Justine walked more quickly, and with each step got closer to Nick. She was going home.

**

Nick was finished with it. A man probably lay dead, and he was a witness. Lee's whereabouts now were anybody's guess, but Nick didn't care about that, and he didn't care about Kay either, with the way she played him like he was her favourite toy of the month. He was supposed to call her and tell her about the events of the night, but he was damned if he was going to do that now. He would jack the job in, scrape what money he had together, speak to Nicole and see if he could borrow more, and he would get on the first plane to Australia. In time, he would forget all about this episode in his life, and all about the beguiling woman that had tricked him into doing her dirty work.

As he walked through the network of passageways inside Kings Cross station heading for the Northern Line, Nick considered that he could send a short text message to Kay when he was back above ground; something that just told her to forget it, that Nick wasn't playing any longer, and that she shouldn't call him; it was over. He couldn't see that working though. She would call him straight away, he reckoned.

Instead he had a better idea, even though it was more of a symbolic gesture than something that bore the real stamp of finality: get rid of this mobile phone. Take the numbers that he needed off of it, which were basically those of Justine, Nicole, and his boss Mike; write them down on a piece of paper, and then throw the mobile away. First thing in the morning he could order a new number and a handset. The only drawback was that Kay knew where the flat was, but he reckoned that after a few days of getting no response to her calls and messages, Kay would finally get the hint. And anyway, in a few days' time he could be Melbourne-bound, if all went to plan.

Nick came to a sign on the wall that directed passengers to different platforms of the Northern Line. Home was via the northbound platform, but something stopped him in his tracks about the one that pointed to the southbound line. The sign read 'Morden via Bank and London Bridge'. He read the two words 'London Bridge' again, and then a third time. Though he couldn't bring himself to smile about it, it was perfect really.

He should finish this thing at exactly the same place where it had started to go wrong; where he and Kay had first kissed that incredible night, just a few weeks before. That was the right place to get rid of this phone which had caused him so much trouble, and had almost cost him his life. In every way, the cold water of the River Thames closing over the phone for eternity would represent a fresh start for him.

He headed for the southbound platform. On the tube train he borrowed a piece of paper and a pen from a woman who was sitting next to him, her feet surrounded by shopping bags from West End boutiques. He quickly jotted down the numbers for Justine, Nicole and Mike, and then handed the pen back, with thanks.

Minutes later, Nick was back in the chilly night air. The temperature had dropped a couple of degrees since he had left Luton, but he defied the cold to do its worst as he strode along the approach to London Bridge and then onto the bridge itself. Further up ahead, halfway across the bridge, Nick could see that somebody – a tramp he guessed – was slumped underneath a blanket. He was too weighed down with emotion to think much about that though.

Stopping short of the hunched figure, Nick turned and looked out towards HMS Belfast and Tower Bridge, cradling his head between his hands, elbows upon the stone wall. On the left hand bank of the river was the Old Billingsgate Market building, where the Bierfest had been, and Nick saw a man and a woman standing down there, almost exactly where he had surprised Kay that night when he had turned up late; where they had laughed before going inside. Don't do it lady, he had joked, as if she had been about to throw herself into the river. He felt a pang of gladness at the memory, but it also served as a jolt to his senses. He had come here for a purpose, and that purpose wasn't to wallow in supposedly happy memories. He steeled himself again.

His mind was made up, he was positive. Just get rid of the phone, before she calls. Throw it as far out into the river as you can, and let it sink forever, deep into the silt at the bottom of the Thames, where it would be just another piece of discarded or lost rubbish. The river kept so many secrets, and this could be just another one. His anger was trickling away though, like grains of sand in an egg timer. He could feel it dissipating with every second, and he forced to the front of his mind once again the recurring thought he had used all the way here to sustain his rage: she had used him; she had played him like a fucking piano.

It was enough to fan the flames of his anger; just enough. Without wasting another second he grabbed his phone from his inside pocket and launched it out into the blackness in front of him.

The regret was instant. Nick felt sick even before he heard it hit the water far below.

His eyes started welling up and a teardrop escaped and rolled down his cheek. He fought back more tears with success, but nothing could protect him from the sense of devastation that consumed him at that moment. He briefly, hopelessly, contemplated following the phone into the river himself – not to retrieve the phone, but just to bring an end to this whole sorry business of his life. He was never to discover if he could have put that idea into practice though, because a voice he'd never heard before suddenly announced its presence behind his left shoulder.

"D'ya think that was a good idea then, sonny?"

Nick had unwanted company. He turned quickly, and found himself confronted by a scruffy old man with patchy bits of white stubble that passed for a beard of sorts. He looks like bloody Steptoe, thought Nick. At the periphery of Nick's vision he became aware that the figure of the tramp slumped further along the bridge was no longer there, but the blanket was flat upon the pavement. This was the tramp then presumably. Nick really didn't want to have to explain himself. The night had been unspeakably bad. His pride was wounded, his anger turning in upon himself. He didn't want to have a conversation about it.

"I don't care," Nick countered. "It's done. That shitty phone has done too much damage already. I'm better off without it. What's it to you anyway?"

The old man smiled. "What's it to me? It's nothing to me, sonny. But this is my bridge, and you're causing a scene, so you are."

The accent was Irish, Nick reckoned; an old Irish feller, living rough on the streets. Probably think you've seen it all, heard it all, got all the answers, he mused. Well, you won't have heard this one pal. Nick still hadn't responded so the Irishman continued:

"I suppose it's all to do with some lass…"

Nick's irritation flared, annoyed that this old man should be so presumptuous, and so accurate as well. He reacted with a sharp denial, even accused the old tramp of being a nosy fucker, and quickly wished that he hadn't. The old guy had opened him up like a can of beans. Faced with Nick's anger, there wasn't even a flicker of concern in the street dweller's eyes though.

"Oh, right you are then. There's no need for all that language now is there. I see you coming along, getting all flustered, and I thought to myself, now there's a lad who would appreciate a few hard-earned tips from the life of old Eddie Finn."

Nick seriously doubted that, but he had a feeling that those tips were coming his way in any case. All he could think of to stop it at this point though was a throwaway remark of "yeah, whatever". The old tramp went on regardless, although he seemed a little put out that Nick had spoken so dismissively.

"Listen, I had a woman once, you know. Beautiful she was – as perfect as a peach. I wasn't in these rags then. But like a bloody fool I didn't realise what I had until it was too late, and I lost her. So don't be like me sonny. Do the right thing now. That's all I wanted to say. It's up to you."

It was all a little too close to the mark for Nick. The old tramp was getting through to him, inflaming his own feelings of regret, but Nick was too proud to show that. "Jesus, are you for real?" he said. "A bloody tramp turned Agony Uncle?"

Even so, odd and unexpected as the situation was, it occurred to Nick that this old tramp was as close to a friend as he had found on a night that had gnawed his nerves to a thread. He regretted snapping at him now. It had been rude and unnecessary, and driven by events that the old feller could know nothing about. "Look...I'm sorry I swore, okay," he went on, trying to smile apologetically. "I've just had a complete nightmare tonight and nothing you say is going to make it better."

"I got a smile out of you though, eh sonny," the tramp said, looking pleased with himself. "I tell you, from under that blanket there I see young guys like you bawling over their ladies every day of the week. It's the story that never ends."

Memories of the evening flashed through Nick's mind as he stood there listening: following Lee from the City; the meeting with Billy; the black youth and his music on the train to Luton; everything that had happened in Luton...Kay...the reality of it all dragged his spirits low once more. He spoke quietly and reflectively. "Well, you haven't heard this story before feller, I promise you. This one is a proper original."

He saw the tramp raise an interested eyebrow. Nick got the feeling that for some reason he was being appraised in a different light now. Instead of being fobbed off, the old guy seemed even more intrigued. It was clear that he was enjoying this, and Nick could understand why, having been on the streets himself just a few years before. If the everyday reality was that passers-by gave you a wide berth and avoided making any eye contact, then even just a few brief snatches of conversation with someone that was living a 'normal' life was a boost to your self-esteem. It might even restore a little hope of bettering your own situation one day.

"I've got plenty of time sonny, so please – do tell. It's not fair to keep a good story like that to yourself," the tramp observed, maintaining an unruffled, good natured exterior.

"No, no," said Nick, with the first laugh he had mustered for many hours. "If I did that you'd have to go in the river too, and that's the God's honest truth."

"She could be trying to ring you right now," the tramp continued, nodding towards the shiny blackness of the river. "How will you make it right if you can't talk to her? You'd better get round there."

Nick's sigh was as deep as the river. It had been a very long and very bad evening. He didn't really want to be reminded that he was being stupid by this philosophical old bloke whose words resounded far too uncomfortably. He was too tired and too unhappy.

"After the night I've had pal..." Nick began saying, but as he spoke it occurred to him that these words might lead to even more questions, and that was something he didn't want to encourage. He changed tack sharply: "It's over, it's done. Now if it's all the same with you, I'm going home."

Nick turned away and started walking towards the tube station at the end of the bridge, but his new-found friend hadn't quite finished.

"Hey, don't forget what I said now. Get yourself round there; take her some flowers. Be a man."

That compelled Nick to stop and turn back to face the tramp, thinking to take umbrage at the implied slight. He looked him in the eye and could see what this conversation meant to him: it was a precious few seconds when an old down-and-out could start to feel like a member of the human race again. Maybe he felt he could even make a difference to someone's life. Nick could appreciate that well enough.

The old sod was right as well, Nick accepted, despite the indignation he had felt during the last hour of his life. Kay would find him, and he would welcome her. All he had achieved by throwing his phone away was to make his life more complicated. Kay would be calling and Justine would be calling, but now he couldn't answer either of them.

What was he running from? Nick mumbled some conciliatory words and went to resume his interrupted walk to the tube station. Something made him stop again however. It was a memory from years before. The dejection of sitting on street corners, feeling invisible, or else feeling a total blankness of mind, lost in thoughts of nothingness. It wasn't a nice situation to be in. Most people ignored you, and even those that did acknowledge your existence usually did so with a mixture of pity and shame. Nick remembered it. It was as if you, the homeless one, were to blame for the remorse they felt at the good fortune which kept them from being in your shoes; as if their soul was impoverished as a consequence.

Nick had been there before, and didn't want to go back. Either of these women in his life could ensure that didn't ever happen. No matter what he had been through tonight, no matter how shocking the crime he had witnessed, Nick felt blessed to have escaped that listless, sometimes angry life.

He would have to do something about Kay and about Justine – that much was clear. He would have to make a choice. At least he had a choice though, which was more than could be said for the old Paddy here.

It wasn't much, but Nick threw the old man a quid and thanked him for his advice. The tramp caught the coin smartly in his metal tin, with a sharp clink of metal on metal.

The tramp looked made up at that – euphoric even. "Cheers! I hope you work it out!" he called to Nick in his thick brogue. Nick was already on his way home. A page was turning in his life, but he had a moment for one last thought before this episode was forgotten about in the stampede of fast-approaching dilemmas: he and the old guy might just have saved each other there.

Printed in Great Britain
by Amazon.co.uk, Ltd.,
Marston Gate.